WARRIORS

WARRIORS

A Novel

By William B. McCloskey Jr.

Skyhorse Publishing

Skyhorse Publishing books may be purchased in bulk at special discounts for sales promotion, corporate gifts, fund-raising, or educational purposes. Special editions can also be created to specifications. For details, contact the Special Sales Department, Skyhorse Publishing, 307 West 36th Street, 11th Floor, New York, NY 10018 or info@skyhorsepublishing.com.

Skyhorse® and Skyhorse Publishing® are registered trademarks of Skyhorse Publishing, Inc.®, a Delaware corporation.

www.skyhorsepublishing.com

10 9 8 7 6 5 4 3 2 1

Library of Congress Cataloging-in-Publication Data
McCloskey, William B., 1928-
  Warriors : a novel / William B. McCloskey Jr.
    pages cm.
  ISBN 978-1-62636-107-2
  1. Fisheries--Fiction. 2. Fishers--Fiction. 3. Alaska--Fiction. I. Title.
  PS3563.A2617W37 2013
  813'.54--dc23
                              2013025361

Printed in the United States of America

For my grandson William Lyell McCloskey

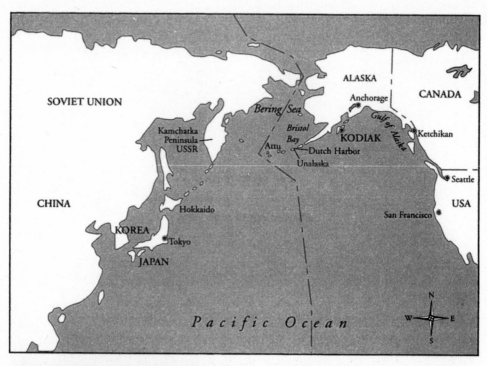

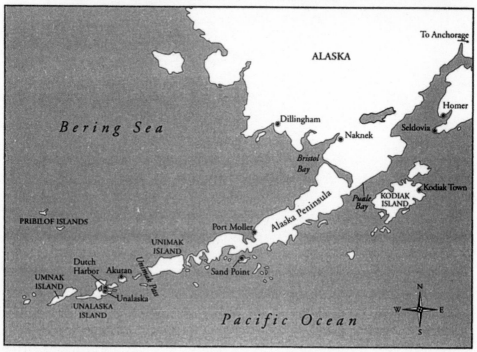

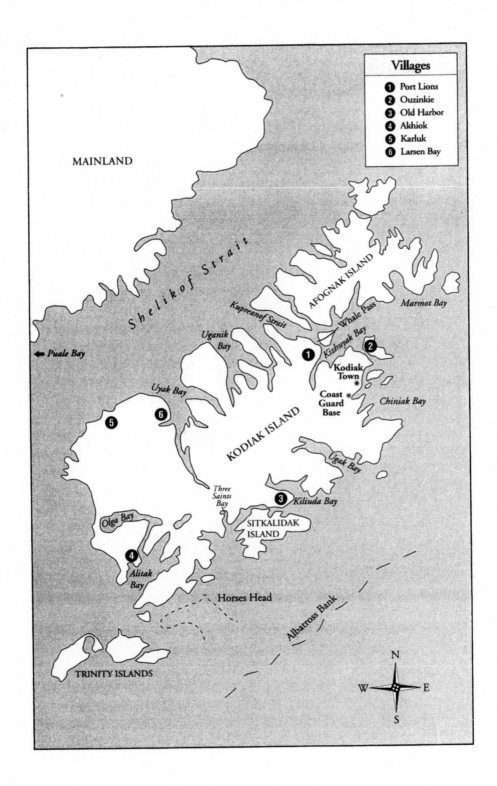

ACKNOWLEDGMENTS

A pleasant task at the end of writing a long book based around facts is to thank those who helped me with the impression of those facts however I chose finally to present them. Also to thank those who looked over parts of the manuscript to check hard information about which there was no room for interpretation. And others who created the climate in which a long book could be written.

The book is dedicated to my thirteen-year-old grandson William Lyell McCloskey. Will is a bright, sassy, inquiring presence, has been a bike and kayak buddy, and a precious friend. That said, the book could not have been written without the support of my wife for more than half a century, Ann Lyell McCloskey, to whom the preceding trilogy of *Highliners* novels have been dedicated with love. Also in a small circle of my support group was my late daughter and mother of grandson Will, Dr. Karin A. Lyell McCloskey. And very much still there for the rest of us is son Wynn, my onetime Alaska fishing companion, now trial lawyer William Bertine McCloskey III of Houston joined by his wife Shawna.

For advice on the Japan portions of this book I'm particularly grateful to Jay Hastings, long an American representative of Japanese fishing interests, who advised in detail on portions of the manuscript. Any slip-up in following Jay's advice can only be laid to my own decisions. Thanks also to Shaya Nakatsuka of the Japan Embassy in Washington, DC, for his comments reflecting a younger generation of Japanese than those in the book. And as always to Alan MacNow, who made possible my commercial fishing visits to Japan from 1980 to the recent present from which I learned respect for Japanese fishing concerns in general.

In Kodiak, as in the past for entree and companionship during my commercial fishing forays to Alaska which have furnished the bedrock of all my *Highliners* novels, I thank Thorvold (once my skipper for king crab) and Connie Olsen, Al Burch, and Tom Casey, all of whom have remained available for advice and support.

Of recent help, my thanks to historian Bob King of Juneau for information and insights on Bristol Bay history circa 1951 at that crucial time when engines supplanted sail on the boats while simultaneously various unions scrambled for dominance.

Further in Alaska: to Alice Ryser of the Kodiak Historic Society for photos of that town before the 1964 tsunami rearranged the town's layout. And for hospitality in Kodiak during my fishing time starting in 1975, still remembered with gratitude, friends and their spouses including Hank and Jan Pennington, Harold and Marcie Jones, plus the late Oscar Dyson and Chris Blackborn with their spouses Peggy and Jim.

In a remarkable accommodation, the Ketchikan Public Library loaned me microfilms of the *Ketchikan Daily Mirror* for the years 1945–47. This was the period when Jones Henry of my present book returned home to Ketchikan from war duty and pieced back together his fishing career. In Baltimore the Johns Hopkins University library received and stored the films while providing me with the means to view and copy them over a period of months. Thanks for this loan in Ketchikan to Tammy Dinsmore, and in Baltimore to the Hopkins Interlibrary Services and Audiovisual Services.

A lucky break for me was contact with Professor Mansel Blackford of Ohio University's History Department. Mansel's dad had been one of the vigorous young World War II veterans who pioneered Alaska's nascent king crab fishery with their catcher-processor vessel *Deep Sea*. Besides becoming a personal friend along with his wife Viki, Mansel provided me with rare material from the *Deep Sea's* days starting in the late 1940s on the Alaska grounds: both original documents and from his own book *Pioneering a Modern Small Business*.

In another lucky break, I established contact with marine biologist Dr. Francis M. Fukuhara. Frank was a young Japanese-American consultant of about my own age in 1952 at the only other time that I had ever encountered him. Back then the Coast Guard Cutter *Sweetbrier* on which I was a junior officer took him from Adak in the Aleutians to ride with the Japanese fishing fleet just permitted back into Alaskan waters. It was a controversial rendezvous at the time. Frank has shared his notes aboard the Japanese vessel of an event that at the time was in my perspective only from the deck of my own American ship.

Thanks further, in no easy category: To veteran Bristol Bay fisherman Dave Milholland of Anacortes for his knowledge of boat engines and gear circa 1950. To librarian Julie Johnson of Baltimore's Enoch Pratt Library system for frequent help with research. And to Gaylord Clark, Baltimore-based seasonal fisherman up in Bristol Bay, for confirmation of traditional grounds along with current updates.

CONTENTS

Part Three

Part Four

PROLOGUE

I

OKINAWA, JULY 1945

*N*othing's *changed about 'em.* Except that now they squatted in a pen—where they belonged. Jones Henry sneered in contempt. *Go on, be scared. Should have shot the whole batch of you when we had the chance.* He regarded them down on the ground below, past the sight of his combat boots, where they squatted, stuffing their faces with American rations instead of rice and fish heads. *Kissed on the ass is what you got instead.* One gaggle even shared puffs on an American cigarette. None looked you in the face. *Thought you had so much honor you'd rather kill yourselves than be captured. All bullshit—that's what your Jap lies turned out to be.*

The prisoners' camp in the heat had its predictable odors of latrine and old sweat and ammonia disinfectant. The stench rose to the guard tower where Jones paced. He'd likely soon have enough of that stink buddied in some snake hole, ducking shells overhead, when they invade Japan itself. *So, you yellow Japs, just be glad nobody plans to shoot you. Unless you get out of line.*

Prisoner-of-war duty at least gave a breather until the big push.

"Patted on the fuckin' head, mebbe," Jones rubbed the smooth barrel of his piece. "But just try to escape with me up here." Out over the hills, past craters and debris, among tile-roof shacks and neat little patches of cultivation, lay the blue ocean—slick and hot under the raw sun. Water he wanted nothing to do with, he who'd once thought water was his only home. Their ratty little boats in the harbor wouldn't last through a storm, and they said typhoons blew regular through here. Boats that would never last a day back home in Ketchikan. Jones Henry could show them how to build a boat to catch fish.

One of the scarecrows below fastened eyes on him. An officer, probably, since he was one of a small bunch that had been cordoned off by themselves: the only way to tell with their muck-caked uniforms in rags. All bones, like the others. Bugs crawled over his face and he made no move to squash them. Eyes narrowed more than just sneaky Jap eyes. Seemed to say "I'm still better than you up there."

Jones scowled back and held the gaze. *Yeah fellah, look at me—a sergeant in charge of enlisted. In charge now of you—an officer. Still alive no thanks to you and your people. In a few weeks I'll be taking fire again from Japs like you while you'll be here, all safe, so don't feel too sorry for yourself. Those cooties crawling over your face—that you're too lazy or too full of yourself to smash—let 'em chew their fill.* Jones cradled his piece for long enough to light up. He let the cigarette dangle from his mouth while he slapped the stock. *Just try to escape, Jap! Give me the excuse!*

Captain Kiyoshi Tsurifune scorned to crush the lice crawling inside his clothes and across his chin. Or to groan from the wound he'd patched with grass and mud to stop the bleeding. The wound now five days old, or six, ached and sometimes screamed inside the remains of his shirt. To eat their food was disgraceful enough. He'd let the time for honorable death slip away when he'd lost consciousness, and now he sat waiting for slow dishonor at the barbarians' hands.

He glanced around. Others watched him with dead eyes. Soldiers under his command who had survived, lice-caked, like himself. He'd failed them, had set no example of dying with honor. They who had heard him day after day shout words of duty from generals and from the Emperor himself. He'd warned of the unspeakable tortures that awaited those taken alive—taken in disgrace. And now he, alive among them, awaited the enemy's pleasure.

How would he face his father if he ever survived to return to Sendai? Father might be glad to have a son back home to help direct the family's small fleet of fishing vessels that were out searching for food in the sea that would feed their countrymen during the struggle against American imperialism. But how would Father and Mother ever again hold up their heads with a son—proudly trained as an officer for the Emperor—returned defeated but still alive?

Let this wound kill me. Let it help me to die bearing pain. Let me do that at least for my Emperor.

Two days before, an American enlisted man—not even an officer—had gone among the captured to cull out the wounded. For treatment, the man had said as he, unbelievably, passed out cigarettes and talked in a friendly way. More likely he was culling them to be tortured and shot so they'd be no more trouble. It was what he himself had ordered for some prisoners, back during his battalion's victories. He barely had enough food for his own men. Back when all knew that being captured proved despicable weakness.

Above him on a crudely constructed platform stood one of their soldiers. Beneath the helmet, the man's face was a blank of lines and eyes, although how could you distinguish the expression on a barbarian's face? They all looked alike. Before he could glance away, the soldier returned his stare.

Even in disgrace, Captain Kiyoshi Tsurifune did not permit his gaze to falter. *Let this soldier from a foreign army know that I will die proudly.* But suddenly the wound scraped at his very heart. Even so, except for one jolt he couldn't suppress, he kept his look cold and steady. Blood seeped into his mouth. He swallowed it back down. His mind dizzied, but he screwed his eyes to hold the gaze. This—now this was important. *Show the victor my resolve until, Emperor willing, I can die and be released.*

Jones Henry wasn't going to look away first. *You'd kill me if you could, Jap, just as I'd kill you, and you ain't getting the better of me on this. Just let me kill more of your little yellow brothers when we invade your dirty Jap homeland in a few days. Then if they get me, at least it'll be some ways even.*

Slowly, the Jap squatting down below began to teeter. As his head hit the ground—with eyes still fixed on Jones's own—blood started to trickle from his mouth.

"One less," Jones muttered. "Good riddance." But he didn't turn away. The Jap kept his gaze locked while he struggled to get back onto his feet.

At last, Jones looked away, then back again in spite of himself. The Jap still struggled, his eyes still fixed.

"Son of a bitch anyhow." Jones turned to a soldier on duty inside the tower. "I don't care what you do, but mebbe you want to call a medic if one's around. Prisoner down there looks like he needs help. If that's what we're up to these days." He thought about it, before adding, "A man who ain't giving up like the rest."

II

OKINAWA, OCTOBER 1945

When word came that he could have five days' leave, Sergeant Jones Henry snorted. Not enough time to fly home to Ketchikan, so big deal. Travel around in Jap-land? The one place he didn't need to go.

Over a brew at the noncom's club, Gus Rosvic raised his bottle, winked, and declared, "You're nuts, man." He too had been given leave. "I'm headed for Tokyo. Nobody's going to hold this boy back!"

"Suit yourself. I'll save my dough for home, where it matters."

Back weeks before and by coincidence of war, Jones had strode into the club and there had been Gus in navy blues. In the darkened room, Jones hadn't noticed him until the familiar voice—grown deeper since Jones had left for the war—said, "Man, if they don't let anybody in here. And if they don't put anybody in a uniform these days!"

When Jones saw that it was indeed Gus Rosvic—Ketchikan born and raised—waving and grinning, Jones could have hugged him for excitement. They had just stayed put, staring at each other.

Jones had been the first to speak. "Navy didn't kick you out, I see. Looks like they even gave you some stripes."

"Bosun First. Looks like the Marines've wasted sergeant stripes on you."

"You here on a ship?"

"Shit Jones, I didn't swim here."

Grinning, Jones asked, "Your dad still trolling for salmon back in Ketchikan?" He couldn't keep the hunger for home from edging into his voice.

"From his last letter, he did good with the cohos last summer and not bad with kings. Main trouble was getting enough gas to run the boat." Gus had stopped to consider. "Same with your dad, I guess."

"That's all I want to do, Gus." Jones had taken an eager step forward. "Get back and fish."

Gus held up a hand, reigning in some of Jones's enthusiasm. "Whoa, man. This boy's going to stick around here first and see the world!" Neither one moved. Except for a scar that now ran from one side of his forehead to his cheek, Gus's broad grinning face had changed little in the five years since they last faced each other across their fathers' boat rails. Rivals for the most fish caught, the fastest boat back to the cannery. "Last time we drank together, Jones buddy, we both had to lie about our age. Remember? You got permission yet to drink legal?" It was a stupid question, Jones felt—Gus always sulked for being a few months Jones's junior.

"'Course," Jones sneered.

"Then it's me's going to order your first brew or whatever today."

So now Jones wasn't surprised by Gus's enthusiasm for Tokyo, no matter that it was prime Jap-land, and was only recently enemy territory. No way he was gonna get Jones to go. In the NCOs' club Gus practically swaggered with know-how and anticipation. He tilted his cap non-regulation style and made the grinning announcement that the would get laid every night in Tokyo by a different broad. "I've heard they just line up smiling and bowing, man. You take your pick! And don't think that the American buck doesn't buy you anything—I mean anything—you want!"

Mebbe I should go, Jones thought. But to Gus, he said, "All Japs. Likely you'll wake up tomorrow or next day with the clap or worse."

"I'll use rubbers—ain't stupid. And the way those broads treat you, man!" he said with as much relish as if he'd been there before. "Soft hands all over. Nice smells. Kissy kissy in places you never thought of before. Think you was a king or something."

"Yeah, yeah." Jones said he might go but for missing the Tigers win a game in the World Series. Gus laughed.

"Think they don't have overseas radio in Tokyo? You sure have gotten stuck on those games since I laid you thirty bucks on my Cubbies."

"You tell me something else here that's closer to the old days. Besides, somebody's gotta call you. Detroit's where they make engines, so the Tigers got to have something. Won three games to your two and on a roll to win the fourth today, and the Series, and my bet to shut you up."

"Yeah, yeah. Newhouser's smart enough to dodge the draft. And Greenberg may be just back from the army, but that's the best your Tigers got against my Bowroy and Cavarretta. We're hot today."

"My Newhauser's going to pitch circles around your Cubs," Jones declared. "That fuckin' thirty bucks I win from you today goes toward the newest style boat engine back home—Palmer Forty at least."

"Bull! Whoever wins today has got to spend it in Tokyo. I need to show a dumbass like you around. Somebody's got to make sure you don't get rolled."

With a shrug, Jones agreed with to go to Tokyo, though he still pretended reluctance. "Nobody rolls Jones Henry!" he declared.

Gus's connections hitched them a transport flight direct to Tokyo. And since Gus knew—or more likely had buttered him up, Jones thought—the pilot, they were invited to the cockpit soon after takeoff, instead of staying strapped to a bucket seat in the cargo hold with the others taking leave.

"Why do we want to do that?" Jones had growled.

"To see the sights, man. Suit yourself. I'm going up."

As Jones expected, there was little to see over the pilot's shoulder that he hadn't already looked at disinterestedly on the ground. Just more of the same blasted out buildings, cratered earth, and squared patches of land.

"So," said the pilot over engine noise, "Who's going to take Game Six? Looks bad for the Tigers."

Jones popped to life. "Who told you that?"

Gus grinned at Jones. "Cavarretta's gonna bring it in for the Cubs, man." He wiggled his thumb against his fingers. "See? I'm already counting my win money."

"You'll count your empty hands. Why am I on this plane anyhow? I should be by some radio for when the game starts!"

"Just wait'll you get to Tokyo," the pilot announced. "Try loudspeakers by the train station. Whole town's likely gonna be there listening." Plainly enjoying himself, he turned to glance up at Jones. "Your Detroit Tigers are in trouble—even if before today they'd got three wins to Chi's two. Chi Cubs are going to take this game today and tie the Series."

"Sonuva bitch!"

Suddenly the pilot turned serious. "Look off to your left."

Jones squinted without interest. "Nothing but clouds. Mebbe smoke. And we're going to miss the start of the game!"

"Smoke, still. Hiroshima. Today's October 8th right? So two months ago, almost to the day. Every time I make this run I change course a notch to see it. May be against orders, but this ain't wartime still, so fuck orders if it don't hurt the plane."

"Yeah? That's the place? Well. Couldn't burn there enough for me." Nevertheless, Jones leaned toward the glass and squinted to see whatever details could be made out. A few black shapes rose from the ground—maybe bits of buildings. He could see little else from that distance. But soon the plane had traversed this part of the scene, and they passed on over patches of water hemmed in by trees with yellowing leaves. "Nope. Couldn't ever be smoke there enough in—what they call it? Hirohito?"

"Killed a few thousand they say," observed the pilot.

"Did even one American get blown up there?"

"Don't think so, Sarge."

"Then it suits me just fine. Mebbe even got the Jap who would've shot my ass in the invasion. Couldn't ever kill enough Japs. And here we're stuck in the sky with no radio!"

The paved airstrip they landed on was clean and open, as was another strip nearby, although further off lay heaps of glass shards and concrete slabs with weeds grown tall around them. Jones headed for a hangar from which a cheer had suddenly burst, but Gus hustled him into the only jeep around that had room to take them into the city.

"What's the score?" Jones demanded of the driver.

"You mean the World Series? You got the wrong man, Sarge. I don't follow baseball. That's why I'm driving today—you can hear everybody else is hangin' around the radios."

"One numbnut they got at this base . . ." muttered Jones.

"Enjoy the scenery, man." Gus produced a pint bottle of whiskey from some recess of his uniform. "Got this at the PX before we left. Figured we'd need to loosen you up." He broke the seal, took a gulp, and offered it to the driver who shook his head, before handing it to Jones. "Not carrying this bottle any further, man, so do your share."

Jones shrugged and drank. They drove through stretches of rubble on either side of the road where only a pipe stood here and there. Past areas that had maybe a building or two intact. Others were roofless, with black holes for windows. People everywhere stooped like mushrooms, picking over things that they put in bags and boxes. Most turned their backs at the approach of the American vehicle. Jones took one more swig and another.

Deeper into the city, the driver steered through streets that had been cleared of rubble, leaving a single lane. He honked nonstop to clear the Japanese to the side, then emerged into a wider street lined by lean-tos and shacks thrown together from charred boards.

We showed 'em, thought Jones dispassionately. What surprised him, though, was the energy with which these city Japs hopped about. Nothing like the ones on Okinawa. These were like the mosquitoes on the islands: sprayed 'em down, you turned for a minute, and back they came in double numbers. Some Japs even waved at them. When, still honking, they slowed a bit, one Jap ran alongside trying to sell a drawing of trees and mountains. By now, Gus held the nearly empty bottle, and he sprinkled the last drops of whiskey onto the Jap's head before tossing the bottle out of the car. It clunked off the boards of a stall where little skewers of meat were smoking, then bounced against an adjoining stand selling pictures. It had barely touched the ground when a Japanese woman ran to pick it up.

"You might've hit somebody," grumbled Jones.

"But I didn't."

"Yeah, you missed."

The driver let them out at the side of a large building that he said was the Tokyo train station. "If you want your World Series, guys, here's the best place."

As the two clambered heavily out of the vehicle, Jones was less than impressed. Japs and Americans stood side by side, practically shoulder to shoulder, listening to the voice from the loudspeaker. "Tigers better win," Jones growled, half-buzzed, to Gus. "Otherwise just standin' around in some shit hole, buddyin' up with Japs for no good reason."

Jones and Gus elbowed their way through the crowd as Greenberg hit a home run over the left-field wall, bringing in two more runs for Detroit. But even as Jones joined in the cheer—looked like the Tigers were gonna win anyhow—he couldn't help but think how there was only one place in the world Jones wanted to be. Home in Alaska. In Ketchikan where his old boat waited.

—★—

PART ONE

I

CAGED

OKINAWA, AUGUST 1945

A pistol would have done it. It could have been with that pistol they took from his belt. The insult! To revive him with medicine when he had ordered himself to die. It was the fault of the soldier whose gaze had fixed with his soon after his capture. Captain Kiyoshi Tsurifune knew enough English to understand the man's order—from English studied long ago, in a different world where dealing with barbarians was integral to the family business passed from father to son for decades.

If only they had shot him during capture as they had some of the others. If he had not been stunned by the explosives thrown into the cave, if he had strode toward them boldly as had young sub-lieutenant Kiji—with a concealed grenade ready to take at least one of them with him. Kiji had died a hero's death. The Americans had shot him in the chest—only moments before the armed grenade blew him apart. This angered the Americans, who had shot others of his group—anyone who made even the least move. In other circumstances Kiyoshi had given those same orders. Shoot the prisoners—even those with hands up for surrender—if they made the slightest step forward.

"That's for my dead buddy you yellow bastards!" one of the Americans had yelled before shooting two Japanese soldiers. Kiyoshi hoped indeed that some of those the American called his "buddies" had been righteously killed for the Emperor.

In the fetid cave where they had lived like rats in dark and mold for weeks, waiting to kill the Americans when the invasion came, hatred for all but anyone Japanese was clear enough. Even worthless local villagers, cringing disgracefully and screwing up their Chinese-like faces, were driven away when they too tried to use the caves after the shelling began. Those villagers that were not even useful for providing food, for they proved to have none themselves; inferiors who would have quickly revealed hidden stores under even lightest torture.

Now he was not even allowed an honorable death through starvation. The captors brought him food. Rice, of course, boiled to a clogged mush. The Americans had no understanding of how it ought to be prepared. Canned meat that smelled like dogs—Kiyoshi had to admit that perhaps it was better than the "meat" that was mostly weeds and sawdust to which they had become accustomed in the caves. But it was so rich that it cramped his stomach and worse. Yet he ate what they dished out onto his metal plate. At first he thought the meat's strange taste was poison, and he prepared calmly for the justified, agonizing death of the defeated. At least he would die without flinching. When this happened, his identity would be found in the worn canvas pouch of letters and photographs that was all he had managed to keep when he was captured. Hope, then, that perhaps merely the report of his death would reach home, but not the circumstance, and Father would be able to mourn a son lost in honorable combat for the Emperor.

Not that the eternal spirits would be fooled. He himself would never be a Righteous Soul enshrined at the Yasukuni Shrine on Kudan Hill, like Junior Sub-Lieutenant Kiji. It appeared it was his doom to remain among the living, the vessel of his own disgrace.

He had prepared himself to suffer greatly as a prisoner. Yet even his wounds healed under enemy care. Now, instead of pain, his body produced such disgusting dysentery that he was often obliged to stagger or crawl in desperation to defecate into a stinking pit. A piece of canvas covering the pit trapped insufferable heat, and the stench attracted insects that bit any part of skin not covered by the rags of a once-proud uniform.

The Americans even humiliated officers as if they were only common soldiers. It was a mere American corporal who ordered them to strip and relinquish their clothes. They were sprayed with brackish seawater pumped by a small, noisy engine through a hose. The sudden pressure slapped their thin bodies against each other until they learned to brace against the gushing water. *(And how the inferior American behind the hose laughed at their struggle!)* Then, by gestures, they were made to cup their hands and scoop a thick, slimy liquid from a large can and smear themselves with it. One captor tapped each man's private and most tender parts with a stick unless the man rubbed in the liquid until it sudsed white. The liquid stung Kiyoshi's open sores and scraped like knives on the sores where the nested lice had bitten in a frenzy.

Then the hose would have been welcomed, but it was left to gush on the ground while their sweat dissolved the pasty liquid into long brown streaks. At last the hose again—washing off with its torrent both the dead lice and those still trying to bite. Finally the Americans splashed a bucketful of fresh, heated water over each man, half into the face and half toward the crotch. *(How good that water felt despite the humiliation. Don't admit it, even to yourself.)* And the final indignity: each man was ordered to pick and mash any lice that remained on the body of the man beside him. The prisoners did so in apologetic shame, avoiding each other's eyes.

The clothes, when they were returned to them, had been boiled clean. They were still hot and soggy, now shrunken and nearly shapeless, but the naked men hurried to cover themselves again.

It was an insult akin almost to torture to be made clean by the barbarian enemy. To be fed by them. Not beaten. Spoken to roughly, yes. Ordered about by the common ranks of their own soldiers. Deprived of an honorable death.

But the sun poured over the camp; it seeped through the shelters formed by swathes of canvas draped across poles. When rain fell, it settled into dripping pockets throughout the canvas. The raw chemical smells of disinfectant slowly replaced the odors of rot—except around the shit pits. Eventually the prisoners' clothes dried and took shape again around their bodies. The lice became so few that they could be sought out and killed with a pop of the fingers—this time, they didn't leave behind a dozen of their vermin brothers to make the picking a useless exercise.

When left to himself in the canvas shelter—the prisoners were too subdued to seek out one another's company—Kiyoshi's gaze wandered toward the sea. It formed lines of purifying blue beyond the fencing and past the heads of restless prisoners. It stretched in distant bands between hills and beyond the broken wings of a plane crashed into one of the squares of cultivated field.

In former days the sea had welcomed him as comfortably as home. From the desolate caves he'd stretched a hand toward goddess Sea. Daydreamed that her clean water washed the filth from his body. Now she beckoned as the ultimate home of the dead. Would drowned souls then live as gods? As restless spirits? As fish? Or, the greatest blessing of all, might the waters close over in simple blackness?

On that unbelievable night they said the Emperor appeared on the radio to announce surrender, when word traveled mouth to mouth among the prisoners, the sudden sound of booming guns made those around him hope. Hah. The surrender was a clever ruse, and now the Imperial troops were arriving to finish off the Americans. Shells exploded overhead, flashing in the night sky. The explosions were so great that hot metal from the broken shells singed through the prison shelters. *Now it is that I am to die*, he'd exulted, *and I will be spared the disgrace of having submitted to capture.* The thought did not fill him with the relief he would have felt only weeks before, even though he told himself—with tears in his eyes—that it did.

And then, after all, it was only the captors celebrating. The Emperor truly had surrendered. Reason enough for tears.

With acceptance that his entire nation was disgraced, Kiyoshi stopped thinking of personal death as the only way out. Surely not everyone should die. Looking back, the cleansing of the lice might have been the symbol of his return to life. All that the incident lacked in importance was the solemnity of a priest, as at one of the great shrines. He began to consider what life—not death—might lie ahead.

A father waited far away. And a mother, of course, both surely still living, although no letters had been exchanged for months. Were able to be exchanged. Father was the one face that remained vivid, the revered one he'd been trained to honor since boyhood. He was meant to follow him in the family enterprise. What of that now? And back home was a dead wife waiting to be mourned. His tender, sweet little Yokiko, who he had barely known except in childhood but married in haste before going to war.

The days after the surrender turned into long weeks. Daily rations of food and cigarettes began to be taken for granted. Anticipated. Criticized, even! And the small soap ration that provided a level of cleanliness beyond imagining during the months in caves and mud-slogged bunkers began to seem stingy in view of the American wealth of food and supplies. Those few prisoners to whom he deigned to talk—defeated officers like himself—complained so much that he felt ashamed. The Americans towered over the defeated. Barbarians, yes: big and loud. Voices deeper than those of the Japanese, less shrill when excited. He watched their confident progress. Men he might have liked if they hadn't been the enemy.

It remained hot even in pouring rain. And boring. Kiyoshi watched as ordinary Japanese soldiers marched off in groups with shovels or picks over their shoulders to do some kind of manual labor. At the very beginning he thought, yes, aha, they were being taken to dig their own graves after all, and his own death was still to come—whether he desired it now or not. But each night they returned, tired perhaps, but joking more and more, with enough cigarettes that they no longer needed to share. Their disgrace forgotten. Reluctantly, he envied them in his own enforced idleness.

With his energy slowly on the rise, he yearned to run and stretch. It so happened that two officers had also once trained in the ways of Jigorō Kanō, and the three of them began to practice judo. Long abandoned during the rigors of burrowing in caves, preparing for attack; such hardships had sapped any will for excess movement. The three men gathered what rags and other soft material they could find for matting against the hard earth. At the outset they felled each other with slow ritual to conserve their fragile energy, though a decade previous, their dojo masters would have punished such soft restraint with shouts and blows. At first, just a few minutes of training left them staggering with fatigue. Days later they found themselves putting force behind basic moves and taking falls with less caution.

Some of the American soldiers began to watch from their lookout towers. Even called encouragement. One day an American shouted out, "Hey! Heads up!" and threw down a rolled rubber tent mat to replace their makeshift creation.

It was the same scowling sergeant who had matched stares with Kiyoshi weeks before. The one who had ordered him medical attention. The two men eyed each other once more. This time, before the sergeant turned away, Kiyoshi made a slight bow.

-★-

2

SEA STORM

SEPTEMBER 1945

One daybreak, as the prison camp was just beginning to stir, a Japanese interpreter suddenly moved among them calling, "War is over. Gather your possessions and be ready to move. There is a ship waiting to take you home!" The rumble around Kiyoshi rose to a roar as the men talked excitedly. Some wept. There was little to gather. Hours yet followed of waiting.

They lined up for a final meal dished from pots onto metal plates (which the interpreter told them to keep for the journey) then at last they were formed into groups of about twenty men. Each group marched out separately, accompanied front and rear by armed Americans riding in open vehicles.

The road was sometimes little more than a rutted path. They passed rusted out vehicles and even a crashed plane—one wing stuck high in the ground like a banner. Green vines had already begun to cover the wreckage, even though most of the terrain was shell-pocked and barren to the rock.

The stones hurt Kiyoshi's feet through boot soles worn thin as paper. The material was dried stiff and rotting, and it chafed raw against each ankle. Officers' boots were not designed for marches but for riding above the troops in vehicles like those the common American soldiers sat in so casually.

Kiyoshi's group passed through the remains of what had been a fishing village—to judge by the scattered nets. Only a few old Okinawan men and women were there to watch the prisoners pass by. Faces more Chinese than Japanese, wrinkled and thin. Short people, brown as the earth to which they seemed anchored. Most of them stared without emotion. Only one, a woman, caught Kiyoshi's gaze. She spat. *Worthless peasant,* he told himself, and turned away. But what would his own father and mother look like after years of war?

Death to expiate defeat would have been the easy way.

The group of marching prisoners had reached the edge of the shore. Small waves lapped nearly up to their feet. In the water waited a boxlike vessel that one had to enter by a ramp.

"Okay, move along. Move along there!" barked one of the American soldiers.

"You must advance quickly with no delay," the interpreter translated. "Go. Go. Others are coming behind you. Do not cause delay!"

"Hai, go!" snapped prisoner Captain Kiyoshi Tsurifune, and he led the way into the water.

Once aboard the vehicle, the seawater that had filled his decrepit boots dribbled through holes worn through at the ankles.

They were packed to standing for the trip to a warship at anchor, supporting each other shoulder to shoulder as the clumsy landing craft rolled and bounced. A man beside him—a common soldier—vomited on Kiyoshi's shoulder. Nothing to be done about it. Kiyoshi stared ahead as if he didn't notice and made no acknowledgment when the man tried to bow an apology in the serried quarters.

At the ship's side they were confronted by a clacking ladder constructed of footboards held together by rope, while their own craft surged up and down against the gray steel hull.

"Grab ahold and climb," shouted a voice above in English. "Look lively there!"

Another interpreter called down in Japanese: "You must one by one boldly grip the ropes and climb upward. This is necessary, so do it quickly."

One man found a handhold on the ropes just as a sea swell raised the slippery deck he was standing on. He cried out, loosed his grip, and fell back against the others hemming him. Some of the men began a mutter close to a moan.

"Oh shit," laughed one of the Americans at the ship's rail above. "This'll be a fuckin' circus. We got some kind of dip net aboard?"

Kiyoshi elbowed his way to the ladder. In the old days as a youth, he had ridden aboard fishing vessels and the mothership owned by Father and Grandfather. He knew what to do now.

"Watch," he commanded and grabbed the rope as the deck rose. "Take hold and then do not let go. Be courageous. Do not let them see you are afraid. Do not be disgraced by their laugh." Step by step he climbed the ladder until he was suspended beyond the surging rail of the barge. "You must move quickly to this height for safety," he called down. "Then, if necessary, stop for breath. Then quickly upward."

Panting, he reached the ship's rail, tried to mount gracefully, and ended by rolling over it on his belly.

"That's the way, baby," laughed one of the Americans, steadying Kiyoshi with a hand on his arm. The touch and voice were firm but friendly. Kiyoshi righted himself to bow, but the man had already turned his attention back to the ladder.

"Name. Rank. Age. Home province," an American sailor with a clipboard demanded impersonally. An interpreter beside him barked the questions in Japanese. Kiyoshi braced himself to attention and snapped crisp answers.

The American sailor stopped writing. A scar down his face exaggerated the hardness of his stare. "Yeah, yeah, fellah, act big. But you ain't a soldier now. Just one more Jap what needs to be shot or fed. How many of us did you kill? Wish I could ask that and put it in your record here. Tell him to stand over there until the rest of them come aboard."

The interpreter, a stiff, slight young Japanese, glanced uneasily at Kiyoshi. "Excuse me," he prefaced, and translated only the instruction.

Two other men clambered up the ladder successfully. Then one, already halfway up, fell back screaming.

"Oh man. Be here all night like this," said the friendlier of the two Americans. "Go tell the captain we'd better break out the fuckin' cargo net."

Thus, the prisoners came aboard like cattle. Belowdecks, the first of the prisoners were crowded into a mess hall with long tables. Others kept coming down the metal stairs. As hours passed, late arrivals were forced to group themselves in the passageways as best they could. Soon the odors of

sweat and rancid breath filled the air. At anchor the ship barely rolled, but
even this motion was enough to make some vomit. Any trip to the toilets
required stumbling around others, then waiting in long restless lines.

Word spread that they were being transported to the Japanese mainland.
It would take more than a day to reach a port on the southernmost island of
Kyushu. What then? Were they still soldiers? Were they to be released and
allowed to find a way back to their homes? For Kiyoshi, the journey north
would need to cover some thousand kilometers more.

With such crowding, they received only boiled rice passed in pots among
them to be scooped out by hand.

"Better than you yellowskin bastards ever gave my brother in Bataan,"
muttered the cook who distributed the pots from the galley. "Just give me
my way here for a day—."

Kiyoshi looked in disgust at the clotted white mess that grimy hands had
already stained brown. He started to refuse, then thought of the strength
he'd need to reach home. He scooped himself one mouthful, then another
before the pot was pulled away.

Throughout the day, the crowding steadily worsened—along with
the stench. The prison stockade had held about three hundred men by
Kiyoshi's estimate, while the landing vessel had carried only about twenty
per hour-long trip. Kiyoshi decided to try for air. He elbowed through the
others, stepping around vomit, until he reached the metal stairs that led to
open deck. A single armed American guarded it. When a new Japanese group
descended in a pack he wriggled among them like a fish moving upstream,
and then, at the top of the group, he crawled aside. The sky was already dark.
He slipped unchallenged into a sheltered corner by an open doorway.

Through the doorway could be heard the roar of unseen engines below.
The air that blew from the opening was hotter than even that from which
he had just escaped, and thick with oily odors, but Kiyoshi felt a rush of
excitement. It was the first time in months that no other bodies were pressed
against him.

At long intervals, prisoners continued to arrive in bunches, igno-
miniously in a sagging cargo net. Cattle indeed, all his countrymen, now.
Dishonored.

Two men clambered up a ladder from the engine room and out onto
deck for a smoke. Kiyoshi crouched in the dark, and they did not notice
him.

"Shit. No cooler up here," one of them said. A short while later, they ground out their cigarettes and returned below. Alone again, Kiyoshi crept from his corner and grabbed the two butts. One still had a spark of glow. He drew on it and extracted a lungful of comforting smoke before the spark died.

At last, the cargo net was dragged off, and the loading appeared to be finished. Sailors hosed the deck with seawater while a static-laced voice issued orders over a loudspeaker. From below, the noise of the engine grew louder, and the deck where Kiyoshi stood began to throb. He heard a distant thump of what might be the anchor chain. *Yes. Leave this cursed Okinawa—*. Whatever might be waiting for him in the homeland.

They moved past the lights of other ships, then beyond the harbor, into the dark. The ship began slowly to roll. *Yes!* Like in the years before the military when he'd traveled aboard fishing boats belonging to Father and Grandfather's small company, the nosing of this vessel into the sea signaled severance from land and all that remained upon it. He dared not venture into view on deck for a taste of breeze caused by the ship's motion, but even the air around his corner began to lighten. Whatever lay ahead, Kiyoshi recognized for certain now that he no longer yearned to be among the honorably dead. Perhaps they were passing out more rice below? That meant returning to that cramped space where he felt like cargo and perhaps not being so lucky a second time to escape. Hadn't he learned by now, through necessity, to live with hunger? He chewed the tobacco shreds from the two precious butts. They released a raw flavor that itself gave comfort. Each morsel was savored and slowly swallowed. When the last shred was gone, Kiyoshi doubled up in his corner against the hot metal walls to allow only minimal visibility and prepared to pass the night. Survival would need to be done an hour at a time.

Later, still in darkness, Kiyoshi awoke from a dream: chased by faceless enemies as he fell from the edge of one cliff to another, ranged like terrible steps. Wind-driven rain now slashed across the lights on the deserted deck. He was shivering, but it was not from cold—not in the still-thick heat. An overhang sheltered him from the rain and the eyes of the Americans. The swallowed tobacco had given him diarrhea. Go back safely below with the others?

No, solitude was surely too precious. Instead, he gripped a handrail, swung around so that his buttocks faced into the rain, and defecated. Back in his shelter he huddled once more and prepared to return to sleep, despite the malaise of the dream that remained strong.

He woke next to water splashing over his body. It was daylight, but the sky billowed in shades of deep gray and black. He rose against heavy motion, gripping the handrail for support. The ship swooped high, thudded down, twisted, pitched. Wind blew through the ship's rigging with the sound of a human whine. Objects unseen clanged and thumped. Beyond the rail, waves roiled in dark foaming walls. With the ship's roll, the long deck he faced sometimes slanted clear to the water. And then, rearing in the opposite direction, it carried scoops of sea that raced in to his corner and bubbled around him. It was only because he had wedged himself in that had he not been swept out or overboard.

He watched three American sailors labor their way across the deck. They were made to bend forward into the wind, moving by spurts in the moments when the deck stabilized between rolls. Finally, they reached a lifeboat— its canvas cover flapping wildly loose. The wind nearly drowned their shouts and so pressed against their pants that the contours of their knees were clearly defined. The Americans tightened the canvas with heaves on its guy ropes. At times, seawater rushed so high against their legs that they needed to grab hold of some part of the lifeboat for support. When they turned to leave from the direction they had come, the wind pushed them from sight as quickly as if they had been running. Kiyoshi heard footsteps on the engine room grating, and clutching the rail, he swiveled around the corner and out of sight. The hatch of the door thumped shut. He looked in time to see the handles that secured the door turn from the inside to lock it. Now he was truly alone. And he was hungry. At least when he extended his raised face beyond the overhang he could lick fresh rainwater from his lips.

Long hours passed. At one point an edge of canvas on the lifeboat flapped loose. The wind, like a beast at its meat, tore and tore until only shreds of cloth remained. Finally, the shreds themselves flew off in pieces. No men appeared now on deck. The black seas swelled and deck lights glistened on the walls. The foam on their tops gleamed whiter than anything else in Kiyoshi's horizon. Unseen objects still crashed with booming thumps, and the wind swept deep ripples in the water that scudded steadily across deck.

Seawater, sometimes as high as his knees, surged into his corner, drenching him. The seas began to seem full of life, trying to pull the man away with them. Kiyoshi gripped the rail tighter.

Suddenly the deck rolled deep into water, and a great waved crashed over the lifeboat. When the water surged away, the lifeboat was gone. Only pieces of rope remained, flapping wildly from a broken davit.

Kiyoshi began to laugh. He started cautiously, afraid to be heard. But the roaring wind drowned the sounds even from himself. He was free to shout as loud as he pleased. Shout till his throat burned.

"Ai! Ai! Why has Japan suffered disgrace?" He shouted it. "Japan has been betrayed!" He shouted this too. "Honored Supreme Emperor, why did you allow this? Are you guilty? *Who* is guilty? What becomes of me? Of my father? Of sacred Nippon itself? Ai! Ai!" He shouted it all until he doubled over, coughing. The wind and rain blew into his tears.

The handles on the hatch to the engine room grated loose one by one, and a man threw open the heavy steel door. "Hey," he called. "Fuckin' Jap out here, Mike—that's the noise. Watch out. Maybe he's tryin' to blow us up somehow."

Kiyoshi gripped the rail and edged away. *I'll defend myself*, he decided. *They won't catch me alive.* Then he stared down the slanted deck at black waves foaming where the lifeboat had been. Death was waiting, if he let go of the rail.

Not ready any more.

"Oh shee-it," the man called out again. "All skin and wet—no place on this one for a bomb. He's just stuck in the blow. Hey, Jap, you! What the fuck you doing out there in typhoon season? Get in here!"

Another man appeared in the doorway. He also wore a white seaman's hat. "Get him in if he'll come," he said. "Otherwise let him blow away—one less Jap. We've got to batten down."

"Grab my hand, Jojo," called the first sailor.

Kiyoshi stared at them. He understood but did not move.

"Nobody's goin' to hurt you, Jap. But ain't coming for you in this, either." The first man gestured with his arm. "Closing this fuckin' hatch, Jojo. Get the fuck in here!"

Slowly, Kiyoshi edged toward them. He came close enough that the man grabbed his arm and yanked him inside. The other helped propel him through the opening, and Kiyoshi landed on his back. He heard the clang of the heavy door and the scrape of the handles. Rough metal grating pressed through his threadbare shirt.

"We're on typhoon shutdown—no time for this," said the second man. "What's around to tie him with?"

"He ain't going anywhere, Mike."

"Geez, Tommy. Still don't know much about Japs, do you? They're treacherous."

The two Americans ended by directing Kiyoshi to go before them, down flights of metal stairs to the level of the engines. The heat and noise increased at each landing. Massive blocks of machinery moved with the ship's sway. Some spouted oil. Every handhold was slippery. The men now had to shout to be heard.

"Look what we caught, Chief!" exclaimed the man named Tommy.

The man named Chief, older than the others with a face that was red and blotched, began to curse. They started to argue over what to do with the prisoner.

Kiyoshi stood. He felt dizzy, but out of pride he controlled the impulse to sway. There in a corner, strapped against a wall and covered by a lid, stood a large glass container full of water. It splashed with each roll of the ship. Clear and pure. A ladle rested beside it. The three men turned and looked him over. Kiyoshi bowed and pointed to the water, trying not to appear desperate.

"Oh, now I guess he's thirsty," said the hostile Mike.

"Then give him a drink," said Chief. The man named Tommy unscrewed the top and plunged the dipper in.

"Not in what we drink out of, shithead!" shouted Mike. With a grin, Tommy drank a sip himself and wiped the rim with his finger, before passing the dipper to Kiyoshi. Tommy towered a full head over Kiyoshi. Light-colored hair stuck like straw from beneath his cap.

Kiyoshi bowed. He tried to control himself, but instead drained the contents of the dipper in a gulp. The water was warm—not refreshing—and he swallowed so fast that he choked some of it back up.

"Better than what you gave some of our boys took prisoner," muttered Mike. He was likewise tall, but with dark hair cropped close to his head. His eyes glared from a sunburned face that was all bone. Kiyoshi started to bow again, stopped himself, and instead glared back. *Let this one be angry,* he decided. *I am defeated, but I'm not your dung.*

"Huh," said Mike after a pause. "Guess he's thirsty after all. Might as well give him more, now the dipper's fucked till we wash it anyway." He shrugged, went to a corner, and returned with pieces of cheese wrapped in a napkin. "What the hell, Jojo. You hungry too?"

Kiyoshi hesitated, then accepted with the slightest nod. He ate slowly, remaining dignified despite an impulse to tear into the food. At a clang on one of the metal walkways above them the Chief looked up.

"Uh oh. Word gets around fast. Here comes the Exec."

An officer arrived at their level. He frowned at Kiyoshi while wiping his hands with a cloth.

"Just happened, Mr. Crawford," said Chief. In surprise, Kiyoshi noted how this engine room worker did not address his superior by the proper title. Far too informal, almost friendly. There would have been great punishment had one of the men under Kiyoshi's command spoken to him so. "Too rough on deck to send him back with the others till the storm's over."

"Guess you're right. He giving you any trouble?"

"We could take care of anything like that, sir!" offered the seaman Mike.

"I don't doubt that, Petrofski." The officer, a man younger than Kiyoshi, had the straight bearing and intelligent face expected of a man in charge. He turned to Kiyoshi. "You. Speak any English?" His words were harsher than his tone.

Kiyoshi drew himself up straight. "Little much. Little much only. Captain."

"Well, that's something. Just have to keep him here till we get out of this. If he tries anything you'd better . . . hell, bang him over the head, I guess."

Chief laughed. "No problem, sir!"

"Got a new kid back home, Chief, I hear. Boy or girl?"

"News travels fast, sir. Just got that letter yesterday before we sailed. A boy. You got a boy too, right?"

"Well, he's almost a year now. With this thing over, thank God, we'll both see our kids before they're much older."

"Wife and I agreed if it was a boy we'd name him Charlie after me. What's yours named, sir?"

"We did the same. Henry, after me. Maybe call him Hank, then. Here's to getting home fast, Chief."

"Aye, aye that, Mr. Crawford."

The officer turned back to Kiyoshi. "Do what they tell you, and nobody'll hurt you. Right, Chief? Guys?"

Kiyoshi watched the officer climb back up the ladders. Clean uniform, strong bearing, none of the distance he himself would have kept between him and his inferiors in rank. These were not the barbarians he'd been warned to expect in leaflet after leaflet.

The ship's motion increased. Sometimes the entire vessel plunged, seemed to hit a wall, then shuddered to a halt while the engines around them sputtered. High above, seawater dribbled down through the hatch from the main deck. Once—most terrifying of all—the ship rolled so far that Kiyoshi lost his balance and the deck remained slanted while he stared up at the chugging pistons that were now directly in his face. Before the night ended, he was caked in grease, sweat, and seawater as he collected spilled oil and water into cans and helped in whatever ways they directed him. So much bilge had seeped through the holes in his boots that his feet squished in liquid. The American sailors accepted him enough to beckon him to them with "Over here, Jojo" when they needed help. Finally he drank dipperfuls of water without asking, while they shared their food with him—including an impossibly delicious apple. When the next watch came to relieve them, they all stayed on duty together for the emergency, and the two watches joked back and forth about "their Jap."

"Got to admit," Mike said. "Our Jojo's done okay tonight."

Kiyoshi felt both humiliated and surprisingly charged with happy energy. He grinned for the first time in months—perhaps years—and declared with a new English word learned during the night: "Fuck you, Mike."

Mike returned the grin. "And fuck you back, Jojo. You're okay. For this night at least."

3

KIYOMIZU LEAP

The next week was confusion. The American sailors from the engine room saw to it that he had new clothes and shoes to replace the threadbare uniform that had been drenched with oil and grease in their service. By the ship captain's orders, however, as soon as the seas subsided, he was returned to the crowded, stinking spaces where his own countrymen were imprisoned. The Americans, concerned now with the damage from the storm, which had swept much of their main deck clean and capsized smaller vessels, gave him no further thought.

Among his countrymen, he alone wore stiff new denims and shiny black shoes like an American seaman. It separated him. While in the prison camp, those who had been under his command in the caves had continued to address him as "Captain." Now others did too. But when the pots of rice were passed, everyone grabbed equally for a share. No one noticed that he alone—with a belly full through the kindness of the sailors during the storm—chose not to cling greedily to the pot but allowed it to be pulled onward.

The ship, delayed nearly a full day by the storm, landed at last in a port on Japan's southernmost main island. New Americans came aboard, accompanied by a female Japanese interpreter who blew a whistle for silence before making announcements. First, she instructed them to open a way for the stretchers carrying two wrapped bodies of prisoners who had died during the stormy crossing from Okinawa. Neither American nor Japanese questioned how they had died: death had become routine for all. The woman interpreter then declared, "Form in silence two by two, for orderly departure." She pointed to rusted trucks that waited at the foot of the gangway.

The Japanese men were not accustomed to receiving commands from a woman. They began to murmur, without moving. Kiyoshi watched as the Americans grew annoyed.

"Do as you are told," he barked in the tone he had not used since the caves. The others followed as he led the way. At the truck, a Japanese clerk compared personal data to the lists he held. The man was hollow-chested and middle-aged, with hands that trembled. Thick glasses kept slipping down his nose.

"How is it now in the homeland?" Kiyoshi asked. The man shook his head and gestured him on.

Two open trucks packed to standing jostled over roads cratered with holes. Outside the vehicles, red roofing tiles lay scattered around charred buildings. Some men were nailing stray boards into the shape of a shack. Kiyoshi saw no young women. Had the Americans then raped and murdered them as the government leaflets had promised? What of his own mother and sister? Could he arrive home in time to protect them? And what if he had to kill Americans while protecting them? At least then his family would all die together.

It began to rain. In one field, drops splashed into water already standing in bomb craters. Peasants were raking the holes level, bent like mushrooms under wide straw hats. They straightened to watch the procession pass. All were old—grandmothers and grandfathers—and expressionless, except for one man, who glared at them. The other prisoners looked down or away, but Kiyoshi bowed an apology as best he could while maintaining balance in the moving truck.

The rain increased and grayed out distant mountains. The trucks stopped by a long, open shelter beside a train, and the drivers told the prisoners to go. Other Japanese, wearing the uniforms of civilian officials, examined what papers they had and stamped documents permitting them to ride the trains to their home destinations. No Americans anywhere. They might have conquered, but they appeared to be taking possession slowly.

Two days later, with little food provided except for the two small cans of American meat rations given to each man upon boarding, Kiyoshi rode a slow train with others bound for northern destinations. He still wore the same American denim clothing. Those around him sometimes touched the stiff fabric enviously. The new cloth dye, bled out by sweat and rain, had stained his legs and arms blue.

A single car of the train held some Americans and a few official looking Japanese civilians. The entrance to that car stayed locked to the scruffy, sweating soldiers.

Only a year before—so long ago—he had ridden a similar train in the opposite direction, en route to defend the homeland from American bases on the colonized Ryukyu Islands. Despite wartime privation, he'd ridden in a separate car for officers. The talk had been of duty and sacrifice. They had raised cups of saké to the Emperor and, with choked emotion, had pledged him their lives. At the time, he'd written letters of farewell to Father and to the wife he barely remembered. He had expected to return only if victorious.

People brought water at the way-stops, but seldom gave food except for money or barter. One woman on the platform, who stood up straight even though her clothes were close to rags, handed him part of a rice cake.

"You have failed us," she said.

"Yes," he acknowledged.

His worn canvas pouch held the document of free passage as well as old letters and photographs. But he had neither money nor possessions to barter. In the prison camp and on the American ship, such food as there was had been simply handed to him. Now, somehow, he was expected to survive on his own, as were most of the others who called out to ask for food and water whenever the train slowed. Only a few had been canny enough to steal items from the camps and from the ship and hide them beneath their clothes. All Kiyoshi possessed besides the pouch were the metal dish and spoon issued him. They were soon traded. He had foolishly discarded the cans of American meat after emptying them—or rather, had set them aside without thinking and they had disappeared at once.

The train, he knew, took them north along Kyushu, the southernmost of Japan's four islands. Then it connected to Honshu, the greatest island, where the rails led through Hiroshima and Kyoto to Tokyo, skirting mountains all the way. In Tokyo he'd need to find another train north to Sendai, then reach his hometown along the coast by some other means. He'd go by foot, if he had to. Let this train hurry!

But in the dark on the painstaking trip that had started shortly after daybreak, the train halted. "All must get off," called an official. "The train goes no further. You must take a boat to where the train resumes. Go. Walk to the boat. Anyone will direct you."

Like the others, Kiyoshi walked along the few streets of stalls and houses in the town. Only a few inhabitants remained outside as they approached. Too proud to beg, he asked only for water. Using chopsticks, one man placed a few noodles from the bowlful he was eating into Kiyoshi's cupped hands. An old woman gave him a small piece of fish. Both avoided his eyes and said nothing when he thanked them.

The boat would not leave until morning. The passengers (except for those from the special car, who had been received in a house) had no place to pass the night but under the roof of an open shed that stood near the boats. Rain poured outside. They huddled away from the patches of water where the roof leaked, at first considerate of one another, but soon pushing without regard for any but themselves.

At last they boarded an old wooden vessel with heavy scuffed rails and a battered engine whose shaft poked unhoused into the water. The boatman, elderly and bent, accepted Kiyoshi Tsurifune's travel document.

"A slow way home when I have so far to go," Kiyoshi observed politely.

"You can't travel on tracks that are melted, can you?" the man snapped. "Thank the barbarian Americans. Not a building or a person left in Hiroshima ahead, and the air itself poisoned, they say. Barbarians who stop at nothing. Criminals. I curse them!"

"Yes? Yes? Is that so?" News of the Hiroshima bombings had passed among the prisoners of the camp, but not the extent of the damage.

"And what did you soldiers do to protect us? Or to save the Emperor from disgrace!"

Among the islands, the first of the autumn leaves were turning red and golden on the highest hills. Gnarled pines bent to the breeze. Mists like those in classical paintings lingered among the branches. Nothing of war had changed their beauty. Kiyoshi gazed and gazed, and his throat tightened.

When the boat landed, a vehicle waited for the Americans and the officials, but the rest had over a mile to walk to the waiting train. The road, although it had not been bombed, was so rutted with gaps and holes that it might as well have been. Now they encountered only Japanese. An old man at the roadside gave Kiyoshi water.

"You've come from the hairy barbarians?" he asked. Kiyoshi nodded as he drank, careful not to stop for fear the pitcher might be taken back.

"As bad as they say? Tell me. Our women will hide. At least some may escape the rape." The man's voice quavered. "How do they torture? Beat with sticks? Whips? I've endured that, sir, with our own. But . . ." The man lost his voice and quietly resumed. "Break bones? Burn the skin with hot iron? All this they say, and more, more. How can we prepare? Such is fate, but we're no longer strong."

Kiyoshi made a gesture of reassurance, but it was a weak one. He too was uncertain.

"Listen, sir. Do you think ghosts can protect the living? Our son, you see. Protect at least his mother and sister. He gloriously fought and died for the Emperor, you see. But we have no offerings left to burn, and do you think his ghost can still pay attention?" Kiyoshi let the question go unanswered. Had he not wondered the same himself often enough? Undeterred by the silence, the man ventured a final, trembling question. "In the places you've been, have many survived?"

"Many, old father. And I've seen no torture. But that means nothing. Make the women hide."

The train crawled, as weary as the people and villages it passed. Outside of Kyoto it slowed more and more, then stopped. An hour later, a conductor announced: "Power is gone. Tomorrow they say, perhaps. Stay aboard if you wish."

A rickshaw driver pedaled up on a bicycle rusted wherever the old paint had peeled away. He quickly discovered the railcar with the Americans and began soliciting them in Japanese as they alighted. A sleek-haired Japanese man in the car joined the Americans and brusquely appeared to take over. Two other rickshaw men arrived, applying with equal urgency.

Kiyoshi wandered out into a field beside the train, squatted on his haunches, and chewed on grass to ease his hunger. Nothing to do but wait. Two American officers smoking cigarettes stopped nearby. One looked around. "Good," he said. "He ain't following, that pushy Jap interpreter. So busy covering his ass you'd think he'd *personally* advised the Emperor not to fight us."

The other held an open book. "Looks like this is the temple place, Sammy. Now get this one. Famous temple that's only sand and a few rocks. These Japs get excited about funny things. Think it's worth the trip to go in and look around?"

"Not if that's all they've got. And sure not with those Japs on the train we're stuck with, whether they talk English or not." He was the biggest of the officers, tall and fat by any standard. His khaki uniform stretched tight around his shoulders and waist.

"Well yeah. But, if we're stuck here . . ." The American with the book was also tall, but thinner and more deliberate in his movements. His uniform had crisp lines. "Might as well see something other than bayonets and helmets." He noticed Kiyoshi on the ground. "Hey. See you're wearing our sailor dungarees. You an interpreter? Speak any English?"

Kiyoshi rose, understanding the question, although not all the words. "Yes? Yes?" he said politely in English.

It certainly was a stroke of luck. Nearly a decade ago, when Kiyoshi was twenty years old, his father had sent him to make offerings for their company's prosperity in the great temple cities of Nikko, Nara, and Kyoto. With gestures and easy laughs from the Americans at his efforts, Kiyoshi named some Kyoto shrines and temples he'd remembered. "Number one, famous Golden Temple. Another number one, Temple of Thousand Buddhas, all one-two-three. The name, yes, I remember, Sanjūsangen-dō. You find in book, sir."

"Buddhas?" declared the fat American named Sammy. "Then forget it. We've already seen more Buddhas than any Christian needs, so just forget it. Give this 'ol Mis'sippi boy a nice clean church. We'll just stay here thanks."

Kiyoshi realized he would be a fool to let this opportunity escape. "Ah. Best number one—. No many Buddha. Good temple with . . . mizu, mizu . . . water! Kiyomizu-dera! Big. Beauti . . . ful. Good every, every . . . thing. No many Buddha."

The lean American turned some pages in the book and read for a while. "That looks like an okay one, Sammy," he said. "Don't make a big deal over its Buddhas, in any case, if that's what bugs you. Anyway, no harm in seeing what they've got." He turned to Kiyoshi, "What the hell, you want to come show us?"

They whistled over to the three bicycle rickshaws. Each driver wore only a top, shorts, and sandals despite a chill in the air. Their frayed shirts flapped over thin chests, but their legs had muscles knotted like vines on a pole.

The fat American leaned from his rickshaw and asked in a drawling voice, "What's your name now, boy?" Kiyoshi drew himself up and gave his full name. "How's that, now? Say it again, slow." Kiyoshi repeated it four times on request. "Shoot, who'd ever remember that? Might call you 'Foonie' but that sounds wrong. How about something easy like, well, Willie? That okay? Willie?"

"Hai. Yes." Kiyoshi's few words of English—long left unused for fear of inviting charges of treason—now served him well. The rickshaw drivers spoke only peasant Japanese. He named their destination to the one who seemed to have taken charge.

"No, no, sir. Far away. We'll go to Thousand Buddhas. That's the good one for the Americans."

"I told you Kiyomizu-dera."

"Sir, the priest at Thousand Buddhas has little Buddhas to sell. That's what the Americans want. Souvenirs to buy. About ten days ago I brought other American soldiers there, the first ones here since the surrender. At first I was afraid, you know—they're so big, and you know what we've been told, but . . . Well, they bought. Bought! Bought all the little Buddhas the priest had and wanted more but he had only four or five for the few Japanese pilgrims who come nowadays. All the priests at the temple started carving— all night long!—and now he has more. Some aren't very good, but Americans don't know the difference. Two I took yesterday, they bought many also. So that's where we'll go, eh? To make your Americans happy."

If his American named Sammy became angry, Kiyoshi knew, he might lose them. But he considered, since they might indeed want souvenirs.

"Priests at Kiyomizu-dera also sell offerings," he said.

"Not little Buddhas, sir. That's what the Americans bought. What they all want. We'll take them to Thousand Buddhas. They won't know the difference from Kiyomizu-dera, which is far, far away from here."

Kiyoshi decided. "No, straight to Kiyomizu."

The rickshaw man muttered to the other drivers, but they started without further argument. Buildings along this road were undamaged. They passed gardens and small shrines. It was only the people that looked worn. After the destruction of the day before and of that back on Okinawa, Kiyoshi found it a sight to awaken hope. Perhaps the Americans had devastated only the islands furthest south. Suddenly there came a roar overhead, and Kiyoshi looked up to see six American planes approaching in formation. He readied to cry warning, leap from the rickshaw, and find cover at first sight of a descending bomb. But the planes passed on, out of sight. He regained his composure.

"Americans up there too, sir," observed the rickshaw man. "All the time fly over, for months."

"They never dropped bombs here?"

"Sacred city here, so Buddha protects us. Other places like Kobe, sure. All the beggars we get here from Kobe. Think they'll get our rice. What rice? Phew! Kobe beggars need to stay in Kobe. Bombs in Nagoya and Osaka they say. And they say bad, bad last month on Hiroshima and the place called Nagasaki. But I've never been to such cities so I don't know." After a pause. "Sir, Thousand Buddhas is coming soon, so we'll stop there. It's a long way to other temples."

"Kiyomizu-dera only I told you!"

The rickshaw man stopped pedaling, and the others followed suit. He faced Kiyoshi with eyes narrowed on a face of browned, wrinkled skin stretched taut across bone. "Listen then, sir. These Americans are rich. The priest at Thousand Buddhas now gets from Americans anything he asks for the little Buddhas. Twenty times the old price! Believe this: He pays me for every one he sells to the Americans I bring. And to you I will give half of this. Understand? You'll get more today than the price of dinner even on the black market, maybe two or three dinners. Eh? All this while you sit easy and I do the work."

Kiyoshi barked out before he could reconsider, "Straight to Kiyomizu, or I'll tell them to get other rickshaws. And they'll do it!"

"What's he saying, Willie?" the large American called over.

"Say Kiyomizu-dera good temple, sir. Say get to Kiyomizu soon."

"Fine. Finest kind."

Kiyoshi ventured nevertheless. "Thousand Buddha Temple come first, soon, sir. Have good souvenir."

"Didn't you hear us? No thousand damn Buddhas." Sammy turned to his fellow-officer. "Don't you just love it, the way they mess up the English language?"

The Thousand Buddha Temple faced the road with an unremarkable façade. "Pay attention! I meant what I said," warned Kiyoshi in Japanese, and the rickshaw men continued without stopping.

They passed a stall with a single steaming pot stirred by a woman. "Hey, John, you hungry?" Sammy called. "What's that cooking, uh, Willie?"

Kiyoshi asked, and reported back, "Nooders, sir. With . . . don't know word, sir—"

"What's that? Oh, noodles. Well, what the hell, let's try whatever it is. Tell our guys to pull over. Want some, Willie?"

"Yes, sir."

The Americans even bought food for the rickshaw drivers. Kiyoshi forced himself to eat slowly, but the rickshaw drivers made no secret of their hunger. The Americans had barely begun before the Japanese, even Kiyoshi clicked chopsticks against the sides of empty bowls. The American named John watched them and said quietly, "Get more, guys. All you want. Go on, uh, Willie, order it for them. For you too."

Back on the road, Kiyoshi noticed that all the people they passed continued to be either very old or very young. A single exception was an open place between old wooden buildings filled with people of all ages. They sprawled on the ground. Many lay prone. Smoke rose from small fires, and a chilly wind blew. Few of the people wore anything but thin and ragged clothing. The rickshaw drivers quickened their pace. The way that these people's eyes followed the three rickshaws made Kiyoshi wary.

"Who are they?" he asked.

The driver didn't answer until he and his fellows had pedaled beyond the cluster and stopped, panting from the extra effort. "Beggars, sir. From towns bombed by the hairy barbarians. And some now also soldiers, already come back. You saw their uniforms—still in uniforms. Soldiers who lost. Betrayed the Emperor. Then why aren't they dead instead of expecting us to feed them?" He paused for breath and rubbed one eye, which watered and was reddened. "Understand, only reason I took us this way, is it's the main road. Too far around other way. Those beggars steal, so watch out. That's why we went fast. Even though we are tired. And still far from Kiyomizu-dera."

Some dozen children from the camp, tattered and dirty, started to run after them. "Joe! Joe! Give me candy," one of them called in a high voice.

"Didn't they learn those words fast, though," Sammy said in good humor.

"Okay kids," called John. "Catch!" He threw out two large bars of American chocolate. The rickshaw man muttered urgently and the three drivers started again quickly. Kiyoshi's gaze followed the candy bars with hungry desire. The children converged on them like birds to feed and began to fight over the pieces. Two of the boys broke from the cluster of children and ran alongside the rickshaws with hands on the rails, looking up. "Give me candy. Give me candy."

"That's all I have, kids," said John.

"Look what you started," said Sammy. "Well now, wait, let's see what I've got." He felt in his pocket and tossed out a few small coins. "That's it, fellahs. Now scram." By now the others had caught up, and they grabbed the coins first. The two boys persisted with cries of "Give me candy, give me candy." The tug of their hands made the rickshaws wobble. The drivers tried to hiss them off, then pedaled faster, stoically, without turning.

"Shoot, kids, let go!" Sammy exclaimed. "Willie! Tell them to scram now."

"Get away! It's over!" Kiyoshi barked in Japanese. The authority in his voice made them let go. They stood still. He watched their frail bodies recede as they scratched themselves—probably from lice. One of them waved.

At last they entered an uphill road that led to the entrance of the Kiyomizu-dera. The few shops that lined the road displayed an assortment of calligraphy and simple dolls made from husks. The distance had indeed been long. Kiyoshi watched with sympathy as the rickshaw drivers stopped pedaling and walked their vehicles. He himself dismounted and walked. The American named John followed his example.

"Come on, we're paying these guys, aren't we?" Sammy demanded. Then he shrugged. "Okay fellahs," he called. "Stop the train there." And he climbed down.

The sacred Kiyomizu-dera. Kiyoshi stood before the entrance with its guardian mythical beasts and wide stairs leading up to the first of the shrines. The curved pagoda rooftops of the vast temple complex loomed beyond the stairs. He bowed before the sight—several times from the waist—while he regained composure.

Nothing here had changed. Just as it had been when he stood here a decade before as a smooth youth engrossed in family duties. Happy time. Whatever else was churning in the world back then, times were prosperous for the Tsurifune family—from grandfather to cousins. Father had even visited America to meet with others in the fishing business and to make agreements. Had that journey to Kiyomizu-dera been in 1935 or '36? The Nation had already occupied Manchukuo—liberated it, so those in power said—and the arming had begun to liberate the rest of Asia from the decadent

West. By then the Imperial Presence itself had issued a rescript declaring military fitness to be the dedication of patriotic youth. He himself had been inspired, but Father prevailed and he was excused because of the family's food-gathering ships. Then, by the time he'd prevailed to serve the Emperor in heroic uniform—on a ship or even in the navy's airplanes, he'd expected— it was too late to choose and they'd assigned him arbitrarily to army officer training. It was his younger brother Shoji they'd chosen to be a pilot. On the sea or high in the air he'd surely not have been forced to do certain things.

What terrible things had he not seen? Had he not done? Some of those executions ordered in Java—not all surely—had been unnecessary. What of that prisoner he'd ordered tied upright, then ordered supported with ropes around the middle and force-fed to prolong death? Punishment to make others see and obey. Indeed, none of them tried to steal food or escape after that. Harshness of the times, ordered by directives from Tokyo and endorsed by the Imperial Majesty himself. It had given him no pleasure, as it had surely given others. The time was different. The beliefs different. It was the duty of the time to despise the captured enemy's weakness and to find ways to make him obey. Kiyoshi glanced at the two Americans he now hoped would give him money and food for his service. What would he have ordered done to them, three years ago?

At a basin topped by a stone dragon he offered a dipperful of clear water to his Americans. They both declined in good cheer. He himself cupped his hands in the liquid and drank. Then he smoothed a hand over the dragon's thick scales. Indeed, nothing here had changed.

With a lighter heart he led the way up the stairs to an urn filled with sand from which incense sticks protruded. A small old woman sat by a bundle of fresh sticks, bobbing her head to temple visitors. In former days he would have been able to produce money without thought and probably with a degree of condescension. But now, to the Americans: "Good thing, sir. Good luck thing. Make good . . . burning . . . therefore smoke, to spirits. Make good luck . . . therefore."

"Well, what the hell?" said the lean American named John.

"Now hold on," said the other. "We're not talking the Lord Jesus or the Holy Virgin, here, but heathen gods. Bad enough all those Buddhas you dragged me to a couple of days ago, but now this mumbo jumbo."

"Oh come on, man. It's the way they do things here, so what difference does it make? Tell you what. Light a stick and make it to Jesus."

"This is not a joking matter, John."

John punched his arm playfully. "Now don't get me wrong, Sammy. I respect all that Southern Baptist stuff you come from, but this is Jap-land. Okay, okay, you stand back now while I light one of these things. Then you won't get burned if a thunderbolt hits me."

"I still think it might be blasphemy. Except as you say this is Jap-land." Sammy turned cheerful again. "You go ahead. Since we're buddies, I'll just stand by you and take the consequences. But what my pastor back home wouldn't say!"

John slipped a bill from his wallet and handed it to Kiyoshi. "Get ones for yourself and these drivers too if you want."

The old woman squinted as she turned the money over and over. "How can I make change for this? It's over a hundred times the cost of my incense. Enough for days of white rice—even on the black market." Her fingers lingered over the note before she returned it.

Kiyoshi's fingers rubbed the note also before he handed it back to John and explained.

The American considered, then shrugged. "Buck or two of play money? Tell her to keep the change for good luck."

The woman rose, brushed creases from her patched skirt, and bowed and bowed.

"You'll spoil 'em," observed Sammy.

"Aw, what the hell . . ."

"You don't need to use that word all the time now, John."

"Sorry, buddy. I like to see you jump."

The two Americans followed Kiyoshi into the temple grounds. He led then through a wide plaza, giving as wide a berth as possible to a loft where Buddhist priests waited to write blessings for a donation. He also avoided the room with a wide altar at which women knelt and bowed to the floor to become pregnant—the subject of his own youthful mockery when, long ago, he could boast to friends that he had a better way to give women children. After all, what could he show the Americans to make their trip worthwhile—to make them generous with all that money—if there were so many things they didn't like?

They continued through the courtyards of the temple complex and down steep stairs to a forest path that stretched far below the main hillside structures. There it was, just as in his youth: the main fountain of sacred water. The clearest drops spouted from a pipe set into the vertical rocks, splashing freely into a wide stone basin. Despite the trees overhead, the fountain seemed to sparkle. A few Japanese men and women had gathered around to smooth it on their faces and to drink reverently.

"Mizu, mizu. Main-place good water of Kiyomizu-dera," Kiyoshi said. He drank some himself to demonstrate. Clean, pure, cold was the sacred water, straight from the rocks of the earth. He closed his eyes and felt the entrance of a friendly spirit into his body.

"That's fine, Willie. You drink for us, too. My guess is you've already caught all the Jap diseases in there." When he translated to himself what Sammy had said, Kiyoshi stared hard at the ground until he could recover from his resentment.

Further along the forest path stood other, lesser structures, and they wended their way slowly toward them. At last the American named John said mildly, "Guess we might as well go back if this is it . . . uh . . . Willie."

Back at the spring Kiyoshi excused himself and sipped another dipperful. When might he ever return, whatever the Americans thought of it? From the fountain they could look up to the temple complex high above them. Only pieces of the structures could be seen through the yellowing foliage and still-green vines—a carved post with its painted spirit figures faded from reds and blacks, the tiles—some of them broken—of a gracefully curved roof.

"Very old, sir. Very . . ." Kiyoshi searched for an English word to express ancient beauty and settled for: "Very . . . excellent."

"Sure needs repair," observed Sammy. "Bet that ol' roof leaks a bucket when it rains."

"Yup. Nice. Good. Very good," added John. He pointed to a long horizontal rail, partly obscured. "Now what's that?"

"For standing, sir. Good for look. Look down, down far." Kiyoshi had no English word for "auspicious." He settled for another, "Very good to standing on, sir."

"Well, hell then, let's go 'standing on' and look down down. Maybe we'll see something, uh, good."

So, back up they climbed to the great balcony terrace of the Kiyomizu-dera. Blue-hazed mountains ranged beyond the treetops. Kiyoshi leaned over the rail and peered. Just as he remembered, the drop went far below the level of the path and fountain and into an obscurity of trunks and vines. He started to explain to the Americans the traditional meaning of the drop. How, when starting a risky venture, the Japanese termed it "a jump off the stage at Kiyomizu." They listened, but failed to understand.

"Looks like you'd just get lost in that stuff—get all scratched," observed Sammy. "And who'd ever fish you out? So how would you do business after that?"

"Good way to kill yourself," John noted.

Kiyoshi noticed a man in a tattered soldier's uniform, lingering alone at the far end of the terrace. His smudged face remained a mask as he clutched at the rail, looked down, and walked away. But he quickly returned to lean farther out, as if he were testing. The worn soldier moved with effort, head down and shoulders slumped. When another person wandered to his part of the rail, he eased into the shadow of the overhanging roof, pressing against a wall until he was once more alone.

Kiyoshi understood. But what concern was it of his if the man wanted to jump? Yet, with a sudden urge, he called out harshly: "You'll hit rotten tree trunks before you reach the rocks you hope might kill you. It'll just leave you to squirm, and who's going to care for a cripple? But that's not my business."

He felt a rush of excited energy. Perhaps it came from the Kiyomizu water! One thing was certain. Suicide no longer offered his own release.

4

HOME

A t the Tokyo station, Kiyoshi Tsurifune needed to change trains in order to continue north. By now the Americans John and Sammy had long forgotten him and returned to the comfort of their special car. But they had been liberal with their money and had even spared a few cigarettes. Past haggard people squatting knee-to-knee on the floor, Kiyoshi picked his way toward the entrance and the fresh air. An occasional hand pulled at his leg. At the doorway, a voice barked, "Step aside!" Kiyoshi obeyed, as ragged men carried two bodies out on a single stretcher. An arm swayed from the stretcher like a pendulum. He'd seen enough corpses not to care.

But at sight of the landscape Kiyoshi gasped. The sights on coming into the city should have prepared him. Those viewed through the train window, seen around shoulders that had managed to maneuver close to the glass, had included a few scattered houses. Before him now stretched fields of ashes. Everything was flattened. Only a few charred tree trunks with stubbed off branches and, far away, a cluster of scorched concrete buildings interrupted the barren landscape.

A breeze swirled black dust into his nostrils and made him cough. Embers of burnt wood still smoked. Poking up within the level gray mass were random pieces of twisted metal, broken crockery, and green, stone-like mounds of—what? Melted glass? Here and there protruded block-like objects. He recognized some typical household strong boxes made of brick and cement, built to survive fire, as well as three bulky little safes with their doors pried open—probably from shops that had otherwise been obliterated. So this had been—yes, he remembered from other times passing through Tokyo and taken for granted—a whole community of homes. And the people in them.

Only a series of concrete troughs made lines through the debris. He'd seen some of these from the train, when someone had wryly volunteered that these had been hastily constructed for the water used to fight the fires. Although what good had they been in the firestorms that raged from barbarian planes through streets of wooden houses? The troughs now provided footholds for masses of scavengers in clothes the color of ash.

A few people walked slowly along the remnants of a street, kicking gray clouds around their legs. Old, all of them. Stooped and looking down. Not a youth or a girl among them. The few women were poorly groomed, with uncombed hair flying loose. Could his tired mind be showing him ghosts?

"Please, sir," an elderly man said, bowing. The tops of his cloth shoes were torn, he wore a ragged jacket, and his eyes seemed expressionless, but he carried himself with a tired dignity. "You've come on a train with Americans, haven't you? Can you tell me, so that I can better help my family, how it is you escaped their harm?"

Kiyoshi bowed in return. "Nobody tried to hurt me, sir."

"Ah. Undoubtedly they're waiting to strike, then, after more of them have arrived."

His tone made Kiyoshi uneasy. "What information do you have, sir?"

"Where have you been hiding? Over and over we've been informed, in newspapers, on wireless, in leaflets from the authorities, who know. The conquerors have a plan. Rape all women. Abduct all children. Behead all former soldiers, and beat the rest of us—perhaps to death. Our young women and children, of course, are hiding. What comes will come whatever we do, so therefore we must prepare to accept it. But some will surely survive, don't you think, after the American devils grow tired of committing their atrocities?"

"Perhaps you've been deceived," Kiyoshi ventured. But he wasn't certain, and his doubt must have shown.

"Young man. Some of these warnings came from the Imperial Presence itself. Forgive me, but you're foolish to be so conspicuous. They might single you out for the worst. Put on your oldest clothes and keep your head lowered like the rest of us, if you'll take my advice."

Kiyoshi thanked him, and they exchanged polite bows.

Despite the warning, the train north to Sendai—with returning soldiers packed almost to standing in a single dirty car and the trip prolonged by frequent halts—delivered him without incident. But his hometown on the coast was still miles away. He was able to ride part of the way on a rusty bus that puffed black fumes, bumping over and around holes in the road. He'd paid for it with a few carefully doled sen from the money the Americans had given him. But when the bus sighed to a halt, the driver declared humbly that there was no fuel to take it further. Some passengers politely requested a return of their money. Kiyoshi watched the man's hands shaking over each note he found to pay them back. A hungry scarecrow of a man. He shrugged and walked to the door with a dismissive wave. It made him feel in control, worthwhile even, for the first time in months.

At last, moving on foot and tired beyond caring, Kiyoshi Tsurifune looked down from a rocky bluff at the town of his youth. There were, of course, small pockets of charred remains, but also whole clusters of rooftops still intact. What of his own house? It was lost in details but the neighborhood had survived! Boats and small ships lay moored in the harbor. The sun caught on the blue sea beyond, rippling as if nothing had ever gone wrong. Around him, the hills were green with vines, while the maple leaves had begun to redden. In places, small waterfalls cascaded over the broken roadway. He cupped his hands and drank. Pure and cold, like the springs of the Kiyomizu-dera. So. Neither the great temple nor wild nature itself had been destroyed. Nor his home! He threw out his arms and knelt to kiss the earth.

In town he walked through the narrow streets, trying to ignore the stir he was attracting with his stiff American clothes. His stance and stride were such that some people bowed as he passed. Yes. There it was. The wood of its curved roof was paler, more sun-baked than he'd remembered, and the paper covering the windows was browned with age—but home! A figure in a sunbonnet was bent over some greens planted in the narrow strip of earth between houses.

"Mother?"

Mrs. Abe Tsurifune looked up from her work. At the sight of the unshaven, razor-thin man in a dirty blue shirt and pants, she cried out and collapsed, touching her head to the ground.

Kiyoshi knelt down to lift her. "Yes, Mother, I'm home." He brushed strands of graying hair from her face. It was a face grown older than it should have in a mere three years, a face now with wrinkles that stretched around the bones. To hide his emotion, he blurted: "I need a bath. And where's Father?"

The old woman clung to him, laughing in order to cover her sobs. "Yes. Yes, you need a bath—your odor, I bless it, but it's terrible. Somewhere I'll find firewood to heat the tub." When Father appeared, frowning at the stranger through thick glasses, she exclaimed, "See! Just see!" and hurried away, still laughing and crying.

Kiyoshi's father stood less straight than he had in the past. He wore a dark blue kimono patched in several places with a lighter cloth. His hair, remembered as black, had grayed, although the mustache clipped in imitation of the Emperor remained dark.

"We have no food for ourselves," Father declared brusquely. "My wife is foolishly sentimental. But we can't be expected to feed every beggar. Beggars not even in the uniform of those who lost our Emperor's war."

"Father."

"Don't profane that name! I am a father whose sons have both died hero's deaths fighting the barbarians. Move on to some other house, and leave us to our grief."

"Father, I am Kiyoshi."

Mr. Yuichiro Tsurifune, first-generation director of Tsurifune Suisan Fishing Company Ltd., adjusted the thick glasses on his nose. He advanced, one hand stretched out, to touch his son's face. Those fingers lingered to tousle the matted hair, then explored an eyebrow, a cheek, the curve of the lips. At last, he said softly, "You're not dead."

"No, Father."

"Not dead honorably, then, like your brother?"

"Shoji? Dead?"

"You didn't know from my letter?"

"No. No!"

Yuichiro Tsurifune clutched his son's face with both hands. "All this later, then. Only one son honorably dead. Are you a fugitive in disgrace?" He glanced around. "Come inside quickly before the neighbors see."

Kiyoshi bowed his head, and his good feeling vanished. Even though he'd given up all thoughts of suicide days before, suddenly it again seemed the only course.

"I'll go now. Before more of the neighbors see."

"But you're alive? Not a ghost playing tricks?"

"Can you touch the hair and the lips of a ghost, Father?"

The older man slowly dropped to his knees. He clutched his son's legs and rested his head against them. Kiyoshi could feel his father's body shaking.

"My brother Shoji is dead, then?" Kiyoshi kept repeating.

When the emotion had spent itself, Father cleared his throat. "Later. Later. Now help me up and come inside, son." He rose, clutching his son's shoulder, and forced a laugh. "By the way, you smell bad. Have you forgotten how to bathe?"

"There's been no opportunity, Father."

"Hah. How much has changed."

A glance inside the house showed Kiyoshi that much had indeed changed. All was neat, but the house was bare of anything but tattered mats and a hibachi with no coals to burn against the chill. Gone was the precious ancestral cabinet that had been treasured for generations. Only the god shelf, the kamidana with its shrine of beautifully grained wood, remained intact in a corner of the small room off the main living space. Beside a photo of the stern grandfather and docile grandmother he'd never known, dishes still contained offerings of water, salt, and something leafy. The white tablets lettered with names of ancestors and priestly charms still stood upright in the sand. And a vase of artificial chrysanthemums maintained its place beside the photo—now brown and curled—of the Emperor and Empress. But no candle burned.

Shivering in the unheated bathhouse, Kiyoshi scrubbed at the dirt with the small, hard piece of soap his mother handed to him like it was something precious. The water in the tub had been heated only to the point of warmth, but he grunted with relief as he sank into it and expelled his breath with a sigh. Then, clean again for the first time in days, Kiyoshi accepted the kimono offered him. But as he handed over the American denim he said, "These must be washed as soon as possible so that I can continue wearing them."

"Why?" his mother asked. He shrugged, not sure himself.

When he tried again to speak of his dead brother and also of his dead little wife Yokiko whom he'd barely known, Father cautioned, "Later. Later."

As in times past, they settled on cushions around a central platter. The meal Mother served consisted of a scant helping of soybeans and small fish. Even though she'd decorated their plates with cooked leaves, the size of the portions could not be disguised. And a shamed glance showed Kiyoshi that his parents' plates held more leaves than his and only one fish each.

"The ration office had no rice this week for our block of houses," said his mother brightly. "But next week's collection may be better. Have you ever tasted grasshoppers? Like crackers. I learned about them in a paper issued by the government last year, but now everyone has caught so many for food that it's hard to find them, or I'd have been able to fill our plates further. Be sure to chew the leaves. They're very nourishing. The best are tea leaves after they've stopped giving off any more tea, but these from the bushes are also good when you get used to them."

"I should register immediately to get a ration too," said Kiyoshi. "And I've heard I'll get some discharge pay when I apply for it. Even, perhaps, some clothing."

"Where would clothing come from around here?" said Father. "The soldiers, when they return, stay in their brown uniforms. I suppose you're lucky to have that blue shirt and pants."

Kiyoshi picked slivers of meat from the small fish, before sucking the spine of each for any food that remained. The time for salmon had passed, but surely the waters held other, larger fish than these. "Your boats then, Father. They haven't yet delivered today?"

"Boats? Where? They took my factory canning vessel for wartime cargo. The barbarians probably sank it. If they didn't, and it's returned in bad shape, where could we find materials to repair it?" Father lapsed into silence, looking forlornly at the patches on his kimono. Kiyoshi wondered how he ought to respond, when, with some of the vigor of only a few years earlier, Father went on: "For a long time, our fishing vessels haven't dared to leave harbor with the American planes flying overhead. The barbarians would fly low and shoot at us. But even if the water were safe, now our boats all leak for lack of patches and material for caulking. And where's the fuel to take them to sea? One or two community nets fish close to shore, reached by oar when the weather allows. But hold up one of those nets and it'll fall apart in your hands. They're so rotted and patched that they lose more fish than they catch, they say. Especially the big fish that can easily thrash themselves an opening. You see what's on your plate, from the community ration."

After a silence, Mother glanced at her husband to make sure he had finished before adding cautiously, "Like everyone else we live from day to day. And pray that our emperor can endure the unthinkable."

"Endure? Do you think he goes hungry?" snapped Kiyoshi. His own vehemence surprised him.

"Oh, I hope not."

Kiyoshi glanced at his father, who shrugged. They picked at the remnants of their food in silence, morsel by morsel to make it last.

Father spoke first. "I've given up, you see. Strength gone. Empty house. Your sister married a navy officer whose death was confirmed and his ashes returned after barbarian bombings two years ago. She lives with his parents in another town. Without sons, I thought, what did the two of us here need, waiting to die?"

"Well, one of your sons has returned."

"I rejoice at that. But I am still tired."

"He reads the newspaper that comes every day," said Mother. "So he follows all that's happening and tells me about it. There's nothing, really, that we can do. Except pray."

"You go to the priest too often," grumbled Father. "And each time, for some charm or piece of wood he's blessed, he expects five, or even ten, sen. Now, it seems, we spent money uselessly trying to reach the spirits in the other world since we had no ashes of yours to pray over. That priest. He'd even given you messages from this Kiyoshi's heroic spirit."

Mother looked down to avoid answering.

Kiyoshi felt a strange excitement, but tried to make a joke of it. "Well then, what did the priest say about my heroic spirit?"

"Happy in fulfillment of duty," murmured his mother. The words made Kiyoshi feel that he had indeed known death and had returned from the dead.

"Yes, I follow the news," Father declared to change the subject. "The American conquerors have taken over everything after they bombed our cities to pieces. What's this general's name? MacArthur. He's announced that Nippon will never again become a world power. What arrogance!"

In the pause that followed, Kiyoshi put down his plate. "All right now, Father and Mother. I must be told. First tell me of my little wife."

Father shrugged and glanced at his wife. "Well. We didn't see much of her. She continued to live with her mother and father." Yokiko had been the daughter of Father's vessel colleague and fellow vessel owner, Munio Nitta. "If you had given us a son with her it would have been different."

Kiyoshi burst out defensively, "We had three nights together before my leave was up and I went off to war again! You and Nitta-san were so anxious that our two households be brought together. The time had come at our ages, and we liked each other, so we agreed to marry. We tried! I know you wanted a son, but it didn't happen. Not even a daughter." He paused, glaring, then asked more calmly, "How was it she died?"

"All young people were required to do useful work for the war, and she was recruited to cut metal in a small factory. She cut herself, Nitta-san told me, and it didn't heal. And there was no medicine to be had to treat the infection. So it happened."

Kiyoshi closed his eyes to contemplate the information. It was so distant. Even as he tried, he could feel no emotion. Finally "All right," he said. "Now it's time to be told of my brother Shoji."

"Not here," said Father gruffly.

"My final child," murmured Mother. "Dead and not yet twenty. You were nine years older, already interested in your father's fishing vessels while little Shoji grew up. Barely noticed him, I think."

"No. No, Mother. I sometimes hugged him. Shoji was my brother."

"Always happy. My joy. So handsome and straight on the day he left for the navy!" She swayed, dropping her head close to the floor, and she began to sob.

Tsurifune Senior gestured for his son to follow him to another room. He began in a lowered voice. "All right. Your brother heroically crashed his bomb-plane into an American war ship and thus destroyed it. It was on the sixth of April this year, in waters near Okinawa. This ultimate sacrifice for the Emperor was described to us in a letter from his commander."

Kiyoshi bowed his head.

"He volunteered," Father continued. "He was a Thunder God. That's what they called themselves and how he's now enshrined. Thunder God! And their little bomb-planes were called Ohka. You'll see the letter. It's protected from rain in a rubber envelope that I made from torn fishing clothes, housed in a box I made that stands beside his shrine. We had ceremonies with a priest. All the town officials from the mayor down walked in procession to the shrine along with our associates, neighbors, even many strangers. A hundred mourners at least. I wrote you all this."

"It never reached me. By then we were living deep in a cave on terrible Okinawa, to escape from the guns those American ships fired at us. Waiting for their soldiers to land and reach us so that we could fight honorably. Could die when necessary. Nothing you wrote ever reached me."

"And then two months later, another letter came that said you—our oldest son—had also died heroically for the Emperor. Again we went in procession, again without ashes, your mother now barely able to walk in her grief." Father seemed to hold his breath, then asked, "Do you think, if the letter announcing your death was wrong, that Shoji might also be alive?"

"The glorious kamikaze pilots had no chance to return, Father." Kiyoshi said it softly, but his manner was firm.

"Your mother goes almost every day to the town's shrine of heroes. She leaves a flower there for each of you—or at least a twig with a bud or a leaf. That's a woman's way. I seldom go, although my sorrow is equal to hers. Now we should remove your place at the shrine. Do you think we need a priest to do this?"

Kiyoshi shook his head. "I don't know, Father. Don't know."

Father suddenly exclaimed, "And then, tell me what good was heroic sacrifice?" His mouth tightened so that his emperor-mustache stretched thin.

"Don't know."

Father put a hand on his shoulder. "All right. There are other things we must discuss. Tell me frankly. In what ways did the Americans torture you before they let you go? I should know the worst, to prepare for the future."

Kiyoshi thought of his own harsh treatment of prisoners two years before. Should he be honest, or tell Father what he wanted to hear?

"No torture. Occasional kindness. I . . . they aren't barbarians. The ones on Okinawa were harsh sometimes, but they didn't starve me. The ones on the ship coming home put me to work but gave me food and these clothes. The two that took me with them to Kiyomizu-dera gave me food and some money." Father continued to stare. "I . . . I think that I like Americans."

"That's treason!"

"Last year, perhaps. Not now, Father."

"Pay attention. How did the trains bring you home? Didn't you see for yourself? Hiroshima was destroyed by their inhuman bomb!"

"We had to go around Hiroshima. But through Kobe, yes, buildings were leveled into fields. Fire bombs, they said. Nothing left but ashes and posts burned to charcoal. Then Tokyo, where I needed to transfer to a train north. Ueno station is leg to leg with refugees. And the ruins. Ai!"

"There. You see!"

"We ourselves did things as bad, Father. Worse."

"Pfah. Our heroic soldiers were on a mission to save Asia from greedy foreigners and to create the Co-Prosperity Sphere. Whatever our men might have done was done to create peace and prosperity. Now look at us. Because of this atomic bomb, the greedy foreigners have prevailed with their evil. And this American general. He tries to make sure that Nippon will never rise again. I've heard rumors—he plans to destroy the great zaibatsu companies that trade and manufacture. And what after that? I'll tell you. Next to be destroyed will be small fishing companies like my own. Eh?"

Kiyoshi found himself smiling. "You just said that you no longer have a company, Father," he said mildly.

"For others. Others. And I've also heard rumors of what they call 'war crimes trials.' The papers tell us the Americans will be holding these in defeated Germany. What do you think? Will I be put on trial for heading my small company? For feeding the people who are now defeated, thus in disgrace and without rights? In truth, this worries me at night."

Kiyoshi shook his head. War crimes! What of that punishments he himself had ordered, back when a captured enemy was considered less than dung? He fumbled in his pouch—still with him always—and pulled out the two precious cigarettes the American soldiers had given him after the visit to the Kiyomizu-dera. He handed one over to Father and put the other in his mouth. "Let's have luxury for a moment. Let's forget things."

His father examined the cigarette, holding it carefully by his fingertips. "Look how all the tobacco is rolled evenly. It's American! Worth good food if you know where to take it. Don't waste that one in your mouth by smoking it!"

Absently, Kiyoshi removed the cigarette and handed it over. War crimes. Who might have survived to tell what he'd ordered? The prisoners under his direction had lost their rights because they'd surrendered. All the Japanese soldiers back then had believed it. They'd been told so, in speeches and in written directives. And most of his prisoners were still able to walk when he turned them over to the next command.

Father rose abruptly and brushed at his patched kimono. "Come. Let's sell these American cigarettes and have a feast to celebrate your homecoming! For one meal we won't need to look for grasshoppers or pinch bugs out of cabbage."

Kiyoshi rose to follow. For the first time since his son's homecoming a few hours before, a spark of purpose had flashed from Father's eyes.

The way to the black market led through the harbor. Along a pier with missing boards were two trawlers, their hulls and superstructures red-orange with rust.

"You might recognize those from better days," said Father. "They're still mine. But as I told you, there's nothing to paint them with, no fuel to take them to sea, no money for their upkeep. And even if my boats could get fuel and if the government returned my canning ship, I've always depended on the waters north of us—especially for crab. And it is rumored that the damned Russians have closed all of our northern water to us. All our great traditional fisheries around the Kuril Islands! That's the end for me. The Russians mean to starve us to death, in league with these Americans that seem to please you so much."

In the harbor, five old men hunched aboard a clumsy, open boat. By moving a sweep oar back and forth, a younger man propelled the boat along the water.

"They're going to one of the traps I told you about," Father said. "That's what fishing amounts to now. Cuttlefish and small mackerel. Once, just once, a big mambo! They cut it into small pieces so that everybody could have a bite. Ai, the fish that used to swim in these waters . . . before the Americans dropped their bombs and scared them away!"

As father and son walked down the road, children stopped to eye them, and mothers paused by their doors. One little boy held out an open hand and ventured: "Chokoreto?"

Father snapped him away. "You see? Hardly a barbarian yet in town, and the kids are already beggars. They see the clothes you're wearing. Not Japanese, so they must be American. Eh?"

"They . . . fit me."

His father stopped and glared. "Are you pretending to be American, then?"

"No. Of course not. No . . ."

The black market vendor, whom they found on a side alley, was not as secretive as Kiyoshi might have expected. At their call, he emerged from the back of a house—a confident man of about fifty in old army khakis. The sleeve that would have held his left arm flapped loose. Without even a glance to see if anybody was watching, the vendor asked at once, "What do you have?" He examined the two American cigarettes between the fingers of his single hand.

"I see part of one's been in somebody's mouth—too bad. You want white rice? Half kilo for the good one, quarter kilo for the other."

"Kilo each," said the senior Tsurifune. "They're both good and you know it."

The man handed them back. "Good luck somewhere else."

"Instead of your stingy price then," said Kiyoshi, taking over the exchange with sudden relish, "We'll just enjoy a good smoke."

"Bring me a whole pack unopened and you'll have enough rice to carry in both arms and I'll throw in some sugar."

Kiyoshi liked the man's tone. "Army? That where you lost that arm?"

"What's it to you? Were you ever a soldier?" Kiyoshi bowed a polite affirmative. "Well then. Happened in Manchukuo five years ago. You see I've survived."

"Doing this, aren't you afraid of the authorities?"

"Maybe once. But our great Emperor no longer bothers to watch. All he's done anyhow is smell flowers. Now we know."

"That's blasphemy!" the elder Tsurifune declared. His son turned respectfully to hush him.

"Tell the police if you want," said the man. "You'll see how much they care for banzai now. You think they don't get their share?"

When Kiyoshi laughed, the two bowed to each other in good humor. They settled for a full kilo of rice and, for good will between ex-soldiers, a few pinches of sugar.

An aged car drove up. Its faded black hood was polished around spots of rust. Through the open back window poked the gleaming rim of some piece of machinery. The driver shut off the noisy engine, pulled a soft army cap low over his face, and sat back.

"I knew you'd find a way to get that!" declared the dealer. He started over at once, pausing only to call back to Kiyoshi: "Come with bigger things and we'll talk longer."

Back on the main road, the Tsurifunes passed a procession led by a Shinto priest. In the center walked a woman with lowered head. Her outstretched hands held a box covered with a white cloth. Both men moved to the side to let the procession pass, bowing deeply as the box passed them.

The elder Tsurifune cleared his throat, but still his voice wavered. "Many, many ashes have come home from battle. So many heroic spirits now swirl in the air around us." He touched his son's arm, then grabbed it, and pulled him closer for an embrace. "What a blessing. I'll go tomorrow and remove the funeral marker with your name. Then I'll smooth over the spot reserved for your ashes, left open had someone ever brought them."

"I'll go with you, Father!"

"No. No! You'll stay at home with the door closed. What if some true spirits were hovering in the air out there and grew jealous that you weren't among them? I'd better find a priest to do it right, after all."

"I thought you hated priests."

"Not when they're needed. Only when they charge for foolish charms that don't work.

Only half in jest, Kiyoshi declared, "I'll wait for you behind a closed door."

"And then, my son, we'll start to figure how we can save my fishing company for your future. And for your sons when they come!"

5

REALITY

A few days later, Kiyoshi Tsurifune summoned the will to register with the local authorities as a demobilized officer. To his relief, no one looked at him with eyes that suggested he ought to be honorably dead. He received a ration card and a small amount of cash. "Perhaps you'll get clothing later, if some is available," said the official. "One more small payment next month, if we have it." The Americans might now be in charge, but the official and his government agency were still Japanese.

With money in pocket, Kiyoshi proceeded to a house of prostitution he had patronized years before in his youth. Women had been supplied him in his army days, before the battles that required them to live in caves devoid of all civilization. With hunger and the confines of the prison camp, his desires had disappeared. He took it as a good sign that his urges had now begun to return.

Nothing at the pleasure house was the same except for the agreeable odor of perfume. All was shabby, even the sprigs of artificial flowers. Dried bamboo slivers popped from the few pieces of furniture, and the patriotic posters on the walls had begun to peel. One poster—with a smiling girl and soldier standing under a message urging happy sacrifice—had been ripped at a diagonal and the lower half removed just at the couple's necks. The women were now different ones, of course. Children, they seemed.

"I remember you, sir," said the mama, bowing. "Young and handsome, brought first time by your honored father." Although the flower print was now faded, her kimono rustled with the swish of fine silk. Heavy powder and penciled features failed to hide pockmarks on her face. "Don't you remember me? Why should you? I was young and beautiful then. Those you might remember were conscripted to serve our fighting men. None have returned." She touched her face. "I was not chosen to serve."

Kiyoshi bowed, but chose not to comment because, perhaps, he did remember and she might have been beautiful.

They made him bathe in a tub with truly hot water and gave him a kimono which, here, it seemed right for him to wear. He folded his denim clothes—they were fresh-washed now by Mother, but the pants were still stiff—carefully in a corner of the tatami to indicate their importance to him.

The girl supplied him was young, attentive, soft-skinned. Barely before he could enjoy her, he'd been aroused and had ejaculated.

"You finished, darling?" she asked.

"No. Haven't started. Stay here."

She obeyed without question and caressed him for more than an hour before his body summoned the force for another entry.

"I'm glad to hear it," said his father at supper, when he said where he'd gone. "Did they ask about me, from times when I had the money?"

His mother, looking down so that only her forehead showed, murmured, "I, too, am glad to hear it. A man should be satisfied."

"Glad because it's time you started to have sons," Father continued. "You were born in the year that I established my fishing company, you know. A year of my greatest energy. Your sister came before that, followed by two baby sons so weak they died. Then, of course, your now-dead hero brother Shoji, the final of our children. So you see, as the family's only son, how important you are. Now your energy is returning. Time to find you a new wife and start having sons of your own. You are already getting old—what, twenty-seven?"

"Twenty-eight," said Mother softly.

"You see."

"I know no other women, Father."

"We'll correct that. Two other fishing company owners in town have daughters, even though none of us have boats fit any more for sea."

Kiyoshi laughed. "Give me time, Father." He liked having a reason to laugh again. And he enjoyed the new spurts of resolve his father had begun to show.

"By the way, why haven't you called on the parents of your poor dead wife? My colleague Nitta-san has surely been expecting you now for days."

"I've . . . not had the time yet, Father." He had indeed postponed the visit, reluctant to face another challenge to him having survived the war. "Tomorrow."

The Nitta house, like that of Kiyoshi's parents, had a thin strip of land around it for the planting of food. Fresh green shoots sprouted from the earth.

A young woman answered his knock. Her black hair, tied in back, hung as carelessly as a horse's tail. She wore pants and a loose shirt, both patched. All most unladylike. She didn't even return his bow, but exclaimed, "Kiyoshi Tsurifune alive! At least someone came back!" She took his hands boldly. "You've been expected."

The daughter, he decided from her shocking familiarity. She'd become a woman in only a couple of years, unrecognizable from the child she'd been. He couldn't remember her name for a moment, then: "Ah. Miki?"

"Of course. Come in, come in. All the town knows you're home, so naturally we've been expecting you." Kiyoshi removed his shoes and ducked inside through the low doorway.

He entered the family room. Father Nitta, who must have heard his daughter's exclamations, stood waiting. His face, once round, was now drawn taut with yellowing skin. His kimono fell loose around thin legs and slippers. Worse, for a man hardly in his sixties, he supported himself with a cane. At sight of Kiyoshi he extended a trembling hand. "So. My son-in-law, back alive to find his wife, my daughter, no more." His voice broke. Scarcely anything seemed left of the robust father of the bride, who, at their wedding, had managed to provide volumes of food for the guests despite wartime austerity. Nothing of the man who had told endless, often nonsensical, jokes that made everyone laugh and forget the problems of the times.

Little Mother Nitta hurried in. Also now thin to the bone. She grasped his hands and they exchanged repeated bows. "You've come, you've come. Still straight and strong, alive, oh!" She broke down and buried her wet face in his hands.

They settled on the main tatami, with his own place of honor indicated in front of the tokonoma niche with a classic vase and single flower. Mother Nitta could barely keep still. She bustled around, arranging cushions that needed no arranging, while her daughter calmly served tea. Then, with "Ah!" she hurried out and returned with a white silk robe over her outstretched arms. "Her wedding kimono. I brought it out when I heard you'd come home. I never allowed it to be sold—despite everything." She placed it in folds beside Kiyoshi.

"Oh, Mother," cautioned her daughter. She must have noticed Kiyoshi's clamped jaw as he tried to edge away without being too obvious. "Afraid of ghosts?" she challenged him with a bold smile.

Why did she need to say the obvious? Kiyoshi thought, annoyed, as he denied it. He didn't like this girl. This woman.

The parents of Yokiko recounted her death at length, breaking down in tears more than once, as they spoke. How, with everyone commanded by the Emperor to work for the war, and no men to do the many tasks, she had been assigned—despite her shy nature—to operate a metal cutting machine in a small factory that made tank parts.

"Work for which she had no skill," said Father Nitta, shaking his head. "My poor child was raised to keep a home." One day she sliced her arm while handling a piece of rusty metal salvaged from what was most likely a farm structure. The cut failed to heal. The arm swelled and turned purple. At last, after two days, she bravely returned to work, since the war and her soldier husband needed her tasks. But she was told to stay home and nurse her arm. The doctor came eventually, but no medicine was left on any pharmacy shelf to halt the infection. "And so your wife died, in delirium and pain," concluded Father Nitta.

In the silence that followed, Kiyoshi reached over and touched the pile of silk. He eventually stroked it, as he joined them in weeping.

When at last he rose to leave, Mother Nitta gathered the silk in her arms and held it out to him. "Yours now," she said.

He drew back. Then, unable to think of a reason to refuse, he reluctantly held out his arms.

"Oh Mother," declared Miki, as she lightly stepped between them. "Better to leave it by our own shrine in the next room. This is where our Yokiko lived. Where she died." She turned to him with eyes almost merrily narrowed, "Kiyoshi-san wouldn't deprive us of this comfort. Would you?"

With many words he assented, careful to hide his relief. After further bows, Miki accompanied him to the door. She stood patiently while Kiyoshi laced up his black American shoes, which he had buffed with a cloth for the visit.

He looked up. The light caught in gleams on her smooth black hair. Her eyes remained lively. "Do you work now, some place?" he asked politely.

"Once also in the same factory as my sister. It wasn't as bad for me. Until it closed, of course. No more tanks to be built. Now, for what pay as there is, I'm in the office of ration distribution. I noticed you there two days ago, but you were paying no attention to anything but your hands and feet. Ashamed to come back alive, aren't you? Stop being stupid."

Shocking intrusion! "I don't know what you're talking about."

"My parents will be glad to see you," she continued without sensitivity for what she had said. "Any time you wish to call. Of course we'll all cry a little bit, at first. But not forever."

Kiyoshi found himself smiling. She was, after all, being realistic. "I should thank you for keeping the silk garment," he ventured. "I . . . would have had no place for it."

"You are afraid of ghosts!"

"Of course not."

"Don't you ever speak the truth?"

"I will of course call on your honored parents again," he said stiffly, and with a bow, he hurried off.

On the way home he realized that he'd started smiling again. Actually, Miki's silky hair tumbled down her back more like a cloud than a horse's tail.

Next day, without announcing his intent, Kiyoshi walked to the harbor and down the pier, dodging loose planks, to where the two trawlers Father had shown him were tied. Rusty indeed. He climbed aboard the first, kicking beetles off the underside of the railing. A light rain was falling, and drops clung to spider webs thick as cloth around the winch. The door leading belowdecks was bolted, as was that which led up a set of stairs to the wheelhouse. All he could do was to peer through dirty windows at the big steering wheel and the binnacle holding the compass. Loose wires showed that smaller equipment had been ripped out. But most important—and beyond his ability to see without breaking a lock—would be the state of the engines.

He decided to return with Father the next day and make no secret of his interest.

Kiyoshi continued to walk around the harbor. That daughter. Miki was her name? Only a child when he'd married her poor sister. Grown up to be most unladylike. Too bold for a woman. Not like shy Yokiko at all.

On the other side of the harbor lay smaller wooden fishing boats. They, too, appeared idle, except for the open vessel he had seen being propelled by bow oar to a set net a few days before. The same old men were preparing to climb aboard once more.

At least this might show what fish were out there. With sudden purpose, Kiyoshi hurried off the trawler and around the causeway, making running leaps over cracked concrete and loose boards. He soon was out of breath from the unaccustomed exercise. When Kiyoshi reached the vessel, the men had already cast off and it glided from the pier.

"Hey," he panted. "Going to catch fish?"

The five men, all nearly as old as his father, looked up cautiously. They wore torn and patched rubber aprons. Two were barefoot and the others had rubber boots. The rest of their clothing was ragged. A slightly younger, barefoot man stood braced on the raised stern with his arms around the thick sweep oar.

"We have official permission, sir," the younger man said politely.

The gap of water was widening. However respectful they seemed to be, Kiyoshi decided, they wouldn't likely return for a simple request. His own clean denims set him apart—gave him authority—he realized. Rather than asking, he announced, as he would have as an officer to a soldier, "Come back. I wish to go with you."

"You'll get dirty, sir."

"That's my business." Making it up as he went, Kiyoshi declared: "I'm assigned to make an official report. Come back."

It worked. When the boat returned to bump against a piling, he didn't wait for a hand but jumped in. He didn't anticipate the layer of slime on the wooden boards—his rubber soles slipped, his feet shot up, and then Kiyoshi was looking at the men from a puddle that began to flood his denim pants with murky saltwater. What would that unladylike Miki say if she saw him thus? Good that she wasn't there to watch. He forced a laugh as the men rushed to help him.

"You see now, sir. This poor boat isn't the place for—"

He made a joke of it, heartily. They didn't laugh. Now that he'd descended to their level he saw that they regarded him with less respect. But the boat had left the pier again, and he was aboard. He took a deep breath.

How many years since he'd smelled the comfortable odor of old fish, permanently engrained in weathered wood? He rose and bowed.

"I've come for observation only. I don't want a share of the catch, so you do not need to worry."

They still regarded him dubiously. Kiyoshi made himself stand erect, blinking into the light rain. The boat made plodding progress under the thrust of the stern oar. Kiyoshi didn't mind—it enabled him to examine the harbor quay by quay. Many vessels of some five to seven meters in length lay moored. Bare, darkened wood showed through the faded paint on each of them. In one area, other far-seas vessels like those of Tsurifune Suisan Ltd. lay rusting. He watched a rat run up the hawser of one, where the saucer-like guard had broken. A building that might have housed the harbor administration was charred and its windows broken. Beside it stood a structure so roughly made that it could have been assembled in haste from the boards of other, demolished buildings. Along many piers sat old men and boys holding lines dropped in the water. As he watched, one man brought up a flapping fish no bigger than a bite. The man removed it quickly as the others strained to see, laid it on leaves in a box beside him, and tied the lid shut.

Their own boat approached three other small ones tied stem to stern, all open-deck except for one that had a simple shack of housing. Aboard the latter sat a woman with face hidden by a sun bonnet and an old man with a headband. Both held needles as they passed their net between them, mending holes.

One of the men aboard Kiyoshi's vessel threw a line to a man on the stern of the last boat in the chain. Soon their boat was added to the chain. It all happened quietly, solemnly, much like a ceremonial ritual, and without any of the lively shouts back and forth that Kiyoshi remembered from his boyhood.

From one of the quays came a boat under power. It puffed sooty smoke, a sign that it burned wood or charcoal rather than oil. When it reached the front of the little chain, a man standing astern threw a line to the first boat, then continued ahead. One by one the lines connecting the boats tautened and the hulls started moving. In this way, all four boats were towed slowly beyond the harbor and out into open water, where they were released one by one. In Kiyoshi's boat the man at the stern oar resumed the heavy sweeps that provided only a sluggish propulsion. Now in water that rose in low waves, it was obviously much harder work than back in the harbor. His thin arms had tendons that stood out like wires as he pushed and pulled the oar back and forth. His lips tightened in a mirthless grin that showed broken teeth clenched against the strain.

Kiyoshi watched and considered. In the time long ago, fishermen had shown him how to scull an oar, although as a boy whose father owned ships, he'd only needed to do common labors when he chose to. So long forgotten. Hard work, that, in open water. If he volunteered to try it now, he'd lose the status he'd assigned himself. And if he failed, it would be worse.

He stepped up to the raised stern. "I'll relieve you for a while."

The man continued to sweep the heavy oar. "I'm doing it, sir. Best that you sit and observe."

The five old men made a space for him, then politely squeezed away to the opposite side.

They reached the stakes protruding from the water that marked their set net. These, Kiyoshi knew, were cunning traps for fish; a wide, funnel-like entrance grew progressively narrower, until the only way the fish could swim was into the area that was boxed off. Once they swam into this, the fish would not be able to escape. It was an arrangement as old as nets themselves; he'd watched it in careless boyhood and had noted it again only months ago on Okinawa, before the horrors started.

Could it really be believed? The long, terrible war had ended, and the Emperor no longer demanded defenders to give their lives for his honor. Life, regarded for years as something to inevitably be lost in heroic sacrifice, had regained a part in Kiyoshi's future.

The men lined the rail. They bent over into the water and locked their fingers into the submerged mesh of the net. Then, with a common grunt, they pulled the first length over the rail. This motion they repeated, hauling in more and more of the net and dropping it about their feet—progressively diminishing the area of the trap that held fish. Water glistened on the men's rubber aprons. Eventually slime came up too, dripping from the net in globs and splashing onto the feet of the laboring men. Kiyoshi had no protective clothing. He stood apart and watched, restless. The armloads of net appeared to grow heavier from the weight of whatever lay trapped out of sight. The men pulled more slowly, with deeper grunts.

Kiyoshi went to the rail, leaned over, and locked fingers into the mesh with the rest. Strands of net parted like weeds under his vigorous pull.

"You must leave the net to us," snapped the oarsman, who had joined the others at the rail. "See how it tears! We must pull gently or it falls apart. There's no other net to replace it."

Kiyoshi stepped back, embarrassed. Humiliation even here at the lowest level. He had been at the rail only a short time, but his clothes now dripped with seawater and slime and the still steadily falling rain. His feet were now awash within his shoes. He recovered enough to say, with authority, "Of course."

"Come back, sir. We can use your help," said one of the older men. "Look, you must grip the meshes gently, eh, and pull in a straight line with the rest of us. Your way, showing off your young power, only makes the net worse than it is."

Kiyoshi glanced at the oarsman, who appeared to be their leader. He shrugged consent.

"I recognize you," said the old man. "Young Tsurifune. Not dead after all. They said so in town yesterday." The others looked up, startled, and moved away as best they could without releasing the net.

Kiyoshi tried to be hearty about it. "Not dead. Not a spirit either, so don't worry. If I am cut, you'll see I bleed."

"Strange," continued the old man. "Here I'd bowed at your funeral only last summer. Do you know that I was a fisherman aboard one of your father's far-seas vessels? In good times. Yamaguchi is my name, sir. Here. Come pull beside me. I don't fear the jealous spirits of those who are truly dead, if we should brush shoulders."

Kiyoshi removed his shoes and his denim shirt. Then—what difference did dignity make now?—his pants. He returned to the rail wearing only the khaki underclothing that remained of his uniform. He gauged his motions in rhythm with the others. Even so, carefully as if he were handling delicate china, another strand broke loose under his hands. One of the men saw and sucked in his breath, but this time nobody commented.

When the net had been tightened enough that they could see fish swirling in the green water about a foot below the surface, they stopped pulling and brought out a wide dip net. "We'll pull our poor net no higher, like we might have in old days," explained Yamaguchi. "Make no more weight than necessary, you see, or the net rips further."

The water above the fish churned now, while occasional fish tails surfaced with foamy splashes. The fresh smell of sea salt and fish surrounded them. Kiyoshi breathed it in with growing excitement. For years, nothing had filled his nostrils with such memories nor with such pleasure. The prostitute's perfume was nothing to this, nice as that had been. And when the dip net had begun to dump fish around their feet, the feel of this vibrant sea life! Flattened bream with their wide, dark stripes, tentacle-clinging cuttlefish, a big sluggish turtle that he, with his feet bare, needed to avoid, and scores of assorted flapping fish. The abundance lasted only for three or four brailer-loads. Then they pulled the net, now relieved of its main weight, to tighten it further and scooped out fish so small that they would be barely enough for a mouthful. It was the first abundance that Kiyoshi had seen since the early years of the war. Why was anyone in town hungry when this much food lay just off shore and rations were divided evenly?

Over the sea splash came the put-put of an engine. A boat approached rapidly, driven by gasoline, to judge from its lack of black smoke.

The steersman leapt on the raised stern and, as the vessel coasted toward them, called out, "Not today! Go! Nothing today!"

The boat continued in. A few feet away, the engine stopped and it drifted closer as the man behind the wheel stared over at them. Suddenly the engine started again and the boat veered away. Just then, a man stepped from a small cabin shelter and peered over through a pair of binoculars.

Again the boat changed course and now came to drift alongside them while the man with the binoculars threw out a line. He laughed.

"So!" he called to Kiyoshi. "Are they afraid you'll tell if they have a good catch to sell me?" It was the black marketeer the two Tsurifunes had dealt with earlier. "Got more American cigarettes from we-don't-say-where, hey?"

Carefully, hand by hand, the crewmen placed all but the tiniest fish into the nets thrown over from the powerboat. The dealer scribbled the details on a thick pad. When they had finished, he calculated, then counted out a sheaf of yen notes to the steersman. Within minutes the powerboat had sped off with most of their day's catch.

The oarsman counted out three bills to each of the men. They received them with a bow and tucked them inside their shirts. He hesitated, then handed Kiyoshi a pair of notes. "Please make that do. We're only poor fishermen. Try to get one-eighth of that at the ration wharf!"

Kiyoshi refused with a dignified wave of his hand. "Don't insult your guest. Your secret's safe."

When the charcoal-powered boat came alongside to tow them back to the harbor, more yen notes passed over the rails. At the wharf where they delivered the small fish, a man with spectacles peered down and shook his head.

"Miserable catch again today, I see. Miserable ration to the households. I'm afraid you won't get paid much for your day's work."

"Terrible, how stingy the sea spirits are lately," observed the oarsman coolly. Kiyoshi shrugged. He felt both angry and detached. What would the practical, unladylike Miki say to such lying? Not that it made any difference.

-★-

6

TOKYO

At home again, Kiyoshi bathed and, later while he and his parents sat at supper, he reported selections from the day's happenings with an amused good-humor.

After the black market boat had left, the net puller named Yamaguchi had produced a fat bream he'd concealed from even their leader. With hungry glee, the men (even the oarsman) sliced the still-living fish and savored the flavorful strips of sashimi. Before the others had a chance to wolf down all but the bones, Yamaguchi had sliced two strips to set aside for Kiyoshi's parents. With a bow, he handed them to Kiyoshi, saying, "Please give respectful greetings to Company Director Tsurifune from one of his old crewmen from better days." Kiyoshi had bowed acknowledgment and found a shred of paper with which to wrap the precious gift.

His parents relished the strips of fish, taking only small bites in order to make the delicacy last.

"Yamaguchi, oh yes. He is remembered," said his father. "Not very well remembered—merely one of many—but . . . remembered. Had a habit of spitting into the wind to tell its direction, despite the disgust of other crewmen when it landed on them—if I have the right man. They complained to me in my office. I sent back instructions that he must stop. He did, of course, I assume. Please acknowledge the gift if you see the man again. But these strips came from a large fish indeed, from its taste of bream. No such fish appears in the ration allotments, and we've been told that the nets no longer catch them. You found extraordinary luck out there today."

Kiyoshi could have reported that many such fish had been harvested in a single haul but had been bought by a black marketeer. Did his father, once a shrewd and commanding member of the community, know so little of what went on now?

"Do you see much of the other small fleet owners these days?" Kiyoshi asked.

"Nothing to be done," said his father abruptly.

After a silence his mother said, in a voice lower than usual, "Last year, the authorities took Mr. Tamai to be questioned. He has not returned since." She looked around. "That was after he spoke out about the way government officials took possession of fishing vessels without compensating the rightful owners and left others without fuel to reach the fishing waters. Your father and the other vessel owners think it unwise to be seen together anymore."

"It should be different now, Mother." But Kiyoshi said it without conviction. As of yet, he realized, there were no Americans in town to take over.

Two days later, a young man in a worn khaki uniform appeared at the doorway, bowing. Mother, the first to see him, cried out and fell to the floor. The bows continued—silent. Kiyoshi and his father hurried over.

Unlike others in town, the man appeared healthy and well-nourished, but the hunch of his shoulder blades made him appear small. His face, while full-cheeked and youthful, had a stone-like rigidity.

Kiyoshi did not recognize the bowing man until his father said quietly, "Akira. Akira Nakamura. You are alive, then, and have come to see us." It was the boyhood friend of their heroic dead son, Kiyoshi's brother, Shoji.

"Will you receive me in your house?" Akira asked in a voice barely audible.

Mrs. Tsurifune rose and pulled him in by the hand.

"So. As you see. I am not dead."

"Yes. Yes," said Tsurifune senior. "We see." He glanced outside, then closed the door quickly and led they way to the family room. "We are . . . glad to see you alive." He gestured toward one cushion and eased onto another.

Mrs. Tsurifune had not let go of the man's hand. She stared at his face, crying, then released her hold and gestured for him to sit. "I'll make tea." She started off.

"Bring saké instead," her husband commanded. It signaled a special occasion, since the household afforded only one bottle.

Kiyoshi hung back. No one had drawn him into the scene. Yes. He remembered Akira. The youth who had been best friends with the now-dead brother. The two had gone off to defend the Emperor together, had become pilots together, and then had proudly volunteered together as Kamikaze. Now, this one returned alive . . . alone. Like Kiyoshi himself—alive after all. Akira was seven or eight years younger than Kiyoshi and thus had been of the age to be stirred by youthful sentiments and ideals when the high command initiated the suicide bombings. A destiny Kiyoshi himself might have chosen, had it been offered during his youth. Kamikaze were not expected to be standing now in doorways, alive.

In a low voice, Akira said humbly, "I have no ashes to bring you."

Father acknowledged this stiffly, from the waist.

"I was assigned a different mission. It did not take place."

"Understood."

"I wish that my mission had been on the same day as Shoji's." Long silence. "That we had sacrificed together."

"I understand." Father considered, glanced at his wife, then added: "The family Tsurifune understands."

Nothing more was said. Mrs. Tsurifune brought a carafe of saké and two cups. She held the tray between the two men, while she stole looks at the young man's face. Father filled one cup with a hand that shook and pushed it toward Akira.

"May I be granted the honor of filling your cup, sir?" Akira asked. Father nodded. The young man's hand also trembled. The two men regarded each other and drank.

After another silence, Akira made to rise. "If you permit me, I will go now."

"No. Stay." Father gestured for his wife to sit beside him, and he filled the young man's cup again.

Akira gulped the newly poured sake, then remained cross-legged with head bowed. His black hair—grown longer since, undoubtedly, a final military cut weeks before—covered his forehead so that his face was barely visible.

Mrs. Tsurifune reached over and again grasped the young man's hand. At this gesture, Akira's hunched shoulders began to shake. He broke into sobs. She too cried out. Father remained straight-backed, with eyes vacant.

Kiyoshi stood apart. The air in the room was heavy now with an odor he knew to be of clothes and bodies long unwashed. He'd since bathed enough times that the smell could now offend him.

At length, with no further words spoken, Mother released Akira's hand. Father had not stirred. The young man rose, bowed, and turned to leave.

Kiyoshi walked from the shadows to open the door.

Akira regarded him with red eyes and a face turned again to stone. "You, too, remain alive, then."

"As you see."

"This burden. How does one bear it? I . . . can't . . ."

Kiyoshi held his breath against the youth's odor and considered. Then: "Wash yourself. And get over it."

"Easy for some of us. For you, I hear."

"Your parents should be glad."

"They're humiliated in front of all."

Kiyoshi considered the terrible truth they shared, then found himself muttering roughly, "They'll recover. If they don't, too bad for them! Who cares?"

The reddened eyes regarded him in judgment. "Some of us can say that."

"I tell you, get over it!" But the spur that had driven him home by ship and rail, that had sent him into dealings with the black market and nets, suddenly evaporated.

For the next two days Kiyoshi laid on his futon. He covered his head with a towel and mumbled excuses whenever Mother tried timidly to rouse him. All the while, his mind obsessed between despairing shame and ideas for survival. When he did manage to sleep, he woke with the conflicting thoughts waiting to be thrashed over again. Occasionally, he tried to mourn his dead wife but her face kept fading. They'd barely known each other in adulthood. In her place drifted the challenging, merry eyes and smooth black hair of the sister—Miki—who would only laugh to see him thus. Yet he could not bring himself to rise.

At length his parents stood over him.

"We rejoice that you've come back alive," declared his mother in her soft voice. "What else could matter to us as much as this?"

Father cleared his throat. "Return to life and be our son. I heard what you told Akira. You also, my Kiyoshi-san. Get over it."

Kiyoshi removed the cloth from his eyes and sat up slowly. His mother wore a sunbonnet and apron. She must have come in from her endless plucking of beetles from the few precious cabbages and sweet potato sprouts they were able to grow. By now, he'd watched her do it several times, over and over in what was almost a ritual. Father held a ledger and looked down at him through thick glasses. His cheeks sagged with weary lines. Both watched him anxiously.

"Shall I bring saké to raise your spirits?"

"No, Mother, save it. Make me strong tea." Kiyoshi glanced through a papered window that was partially open. The sky had begun to dim against darkened leaves.

"Is there supper? Is it that time?"

Seated cross-legged on the tatami around the low eating table, Kiyoshi gulped the strong tea like medicine. His own bowl had more rice and cabbage than those of his parents, as well as a small piece of meat not replicated in theirs. He divided the piece into thirds with his chopsticks and distributed it.

"No, no, we're not hungry."

"Take it, Mother. You make me ashamed."

Silence. They finished eating.

"So," Kiyoshi declared at last. Another silence followed.

Kiyoshi shook the pot that now held mostly over-steeped tea leaves and drank the tea that remained—now cold and bitter. "So. We've been defeated. In disgrace. The Imperial Presence is proven not to be divine after all."

"No! Don't say that," his mother exclaimed.

"And those of us not killed honorably . . . feel that we should be dead."

"No. No."

"I'm saying what's in my heart, Mother. And Father. You may as well know it. Can you understand? Never mind. But everything they've told us for years turns out to be . . . shit."

At the crude word Father snorted in what sounded like agreement, but Mother covered her mouth. Her shock chastened him, but he chose not to apologize. Too much now had to be said, before he lost energy again.

"You still have two boats, Father. The vessels of the Tsurifune family. Idle, rusting. No parts to fix them. No paint. No fuel to run them. What now? Let me tell you: There is more than little fish out there to be caught. You never see the big fish because they go off somewhere—black market, Tokyo maybe. We'd better do something for ourselves besides go hungry and hope for the best. We should get the boat owners together and forget the risk. I think the risk has gone. I'll be the risk. If they arrest anyone, it'll be me."

"Oh no, oh no!" exclaimed Mother.

"Father. You tell me to get over it. So, also, you yourself. Go to the other owners, and bring them here for a meeting tomorrow." As an afterthought he added, "Perhaps I'll go to the house of Father Nitta and invite him myself."

It was done. At the Nitta house, the girl Miki was off visiting friends. Just as well, he told himself, disappointed.

Next evening, six men came to the house, one by one. Each gave a cautious look round before darting inside.

When they had all seated themselves on cushions around the low table, Kiyoshi waited for his father to take the initiative. Nothing happened. His mother brought tea and bowed herself away. They all sipped politely, all of them uneasy. On impulse, Kiyoshi took down the guarded single bottle of saké and emptied it with a half cupful for each. He raised his own cup to each man in turn, and with a "Kanpai!" forced them to drink.

"Yes," he challenged, "You see that I'm alive. I failed to die heroically. Thus, am in disgrace, don't you think?" Two of the men looked down. The others met his gaze, but their faces remained uneasy.

Kiyoshi turned to his one-time father-in-law. Indeed, as he'd noted sadly before, a man now wasted both in manner and body. "Honored Father Nitta-san. Your daughter, my wife, is dead. We've mourned together and I have . . . continued to mourn. Forgive me today while we speak of other things." Munio Nitta clutched his cane and bowed with effort, as though his body hurt. He was one of those who had looked down.

Kiyoshi turned again one by one to the others. He'd known them all— only years before, but so long ago. There was Mr. Shoichi Hosono, former net fisherman, bent from some distant boating accident. He had always been bony and shrewd-eyed but was now more so in every way. The left side of his lip twitched upward in a permanent scowl. And Mr. Susumu Nojiri, another former fisherman, burly yet still with the same angry challenge that mobilized all his features and allowed for no disagreement. He alone held the gaze of young Tsurifune without faltering. And quiet Mr. Hitoshi Uchimura, the only one who still had some unlined flesh around his face and neck, as if he were still getting enough to eat. Once a clerk and never a man of the sea, Uchimura had saved his money and invested one after another in four fishing boats—at least one more than any of the others had. Had—at least in the past—even covered all possible circumstances by owning a hand liner, a small long liner, a crabber using pots, and a seiner. Lastly, representing his father Masashi Tamai—who had been taken by the authorities and never seen again—was his son Muritaka, a man in his thirties who had said nothing even in greeting. He too had been discharged from the army.

"We here are the six families of this town who once sent out vessels that returned with fish, crabs, and eels. What can we do to make this bounty return? Now, when the town lives on little but . . . radishes and mere minnows—and those only when we can get them."

Nojiri, who had not relaxed his gaze, stated, "For this, we can thank those soldiers who failed to defend the homeland with that final dedication against the American devils."

Kiyoshi felt afresh the dreadful shame. He so wanted to return to bed, but he forced himself not to look away. No one else spoke, not even Father. At length, Kiyoshi bowed slightly and continued.

"Therefore, the question is, what must be done to put our vessels back to sea?"

"Nice to talk about this, but beware!" exclaimed the former clerk Uchimura. "If the Americans know about us, they'll try us for war criminals. As now happens in Germany, the papers say. Anyone who is the head of a company that did anything to help its people. They'll call our business an atrocity and shoot us. Or worse."

"We're not a great zaibatsu making guns," said Kiyoshi. "Only little boat owners." His confidence seemed to reassure them, but he wondered again what would happen if someone revealed the terrible things he himself had done to prisoners.

"What hope is there, even with all of us together?" Hosono demanded, his lip twitching. "The foreign devils now have it all. They plan to starve us. Sea of Japan that we once owned? The Russians just closed it to us. Worse, those pigs of Russians have grabbed our Kurils to the north. Stolen! Now our crab canning fleets have nowhere to go. So, therefore, if that's from the

Russians, what can we expect from the even worse Americans? They control all South Pacific waters. Took it from us island by island! And we can forget all the way east to their Alaska, which we once fished." He peered around. "Waters of the harbor here. That's all there is for us. Village boats. Whatever they pull up. Not much that I've seen. Pitiful!" Father, Nitta, and the silent son of Tamai all shook their heads in sad agreement.

"Yes, yes," echoed Uchimura. "Pitiful."

"Pitiful what fish come to shore, you mean," snapped Nojiri, and he turned to Uchimura. His tone brought the others to attention. "What kind of memorial is this to our colleague Tamai, who disappeared trying to help us all? Do you think it's a secret, whose man it is that buys all the big fish before it gets to shore. Sneaks it onto the train at Sendai for sale on the black market?"

Uchimura's fleshy cheeks began to quiver. "What does that mean? I can't help rumors. Rumors, that's . . . all it is." No one spoke. "What are you implying? Prove something if you can. I think you cannot."

"The ration board in town should prove it. But there's not enough money around to counter the bribes that have already been given."

Instead of angry denial, Uchimura simply looked from one to the other of his peers. "What an implication. If somebody is doing this, nobody can prove it's me." Silence. "See here. If one man doesn't see the opportunity and take it, another man will."

Kiyoshi Tsurifune turned to his father, who as host reserved the right to intervene, but Father—his expression one of shock—looked away. Kiyoshi wondered if Susumu Nojiri accused unfairly, as he had just minutes before with his barb about Kiyoshi's return. Or was this accusation real?

Their uncomfortable silence continued. Kiyoshi took a breath, and though he arched his back for increased stature and confidence, he forced himself to speak humbly. "With deepest respect to you, my experienced elders, please allow me to change the subject." He bowed in turn to each of those seated around him. Nojiri inclined his head curtly, the others with apparent relief.

"Forgive my boldness. But what we should discuss, with everyone here of importance, is the future. Surely we still control the fishing water a few miles out from harbor. How many vessels do we have—do the six family enterprises have—that are seaworthy to fish in whatever of our poor nation's territorial sea remains ours?"

"Poor? Never say that!" exclaimed Nojiri.

Suddenly Munio Nitta grasped his cane and waved it at Kiyoshi with unexpected levity. "You mean if we had enough oars to row them out? Hundred oars for each vessel, eh? I'll start by donating two rotting oars abandoned against the side of my house. That does it. Off we go!" His outburst broke the tension enough that even grim Hosono chuckled and the belligerent Nojiri exclaimed "Ha!" in good humor.

"Fuel, young man, fuel!" continued Nitta. "Find me diesel for the engines, and my vessels can work a few miles offshore—even if we need to wipe rust off the first catch from the equipment that has been too long idle."

"All very good," said Hosono. "Except that the American devils want to starve us into submission. Count on it, they won't let us leave the harbor."

"Respectfully, about the Americans," ventured Kiyoshi. "The ones I met, coming home from war were stern, but not unkind."

"You're young," growled Nojiri. "Didn't the war teach you anything? The Americans hate us as much as we hate them. They'll do anything to destroy those of us they haven't killed with their barbarous atomic bombs."

"Respectfully. Not the ones I met."

"Fool!"

Father at last raised his head. "I think that my son is not a fool, Nojiri-san. Maybe he's seen more of Americans than the rest of us. Be generous enough to let him speak." Nojiri shrugged permission.

Kiyoshi described the more reasonable of the Americans he had encountered on his journey home. The boat owners listened out of deference to Tsurifune Senior, although it was plain none appeared to believe what they heard.

Finally Nojiri himself declared: "Very well. Hear my proposal. Between us, we'll find the money—not much—to send you to Tokyo. Out of respect to our colleague your father. See if some American who's taken over our country can find us fuel for our vessels. And see what they plan to do about criminal trials, to reassure us. Ha! Go bow before this great General MacArthur—if he's real and you can find him. If you dare! Then, young man, if you're wrong, we'll at least know which of us sees the truth. And then—." He glanced at Uchimura. "Then, perhaps we'll all decide to crawl like worms into secret black market deals and take our chances."

OCTOBER 1945

Three mornings later, a freshly energized Kiyoshi prepared to set out for Tokyo. On impulse he started to put back on his blue denim—American clothing. The garments, now washed often, had lost their initial stiffness.

"Why this?" challenged his father.

"The Americans might be more willing to talk to me. It shows that I've made connections with them. That I'm not just a mere, defeated—"

"Have more pride! What are you pretending? Face them as a proud Japanese!"

Chastened and quickly shamed, Kiyoshi changed clothes. When he boarded an early train in Sendai, he wore a suit purchased for him long ago in times past. The jacket smelled musty and it hung loose around his shoulders. Without a belt to hold them up, his pants bunched uncomfortably from the weight he had lost.

At the station in Tokyo, nothing at first seemed changed from his passage through the city nearly a month before. Haggard and restless people still squatted virtually knee to knee in any open space. But now, the odor of filthy human bodies made him clap a hand to his nose. It was much worse than before, back when he had stunk as much as they. He had come this far back to normal!

From the station entrance a month before, he had watched a breeze kick up black dust and fan still hot embers from buildings burned to ash by the bombs. Everything had been flattened and still smoking. Now he looked at ground more akin to the colors of earth than that of ash, and primitive structures now rose from it. Men and women moved everywhere. They had begun to rebuild their houses, using half-charred boards and with a strange mix of sandbags, petrol cans, wire, and pieces of twisted metal. Vegetation was already twisting around some of the hovels. Two children ran, playing, from a doorway in one of the structures.

The concrete troughs had been swept to reveal pavement and roadways. Streets had opened and were now crowded with pedestrians and honking vehicles. Further off in the orange haze, the long cars of a tram snaked between buildings—some in shards and some apparently intact.

People! That was the great difference between Tokyo and the small town he had just left. And not just the ragged Japanese on the floor of the station.

People were everywhere, knotted along the opened roads where they seemed to move in slow motion, in competition with the vehicles. Some of the women wore traditional kimonos in bright colors: women both old and young. They were no longer dressed all in gray and hiding away as they had been a month before. Even customers could be seen gathering around make-shift stalls. Kiyoshi could see into one stall where a man held out a sheet of rusted metal. Another displayed bicycle wheels. Steam drifted from yet one more, perhaps coming from a boiling pot.

Along the sides of the main street and against one wall of the station, there slumped scatterings of Japanese men in the poorly made and poorer fitting brown shirts and wrapped leggings of former soldiers. Some merely stared, some stood by with small items to sell. A few men sat with an open hat at their feet. Walking in groups separated from the Japanese, who made space around them, were American soldiers in their khaki and American sailors sporting dark blue. They strode confidently in uniforms that were both tight-fitting and clean. Some stopped and pointed cameras in every direction, even boldly into the faces of approaching Japanese—who, of course, shied away.

A loudspeaker along the side of the station blared voices alternately in English and Japanese. Occasional shouts and laughter accompanied the crackling transmission. Kiyoshi clutched his traveling bag tightly lest some-one steal it and walked toward these refreshingly human sounds. A cluster of people, all men, stood shoulder to shoulder. Americans in uniform and Japanese—together. Standing high above them on sets of boxes, were two American sailors, and opposite them were two Japanese civilians. One man in each pair held wads of money and the other a pencil and notepad.

At an enthusiastic statement from the loudspeaker—which included the English word "Tigers," Kiyoshi recognized—many of the Americans cheered and waved their arms. Several Japanese joined in when the trans-lation followed. Others groaned loudly. The men holding money disap-peared amongst an array of hands, while the markers scribbled notes.

"What's going on?" Kiyoshi asked of a Japanese on the sidelines.

"Shhh! Why did their great southpaw ace Newhouser fumble? Run just made. Bad for Tigers, bad for me." He pronounced "southpaw ace" in English.

"Baseball, is it?"

"Of course. World Series in city of Chicago. Detroit Tigers and Chicago Cubs, deciding game. Shh!"

"Haha!" exclaimed a different Japanese, who accompanied the first, in a voice that could barely contain his glee. "Clearly now, Chicago Cubs will win the entire World Series today. The great pitcher Hank Borowy shall see to that, as he did three days ago—and you, Hito-san, will pay! Soon you'll be forced to pay me our wager."

"Early inning. Early inning only," grumbled the man named Hito.

Kiyoshi lingered for a while to listen. It was pleasant, to see people excited by something other than war.

"Forgive me," he ventured of the two men during a lull in the game. "Do you know where in the city it is that the Americans have set up offices to make decisions?"

"Everywhere. Nowhere. Akasaka district perhaps."

"No," said the other. "Americans like the girly-girl places in Roppongi district. That's where they'd have offices, maybe."

Kiyoshi shrugged and left them. He'd approached no American now for weeks, nor essayed his English, and he felt timid about it. But here, in this one place, they stood easily next to Japanese. He approached two, one of whom wore the splendid, gold-trimmed uniform of the American Marines, and in halting English politely asked the same question of the one facing him.

"Hey, you spikka English," said the American in navy blue jovially. Kiyoshi smelled whiskey on his breath. "Well, bud, I don't know where you'd find headquarters, but good luck in this mess of a town. Say. Who you for, Cubs or Tigers?"

"How would a Jap know the difference?" muttered the marine without turning.

"More important," continued the first, "you got a sister go bangy-bangy?"

"Leave him alone, Gus," said the other. "Sister prob'ly give you clapp."

"Now, Jones buddy. We might have grown up together, and now we've been here smashing Japs in the Pacific, so I ain't disagreeing with you so soon. But, ever hear of penicillin, you dumb fuck? You gotta relax, Jones Henry. It's over now. We're sure gettin' banged somewhere today." He wrapped his arm around the other man's neck and nearly lost his balance to lean on him.

"Banged later mebbe," declared the soldier named Henry or Jones. "Get off my neck you slob . . . Slav . . . whatever. Let go, man! Rosvic! Let the fuck go. We're gonna hear this game first." Over the loudspeaker, the announcer excitedly marked a run for Detroit, to cheers from the listeners around them.

"Ha!" The Henry soldier smacked a fist into his hand and turned, releasing himself from his friend's grip as he exclaimed, "Lump that, buddy!" A cigarette dangled from the man's mouth. His whiskey smell was even stronger than that of the other. Eyes in a deeply sunburned face fixed on Kiyoshi. "Say . . ."

It was the sergeant from the Okinawa prison camp—the one who had stared down at Kiyoshi in hostility. But also the one who had seen to it that he received medical treatment and, later, a mat for judo.

Kiyoshi backed away, startled. "Forgive me, I am not wish . . . trouble . . ."

"Now here's a man looks familiar," muttered the sergeant. "Course, you people all look the same." He swayed in front of Kiyoshi while surveying him from hair to shoes and back. "Think mebbe I've seen you before. Where were you back when Japs strung up their prisoners for bayonet practice? Right out there I'll bet. Times were I'd have shot you straight in the face. Like you'd have done me. Any of that changed?"

"Ahh Jones, buddy, knock it off. War's over. We took their shit but now they got to take ours. Our American HQ, where is it? That what you want to know? Seemed it was somewhere around what they call the big palace. Big main palace, got it? And a hotel called Imperial where the officers bunk now." He pointed. "That direction."

"They prob'ly kick your ass before they'd let a Jap get close to any of our HQ. I would if it was me. Never turn my back on one of you Japs. Now scram before I remember where I've seen you, because it mebbe wasn't good." The sergeant named Jones leaned close to Kiyoshi's face with his eyes narrowed. The whiskey smell intensified. "But first, just tell me this. Why're you Japs fuckin' around with our World Series anyhow? Belongs to us, not you."

A light rain began to fall as Kiyoshi hurried to lose himself in the densest crowd on the road. He made for the makeshift stalls. Kiyoshi pulled a small umbrella from his bag, packed at Mother's urging, and opened it with trembling hands. Suddenly he needed food to assuage the humiliation. The smell of it filled the air. He had eaten sparsely hours ago, before leaving on the train. One stall sold noodles, the adjacent one yakitori. The meat chunks on the yakitori skewers sizzled over a charcoal grill, emitting odors that made him salivate. He priced a single skewer. The cost was frightening.

"You think this meat comes from my poor ration card?" the proprietor demanded. Three American soldiers wandered into the cramped stall. They casually crowded Kiyoshi to the side while they debated the food. "Single stick of this couldn't feed a pigeon," one declared. They held up their fingers to order six skewers each and noisily sucked them clean. Kiyoshi hurried to the adjacent stall and bought a small bowl of plain noodles to appease his now dizzying hunger. He ate the noodles slowly, combining each mouthful with a breath of the meaty yakitori odors. *Wait a few minutes,* he decided, *then eat more noodles and deceive yourself.*

Kiyoshi moved on to where a woman was selling pictures. He idly fingered the images in order to linger at the stall, so that he could continue to breathe in the yakitori, even though the smell was torture. In his student days so long ago, the work of artists had pleased him. Had set him daydreaming. These clearly were mere reproductions, some perhaps from magazines printed years ago before the great austerity, and glued to backings of nothing better than stiff paper. They depicted mountains, twisted pines, flowers, water, pagodas, robed sages, and cone-hatted peasants in slanting rain, round white moons in fullest glory. All in perfect harmony. Two by the revered Hokusai depicted views of Mount Fuji, one with cherry blossoms in the foreground, one with snow on drooping branches. Another, by the revered Hiroshige, showed cranes by a stream in ancient Edo. Some day, might he ever own pictures like this? Own them on better paper, of course. Perhaps own some directly from the artist's brush. Maybe even signed?

All at once and with all the intensity of pain, Kiyoshi felt the call of beauty. It had stopped being a part of his life. What of old days with a sister and brother, together with their parents, climbing to a hill at dusk to watch the rise of a full moon? They'd contemplate its silver light on branches and take turns inventing haiku to describe the lovely sight. A few months ago on terrible Okinawa, when he'd crawled to the mouth of a cave to breathe air that hadn't been contaminated by sweat and human waste, the clean glow of a full moon over neat little fields of rice had, without warning, brought tears. And later in the prison camp he'd watched another full moon unblinkingly, dead to emotion. But now his eyes welled up again as he looked at the pictures.

"Very cheap, sir," urged the woman, who ran the stall. "For American soldiers the price is thirty times what I'd charge you. Forty, perhaps!"

Kiyoshi nodded, abstracted. He had even forgotten the nearby odors of meat.

"Also, over in this corner if you're interested, two very curious pictures from America. Taken from a magazine some wasteful American dropped and never returned to claim. Nothing but paint scratches. All kinds of twisted shapes. I have them so perhaps other Americans will buy, you understand, since that's what they like apparently. If you ask me, foreigners who paint such pictures won't long be happy in Japan and therefore will leave soon."

"Or they'll change our ways to theirs."

"Humbly, sir, I can only laugh at that." Kiyoshi turned to look at her for the first time. Black hair worn carelessly long, broad peasant-like face without any sign of makeup. Bold, unlike a cultured Japanese woman, although her voice was high-pitched. "Barbarians may try, sir. But our culture is ancient. It will last forever. Theirs will vanish—poof!"

"Well. Show me these laughable pictures then."

The pictures consisted of paint splattered and slashed. No recognizable images. No relation to human beings or nature. He dismissed them with a grunt of contempt, looked once more in spite of himself, then firmly replaced them on the rack.

"You see. You see what I mean," continued the woman. "I'm an artist myself, you understand. Even though I worked in a factory all through the war, making torpedo shells—can you imagine?—I painted when I could. That is the artist's necessity. I've studied the great traditions, so I can distinguish between what's good and what is merely trash like this. Except that this you hold is perhaps the sort of thing Americans might buy, and how else can I make enough money to live now, with the factory closed? Would you like to see one of my own paintings?"

"Yes. All right," he said in dutiful politeness. With careful ceremony she uncovered a painting from a group of three stacked by themselves. It was a picture of Fuji with a branch of autumn leaves in the foreground. Nothing about it differed from the classical renderings except that it lacked all vestiges of the lovely shading and subtleties that were obvious even in old magazine prints.

"No compromise with the traditions, you see," she said with satisfaction. "But in a style more direct and modern."

"Yes," he said politely. "Indeed." To himself he thought: *Have all women now grown bold like this?* Beside this would-be artist, though, that Miki had a boldness that was at least entertaining. One that could be tolerated. Eyes with fun in them. Talk that might be enjoyed. *Miki.* Did she have friends? Men, that is? No reason not to call again on Father Nitta. When convenient. With, perhaps, a small gift.

He started to edge from the stall, then eased back for another look at the American pictures. "You're right," he said to justify his interest. "Nothing but paint splashes." He peered at the captions under them in English and tried to translate while pretending disinterest. The work of a painter named Pollock, or Jackson. Neither seemed a first name. Not sure how the Americans wrote their names, as with the insulting sergeant named Jones, or Henry.

"In New York, I hear," the woman continued, "that's all that the artists do. Make paint splashes. At least that's what somebody tells me the magazine writes. Decadent! What's that thing called you're holding? 'Guardians of the Secret,' it was translated for me. Some secret! Big rectangle of squiggles that look like garbage in a river—no, vomit. Excuse me!" (At least the woman covered her mouth at the crudeness.) "And that other one, called 'Moon Woman,' ha! Find me a woman in it, much less a moon! The secret is that anyone pays money to buy even a magazine with such scribbles. Well, they waste money, the Americans, I've seen that already. As I said before, if that's their culture, I'm not worried. Poof! Eh?"

"Yes. Shocking." The more Kiyoshi's eyes explored the paintings, the more their energy held his attention. In the images he could see both chaos and a wild discipline. It made him feel uneasy but also happily excited. New York, then, where such bold paintings could be created, would be one of the greatest places in the world! He lingered a while longer to look at the paintings again, while he invented polite compliments to the woman on her own uninteresting work. Some day, perhaps, he decided suddenly, why not be rich enough to own one of these American paintings also? In order to remember the strange American energy.

Out on the crowded road again, he could now smell the yakitori with a shrug and continue on. And then, where to? How to find the Americans in authority? He started toward a cluster of tall buildings that still stood intact. And then, how to convince Americans that fishing was necessary to feed hungry Japanese and therefore, a generous ration of fuel was needed for fishing boats?

On the way, from the occasional stall radio and then from a loudspeaker mounted on one of the buildings, a sweet, easy tune played over and over. The melody, soothing as sugar, was delivered in the high female singsong of popular music:

Shall we sing the apple song?
If two people sing, it's merry.
If everybody sings, it's more and more delightful.
Let's pass on the apple's feeling.
Apple's loveable. Loveable's the apple.

He asked someone about it. "Where have you been all week?" the man replied. "See that line of people outside the movie house over there? Everybody knows 'Ringo no Uta' from the new movie. It's the latest sensation. Makes you forget all the troubles, doesn't it?"

At last, in an area of buildings that hadn't been bombed, although most of the windows were shattered, Kiyoshi felt that he could receive proper directions.

"Don't know," one man answered quickly, and he hurried off as if afraid to be seen discussing the matter. The crowding increased.

"Go that way, where the street rises over a hill," said another man with more confidence. "That's where the bombs didn't fall—maybe on purpose by the clever, treacherous Americans. The buildings don't even have blown up roofs. Dai-Ichi Seimei building. Imperial Hotel. Taken over by the great General MacArthur, most of it, they say. But don't expect to get there now. Stand back."

Japanese policemen arrived in a truck. They dismounted in order to push people back against the buildings and to clear the road. Other Japanese policemen began to arrive on motorcycles. Then, more slowly, came the American soldiers on motorcycles. They drove flanking a white jeep that was followed by three long black automobiles flying American flags on their bumpers.

"If it's what I think," said the man who was directing Kiyoshi, "prepare yourself. Watch if you can see into the second car."

All the cars contained important looking American officers wearing caps crowned with insignias. In the wide back seat of the second car rode two stolid-faced Japanese wearing high silk hats. Between them sat a small man with a mustache who wore a soft civilian hat. While the car passed, the onlookers stopped murmuring and bowed all together, almost as one person. The man beside him bowed and Kiyoshi followed suit automatically.

"High officials?" he ventured after the procession had passed.

"You're only a country boy yourself, then? The man in the center with the civilian hat? You have just bowed to your Emperor. No longer hidden in his palace and seen by no common man. On his way up over the hill, perhaps, to meet with the great General Douglas MacArthur who doesn't come to him they say."

Kiyoshi gasped and started to bow again as his throat tightened.

Apple's loveable. Loveable's the apple . . .

The pretty song sang on.

7

BORN ON THE FOURTH OF JULY

KETCHIKAN, JULY 1946

High above Ketchikan, Jones Henry crouched in a pocket of late snow that had been preserved by a shadowed gulch of rocks and pine. From such a height, it all looked innocent enough below. *Rain mebbe, later.* Such cloudy gray on branches and rooftops suited him today, more so than the water beyond sparkling from the sun that poured through a cloud opening. Revillagigedo Channel was busy with boats coming in to make deliveries from a shortened fishing week before the fun started. Boats where he still ought to be. The stink of rotting bait had started the malaise. With no thought beyond a physical urge, having pewed his fish up at the plant, Jones Henry had tossed tire bumpers against his hull, tautened the mooring lines to absorb a rising tide, and heaved himself up the kelp strewn and barnacled ladder. From boardwalk pier to street he had strode, without a word to anyone—even those few on the other boats who called to offer him a beer.

By the stores that lined the main street through town, people were mounting the Stars and Stripes everywhere in preparation for tomorrow. *Let 'em.* He didn't need a flag to know where *he* was, but mebbe *they* did. Others were nailing together a raised boxing ring for the matches that would occur later that day.

"Hey Jones, not too late to sign up," called Knute Jensen. Jones waved him off and kept going. Let others punch each other around for fun. He paused at the walkway on pilings that wended to the little whorehouses of Creek Street. But he rejected the option and instead passed behind more storefronts onto the paths that skirted the creek. *Come on, pull it together*, he told himself. Fish rot is nothing like corpse stink. But still he gasped for fresh air as if the other smell would never leave his head.

Some kid was poling a line into the water to snag a fish. *Do it, kid*, he thought. *Just like I used to do, right where you're standing. Then run the other way if a war starts and they try to get you. That's what you'll see me doing if the Russian commies start another one. Just let me catch fish for the rest of my life, and everybody stay clear of me otherwise.*

His legs had kept him moving past the baseball field being limed for tonight's games against Prince Rupert, toward the trail that led up the mountain. As a kid, he'd seldom climbed it since he lived down on the water. Grew up watching the old man toss up fish from deck until, at seven or eight years old, he'd grown big enough to fill a pair of oversized boots and was allowed to ride aboard and help. Finally got his own boat at seventeen. Dreamed through four years of war to be back on that water flashing blue far below. Now here he was, back with big enough pay saved to buy a small troller outright and live aboard her. Yet nothing made him content, not after all the dreaming over how it was going to be. *Come on, face it: Jones Henry's in luck*. Still had both arms and legs. Lived through *it*, while buddies died all around him. His life had resumed as if nothing had broken into it. Seemingly.

A few months ago when he'd demobilized, anything pissed him off. Everything! Strikes all over the country, as those who didn't go to fight tried to fuck the men who did and who were now coming home. All that talk about GI loans, but the bureaucrats got so snafued that the applications never even left their desks. Not to mention the so-called vets who'd spent the war behind desks and were now pouring into Alaska from below expecting to be given a homestead and bitching in the bars every night about their rights. No wonder Jones kept to himself. And some virgin preacher in town trying to close down Creek Street. And—unbelievable—he'd read in the Ketchikan paper that the Japs were whining that they couldn't fish in American waters like they had before Pearl Harbor. Send Jones Henry back to Jap-land and he'd set them straight.

From Ketchikan Creek, he'd continued up the log-blocked trails. Jumped over stumps rather than clamber through the thick bush around them. Exploded at last into a run, until he came panting out of the dark canopy into the bright scrub above the mountain's timber line. A year ago he wouldn't have panted: wind was steady as a rock, and no apology. He'd been a rock. Like all the buddies around him then.

"I'd never've let you down, any of you!" he burst out. *Guys whose shoulders bumped mine, sweat to sweat.* "Count on me, like I counted on you!" Until some became arms and legs on stumps that oozed, faces black with hungry bugs dug so deep you couldn't scrape them off. *And here's me still alive, Jones Henry, spun home free and intact.* Returned safe. To all this spread out below, to blue water catching the sun. *And you guys—Sokovich, Chuck, Sugarmouth, Jimmy Sleeves, Callihan—you guys left under crosses no thicker than sticks.* Leastwise, those parts of 'em not blown off and melted into the water and mud. *You watching me? Jones Henry, who made it back with no wound that couldn't get patched? Look at me here now, safe with not a Jap in a thousand miles and people asking me to fight my own kind for fun.* He snapped sticks covered with lichens and tossed them at random. He balled snow and sucked it to liquid. He yelled.

Nobody to answer to except Jones Henry. You couldn't beat that. He held out his left hand. One knuckle missing on the index, that's it. He bit the ball of each remaining finger one by one. Each little pain proved he was alive. Not down in mud beneath some stick of a cross, side by side with buddies. Did the dead talk amongst themselves, keep each other company after they'd left the living abandoned and alone?

Don't want to do that Fourth of July parade tomorrow. No, fuck, I want to. No, I don't. Lead the parade in my Marine dress with everybody watching. If I started to tell them what really happened, they'd run away.

He felt noise scrape up from his throat. It ended with smashing heavy, dead limbs to pieces against a solid trunk while howling to cover the sobs. Then, feeling raw, he walked back down past the creek and past Creek Street with its friendly whores, back through town toward his boat.

"Hey, Jones there," called the skinny 4-F who'd taken his photo for the paper when he'd returned home months ago. "Found you finally. I need an article on colorful war experiences, so slow down. Let me catch up."

Jones Henry broke into a trot to avoid him. The rain began before he reached the pier, and he made no attempt to shelter himself. By the time he'd climbed down the slippery ladder and strode the couple of paces across the deck to the hatch of the tight cabin, water streaked into his eyes and down his neck. He snapped the latch behind him and fired up the stove. Rain drummed overhead on the cabin's boards. No leaks. He'd caulked enough. Never again would he dodge splashes of water like those that slipped through a poncho stretched over a foxhole. *Deep in mud.* He sat with his hands clenched into fists on the table, making no attempt to remove his drenched clothes. Gradually, the stove's heat warmed the wet against his body.

Wouldn't feel so alone if they'd ever decommission Gus Rosvic and send him home to fish. Then there'd be somebody to talk to who understood.

"Oh my, just look, Daddy!" exclaimed Helen Henry the next day, when her son emerged from his old bedroom in full Marine Corps dress. "To think this was the scrubby little fellah I always wondered about what was next. Oh my!" She threw out her arms, but kept them spread as she kissed him. "Oh honey, you're so neat and pretty I'm almost afraid to touch you." Her voice caught as she said it.

In spite of himself, Jones half-enjoyed the press of her soft lips smooching his own hardened cheek. So long as she wasn't doing it in public.

"Leave the boy be," gruffed Roger "Buck" Henry. "I never seen his face go red like that before."

"But I'm so proud of him! And today's his birthday. Twenty-five and home safe from that terrible war! Now we can all forget it ever happened."

"It's okay, Ma," said Jones quietly. He knew he looked good, from the reflection he had seen in the mirror while dressing. Straight shoulders, full chest, hair still kept short and bristly in Marine Corps style, expression that said "Don't mess with me." Not bad. The rest was a roadmap of what he'd done. Sun-scorched face tight at the cheekbones. Cool eyes surrounded by squint lines—enough to no longer be a kid's. Nose a little bent from some fight too many. Scar down his left temple—all that was visible of the scars that ran down his back and right leg, hidden by clothes. The scars still sometimes itched and throbbed. Not a bad thing, though, lest he forget.

Jones Henry noted two packages tied in ribbon, half hidden behind his dad's easy chair stuffed to match the sofa. Still needed to go through gifts with them after the parade. Then maybe he could be off by himself again.

"Well, let's get this marching shi— . . . stuff over with," he said firmly.

Outside, Buck looked up at the flat gray sky. "Going to dump again pretty soon."

"Oh, it wouldn't, Roger. Not on parade day."

"Mark me, Helen. Blowing southeasterly still. Rained out the boxing and one of the ball games last night. Mebbe hold for the parade, mebbe not."

They walked down together, from the house four ridges up the hill, to where the parade groups formed on the wide ferry pier. His dad led proudly ahead, single file on the wooden staircase that connected the levels. Jones descended stiffly, eyes ahead and chest pushed out. From the pier rose the sounds of the Shriner band practicing "Stars and Stripes Forever." And suddenly his mood lightened. He felt, rather than saw, the clean golden trim of his dress uniform. Careful not to grin and spoil the picture. The coat smelled of the mothballs his mom had packed them in when he'd returned as a civilian last December. He'd thought at the time it was the last he would ever wear a uniform.

A few years ago he'd have grinned enough. Kid still in his teens and already the owner of his first boat bought with the pay saved from years of fishing for the old man, hell-bent to beat other boats to harbor for the Fourth, the ol' cock tugging against his pants for every girl he saw. Older fishermen laughing at the eighteen-horsepower Palmer he held together with wires— after the old man had made him disassemble and clean every part and renew each hose. No, Dad hadn't changed, descending the stairs now in front of him—with the same shaggy hair and wide shoulders. His words back then still held true: "Never go short on your engine, boy. The one thing you can't afford, you don't risk is to let your engine die on you."

Without warning Jones felt his eyes turn wet. He reached out and touched his father's torn jumper, lightly enough not to draw the old man's notice. Had promised himself never to cry again, after losing it when the Jap sniper blew a hole through his pal Jimmy's forehead, just above the eyes. And now, almost with people watching, he had to bite his lip to hold it back.

Was that carefree kid's time only five years ago? 1941? No, by '41, just turned eighteen on that Fourth, he'd known the draft would soon get him; had already signed with the Marines, and waiting for their call left him both scared and excited. That summer it hadn't been easy to pay full attention to catching pinks and cohos. It was 1940, the year before, that was the best Fourth—so long ago. Could have been twenty years instead of six.

Close now to the ferry pier, not only was there the sound of the band's warm up but a steady buzz of voices. Clusters of people had already gathered by the storefronts. Flags and bunting flapped everywhere, riding puffs of breeze. Off to a corner, by the fishing gear store with boots in the window, they'd set up a big sandbox where little kids scrambled to find buried treats. *Need to buy new hip boots*, Jones noted to himself. Too many patches in the old ones to hold up any more, after years of closet rot. Even though old fishing clothes reminded him of good things.

Somebody from the pier looked up at the hillside stairs and called: "Hey, here's our lead marcher, our marine. Hurray to Jones Henry!" Other voices joined in the cheer. A bright young woman approached immediately.

"Well, don't you look good!" she exclaimed. "My name's Adele Johnson, from the USO. Now why don't you ever come join us there? Dancing? Eats? Well, later for that." She took his arm firmly. "Come along now. I'm to make sure you get set up right at the head of the parade." She tightened her grip. "Goodness, what a muscle in that arm!"

Jones felt the grin coming on again. Harder to hold it in but he did. He squared his chin and straightened his shoulders even further. But it came to him in a flash. *Time to stop mourning dead buddies.*

He was so full of it that Fourth of July back in 1940, with his own twenty-foot troller and not even out of high school—for whatever school mattered. Because of the big events planned in Ketchikan for the next day he'd made a short week of it; had pulled in the last of his four trolling poles a few hours early—a Wednesday was it?—aboard his *Helen J,* named for his mom's maiden name, and, once he'd cleaned his cohos, stowed his gear, and had hosed down, the sun was still resting above the tops of the spruces back on the low mountains ashore. About six o'clock. He had gunned for town to deliver before the line started at the cannery pier.

He passed his dad's thirty-six-foot *Helen H* by the curve around Gravina Island and shouted over his intentions. The old man, with legs solid on deck, kept right on working his lines but called back, "Mebbe follow, mebbe not. You take care to stay by the markers. No shortcuts around Henderson Point. You hear?"

"Yes sir." Next he passed the *Susan Ray*, a troller the same size as Dad's, owned by John Rosvic and worked with his boy Gus. John was lashing in the poles and barely nodded. So they were heading in early too. Gus, just a few months younger than Jones, looked up from the gutting plank.

To Gus, Jones announced: "Be in town, all delivered and truckin' before you even deliver."

"With that old tub of yours? Once we get going, you'll wipe our wake outta your eyes, man."

Jones brushed back the hair that was flopping into his vision and throttled his Palmer Eighteen for all it was worth. The clatter had its effect. Gus's eyes widened in envy. The engine vibrated so hard that it shook the plyboard housing right by his head and puffed gas fumes throughout the cramped wheelhouse, but he could see the satisfying wake it churned behind and that was what mattered. That engine wasn't going to let him down after all the maintenance he had done. He kept gunning and shouting to himself above the noise.

The channel cut deep into Nichols Passage, but then there were the Walden Rocks that hid shoals at high tide if you didn't know. No problem. Tide rising on flood, but after fishing with the old man for five summers, Jones was able to recognize the swirls that betrayed rocks just inches underwater. He knew all the waterways they fished, all the turns and cautions. Had it all in his head. "Yahoo!" he shouted.

A current just at the entrance to Nichols Passage pushed his bow and vibrated a cup against its plate in the rack above the wheel. Current flooding to north. His boat rocked to it more than Dad's larger boat would.

"Then rock to it, baby!" he called to himself. Man with his own boat! The bow dipped, then rose under a fan of spray that splattered past the open window and onto his face. "Yahoo!" His boat creaked and groaned like a boat should, but the caulking that he'd squeezed into open seams held fast. She nosed into the water, then sprang back up spitting. Kept plowing right through. His own boat. First boat of Jones Henry, able and seaworthy.

He entered Clarence Strait singing and shouting. "Man in charge, that's me!" After the narrow passage hemmed by hills and trees, the sky was suddenly bright and open water rippled ahead. Current going northerly.

Needed to buck it down past Annette Island, then into Revillagigedo and free-ride with the current straight toward town. Who needed a chart when you knew the way? Clear through to the New England Cannery dock. Deliver, tie up, change, then stroll into Ketchikan before Dad or the Rosvics had even made it around Gravina Island. "Where you guys been?" he would ask, cool as ice cream.

Behind him, a whistle tooted, then another. There, just entering Clarence Strait, was his dad's *Helen H*, followed bow-to-stern by the Rosvic's *Susan Ray*. "Shoot—shoot!" Jones pushed his throttle harder, to no effect. Before long, the larger boats had caught up. On deck, Gus cheered, whistled, and waved his arms like signal flags as the Rosvic's boat passed by, churning a wave that rocked the *Helen J*. Jones gripped his wheel and looked straight ahead, ignoring them.

That day, his own dad eased the *Helen H* to align her bow with his son's pilothouse, then slowed to Jones's speed, leaving the smaller boat with a few-foot lead. Together, the two negotiated the spruce-lined waterways. Long before Ketchikan itself appeared, an umbrella of smoke from the sawdust pile burning at the lumber mill appeared above the hilltop to announce the town. They waited together at the cannery dock for the *Susan Ray* to unload, adjusting speed to ride with the current while the tide rose. When the Rosvics moved, Buck Henry moved his boat in to throw a line around the barnacled pilings, and Jones tied rail to rail on his dad's outboard side.

At the halfway rise of the twenty-foot tide, they still bounced far below the top of the pier. Jones, as usual, jumped lightly over the rails to his father's deck and scrambled up the long slippery ladder. As the two men had done countless times before when they had worked aboard the same boat—sometimes shifting positions for variety—one checked the scales above and the other loaded the catch below into the cannery's bucket. The only difference now was that they each oversaw their parts of two separate deliveries and tabulations.

The two Henry boats, having made their delivery, tied alongside the Rosvic boat. Gus, waiting to take their lines, had already changed into clean dungarees and shirt.

"Hey Jones!" he yelled. "What took you so long?"

Jones Henry remembered how he'd removed from his pocket the fish ticket he'd just received and unfolded it elaborately. "Guess some of us got more business needs attending to than others." He'd savored the respectful look that Gus had given to a man with his own fish ticket.

"My goodness, the things you must have done and seen!" exclaimed the girl on his arm—Adele. She looked up at him with an expression both serious and playful.

"Well, yeah." He liked her spirit already, but the tone made him cautious. "Seen some things, I guess," he allowed, hoping she wouldn't spoil the moment by asking for war stories. She was shorter than he by almost a head—about the height a woman should be, he felt. He'd almost forgotten, after the Jap whores (who might have been short but that didn't count the same), how nice a good American girl could look. Light skin all scrubbed, pink sort of cheeks, brown hair with a bit of curl. . . . She had escorted him past young girls practicing waving their pompoms in unison to the clapped beat of a teacher, then past boys in band uniforms tooting their trumpets and trombones. *All those kids, they don't know a thing*, Jones thought. *Get yourselves out now, no war left, you'll never know a thing. If you stay lucky.*

"Tell me now. Frankly." She looked straight up at him. "Do the Japs really have slanty eyes?" It was a question he could answer.

"Yup, slanty eyes. Every one of 'em." He considered whether to open the subject further, then added, "And I'll tell you, slanty minds to go with it."

"Really? And you've been there so you know. My goodness I'm learning a lot."

"Just my opinion, of course."

"I'm sure your opinion is very accurate."

"Well . . . let's just say, you should never turn your back on a Jap."

"I'm not surprised. I'll be sure to remember that. Although I'm never likely to see an actual Jap in person."

"Just as good you don't. My opinion, anyway." Adele squeezed his arm in a way that Jones took to mean that she understood. They continued toward the band that would lead the parade, past the members of Buck Henry's lodge puttering around their float. Dad had already joined the group and was standing on the truck bed with two others trying to stiffen a flopping paper palm tree.

"Right there goes my son, fellahs," Jones heard Buck say. "Marine. Back from the war after licking the Japs."

"Got a right to be proud there, Buck. Fine boy. Fine man. He does us all proud."

Jones tried not to puff his chest too wide, but he felt it expand against the stiff cloth of his uniform. A drop of water hit his face. Suddenly there were little cries from people all around. It had begun to rain.

"Oh my goodness," the girl squealed. "My permanent—I just got it yesterday! And my new dress!"

Jones thought about it only for a second. Nearest cover was the pier's warehouse. It wasn't close and people everywhere were mobbing toward it. He clapped his white dress cap on her head, then quickly unbuttoned his jacket and draped it around her shoulders. His arm held the jacket in place as he guided her to shelter.

By the time they reached the sliding doors of the warehouse and pushed in amongst the others, the rain fell in such torrents that it splattered up from the boards and drenched their ankles.

"By golly now, der you got it," grumbled a man with a beard like a tangled mess of netting. His shoulders bulged from a gray coat embroidered with green stripes. A sash across his chest proclaimed him a "Son of Norway." "Boxing rained out last night, first t'ing. Den ve play only half the double header against Prince Rupert and even that ve got to cut short with a tie. Street dancing last night? Har har! You liked hoppin' around in wet boots, Mama?" He looked around. "Vat now, eh? No parade. No log chopping later, too, I'll bet. Might as vell stayed fishing."

"But you're here with family," said the woman beside him. Like others around her, she wore a flowered headpiece and a white dress covered with larger flowers. "Ve hardly see Papa from spring halibut to fall kings, except Fourth of July."

A deep laugh from the man. "Ain't vinters enough for you, I t'ink?" He gave the woman's waist a squeeze. She jabbered something in Norwegian and squirmed away.

Jones watched the water coming away in sheets from the warehouse roof. His dad and the other lodge members had stuck to their jobs. They were trying to stretch a tarp over the central battleship on their float. The palm tree beside it had so collapsed in the rain that its colored paper hung limp around a metal rod now seen poking through the trunk. Red ink dribbled across black on the banner lettered PEARL HARBOR REMEMBERED FOREVER! Maybe he should go help them. But the girl's hand was on his arm again. Name: Agnes? No, Adele.

"I just don't know what I'd have done without you," she exclaimed as she returned his jacket. "I do hope I haven't ruined it." Jones shrugged and put it back on, dripping wet. As for his white dress cap, she held it, touching the emblem before handing it back.

From a group of men—most of whom wore checked wool shirts—a big guy whose black hair poked from under a wool cap declared: "Well, count me in if we still log-buck and chop later this morning. Slippery, but yeah! That's what we come in for."

"Sure, day in town for everybody. What the hell?" said another. "Jeannie gets antsy out there on the boats, and it's been a month since we came back to civilization. If the ladies get their fill of shopping I'll call it a good day."

Men and women came over to shake Jones's hand and to clap him on the back. In the months since his discharge he'd avoided such contact. Now, suddenly, he found it wasn't that bad, with a bright girl beside him.

Up came John Rosvic, Gus's dad. Unlike the others, he wore boots and oilskins. As always, he was clean-shaven.

"Just delivered," he explained. "No call to take off early till my boy Gus gets home. Writes he's having a good time in Tokyo, helping to straighten out the Japs."

Jones shook his hand gravely. Like his own dad, John Rosvic, with his square Slavic face and calm, sturdy manner, was part of what Jones had daydreamed of seeing again during all the mud and chaos of the war.

"Well, sir, like I said when I first got home, when I left him, Gus was doing okay there in Jap-land." And as earlier, Jones didn't bother to mention that Gus had begun to have his pick of the Jap girls any night he pleased. Had often seen to it that his buddy Jones, shy with girls, got the best of the leftovers.

"Writes that since the time you buddied with him last October you wouldn't recognize Tokyo—its gotten so lively. Misses you, Jones."

Jones deepened his voice. "Write Gus I sure miss him too, sir."

"I know you enlisted earlier than Gus so you had the discharge points." John Rosvic looked around and saw that others were listening. He raised his voice to include them. "You know my boy Gus is helping guard American headquarters over there. Writes he's actually seen General Douglas MacArthur. Seen him more than once. Once got a salute back from the

General. And for that matter, he's even had a look at the Jap's Emperor Hirohito. For what that's worth."

"Just think of it," said one of the women. "Little Gus over there a friend of General MacArthur."

"Now Jones, son. Don't be such a stranger. Hardly seen you at all since you've been back, after you first came to call. Fishing alone on your boat, off from the rest of us, most times. Why don't you come tie with the other boats at night, son? We want to hear your stories. You know how welcome you'd be to come have dinner aboard whenever you please. Or back here at the house for that matter. The wife, too—she wouldn't mind hearing a few war stories."

"Thanks, sir. I'll sure keep that in mind."

The rain continued to dump. In one corner of the warehouse, boys from the high school band had settled themselves atop coils of black pump hoses as they played patches of "Stars and Stripes Forever" without any coordination.

At last, people left Jones alone. He sought a corner, hoping that the girl named Adele would follow. She did. Now he didn't know what to talk about.

"Been here long in Ketchikan?" he ventured.

"Seems more like two years than the three it's been. That's how much I've settled in. My pa came up with the Coast Guard, you see. But now he's reassigned to Seattle and moved there with my ma and younger brothers."

He liked the sound of her voice. A little bit husky, but clear as a bell. Despite the loan of his jacket, she was wet enough that her hair had lost some of its curl and her pretty green dress hung damp against her knees, but she didn't complain.

"To tell you the truth, I like it here," she continued. "I have a nice job at the bank, and anyway it's time to be on my own. You know, growing up with the military, you're never in the same place all that long. Now I have all kinds of friends in town."

"That's . . . good."

"I think so." She faced him. Expected him to speak next, it seemed. He glanced out the doorway where rain still fell like a curtain. Suddenly he wanted to hold her. But what if she drew back and walked away? She wasn't just some kind of little fluff of the sort he joked about with Gus—that you could just shack up with. Should he risk telling her she was pretty?

Instead: "Your dad's Coast Guard? Good boys out there, Coast Guard. Men, that is." He'd not considered it before, during the tension of battle landings, but now he volunteered, "They didn't ever have to go ashore, of course, so they got off easy that way. But, you know, they brought us in their landing crafts straight through fire as close to the beach as they could. Times, some weren't lucky. But others of them kept coming. Once—" The memory of it stopped him.

"Oh! Tell me more!" She waited so long without speaking further that he felt obliged to say, "That's it. Nothing more."

He hadn't expected her eyes to mist and her voice to soften with: "Thank you for saying that much." *What should I do now?* he wondered. Arm around her? Leave her be? He'd gladly have kissed just her brown hair that still held its sort of curl despite the rain. Hell, anything, gladly!

Action (or rather, nothing) was averted when a man announced through a megaphone: "Okay, everybody. Decision time. We've got to parade in the rain or not at all. That's how it looks. Are we rainbirds here in Ketchikan or are we not?"

Good-natured groans greeted the announcement.

"Ah, Yon, you're vet already anyhow," said Knute Jenson to general laughter. "I t'ink you can't get vetter!"

"Knute, you old square head," laughed the announcer. "When would you ever be dry enough to notice anyhow? Now. I've been watching all the floats out there. Nobody's given up and they ain't getting any drier. Not only floats from VFW, Elks, Eagles, plus their Auxiliary, Emblem, Moose, and Lions, but I see the floats from Brownie Scouts and Mount Point and the Hospital folks and even our fair Queens all still holding out. And the Filipinos from the canneries on their float, all cooked up to celebrate new independence back in their home country, since we kicked out the Japs. Shrine band says it's ready to go. Marchers I've talked to—Norway Sons and Daughters, VFW, Sea Scouts, and Girl Scouts, Coast Guard color guard, Pioneers, they all say go. So we're going! Parade's making up again for everybody who's up to it."

Amidst scattered cheers the warehouse shelter began to empty. The girl named Adele turned away with an embarrassed smile, and when she looked at him again her eyes were clear.

"Do Marines mind getting wet?" she asked with unexpected boldness.

Jones Henry felt himself to be a man of the world at last as he declared, "Not if somebody cares to show them where they're supposed to go."

She took his arm firmly—not with a half-cling as before. "Then you just come along!"

8

FISHBOAT

Jones Henry woke to the buzz of the alarm clock, but the dream continued. He clutched his hands in panic when the rifle slipped away. Even felt sopping mud against his legs. With a groan he opened his eyes. There, through the hatch, which had been left open for ventilation, shone the dim early light silhouetting the points of spruce across the water. The malaise lingered, even though every bit of his legs and feet were dry and warm. Sweat still dampened his chest, from the dream that had him staring into a Jap's slanty eye before both men pulled their triggers. He wriggled his toes in the sleeping bag and folded his arms behind his head. The action released a mildly sour odor from the armpits of his long john top, which mingled with the smell of an untraceable gasoline trickle from the engine into the bilge. Boot socks and gloves hung on a rack over the stove, swaying gently with the rocking of the boat. But for being a man, he would have put an arm over his eyes and sobbed for relief. Did. Then, quickly, he anchored his feet on the chilly deck and started moving.

He lighted the single burner under the coffee pot. The boot socks were dry as he slipped them on. Hip boots too had stayed dry inside. Wool shirt, dungarees, wool cap, all dry. He scratched a bit, then clumped outside, still stiff from the tension of the dream.

A deep, slow lungful pulled in the clean scents of spruce and salty water. Amidst the chirping of birds, his piss splashed lightly overboard. Mist puffed over the surface of the water and made hazy the lowest trees on shore. But for all that had come in between, he might still be the young kid out with his dad in the same cove only six years before. No hurry today, if he wanted to take his time. His eyes scanned for any fin or jump of fish, but the water gave back only reflections.

What? Astern and at first hidden by the cabin, there lay another boat at anchor! Only a couple hundred feet away. Snuck in late after he'd closed down for the night. If he'd craved company he'd be anchored with Dad and old Rosvic and the others, not in a cove with tricky shoals that he had sounded fathom by fathom to be by himself. Everybody knew he wanted to fish alone.

With a squint against the brightening sky, he made it out to be Nels Knutsen's troller *Gunvor*. Two figures at the rail were pissing to starboard, rather than the usual one. Then, the bigger of the two—Nels for sure—raised his big muscled arms for a yawn.

"Ja, Jones, good morning," Nels called.

Jones started to turn away, to pretend he hadn't heard, but then out of civility replied, "You come in late."

"Ja. With now my cousin from Norge. Yust arrived here not long ago. Now fishes with me."

The second man on the *Gunvor* climbed around the housing to the bow and started to pull in the anchor, hand over hand. Jones had heard about some cousin of Nels's who'd fought the Krauts. Nothing he needed to hear. Enough to have his own memories. But: "Looks like you got a good man there," he called to compensate for his evasion.

"Ja. Not tall, but strong arms. Ve go now."

Jones watched the *Gunvor* glide from the cove. The cousin began to lower the trolling poles while Nels himself stayed free to steer. Company at night, that would be. But at work? He'd had enough of bumping against other shoulders. Alone, you went where the fancy took you—and kept secrets to yourself. Jones returned inside. The water in the pot was boiling. He dumped in two ladlefuls of coffee grinds, stirred the brown mass while it dispersed among the bubbles, and slid the pot to a cool part of the stove to steep. Nels on the move. That changed things. Let it be a race, then! He turned the key to start his engine. It gave its usual sputter, along with a fresh whiff of gasoline, but soon began to idle smoothly. He poured coffee and swirled in PET Milk from a half-clogged hole punched in the can. The hot liquid jump-started his energy. Yeah, Nels and that new cousin might top his catch if he didn't move fast.

Outside once more, early sun had begun to streak through the treetops, shooting beams of light into the misty air. Gray clouds rose in the opposite direction though, so with the lay of the breeze Jones figured it would probably rain. The anchor came up chain by chain in his bare hands. Cold, but unnecessary to wear out gloves and buy new ones—the supply bills were already too high. With the first kick into gear the engine lurched and took hold. His boat chugged ahead, leaving a wake as slick as pencil lines. She sustained the easiest of rocking, almost like a breath. The four trolling poles began to clack in their lashings, while the boat's wooden hull groaned comfortably throughout its seams.

Jones switched the engine control from wheelhouse to deck, pulled up his boots, snapped into his oilskin coat, and stepped aft into the sunken trolling pit to start his day. A piece of gut he hadn't noticed during last night's wash-down clogged the scupper. As soon as he flicked it over the side, a gull glided in from nowhere to grab it. The V-shaped cutting board, scrubbed the night before, still smelled faintly of disinfectant, but the fishy odor had seeped into the wood long ago and was stronger. Good smell. He honed his knives and replaced them in their slots handy to the board, then scooped some herring from the ice chest and slapped them down alongside the knives. At last, one by one, he unlashed and lowered the forward poles port and starboard, followed by the two longer poles astern. He adjusted each pole's wing-like stabilizer and guided the assemblies to their working angles over the water.

By the time he entered the wide sweep of Clarence Strait beyond the shoreside rocks, his boat, with its graceful poles extended, swayed like a dancer. A southeast wind sang a high note through the taut stabilizer lines. As he knew from the tables, flood current had just begun. He steered into it. Before getting competitive this morning, he'd planned to take his time and catch the flood an hour after it started, when experience told him the salmon turned livelier, but today with the *Gunvor* ahead of him, every fish might count. There she was, Nels's boat, just ahead and already baited and fishing—to judge by the birds that swooped around his stern. Catching anything? Not enough birds hovering at the rails to signify more than tags of bait, it seemed. Jones squinted for better detail but couldn't see signs of action. No other boats in sight at least. *Well damn*, he decided, *I'll catch more than those two together today. Show 'em. Hope then they'll go somewhere else.*

He knew the coast well enough to eye its points in his head relative to each other and know the depth he trolled through. With that knowledge he set course a quarter mile astern of Nels's wake and, after considering, a few feet to portside closer to the rocks, where two weeks ago, he'd fished best. Still on the same fathom curve some thirty to forty before the hundred-plus dip into the channel, to judge by quick sightings from shore. And from experience! The breeze blew off the oily boat odors along with the exhaust from the engine pipe. Jones breathed the fragrant air of trees and water, and without thinking, started to sing in a low grunt while he baited. Now. To it! He'd been toying with a new idea while still adhering to the method used by his dad and his grandfather before him. In the old way, Jones buried the hook in a whole herring—speared crooked so that it flapped in the water when under tow. In the new way—call it the Number Two way, that used baited artificial lures—he hung either a plug or a newfangled hoochie. He alternated the methods on the six hooks that each pole would tow through the water. On one pole he played it one-two one-two one-two on varying lengths of leader, thereby reaching different depths. On another he made it one-one-one then two-two-two. Scribbled it down in pencil, although he kept it in his head as well. A true fisherman used science. He also fixed a longer spread to the lower leg of each line in order to lure any deeper-swimming king. When kings arrived in force, time to target them exclusively. Use strategy. Wait until that boat ahead of him might have gone somewhere else.

Under his breath he still voiced that "Da-da! Da-da-da! Da-da-da!" He had baited and lowered the aft starboard pole and started on the pole portside before he finally placed the tune. "Stars and Stripes." That was it. "Stars and Stripes Forever." From three weeks before. The thing kept returning, wouldn't leave his head. Marched to it in such rain that, before they'd gone for two minutes, his pants clung to his legs and shoes sloshed with water. Still, wouldn't call it a bad day. Dried out, or at least warmed up, with a beer or two in the Legion Hall after it was over. More brews bought for him than any man in his senses could drink and everybody wanting to shake his hand. The old man proud of him—that was nice—getting sent free beers as well.

Fireworks at dark when the clouds finally cleared. That girl Adele's head on his shoulder for a while during the fireworks.

After a while the sun rose above treetops and sparkled on the water. "Da-da! Da-da-da! Da-da-da!" Sonuvabitch. All he'd ever wanted, right here! With each baited pole he let the gurdy spin so that the cannonball-shaped sinker hit the water with a satisfying plop.

The little bell on the end of the forward starboard pole tinkled once. Jones's quick eye caught a single bend of the pole's tip. Then the pole straightened again except for its normal quiver from the boat's forward motion. He watched. The tip did still bend a bit without straightening. Meant the drag of a single fish that showed no more fight. Coho, then, if not seaweed or some trash fish that wasn't salmon. He judged it to be on hook three or four of the pole, so it could be either type of lure. After a minute to see if any of the pole's other hooks would grab a fish, Jones reeled in the line. Nice little coho flapping there. Sure enough it was on hook four and thus, on that particular line, had struck the squid-like rubber hoochie. No mess with Japs had smudged his eye for trolling, learned trick by trick under the tutelage of the old man. The silvery fish flapped on the hook. A thump to its head ensured it wouldn't twist free while he gaffed it aboard. Judged it a five- or six-pounder dressed. Hadn't even gotten to swallow the bait that had hooked him.

"Better luck next time ol' fish. Mebbe," Jones muttered in good humor. As for the chunk of uneaten herring, it was still soon enough after casting that it wouldn't have lost its flavor, so Jones left it on the hook for another round. With a finger locked into the red gills to keep the fish steady, Jones quickly sliced out the whole gill structure and zinged it overboard. Quick enough that only a minimum of blood and gurry splatted on the deck. Predictably, screeching gulls converged to fight over the mess as it floated astern. A long slit up the belly opened the fish. His hand grabbed the gut assembly and pulled it free. Female, since there in the slimy pink mass lay the maroon roe sack. The cannery had announced only a week before that they'd now pay extra for roe. They shouldn't have told him it was for the Japs. So the little slant-eyed fuckers already had the money to buy something he had to sell. With tightened lips, Jones Henry tossed the roe overboard with the rest of the guts.

"You Japs get nothing from this man, even if you do pay well," he muttered. "Not from Jones Henry you don't." A second incision sliced the fish belly's membrane, and a following swipe of his hand left the carcass clean for the cannery. He laid the dressed fish atop ice until he had enough of a catch to bring it to the hold. A man who'd watched his buddies die with no more than a quiver couldn't worry over the death of a fish. But it was just as good that the carcass, with its head still attached, didn't twitch.

"No sir, Japs. You get nothing from this Jones Henry except mebbe the back of my boot." The speech sounded good enough to his ears that he repeated it a couple of times. But by the time three other cohos had been gaffed aboard and he'd entered the day's fishing rhythm, he was back to "Stars and Stripes Forever."

The sun had barely risen high enough to gleam in his eyes when clouds obscured it and rain began to dump. The inverted lifeboat sheltered the trolling pit and kept the worst of it off him, although the diverted water sluiced on either side to rise around his boots faster than the scuppers drained it off. Like a curtain, it dimmed Nels Knutsen's boat and obliterated all of the shore except only the nearest rocks. People said that soon there would be something for fishing boats that the navy had developed during the war, a gadget that gave a picture of the shoreline. Called it by a word like "radio." Be handy if it worked.

As the rain increased it grayed out the rival boat and left Jones alone, as he had wanted to be. Answering to Jones Henry alone. Engine exhaust puffed in a slow-speed murmur from the pipe. Water lapped against the hull. Gulls spun slowly overhead, alert, whimpering for the next toss of guts. When fish struck, bells on the pole tips tinkled a virtual tune. Jones entered his rhythm. Now and then he spat red juice from the snoose he chewed like the old-style squareheads—including Nels Knutsen. With gurried rubber gloves, it was no use trying to keep a cigarette dry long enough to smoke it down. With his body in tune like the well-maintained machine it was, he cranked the hand gurdy to bring up fish weighted by the sinker, gaffed in his catch, rebaited hooks sometimes with different combinations of lures and herring, and then sent them back over. In between, he gutted the catch and iced it down. Now and then he drew up bucketfuls of seawater to clear the blood and slime. All in a rhythm, with mind focused and no need for any other thought.

Just the same, that girl Adele crossed his mind occasionally. And that Jap prisoner in the camp, the one who stared back at him like "fuck you," even while he nearly passed out. Wonder how he made out? Didn't matter.

All Japs were the same underneath. Man was probably dead by now and so what? But just the same. . . .

After a few hours, begrudging the time wasted, he hosed enough gurry from his oilskins to reach into the galley for a can of baked beans he'd left open to warm on the edge of the stove. Down it went with bread for a spoon. Then the empty can went over the side with a snort at the gulls who thought at first it might be dinner, and back to the fish.

By day's end around 10:00 p.m., Jones had caught, gutted, and iced down eighty-three cohos and seven kings. Not to mention a couple dozen undersized shakers that he needed to release carefully so they'd live and grow to keeper size. Lunch, when he gave himself time to grab it around 4:00 p.m., consisted of Spam and peanut butter, washed down with a Coke he'd crammed into the ice among the bait herrings. By now he'd sung and muttered to death the "Stars and Stripes" tune and had thought once or twice more about that lively girl named Adele. Even wondered, if he found the phone number she'd given him the second time he'd asked, whether she might care to see a movie some Saturday night after he'd tied his boat up for the weekend.

As his boat re-entered the cove for the night Jones spat the last mouthful of snoose and hung his dripping oilskin coat on a sheltered peg by the cabin door. Once inside the dry cabin, he lit the kerosene lamp (no need to tax the batteries just to run a bulb), then the diesel stove, and finally a cigarette. Rain drummed comfortably overhead. He cut open a package of hot dogs and dropped a half dozen into the pan along with a dab of lard, slapped slices of bread onto a paper plate, and took down the bottles of mustard and ketchup from the overhead rack. As he waited for the hot dogs to blister and sizzle, he relaxed with another cigarette while opening a can of pineapple rings. He ate them one by one, speared on the end of his knife. As confirmed by the tide tables, the main thing was to get to bed and be up again just before sunrise to intercept cohos at the start of the next flood in from the ocean.

Not bad altogether—eighty-three cohos and seven kings. He'd pushed especially, in case it came to a competition. But, during the course of the day, Nels Knutsen's boat had trolled up the Strait out of sight, so good riddance. At one point Dad's boat had fished close enough for them to exchange cheerful insults. And other boats had passed, all of them towing baited hooks through the Strait, using knowledge they'd learned the hard way and kept to themselves, so that whatever word the fishermen called to each other about their catches could be counted on to be lies—like his own. (If his old man had seriously wanted to know his catch and where best to get it, that would have been different, done in their private code.)

Damn right, good riddance that Nels went off to another cove for the night, probably with all the other boats. The dumb thing was, a little company might have been nice for a change. Shoulder to shoulder might not always be bad. That is, if you knew that next day you wouldn't chance to find a piece of that shoulder in the mud by your feet—another buddy blasted to pulp. But who around here understood? If only Gus Rosvic had taken his discharge and come home, instead of hanging around Jap-land. Had used good sense, like Jones Henry here keeping himself company. Only Gus would understand some things.

Jones scrubbed his pan and galley table with seawater. Save the fresh water in the small tank for drinking. He'd hung his socks and sweated jersey over the stove to dry and was having a final scratch under his long johns, which he never removed during a trip, when a bump jolted his boat. Barefoot, with a yell, he reached the deck in seconds.

There alongside, buffered by two worn tires squeaking between their hulls, bobbed the rail of Nels Knutsen's boat *Gunvor*. And Nels himself, old eyes bright under his boat's deck light, his lined hound dog face poking from a watch cap. His oilskins glistened in the rain. The cousin, about Jones's own age, stood behind him, frowning.

"Ja, Jones, you busy?" Nels asked in his mild singsong. "Come over visit for a little bit."

"It's rack time, man!"

"To meet my cousin here."

Without considering the consequence Jones growled, "Already got my shoes off."

"Ja, den, ve come over to you."

Before Jones could object, the cousin grabbed a line and put a leg across the rails and onto Jones's deck to moor it.

"Stop there! Just you throw it here." Jones strode barefoot to catch the line and secure it.

Nels laughed his big Norwegian har har. "I forgot, Arnie. Nobody on Jones's boat comes aboard except Jones and de fishes, except maybe if he invites."

Jones wanted to be pissed at the intrusion so late at night. Instead, without admitting any pleasure at the company, he muttered, "For just a minute then, okay, I guess." He tried to make it sound reluctant.

He led them inside, self-conscious for once of his galley's helter-skelter. He stopped himself short of wiping a wet rag over the bench by the table. *Ain't like I'm some woman in her damn kitchen*, he reminded himself. But he hoped they weren't looking too hard. Nothing to admit out loud, but company with the right kind of people wasn't too bad.

"Okay, Jones, you meet my cousin Arnie." Jones shook the proffered hand cautiously. He hadn't yet forgotten the fact learned during the war that if a stranger held one of your hands—making it inactive—his other hand might hold a grenade.

"Yo," he said without warmth.

"People call me Swede," said the man dryly, in good English. "You might as well call me that." His eyes appraised Jones coolly. He wore a billed cap pulled tight over straw-like hair. Square, serious face. It showed none of Nels's easy but rough joviality. Had no more humor in it than that of Jones Henry himself.

"Svede, pah!" exclaimed Nels. "No fucking name for a good Norwegian, eh Jones? I tell Arnie to call himself Arnie again. Vat did the Swedes do when came Hitler? Said march through here, Hitler, here's my ass you kiss it good but don't hurt me since I'm neutral. Pah! Arnie here, he's got a Swedish papa but a Norwegian mama, both good people. They live north from Göteborg, you see. Water close to Norway but in Sweden. So Arnie's papers are Swede, yah? Arnie here, he can talk like a damn Swede so the Germans think he's okay."

"This is not necessary to say," Swede muttered.

"Arnie here," Nels continued, unperturbed. "His papa during war runs a little fish plant."

"Big damn fish plant!" Swede exclaimed, then added less aggressively, "If you are going to tell it."

"Ja, ja okay, big fish plant. And papa, he vas on committee the German bastards started, to make sure they get most of the fish. So Arnie here, he finds a way to hide half of de fish ven it come delivered. Svede fishermen, not like other Svedes, they deliver to secret places half their catch, and dis fish goes a lot across the border to feed Norwegians, like my family that the German bastards try to keep hungry. Eh? Stupid Germans think the water gives up yust little bit of fish. Eh? Eh? Ha!"

"All this now finished, Nels. This man cares for important . . . matters of his own."

Jones made a deprecating gesture, but he listened with more attention than he gave most people these days.

"And the German bastards took his papa, and—"

"Finished!" exclaimed Swede.

"Yes, okay, Arnie. So! My cousin here gets also Norge freedom fighters safe across the border and off into England. Onto fishing boats that go to England. Finally the German bastards get suspicious and Arnie got to escape himself. To England. Den over to Seattle, here in de States. Joined de Quartermasters to help fight those German butchers. So Arnie, you don't need to call yourself Svede no more I think."

Arnie—or should he say Swede?—turned to Jones. "Do you make us welcome on your ship, sir?"

"I'll put on coffee." Jones quickly wiped a half-clean towel inside the coffee pot to clean out old grounds and started fresh water boiling.

Nels settled with his big puffy hands clasped on the galley table. "Arnie. Tell how you smuggled out de fish past the German bastards."

Swede ignored his cousin. He surveyed the galley from stove to cup rack to bilge hatch. "You fish alone, yes?"

"You fuck up, it's nobody to blame but yourself," said Jones, half defensive. "Then payday you don't split nothing."

"Understood. How also I should do, if I fished only. I now work a little bit with Cousin Nels until there is a fish processing factory that gives me work. Fish processing is my business, you understand." He considered, then added, "It is not wise to push what you call the gaff into the body of a fish, as I see sometimes here. Pardon me, but at home we would not buy fish pushed that way, making a hole in the side."

"Okay then, Arnie," Nels persisted. "Yust tell Jones how in England after you escaped, with the Resistance fellows from Norge—all of dem fishermen, Jones—they pull so strong on oars—training, you see, for boats they need to sneak ashore quiet in de night. Ha, they split dose oars in half! Need to cut big holes in de oars so they don't break, eh? Dot's how Norge fishermen grow up, Jones. From kids. Pulling de oars!"

Swede continued to ignore Nels's running narrative. To Jones, he said, "You catch the coho salmon here, like Nels. I have watched through the glasses. However, then, sometimes you take your ship close to shore near the rocks, where we don't go. I think you are taking risk for bigger fishes?"

Jones laughed but said nothing. He liked this man. Swede's square face gave its first hint of a smile. "Not that I ask for answer to your secret, sir. Only observe."

"Not that I'm telling." Jones tossed ground coffee into the boiling water. He let it steep, then held out the pot. "Steady your mug. Sorry I've got nothing stronger."

"Then you come on to our boat, Jones," said Nels. "Little bigger anyhow. Ve have some hjemmebrent."

So my boat's not good enough, thought Jones. He started to refuse. Swede spoke before Jones could start. "I shall bring here the hjemmebrent. If you will drink some Norge viskey with us, sir."

Jones relaxed. "I've scorched my throat with worse, now and then."

9

ARNIE SKOVKUS

AUGUST 1946

Arnie Skovkus had his share of bad dreams. They were his own, nothing
to share with Nels or Helga, safe in Ketchikan now. He had nodded in
grave good humor when Nels mentioned—with fumbling apologies—after
the first week of his stay, that he cried out so much in his sleep that it kept
the kids awake at night and left them groggy all the next day at school. It
had meant that they needed to move his sleeping quarters from the cozy
warm house to the outbuilding where Nels kept his gear. Fortunately, the
shed had a small wood-burning stove for heat. And they had moved Nels's
grinder aside to make room for a padded chair in front of the tool bench.
Helga had done her best to make up a bed with unnecessary ruffles around
the base. She even sewed a small lace curtain to put across a square window
in the shack. It blocked half the light but did give more of a vestige of home.

Indeed, under a thick quilt and with rain often tapping or thumping on
the tin roof overhead, Arnie did not always need to be a polite guest. With
such privacy there was no cause to worry about crying out in his sleep, if that
actually happened. Or then, lying awake, tensed and shaking, even though
he knew he was safe. Anguished, even though he knew the past was past. He
could reason out loud to himself without disturbing anyone.

No question that he was always welcome at the table. And Helga prepared good filling meals. She and Nels had settled in America before the war. They knew what their countrymen had endured, even though they could never have understood all of it without being there. But Helga, despite her good intentions, was rigid and judgmental. Church played too great a part in her life, especially when it came to looking him over, as well as Nels, if they came home late from town. Nels took any scolding in submissive good humor. It was probably good to have a woman care about you. But devil to it all the time. It was Helga who first told him outright to stop using the nickname Swede. It was, then, probably out of stubbornness that he continued to use his Resistance code-name.

"Those Swedes stayed neutral," Helga had declared in Norwegian, her hands planted against the tucks of her apron. "Traded with Hitler. They didn't suffer like we did."

"Gave our men an escape route if they couldn't make it by sea to Scotland," he countered. "Hid and protected us."

"But they didn't suffer like you did. So Arnie, you should stop calling yourself 'Swede.' Even the ladies at my church tell me this."

What argument could have been better for keeping the name! While big Nels retreated to a corner, he'd settled to argue it to her logically. "Swedes saved many of us. Their country mobilized its army. That's why the German bastards left them alone and occupied only Norway and Denmark—the ones that didn't wake up in time, started only to make a strong army as soon as they saw Hitler take over Poland in . . . when? Half a year before they invaded Norway! No, Sweden started more than a year earlier, when Hitler went into Austria. What did we do?"

Helga shook her head. "Oh Arnie, for shame." But she said it without conviction.

"Helga, even our Norwegian language is no more than a bastard combination of village dialects and Swedish, you know? Coded for us by the Hanseatic League so that thickheaded village fishermen could do business with other places."

"Arnie! What your mother would say?"

It was getting too serious. He had forced a smile but couldn't stop arguing. "Father sometimes traded fish across the Baltic with Gdynia in Poland. He'd send me to learn the business. I dealt over there with a big, laughing Paz, Kosiki his name was. Suddenly, one day it was a German named Herr

Schmidt, who never smiled. When I asked about Kosiki he shrugged with something in German like 'Bad man, he's gone.' That was half a year before they captured us in Norway. Most of us were out skiing for fun while the Swedes were marching with guns."

Helga shook her head, although she sturdily gave no ground. "Just the same," she concluded. "I will call you only Arnie." She glanced sharply at her husband. "And so will Nels!"

Nevertheless, he repaid their hospitality as best he could by working hard on the boat. Jumped to relieve Nels of any task he could. Said nothing of a possible crew share, just thanks for whatever Nels paid him. Sometimes he did choose to sleep the night on the boat's hard little galley bench, relieved from all the lace, and free to wander the town without explaining himself—although mostly he just watched others through open bar doors. This also left him able to maintain his welcome by firing up the stove, so that when Nels arrived in the cold dawn the icy cabin had warmed.

The dreams at night weren't bad when they merely had him crossing four hundred miles of sea to Scotland in that fishing boat, jammed with others escaping the German bastards. Rough seas, wet, cold, and harsh, joking about their odds of survival. But sometimes a nightmare took him rowing in with padded oarlocks from that leaky offshore boat, back to Norwegian shores under cover of black night and rain. Betrayed from somewhere and with German bastards in wait. Torstein shot and quietly begging to be killed rather than captured and tortured with methods unknown. Others scattered, never seen again. Frozen, hiding, alone. He'd hurdle awake sweating and short of breath. Kill them before they—. Whatever was needed. Would he have broken under their electric fire or other tortures?

The worst: Sometimes in dreams he became his father, arrested by the German bastards for a son escaped to the Resistance. Tortured how? As if him becoming Father could share or lessen the pain that he almost wished for. What had been done? A hardy, jovial man turned frail and silent even after liberation, who patted his son—granted a too-short leave from the Quartermaster corps to return home—on the cheek and within weeks slipped into death. Joining Mother, whose cause of death no one could tell him.

Neighbors in the village even tried to prevent him from examining Father's body. But not before he'd seen and touched, weeping, the long blackened stripes welted on Father's back. Some so thick they merged. And saw the right leg with terrible scars and a hollow indentation below the knee. No wonder Father had never undressed before anybody, had walked bent with a cane! And all for a son still alive and healthy.

Thank God he'd gotten to kill some of the bastards! Yet the German guard he'd choked to death with his bare hands would cough and rattle sometimes in his dreams, so that he woke to the same sounds in his own throat. It was only the ones shot from afar that played no part in his nightmares.

One day on the water, he and Cousin Nels were busy bringing aboard the salmon they called cohos. He himself stood at the gutting table, awash in fish blood that covered his gloves and apron, cheerful and still pleasantly groggy from the hjemmebrent the night before, although wishing that fish blood wasn't so red as to remind him of other things. Suddenly Nels muttered in Norwegian, "Quick. Take my line here, gaff this one fish coming up. Don't pull any more, just clean what you've got. I must go down to the cabin fast." In seconds he'd hung his oilskin coat on the hook by the cabin, and without taking time to draw water and slosh off his boots, he had disappeared below.

They were fishing part of Chatham Strait in sight of the troller run by the mysterious Jones Henry. There, nearby and looming motionless, was a black-hulled ship. From it moved a white boat rowed by four men with long oars, steered by a fifth man working an oar attached astern like a rudder. Nels seemed frightened at this. Pirates?

The pulling boat moved alongside that of Jones Henry, who threw it a line. The man astern climbed onto Jones's troller along with one of the other oarsmen. Swede called down the information to his cousin.

"Ja, ja I saw," snapped Nels. "Coast Guard coming for inspection. Just clean the fish. Pretend that's all we're doing."

"Government? This is the government coming? What are they going to do? Is it wrong that we're here fishing?"

"Fish. Fish. Sure. We fish till they come bother us." A few minutes later Nels emerged on deck, holding a bucketful of greasy water with hands that were now equally greasy. "Where are they now? I don't see them."

"Only on the other side of us, where you can't see."

"Current. Must be sure. Here, take the bucket, don't spill, don't spill!" Nels fumbled around in haste. "What floats a little?" He grabbed a half-worn rubber glove from the gutting table, hurried astern around their gear, dropped it in the water, and watched it move away slowly. "Okay, so, anyhow, current now moves from us both, so okay." He reached out with a gaff to retrieve the glove, but it filled with water and sank. "Devil! Well, hand around the bucket. Don't spill!" He poured the bucket's contents out in a slow oily stream and the current bore it away.

"Nels! Is the government coming to hurt us?"

"Not now anymore. Just coming to inspect. Last time they found oil in my bilge and wrote a report. Ten dollar fine! Even though it wasn't enough to start a fire, like they said. But back just then, only a little time before, it was Trygve Jenson's troller exploded and killed him, poor guy. So it wasn't good for a bilge floating even a little bit of oil. Maybe still."

"But you cleaned there just since I've been with you."

"So. Just to be sure. I don't want to tell Helga I must pay another fine."

A half hour later the Coast Guard boat cast off from Henry Jones's troller and moved to theirs. Swede watched the four men pulling in unison at the oars. Just like the training in England for the Resistance. It hadn't been so bad, he could now admit, to dip an oar blade into the sea and pull against the water's pressure, over and over like the pendulum of a grandfather clock, creating a swift whish of motion against the hull. The men here, in lifejackets with a thick collar that puffed around their faces, did not seem to be enjoying themselves the way he remembered of himself. All business. The same went for the man standing with such a frown at the tiller oar, his ruddy face marked by thick black eyebrows.

When the man with the prominent eyebrows came aboard, he was polite, although he held himself with the authority of one in charge. He was older than the others and wore a khaki shirt and billed hat while the others wore blue denim and white sailor caps.

"Check your documents, sir," he growled without preamble, and after a glance at the papers Nels handed him, said, "Okay now, let's see your lifejackets." From under his bunk, Nels produced two floppy vests of cork strips sewn into canvas. "Yeah. Regs say that's okay. But you know and I do, those things might float you, but they won't keep you from freezing to death in this water. Give you five minutes if you're lucky. The padded ones like this on me, they might just keep you warm long enough to make it to shore."

"Ja, ja I see," said Nels dutifully. "T'ing is, I don't fall over. Har har."

"Yeah, we both know that too."

One of the oarsmen peered from deck into the cabin. "Running lights all check out, chief."

"Okay then. Last thing on the list. Let's see your bilge."

"I think that you will find it very clean," said Nels. He pulled up the deck board with a flourish. A mere puddle of dark water sloshed against the boat's strakes. The chief shone down a flashlight and then dipped a finger into it. "Just like I figured it would be. So that completes things. Keep fishing."

"You see. Vas very clean the bilge, ja?"

"That's 'cause you flushed it five minutes ago, cuz," the chief said in good humor. "You think from the ship they didn't have binoculars to watch you dump it? Then they walkie-talkied me. Like I said, good luck fishing and don't fall overboard." He nodded to Swede. "You too."

"Thank you, sir," said Swede. *Yes, I do like Americans*, he thought, not for the first time. *They do business, but they can laugh.*

Well, so maybe he'd decided to hold onto the nickname Swede for no reason greater than to irritate Helga. Just the same, he'd already changed his good Norsk family name "Skovkus" to one of indeterminate nationality: "Scorden." (What the hell let 'em guess!) In this way, people in America could stop stumbling over it. Now that wartime commitments had ended, he meant to be American all the way. Worked daily to hone American English from the British version he'd determinedly taught himself while in England with the Resistance. To get along in the world, you must leave no room for apologies.

Most important over here, don't pretend at divided nationality. Don't, even when vouched for by well-meaning cousins, bunch yourself with the heavily accented Norwegians who had no intention of improving their skills in the language of their adoption, so complacent were they over their damn heroism. He had encountered it first in Seattle, now in Ketchikan, and he was told it was worse in Petersburg—where they had first arrived. He wasn't going to be a half-country patriot who kept one leg here in the States to make money, without ever removing the other leg from the old country. If somebody wanted to make something of that, Swede Scorden stood ready.

It was right of Cousin Nels on Mother's side to help him over the first hurdle. An okay guy, Nels, as Americans would put it. But come on, Nels, no more bragging to strangers of a cousin who fought the German bastards. So did every Viking son who was able.

With all this in mind, Swede was grateful enough to work aboard his cousin's boat temporarily. Hard work was always good. But he knew, from growing up with a father who owned a fish plant, that while any strong man could pull oars or work nets and lines if need be, the real adventure for him would lie not in rugged labor, but in the buying and selling of fish. Most important then: crewing on the boat enabled him to observe the practices of the fish plant when they delivered each day. There was no question that fishermen were not free to roam the cannery premises. They brought in their catch, perhaps might climb to the wharf to sign a fish ticket rather than have it passed down, but then they were expected to move quickly from the pier and make room for other boats. No lingering allowed. Then the boats proceeded down the Narrows to the city pier at Thomas Basin where they tied together in their own community of fishermen.

Father's lilting voice from the old days would come to him when waiting as they or other fishermen delivered. "Be easy, easy," Father used to cajole, one hand on the boy's shoulder. Trying to train his son in the business of buying fish. "Watch the scale carefully when those boats deliver. Fishermen are good fellows but they're full of tricks. Don't you understand that a netfull raised at once to the scale weighs at least a kilo, maybe two or three kilos more, before all the water and slime drains off? Talk a minute before you write down the weight."

Good advice and he'd followed it, until he'd trained in the Resistance with fishermen. They were good fellows, strong and generous, able to march without tiring and then to joke quietly in the barracks at night. They'd included him when passing around bottles of hjemmebrent. They'd tell him, mildly, without rancor, "Sure Arnie, you think we don't know? Fish plants always try to cheat the fishermen. We work all day in cold water. Then you walk out of a warm office and try to cheat us."

"Sure. And if you sneak us a bad fish and nobody buys it from us, who suffers?" Everybody would then share a laugh.

Trying to learn the ways of the Ketchikan cannery became an agree-able form of the subterfuge he'd learned for survival. He needed first to be tolerated by the dock foreman. After a few days, he asked politely to use the bathroom, then lost his way, with apologies to whomever he saw, in order to view parts of the plant operation. Never touch anything along the way. Never, of course, stop too long at any location so that it looked like he was actually studying the operations. (And boy, oh boy—to use a phrase he'd picked up—how careless they were in keeping the catch fresh. Given charge, he'd sure change some things fast!) Some of the Filipino women in rubber aprons cutting fish murmured as he passed, but he studiously ignored them so as not to draw attention. The Filipino men seemed to have no such curiosity. They kept their eyes on the conveyor belts while their hands sorted fish. They, at least, were efficient. When any of the foremen regarded him, he asked questions so politely that they felt bound to answer rather than challenge his presence. Bit by bit, he became free to wander. Was even allowed to change from gumboots into shoes that made walking easier in the parts of the plant that weren't streaming with hose water.

Seeing his interest, Nels often said with a friendly shrug, "Sure, see you at de harbor later, I wash down." Then Swede could pass through the plant into even the storage and office areas before jogging the mile of shore side road to meet Nels at the city pier or back at the house.

Such it was this day. At town's edge, he passed the few bars in their low frame structures—dark little places despite the neon signs—that were only just beginning to open as the boats were still delivering. He'd visited these only once when some friendly fishermen had insisted on taking him. Then back at the house, Helga had immediately sniffed the alcohol on his breath and delivered a lecture on the money fishermen kept from their families when they went to bars. Nels had listened without interfering, a half smile on his heavy face. Big as the man seemed on his own boat, he appeared much smaller the moment he entered his house. Cousin Nels did not drink alcohol during the week. Not with Helga waiting at home. Only on Saturdays, if the Norwegian community had a dance, Nels once said with a wink. Swede knew he himself would marry some day. But first he would look the woman over hard.

The road passed over the rapid mountain stream that skirted the town. He slowed to glance up at a sturdy boardwalk fronting small houses on pil-ings. A sign announced this to be Creek Street. The town whores kept the houses and did business there, he knew well enough. But the boldness that enabled him to make his way through the cannery deserted him here. He watched two men from the boats jaunt up the boardwalk to enter the open doors, and he envied their confidence. But he didn't want grave lectures from Helga, to whom the church dictated in all matters. She thought all unmarried Christian men should remain as deprived as all unmarried Christian women.

Today he made a detour around the boat harbor to walk through the main part of town. Here he slowed to note each bank, store, and building that might contain an office. Even along Main Street, most people wore rough clothing. It was, after all, a hub for fishing boats and logging camps, while barely within sight rose the high burner for the paper mill. Nevertheless, some men did wear suits. These he watched closely, wondering where they came from and went. Entering the largest bank was Miles Jackson, manager at the cannery, where he sat at a desk behind a glass barrier. Swede had watched him whenever possible, but did not yet feel ready to introduce himself. Nevertheless, he nodded and Mr. Jackson, probably not placing him from the boats, was polite enough to return the gesture, albeit with a frown. The man had about him the manner of confident authority. Perhaps this was only because he wore a suit and tie, but just the same.

It was all right to wear rough clothes and do work that kept you wet and sometimes cold, but not for a lifetime, Swede thought—if you could help it. Back home in the fish plant office, his father had always worn a coat and tie. When young Arnie himself was brought into the office after training at the delivery bins, he dressed with like formality. It gave him a comfortable feeling to know that he could still handle fish slime, that a wet life on the water did sometimes give an excitement unmatched within the safe walls on shore. But it was far more satisfying to make decisions that affected more than one boat, to barter and bargain with authority, to refuse and walk away, to manage people rather than be managed himself.

In town there was a single clothing store whose window displayed a suit, instead of the usual heavy checked wool shirts, long red underwear, and high rubber boots. Today, as occasionally before, he entered to walk among the stacks of white shirts and shelves of leather shoes cut low and polished to a shine. Those shoes, unlike the heavy brogans he wore, were not made to walk on wet decks or sluiced concrete floors, but to stand high above on dry flooring.

At last, Swede walked back to the assemblage of masts and hulls in Thomas Basin where the fishing boats were tied. With a halibut opening in progress, the wider schooner slips stood empty, but the slips for small trollers were already packed rail to rail with boats in from the grounds. The forty-foot *Gunvor* of cousin Nels bobbed second rail to the troller *Midnight Sun*. There was Nels on deck, still in hip boots, one foot braced on his rail as he chatted with Sven Torgersen of the *Midnight Sun*. Clouds of smoke rose from both men's pipes. The two were undoubtedly talking in Norwegian rather than English, and in their regional Vesteralen Norsk at that, not Oslo. Swede stood watching, unnoticed. All of Nels's gear appeared scrubbed and stowed for the night, so nothing remained there for him to do. A deep, hearty laugh exploded from both men. Part of him wished to share such a laugh. His other half rejected this vestige of the old country. Don't join them, then, at least not until Nels appeared ready to go home. He looked around. There, tied in another section of the piers away from the Scandinavians was the troller of that American named Jones, or something, whom they'd visited two weeks before and who they had since anchored with now and then; the fellow with that shutdown wall to his face and eyes that Swede himself understood. The man was working on something, under his canopy, out of the rain.

Swede walked down the other float pier with purpose and then stopped. He himself hated intrusion, and this Jones's boat was moored third rail from the pier, making it far more difficult to be casual. Moreover, this Jones had a scowl no more friendly than when they'd first faced each other rail to rail. He'd pulled the visor of his cap down practically to his eyes, while cleaning the disassembled pieces of a wheel. Finally Swede coughed and ventured, "Good evening. You fish good today?"

No answer. Swede, embarrassed for himself, started back the way he'd come.

"Talking to me?"

Swede turned. "Yes."

"Fish today? Can't complain. You?"

"Also. Cannot complain."

"Fuckin' gurdy here. Got jammed."

"I am sorry to hear it."

After a long silence Swede decided he'd intruded enough. As he started away, that Jones growled, "Could mebbe use an extra hand to hold this piece steady."

"Shall I come there to hold it for you, then?"

"If you got nothing better to do."

Swede walked carefully over the deck of the first boat by the pier then stepped with greater confidence onto the deck where he'd been invited. The American gestured to the metal part he wanted held and, without speaking, reassembled the wheel.

After the gurdy was returned to its place and secured, Swede ventured, "You are a good fixer. At fixing."

"Fucked otherwise out here. Need to clean my bilge inside now." A pause. "Follow if you want."

They entered the cabin. "Sit there," the American directed, and pointed to the far edge of the bench.

"Perhaps I shall help you?"

"Nothing to help with. One-man." A long silence as Jones moved a deck board, reached down with a tin can, and bailed up oily water into a bucket. He finally straightened and wiped grease from his hands. "So they had to drill holes in the oars you pulled. So you wouldn't break them. Eh? You don't look that strong."

"Others. Stronger than me. Cousin Nels, he talks . . . much, a little."

"So that's what you did—just fuck around with big oars? Or did you use all that training to get you some of them Nazis?"

"Ha. First the oars. Then the other." With the opening made, Swede ventured further. "Four German bastards that I get for sure. Got. Three others maybe. You did the same, maybe. With some Japanese bastards?"

"Mebbe," the American muttered with a shrug.

"Then, perhaps, we are the same? But now I think how good that we kill only fish."

The American's eyes narrowed. Finally he said, "Yeah." After a moment he added: "That's the only good part of it. Don't matter if you kill fish. Don't even matter to the fish, far as I know."

Another long pause. Swede decided it was time for him to leave, that in any case Cousin Nels might be getting restless to walk up to the house. He started for the doorway.

"Well," said Jones. "I ain't eating Spam again tonight, I guess. Mebbe go grab a piece of real meat or something at the diner up the road. Come if you want."

Here was the problem of not being paid! "Thank you. But I will not."

"Don't worry, I settled a good fish ticket just now, so I've got money."

Swede hesitated. "You understand, I shall pay you back?"

The man named Jones studied him, then nodded.

"Then yes! Sure! I will go tell Nels."

"Afterward, up to you if you want to come, I'm going to grab a piece of ass down at Creek Street. Seventy-five cents for a drink in what they call the parlor, four to six bucks for a job, depending. I got money to lend anybody · who killed a few Nazis. Suit yourself."

Swede felt a rush of pleasure and gratitude. "Sure! Okay!"

10

CREEK STREET

The American fisherman Jones Henry started to knock with American assurance when the door opened by itself.

"Why come right in, boys. Miss Eva'll be glad to see you." The woman wore a maid's apron over a bright blue dress. "Just make yourselves comfortable."

Swede braced for red velvet everywhere, for heavy perfume, and for women barely clothed. Instead, the small room was mostly brown in both wallpaper and upholstery. The air, heated against the chill outside, smelled of coal dust. In a corner slumped two men, who glanced up just enough to take in the newcomers. A lace-covered table standing between their over-stuffed chairs held two glasses, as well as a tasseled lamp with a dark yellow shade that glowed from the bulbs behind it. The place could have been the living room at Nels and Helga's, or for that matter, at his parents' back in Norway.

"You boys thirsty today?" asked the woman.

"Make it two," said Jones Henry.

"Scotch or bourbon tonight, honey?"

"The second, I guess." Jones turned to him. "Tell the lady which you want."

What will this cost? Swede wondered. He started to say he wasn't thirsty, but at a cool appraising look from Jones Henry, he declared, trying to sound experienced, "Ja, vell. Maybe yust . . . Scotch vhiskey? Dis time!"

The woman patted his cheek. "Just off the banana boat I see. Now aren't you yust the blondest thing and look how red his face is."

All his carefully rehearsed American pronunciation had abandoned him! He indeed felt himself blushing. It didn't help that Jones Henry gave a dry laugh. Worse, the two men in the corner glanced up with something like amusement. One of them, with black eyebrows thick as fur, seemed familiar. Did then many Americans look like this?

He and Jones settled in two of the room's other armchairs, away from the earlier arrivals. The cushions sank with his weight, even though he tried to sit upright.

"Still soppin' out them bilges on the run, cuz?"

It was the Coast Guard officer! Instead of khaki uniform and a cap pulled down to his forehead, the official now wore a flowered shirt, while his bared head revealed dark hair combed back in a slick wave. Swede automatically scrambled from his chair and stood. "Sure! We clean often the bilge."

"That's news. Something just bite you there?" The others laughed. Swede sat again, feeling foolish.

"Leave the man be, Jimmy," said the officer's companion, an older man with a leathery face and graying hair. He turned to Jones Henry. "Your pink salmon come in yet?"

"Ain't my pinks, I troll for kings and cohos." Jones replied easily. "Leave the seiners and them damn fish traps to fight it out over pinks while I'm off to try for halibut."

"Lucky for you. Pinks already two weeks late, still not in sight, seiners and canneries bitchin' everywhere . . ."

"Their problem."

The woman brought drinks for Jones and Swede on a tray set with a lace doily. Each was in a plain glass overloaded with cubes of ice. Swede's first sip tasted strongly of the whiskey, but when he pushed down the ice the liquid mixed into a flavored water. A relief. He didn't want to become drunk and turn even more foolish.

A door at the far end of the room opened and a plump woman came brusquely in.

"Evening, boys!" she declared. Red hair was piled on her head like a grand wedding cake. The clothes she wore were silky and light and covered all of her body except for the top curve of her breasts. Swede stared in spite of himself. Fine large breasts! They quivered against the tight silk as she walked. He had to fumble his hands to cover a sudden erection. Like a schoolboy so many years ago. The memory made him want to laugh. Something was still the same! At least, his body remained young. In fact, despite all, how much luckier he was than many of the others. Yet, among all these lucky people, he had no need to feel guilty or apologetic.

"Coast Guard's back in, I see. To grace my sitting room with its cutter's chiefs. Ed Hancock dear, you're always welcome. But that Jim Amberman, with eyebrows like to burn off his head. Jimmy, should I alert the shore patrol ahead of time?" She turned to Jones Henry. "And my goodness, Mr. Sourpuss with—is that a friend of yours, Jones honey?"

"He's with me, you might say," Jones growled. Swede again rose to his feet, although the others remained seated, and he inclined his head in as much of a bow as he dared.

The woman took his hand and shook it. "Well. Always a pleasure to have a gentleman in the house." She glared cheerfully at the others. "Not like some I know. Now what's your name, sir? I'm Miss Eva Tarkington, in case nobody's bothered to tell you."

"Arnie Skovkus once. But now I am calling myself Swede. Swede Scorden."

"Well then, Swede dear it is. Welcome to my house. You'll find it more refined than, say, two doors up at Lola's. And don't let them tell you that Dolly down the other way gives the boys any better of a time than right here." She turned to the two in the corner. "Ain't that right, boys? Tell him from the Coast Guard."

The older man raised his glass. "No problem here, except I'm empty."

"See to it," Eva told the other woman, who hurried off.

In his daydreams, Swede had pictured whores as hard and thin, like Marlene Dietrich. Women who made men feel ashamed if they didn't perform well. This lady wasn't like that. Not with such gaily bouncing breasts. He'd barely looked at her face except to see that it was bright and cheerful, although no longer that of a girl. A second look showed that pink powder barely covered some wrinkles around her eyes and mouth.

"Well I have to say." Miss Eva indicated Jones Henry. "Mr. Sourpuss might be short on smiles, but July Fourth he was the grandest sight you could imagine, all in his Marine uniform and medals at the parade. I even forgot it was raining cats and dogs when he marched by. Sit down, Swede honey, sit down. So now you boys catch fish together?" She spread her silks and settled into a chair beside him. To the two men across the room, she said, "Thought your boat was out on patrol for another week. I do keep up with the Coast Guard, you know."

"Old story out there, Eva," said the older chief. "Needed to rescue some fishing boat. Engine failed. Pulled him off the rocks and then had to tow him in. We'll go back out tomorrow."

"Oh, you fishermen!" Eva exclaimed to Jones Henry. "You boys live in such danger out there, I can't even imagine it. In the paper just yesterday— yes, I do read the papers—some poor fisherman up in Port Alexander, I think it was. His boat caught fire and sank, and he drowned."

"Man keeps his boat like a shithouse, what do you expect?" muttered the eyebrow chief named Jim. "Then calls us to haul him in. Leave work we got to do, then overtime and no extra pay like the unions. Fishermen! They stayed sober enough to tend their engines, we'd get our real work done."

Jones Henry started to rise. "Who you talking about there?"

"Don't you start anything in my house!" snapped Eva, suddenly all business. "Sit back down, Jones Henry! And Jimmy, you apologize this instant. My stars, talk about too much booze, coming from you!"

"You ever seen me take a drop at sea? Never will."

Eva adjusted one of her scarves as she settled back. "One thing I don't need here, boys, is trouble with the police. What with all this talk in City Council about closing us down. And that minister from his pulpit every Sunday, which people tell me all about, since that's *certainly* not the church I go to. What would all the boys from the boats and the logging camps do if we weren't here? You tell me now!"

"Simmer down, Eva," said the older of the chiefs. "We all know that preacher's got numb nuts. Give you some news there. I hear he says if he can't get the Council to act on what he calls bawdy houses, he's leaving town."

"That's what I'll call good riddance!" She turned to Swede. "Bawdy! Can you tell me what you see here that's bawdy?"

The older chief laughed. "You heard what happened at Ida Mae's last weekend?"

"That was five doors up. I hardly know the woman except by sight. Maybe the paper called it a shoot-out. I did hear a shot or two but nobody was hurt I hear—just boys letting off steam."

"Had to take 'em to the hospital, I hear. Not that they weren't released soon after."

"Well, Ed dear, I never have to worry about you. But I'm here to make a living just like everybody else." She turned to Jones and Swede. "Don't mind those two. They're in no rush. It'll be midnight before they make up their minds, and maybe they won't get out of those chairs even then. Now, are you coming to visit and drink a few?—which is all right, I pride myself on my hospitality. Not like some houses around here. Or for something more?"

Jones Henry gestured toward his companion. "Take him back there with you. I ain't in a hurry tonight." He winked. "Or mebbe I'll go with Angie when she's through bringing drinks."

"I don't mind having a rest, dear. You're not going to make me jealous." She turned to Swede and suddenly stroked his fly. He erected so immediately that she chuckled. "Now that's a response! Don't need to guess what's on your mind tonight!"

Her eyes were both shrewd and merry, he thought. The few wrinkles under her powder didn't matter. "I should like to go with you. Now! If it is convenient."

She took his hand. "You just come along then." She led him back into the house through the door from which she had entered.

Before his eyes had adjusted to the shape of a bed in the near darkness, she was unbuttoning his shirt, and he'd already begun to breathe heavily. Her hair, unpinned, flowed around his face.

He barely reached the bed before he ejaculated. When he started to apologize, she patted his bare thigh. "My goodness, what a man! Now just relax. You've got a whole hour so let's see what more we can do." Indeed, by the time that Angie's discreet knock on the door signaled the approach of the hour's end, she had helped him muster back his manhood and he lay back relaxed and content.

The evening left Swede feeling better about himself than he had in weeks. He slept aboard the boat that night. When Nels came aboard before daybreak to start another couple of days' fishing, for once Swede was not already awake to greet him. With a yawn and a grin he began the day's work slowly.

When they next delivered to the cannery at the end of the week, Swede began his tour of the premises as in times previous. He proceeded to the sliming line and greeted the foreman with the friendly humility that had always worked before. This day, however, the man seemed uneasy and disinclined to talk. All at once, two large men appeared. When he started to walk away, they flanked him.

"Up at the office, they want to see you," one of them said. Their impelling motion left him no choice. The gate to the management space he had never dared to enter now opened automatically at a buzzer, and the two men conducted him past the desk of a frowning secretary to the glassed-in office. Miles Jackson, boss of the whole cannery, sat behind a desk flanked by radio boxes that crackled with static. His wiry neck jutted from a collar stiff enough to have been starched.

"The man delivers exclusive to us or we dump him," he stated into a microphone in his hand. "Yeah, right now. If he ain't ours, no credit for him today or any other."

There were two swivel chairs in front of his desk, along with a simple straight-back chair. Jackson indicated the latter. "Sit him there. Then wait outside." Back into the microphone: "Fuck how desperate he is. This ain't the Salvation Army. Desperate short of sinking, that is."

Swede sat stiffly but suppressed a smile. This was how a cannery manager should talk. At last, whatever the circumstance, he was in the office of management, where he belonged.

Finally Miles Jackson turned to him. "Okay, my friend. We've watched you snooping around all these weeks. Which one you with? I figured you'd find out for yourself that nobody here needs to organize."

"Organize?"

"Unions, unions! We're not as dumb as you might think."

"Unions, sir?"

"CIO or that damned AFL? Go back and tell your bosses, we've got no place up here for unions. We've watched you people pulling the country apart since the war ended. Close the mines and every damn thing else. Block longshore unloading all the way to Seattle and up here. My cannery workers are seasonal and I take good care of them. We don't want you union spies and organizers up here. Watch out. We're ready to get mad about it."

Swede rose, pleasantly excited, and extended his hand. "Sir, I am Arnie Skovkus, now named Swede Scorden, to make my name easy to say in America. I am now fishing with my cousin here, Nels Knutsen. But back in the old country I vas cannery manager. With my father. I am happy to be in this cannery. I wish to work here. I vill help to make this cannery good running!"

The man studied him, but did not offer his hand. "I've got somebody in town can check on that, so don't bullshit me, son." Finally, he said, "Sit back down. Take that other chair with the arms to it, if you want. Stay there quiet for a minute." He walked out to one of the women at a desk, but Swede saw through the glass that the man kept watching him all the time that he spoke to her. She picked up a phone and spoke into it.

"What's your name again?" Jackson demanded through the door. "Your original one?" Swede needed to spell it for him. The manager relayed the information to his secretary, then faced Swede with narrowed eyes. "Don't think I'll forget if you're lying. You got any papers to prove who you are?"

"Yes! Back at the house I have papers. House in town. Where I stay with Nels Knutsen. And Helga."

"I knew you were on Nels's boat. But Nels ain't necessarily that bright about things other than fishing. Cousin, eh? Cannery, huh? Canning what?"

"Herring. Also we salted the fish. And torsk, how is it called here? Cowdfisk?"

"Yeah. Cod. I take it you speak Norwegian?"

"Ja. And Swedish."

"If you check out, I just fired a man this morning. Let's see what I hear and what papers you've got. Call my secretary to make an appointment back here in a couple of days."

"I will run to house immediately and then run back with the papers. If that is convenient, sir."

"Go-getter, eh?" Jackson glanced at his secretary, who was still on the phone. She nodded. The wrinkles around his mouth expanded. "Ever heard of Horatio Alger?" He chuckled and consulted his watch. "Hour and a half before I go home for dinner. Up to you."

The time for the mile run to town and the mile back was extended by only a few minutes to gather his papers and to give Helga a breathless assurance that nothing was wrong on the boat but that he must hurry. He arrived back at the cannery with thirty minutes to spare.

Jackson's secretary hit the buzzer to open the office gate, then gestured for him to sit in a chair by her desk. Swede sat straight, controlling his breath, trying to keep from panting. When her head was turned, he passed a sleeve across his face to absorb some of the perspiration that wouldn't stop flowing. He watched Miles Jackson's movements behind the glass of his office, keeping a steady gaze to catch his attention when he turned.

The manager neither turned nor glanced his way. In fact, he left in another direction and never returned.

At last the secretary, a stern older woman with graying hair in a stiff permanent of finger waves, turned to him. "I'll take whatever you brought for Mr. Jackson. But he's checked you out now so it doesn't matter." Her smile creased, warming the look on her face. "Even your war record. Very impressive, young man. Mr. Jackson said that if you really want to work here, be at the office at seven next Monday morning. Shall he expect you?"

"Yes!"

She held out her hand. "I'm Mrs. Lacey. See you at 7:00 a.m. next Monday and we'll sign you in." She appeared to think a moment, then added, "I lost a son in this terrible war. About your age. He'd be a fine young man now." It sobered him in a moment.

"I am sorry," he blurted. "A terrible thing. I am sorry."

"I see you are. Never mind. Just continue to be a fine young man. Now. I'm not sure where Mr. Jackson plans to fit you in first, so you'd be smart to wear those brogans, but pack along your rubber boots."

By the time he strode through the cannery, noting the operations with a new, possessive interest and had reached the road to town, the somberness of her loss was dissipated. After all, he'd suffered himself and had not survived easily. And now had come his time in the world and his place!

In a buoyant mood he sauntered the mile to town. Suddenly he was going to be a part of the town! He'd possess it! Earn money boldly without apology to any relative, be responsible for himself alone, be in charge. Buy clothes! Afford his own quarters where he'd close the door whenever he felt like it. Tell Nels tonight at dinner. Nels had fished alone before taking him in, so this could not be considered a desertion. But he'd certainly remember his debt to Nels and Helga. Invite them to dinner in a restaurant at least once a week. Yes. Peel off dollars to pay the bill as calmly as breathing!

He entered the fancy clothing store for the first time, with barely a glance at the window where he'd lingered before. The place had an instant odor of things right, of fine cloth, leather, even perfume. Not a hint of all the metallic, oily, rubbery odors that permeated other stores on the street.

There, trying on a silky, embroidered jacket, was a woman it took him a moment to recognize. Her plain, puffy face had no makeup and wore an expression more a frown than a smile. Her red hair peeked out only in a wisp from under a plain felt hat, but undoubtedly it was Miss Eva herself. Of course—there was the other woman—Angie was it?—trailing behind in a long brown coat.

"Good afternoon," he said with polite assurance and a smile of familiarity. "It is a pleasure to see you in the day."

Her face turned toward him, but her gaze fixed on some object beyond.

"The weather is not so much rainy now as it was," he continued.

Her eyes, so welcoming only two nights before, barely surveyed him before turning away. Oh.

Swede decided he would not wear the new clothes he'd bought until the right time, so he appeared for supper as usual in the clean, rough shirt and pants he routinely changed into from the boat. Save announcements also until a bit later, perhaps after the meal.

"Well, I am happy to announce good news at last," Helga declared as she placed a bowl of boiled potatoes beside the fish stew already on the table. "There shall be finished here the Sodom and Gomorrah."

"That's good," said Nels automatically, as he ladled food onto his plate.

"Good indeed! You will eat without me tonight, and take your dishes out to the kitchen when you finish." Swede and Nels regarded her fully for the first time that evening, although both had spoken with her more than once since coming in. She was dressed in the clothes she wore only to church on Sunday.

"Eh? You're going out?" Nels asked.

"I certainly am. To City Council with the Reverend and all the ladies from the church. This is the night."

"Night for what, Helga?" By now Helga had on her good wool coat, and she shook her head in answer, because of the two long pins she held in her mouth. After she had secured her hat, she stated, "If you paid attention to more than that boat you'd know. We're finally going to force those people on the Council to pass a law that drives the whores from our town. That disgraceful boardwalk of houses over the creek will soon be lived in by respectable people, I thank the Lord. It wouldn't hurt if you two said a prayer for this tonight." And she was gone.

Nels passed the two dishes to Swede after he had heaped his own plate, and then poured thick gravy over his fish and potatoes. "Well. At least she didn't say we must follow to the place. The women are strong enough without us."

"Close down Creek Street and drive out the women?"

"Ha, Arnie, I know you went there. No secrets around the boats. Too bad. Young fellows need something like that until they get married. But the women don't like it and that's that. They'll get their way with that preacher of theirs, I suppose. Even though the mayor doesn't want to. Neither do a lot of the fishermen—and the loggers when they come to town from the camps. Next I suppose the preacher and the women will try to close the bars. Then where will the men without wives go? That's why it's good to be married, Arnie. You should find yourself a good woman. Make sure she knows how to cook."

I I

JONES MARRIED

Jones Henry married Adele Johnson in November of 1946, after the season for Chinooks had finally closed and he'd put his boat up for the winter. It was a nice church affair, since that was the way she wanted it. Most of the guests on his side were friends of his parents from around town. Even three Norwegian couples with their accents, although by now most of the Squareheads had gone back to Seattle for the winter. Naturally, Adele's father and mother came up from where he was now stationed stateside on a Coast Guard ship. The girl, for her part, had friends from working at the bank. Women always had other girlfriends, since they always talked so much. With Adele's gaggle of bridesmaids, he himself needed to find at least a couple of guys to stand behind him at the altar. Fortunately, his best man Gus Rosvic was just back—discharged from Japan—so the two of them could stand together in full dress uniform. And—why not?—he'd asked that guy his own age named Swede, who'd come to fish with his squarehead cousin Nels after they'd visited boat to boat and done the Creek together, to stand alongside him too.

He'd even thought of inviting Miss Eva and a couple of her girls from Creek Street. But even before Adele heard—and to his surprise, reacted indignantly with him for the first time ever—Buck Henry had declared,

"I knew you were dumb, boy, but I never knew *how* dumb till I heard this. Know when you're well off!"

Not that he'd need the services of Creek Street anymore. Adele, from the way she looked up at him, was all the woman he'd ever wanted to handle. Bright, curly haired, cheerful always. But so energetic that he sometimes wished she'd settle down. Yet, other times, he'd watch her and find himself grinning at his good fortune.

Everybody at the Elks' Hall reception said they made an ideal couple. He knew it was so. Even Commander Johnson, Adele's father, who gripped his hand—strength for strength, neither man letting go—declared with gray eyes staring right at him, "Glad it's you, Marine. I know you'll take care of her!"

"Oh, leave the boy be!" exclaimed Adele's mother, sidestepping their handshake to plant a kiss on his cheek.

"I will, sir! Sure will!"

After the drinking and dancing, when it was time to catch the ferry for their honeymoon in Seattle, Adele, with a bright laugh, tossed the bouquet. He swooped her up in his arms to carry her out the Elks' doorway. As everybody cheered, he felt her warmth and softness against him. Smelled whatever perfume she'd put on and felt stimulated right there. He couldn't help grinning again. That night, alone at last in their ship's cabin, he knew, if ever there had been a doubt, that he'd done right. Lucky. He began to admit that he likely loved her.

Adele was ready to make a home right away. That suited him. Nobody would ever say that Jones Henry couldn't make enough to afford a down payment on a house. Even though a new boat would have made a smarter investment. They found a small house with a bedroom overlooking the harbor, a living room, and a room facing the hill behind—for a kid, when one came.

He found himself hurrying his boat to town even when his checker wasn't plugged—even making mere daytrips rather than two- or three-nighters on the grounds—and grew impatient if he needed to wait in line for delivery. All of it was time wasted before he could walk in the front door and have her arms around him.

Maybe it had been easy before marriage to knock on his parent's door at dinner time, even if he wasn't expected. But it was nice to open his own door and smell the cooking. Adele prepared food fancier than his mother knew how to, with spices dumped in that Jones had never eaten before. Most of it tasted fine. He shrugged off the rest and ate it when he saw her gaze lingering on his plate, anxious for his approval. One night, they invited the folks over. His mom's warmth toward her as they washed dishes together and his dad's hearty praise for the girl's cooking made him remember once more that he'd chosen right.

And when she came to him tenderly in the dark, no longer a chatterbox, but a woman of soft flesh and firm breasts, and they remained quietly close after the heat of intercourse, he would lie back satisfied for maybe the first time in his life.

A few months later, one Friday evening when he opened his front door and, to free his arms, threw down a load of dirty boat clothes for the laundry, she just stood there in tears.

"Something wrong, girl? Where's my kiss?"

"Oh Jones, dear. It's happened! Doctor says I'm pregnant."

"Hey! Well, good!" He knew it was good, and he held out his arms. As she snuggled against him, suddenly he realized that she wouldn't be all his alone any more. She wanted hugging, and he did so gladly, enjoying her plump warmth.

Things did indeed change. They had intercourse less and less, and if he tried anything beyond the usual she'd murmur, "Careful, dear, careful" with a hand to restrain him. After the fifth or sixth month, when, in any case, she had become large in the wrong place for lovemaking, she insisted gently that they stop altogether. As a point of pride, and of course to save money, he walked from the boat harbor past the entrance to Creek Street without even a glance toward the houses. The tassels and stuffed chairs of Miss Eva's living room remained in his mind like a pleasant scent, but he dismissed it.

He'd never seen his own mother so animated and busy. All the maternity clothes and baby blankets and doodads she bought for Adele, and all the talking they did together.

"Let 'em have their fun, boy," his dad advised, with lines of amusement creasing his weathered face. "Keep out of their way now, if you know what's good for you."

"I could use a beer."

"You know where the Frigidaire is. Get me one too."

While it spooked him, even at her invitation, to lay a hand on her stomach and feel the baby stirring inside her, it made him catch his breath and share her wonder. *With that kind of liveliness it's got to be a boy*, he decided. A few years and he'd teach the boy to be handy on the boat. Adele thought it would be a girl. *Either way*, he told himself. But for sure, he'd felt there the boy he wanted. Would suit to call him Jack, say. Or Tom or Hank—something manly, like the way he was going to be. A good solid name the kid could grow up with.

Still, when a nurse at the hospital came out with a smile to show him a red-faced squalling baby girl, he gladly hugged tight the swaddled bundle and couldn't speak for fear of choking. And a while later, he stroked Adele's forehead as she lay in bed, with curls damp against her skin. He'd murmured: "Nice going. Honey. Dear."

"I know you wanted a boy," she whispered.

"A girl's fine."

"Next time, Jones, dear."

"Sure. Next time." He'd forgotten the bunch of flowers he'd brought and laid beside the bed. When he picked them back up and handed them to her, she started to cry. "Hey, come on, I didn't mean to—." But he could tell it pleased her, whether she carried on about it or not. Women were emotional.

"I like the name Amy, Jones dear. After my mother. Family's important."

"Amy? Sure, good. Mebbe Amy Helen, then, to throw in my mother?"

"Oh yes. Yes."

Now he had another reason to search out the fish. Adele was already saying it would be a good idea to start putting away money for Amy's college fund. As if anyone in his family had ever needed college. Then, his mother said that she and his dad had bought a $500 savings bond in Amy's name, to mature at the time she'd need it for higher education. When women started making plans, there was no stopping them. But none of it was bad.

PART TWO

I2

A SMALL WORLD STEWING WITH CHANGE

Fishing Bristol Bay has become the stuff of legend. To catch an abundance of fish, Alaskans face high tides that sweep over shallow banks and threaten to sink their boats. In the old days many fishermen drowned. Technological advances have alleviated the casualties, but not the danger.

From late June through July, red—or sockeye—salmon pour into the Bristol Bay river systems to create one of the world's grandest storms of fish. The fish, born four to six years earlier in the same waterways, have gone far to sea and matured. They now return to spawn and complete their life cycles. This has occurred for centuries, as past generations of bears and other fish predators could attest. For man, it has been a part of his formal harvesting and processing labors since only as recently as 1884.

One of the Bristol Bay seasons most engrained in legend, remembered directly by old-timers and passed on to new generations, was that of 1951. At stake that year were major issues about the way things had long been done, and they all came to a head at the same time. Some blamed the changes on the perceived spread of Communism, although in reality these changes were long overdue. World War II had ended, and returning veterans who had ventured forth and faced death for their country were not about to resume a Depression-era subservience to authority.

Bristol Bay is a place far removed from the cities that can provide options for work other than fishing. Many converge from faraway places to fish and process there for the brief season but afterward, they return home, leaving the small communities of year-round residents to work lesser bounty for the rest of each year. Resentment over such distant control of a local resource was a large part of the problem that pulled Bristol Bay apart in 1951. Locals started their own union for fishermen and cannery workers, an action that threatened the authority of the Seattle-based union that had, until then, controlled the majority of seasonal manpower. Labor loyalties became divided when dealing with the sole employers: the canneries. These canneries, having stored the boats and shipped all their supplies for the season—into relative wilderness, at that—at a cost beyond the scope of individuals, had always felt entitled to dictate terms. And, as the only customer and only source of revenue and maintenance for the Bristol Bay fishermen, the canneries had been free to set terms, so long as the unions cooperated.

Until 1951, a Federal law under the US Interior Department's Fish and Wildlife Service—and which was vigorously supported by the canneries—restricted access to the fishing grounds of Bristol Bay to boats operating only under sail and oar. This was despite the fact that all other fishing boats throughout the nation—including those of the dangerous Alaskan waters—had been free to run under engine power for decades previous, since the technology had become available.

The canneries justified their stance against engine power by asserting that inefficiency kept the salmon stocks from being overfished. But they neglected to voice that by limiting the type of boat available to them, and by constraining the quantity of fish they could catch, the canneries kept the Bristol Bay fishermen entirely under their control. The company had a "monkey boat" with an engine that would tow the sailboats of loyal fishermen to the fishing grounds, and it would assist a sailboat in trouble. A powered company scow would be stationed in the area to receive the fish, so the fishermen could make more frequent deliveries, thereby increasing their season's catch. The fishermen had no choice but to depend on the canneries' selective assistance. But while under sail and oar, they remained vulnerable to both huge tidal currents and to the region's sudden and unpredictable squalls. Most years men drowned when, for example, wind drove them onto the sands that had been bared by the falling tide, leaving them stranded, then fierce incoming waves from a rising tide would swamp their boats. Fishermen knew that earning a living on the water was tough, but they had long prided themselves on their strength of body and nerve, which had gotten them through many a rough season. Many veterans back from World War II, however, had been tested enough to no longer find charm in needless hardship. Why should they risk dangerous tides and winds through skilled sailing and muscled rowing, and why get hernias, grunting hundred-weights of fish over a roller, if, by the flip of a switch, an engine could do the same work for you?

Meanwhile, veterans returning to local communities in Bristol Bay had begun to chafe at seeing their sea wealth move south each season when most cannery workers and fishermen went home to someplace else. Why should these carpetbaggers dictate terms from faraway places? (It would be seven years before Alaskans achieved statehood in 1958 and thereby gained state control over their near-shore fisheries. Nevertheless, out-of-state management of Alaska's resources from Washington, DC, via interests in Washington and Oregon was already a hot issue.) Even under the threat of being called communist—a ready accusation in 1951 for any organization or individual challenging the status quo—Alaskans wanted to have a louder voice in their own affairs.

In Bristol Bay, old alliances fell apart. Fresh angers flared. A new Alaska-based union called a strike for higher cannery wages and a higher price to fishermen. The Seattle-based union ignored the strike and sent its members to work anyway. This meant some men fished at the start of the season in late June, while others fumed beside their landed boats. And, among those fishing, some eighty had been able to afford the newly-permitted engine boats—finally legalized in 1951—without the aid of cannery money or assistance. Although they now had to earn enough through their catch to pay for their new boat loans, these fishermen could lord it over the thousand-plus who remained committed to company sails and a heavier cannery obligation. To make the scene more delicate yet, Bristol Bay was experiencing a spate of seasons with historically poor runs of fish. The openings, which usually ran from 6:00 a.m. Monday through 6:00 p.m. Friday, began to have mid-week closings. If the Communists could have controlled this poor return rate of spawning salmon they would certainly have been blamed for that too, along with the union and boat rivalries. They probably were anyhow. Nineteen-fifty-one was that kind of year.

Perhaps to those involved at the time, the various interests of the strike were able to be kept straight. In retrospect, it's much less easy. Historian Robert W. King ventured to clarify matters:

> The strike is hard to explain but let me try. Part of it, I believe, was due to local residents trying to flex their muscle and break away from the Seattle-dominated Alaska Fishermen's Union (AFU). It also got caught up in the red scare of the time. Prior to World War II there was very little Native employment in Bristol Bay, but wartime manpower demands changed all that. A resident cannery workers union was formed and was affiliated with the International Fishermen and Allied Workers of America (IFAWA).
>
> After the war, as the iron curtain descended over Europe, the Berlin Airlift began and the Cold War got hot in Korea, IFAWA was linked to communist-leaning elements and was purged from the CIO. The resident union and non-resident AFU aligned with Harry Bridges's ILWU, a CIO affiliate which controlled much of the Pacific Coast ports but was also linked to the communists.
>
> In 1950, Jim Downey of Dillingham organized the independent Bering Sea Fishermen's Union on an anti-Bridges platform and aligned himself with Harry Lundeberg of the Seaman's International Union, an AFL affiliate. A separate resident cannery worker's union was formed, also affiliated with AFL. In 1951, the packers were forced to cut deals with Bridges and the ILWU to load their ships in Seattle, but when they arrived in Bristol Bay the resident AFL workers picketed the canneries.
>
> The AFU and ILWU workers, part of the CIO, did not honor the AFL strike and went to work. Downey held out as long as he could, finally agreeing on July 3 to terms offered a month earlier, including forty cents each for red salmon, less than eight cents a pound. By that time, many of the Native cannery workers had been sent home and missed the entire season. The canners blamed the

strike on jurisdictional issues. Downey said it was all about fish prices and the cannery workers were being used as pawns.

The labor issue was not directly linked to the powerboat issue but I think the powerboat success emboldened them.

13

Promised Land

NAKNEK, BRISTOL BAY, JUNE 1951

Kiyoshi Tsurifune pressed his forehead against the airplane window. The aircraft's wide silver wing obstructed half the view. Ahead and behind it, seen through streaks of cloud, he saw for the first time the soil of America. Streaks of earth colored brown and green. Mountains in late June with fingers of snow. Water with boats. If only, by some miscalculation, the plane would be forced to continue to New York City! Or at least to Chicago.

They circled a nest of squared buildings whose panes, one by one, reflected rays from an early sun, while a voice over the loudspeaker repeated that they must fasten their seat belts for the landing in Anchorage. The city below lay intact. Nothing was scorched nor blown apart nor in the process of being rebuilt—all of it clean and whole. *Bombed us to pieces but stayed clean and whole yourselves. How would you have managed had we prevailed? Would you have rebuilt quickly and with such energy as have the Japanese— have ever recovered—had we destroyed you?*

His anger ebbed as quickly as it had flashed. Good fortune that America was clever enough to invent the atomic bomb and end the war. Otherwise he, Kiyoshi Tsurifune—now no longer starving in a foul cave but the young director of a company with two fishing vessels (and more to come if America opened its waters again!)—might be dead like his honored brother and unable to care for his parents. Worse, might now be one-legged, or eyeless, or broken in some other way.

Beside him, Mr. Itaru Sasaki leaned over with a smile that reflected the gold fillings on his uneven teeth. "These people have everything, you see. So they consider themselves clever. But as we have seen to be obvious, they can be twisted like children. Generous children, but foolish like children."

Kiyoshi pointed to his ears and shook his head while saying in Japanese, "Too noisy." He busied himself with the seatbelt to avoid having Sasaki-san repeat what he had indeed heard.

Despite everything they said at home, Kiyoshi did like Americans. He did not merely tolerate them in order to do business. And now, arrived in at least Alaska, he was closer than ever before to the main thing. On the planes from Tokyo to Seattle, then to Anchorage, he'd kept focus most of the time on the mission he'd been assigned: to report facts on the runs of salmon in Bristol Bay and the Americans' ability to catch and process them. Further, he repeated and repeated polite American phrases learned from language records, to be sure he'd got them right, until Sasaki became impatient.

"Don't forget," Sasaki had said more than once, "we now have leverage that we did not have just two years ago. Where else can they put military bases to fight their war in Korea? It's no longer as it was just after the defeat, when we first requested permission to fish again in the Aleutians, where we have historically fished and thus have great rights. Now we can demand— although diplomatically, of course—to make them feel better. So therefore, you don't have to speak like an American so long as you say enough of their words to convey your meaning. Make them work a little to understand you. This makes what you say more important, you see. Don't forget your proud Japanese heritage that goes back thousands of years before the name 'America' was even invented."

"Yes. Yes." Kiyoshi needed to be polite to Sasaki, who was from the government agency that dealt with fisheries. The man was his senior on this mission. Kiyoshi had been chosen to come at government expense because he'd taught himself English and had become articulate in representing vessel owners and even the processors who needed the fisheries of

Alaska. But Sasaki couldn't object to Kiyoshi studying the map of United States laid out on his lap, even if, in the cramped space of the airline seat, the end part spilled over. What a heart-stopping distance between Anchorage and New York, even when compared to the longer distance from Japan across the Pacific. Sasaki would be traveling on to Washington, DC, while no provision had been made to send Kiyoshi himself any further than Alaska. Not even to stop over in Seattle where important fish merchants lived. He must, at least, find some way to continue on to San Francisco to see the famous hippies. Perhaps a *little* bit further? Chicago to see gangsters. New Orleans to hear the strangely exhilarating jazz. But mostly their greatest city: New York. New York! Where the luckiest people of all lived, including the most important artists. Where it was said on authority that artists' thrilling work could be casually viewed just by entering a gallery.

How foolish his people had been, just months after defeat, to demand access back into American waters as if nothing had transpired between the two nations! No wonder the victors refused. Now, though, after the passage of half a dozen years and many changes in the world, things might be different.

"Don't forget how hard we had it," Father had groused just before Kiyoshi had left for Alaska. They were sitting on the tatami while the servant they could now afford laid out tea.

"Sure, we had it hard," Kiyoshi had said, more boldly than he would have dared a few years earlier, and without even the semblance of a bow to soften it. "We were defeated. Remember?"

"And the Americans sucked away everything."

"No, Father. It was the greedy Japanese black marketeers that did that. Charged us four to five times—ten times—the value of even rice. Until the Americans put a stop to it."

"You forget that the Americans exploded two terrible bombs on helpless Japanese. That's what happened. What could we do?" Father was growing old and his opinions had hardened with the past. Yet of course he still needed to be given all respect.

"Two bombs that killed only a few thousand," Kiyoshi had tried to clarify. "They saved a million Japanese told to defend the homeland. Including me! And they saved us from the rubble of the cities that we'd still be clearing. Bombs or no, our defeat would have been the same." Father shook his head, annoyed, but Kiyoshi could not stop now. "And before those two powerful bombs, terrible, yes? Years before? Who was it who prepared for war, then started it?"

"Our nation had a sacred mission to save all Asia from colonial aggressors. But our soldiers failed us," Father cried. "Not those who, like your brother, died gloriously, thereby inspiring his companions. Others. Those who surrendered rather than carrying us to victory and honor."

"Enough," murmured his mother.

"Then I'll say no more. I'm grateful that I still have one son alive. Yes. Naturally. But just the same. Since in disgraceful surrender we have lost—"

"Enough."

"—we have lost honor."

Rather than argue further, Kiyoshi had begged an appointment and had bowed to excuse himself.

An increasing burden, this. He ran the family company in all but name. Yet it was dutiful courtesy to appear at Father's home every morning, as if to receive instructions. And it comforted Mother. As did the presence of his precious five-year-old son Shoji, whom he brought to Mother daily while his young, beloved wife Miki worked—in true Western fashion—in the fishing company office. Despite Mother's frequently murmured questions of when she'd have more bubbling children to look after on the workdays, Miki and Kiyoshi had decided to wait for greater prosperity before having any further family.

As always after the morning call on Father, Kiyoshi left his parents' house, which was wooden and utilitarian like all others in the neighborhood. With the return of prosperity, its sliding panels and screens were all in good repair. His own home, in a nearby neighborhood once leveled by war and now built fresh, would be empty until mid-day, except for their servant. He turned toward his office by the waterfront. There, moored and being unloaded from the night's fishing, rode one of the two fishing vessels their company owned. At sight of him the captain, Oono and the two fishermen on deck stopped to bow. He reciprocated in full gravity with a shallower bow, as befitting his position, and strode over to see the harvest. It was a catch of assorted fish—none large—already separated by species into tubs, along with a few crayfish with sluggish, snapping claws.

What a difference from the catch of a deep sea trawler if the Americans were to permit access to their waters again! In that event, credit enough would appear in order to refurbish the company's larger vessel that still rusted at moorage. And yet, with all that was at stake in his mission to Alaska, Kiyoshi Tsurifune sat in the plane from Tokyo dreaming over the distance on the map between Anchorage and that golden city of New York.

A man dressed in suit and tie met them at the Anchorage airport. He introduced himself as John Goss of the US State Department representing overseas trade. The three men exchanged cards. Sasaki, who on the flight had said that he had studied English, merely smiled and bowed, appearing somewhat ill at ease. Kiyoshi stepped in at once to use the English he had studied and practiced over and over. Kiyoshi sized Mr. Goss with disappointment. From his bulging waist and unweathered face, he was clearly a bureaucrat rather than a man of seafaring background. Nevertheless, the man was in charge. He decided to try him. With sentences rehearsed during the flight over, "Sir! What is your opinion? Yankee baseball team from the great city of New York. Again this year, shall they play the famous American World Series?"

"My. You people learn fast." Goss ignored the question. "Now, let's get your names straight."

As soon as Mr. Goss had established their names, he turned his attention to Sasaki and handed him a folder of documents. "Read these over during your next flight. They're in both languages. Somebody who speaks Japanese is waiting to meet you in Chicago and see that you get on the plane to Washington, DC."

Sasaki bowed and accepted the folder with a thanks murmured in Japanese. Did the man even understand, Kiyoshi wondered? So much for Sasaki-san's English, and for his boldness on the plane. To show off his own skill Kiyoshi declared: "Weather in Alaska, now I think, is summertime. Yet, however, very winter-seeming. Thus cold snow—I see this through the window, on . . . the high of mountains."

Mr. Goss laughed. "High of mountains, eh? You've said it. Still a piece of snow up there all right. Now, let's make sure Mr. Sakisaki gets on his plane to Chicago. Then we catch a plane later in the day to King Salmon where they're waiting for you. Okay? Frankly, I'm just finding my way around here myself. Place not exactly what I'd call . . ."

At the entrance ramp to the Chicago plane, Sasaki looked back at Kiyoshi with what seemed like agitation. What kind of representative would Sasaki make to the high officials in Washington, DC? Better they had sent himself, director of only a small fishing company perhaps, but ready and eager with talk that might gain their attention.

A small plane flew Mr. Goss and Kiyoshi from Anchorage to a place auspiciously named King Salmon. The other passengers were roughly dressed, tall, sturdy Americans. His own suit and tie, echoing those worn by Mr. Goss, set them both apart. It was a fashion he might have wanted in Japan, but suddenly not in America. Confident people slumped comfortably in the single seats along each side of the plane. Just like their bold new expressionist paintings.

The plane landed at an airport so small that the waiting room was only a shelter a few feet wide. Baggage stowed in a side door of the plane was unloaded into the open and carted directly to a high pile outside the airport door. In contrast to his two neat leather suitcases, which eventually landed on the pile, these men traveled with knapsacks of rough cloth. Some of their luggage was scuffed from wear, some had high rubber boots strapped around the outside. Yes. Only workers, perhaps. But free and bold in their nature. Indeed, he liked Americans.

Several old-looking vehicles were parked to the side, including trucks and a yellow bus. "Where's the car that's supposed to meet us?" muttered Mr. Goss. "This is a hell kind of . . ." A man in work clothes approached them and declared that from the way they were dressed he guessed they were the ones to pick up for Swede Scorden. He led them to a proper automobile parked further away. "Getting worried there for a minute."

Several of the roughly dressed passengers from the plane headed to the bus. It was foolish even to think of it in his position, thought Kiyoshi, but he wished to be with these Americans. They shouldered their assorted baggage and climbed aboard the bus with bold confidence, joking amongst themselves and even two bold women. It would have been informative to watch further. Indeed, admit it: agreeable.

Mr. Goss settled back in to the automobile, offered a cigarette which Kiyoshi accepted, and lit both with a pocket flame machine smaller than a box of matches. "So, Mr. Sura . . . furie is it? You represent—"

Kiyoshi chanced a correction that would have been unheard of to a high Japanese official. "Forgive me. Name 'Tsurifune,' sir. In Japanese these words represent meaning thusly: fishing equipment is Tsuri and Fune is vessel."

The official did not appear to be insulted. "Fishboat nets, that's a good one. And so, Mr. Surafurie, you're here for fish buyers from the companies of your city, right? Frankly, I'm not in the fish business, more in canned beef from South America, but here I am. So, what's the total volume of our uh, salmon, that you want to buy each year?"

Kiyoshi did not trust his English for a matter of such importance. Following instructions from the Tokyo manager who had briefed him, he opened his briefcase and pulled out several pages clipped together. In words that he had practiced for days, he stated: "Here I have official documents which you shall please receive. However, product sales must depend on product quality. Therefore, thus, I must inspect product."

Mr. Goss chuckled. "Well I guess you do. Nothing but the best for you folks now, eh? Okay then, that's just what we're headed to see about right now."

They drove through a swamp-like countryside of stunted brown vegetation. Kiyoshi watched every detail of his first experience on American soil. Not beautiful. But raw, perhaps with wild beasts lurking. Most energetic. They turned onto a primitive road that led eventually to a compound of buildings huddled together in the seeming wilderness. During the drive that lasted at least a half hour, there had been no other sign of habitation. Yes. America. The place of famous wide open spaces he'd read so much about. Desolate perhaps. But indeed wide and open, not crowded with people.

14

Boss Swede

The first thing Swede did at 5:00 a.m. one morning halfway into June, was to tear May 1951 from the calendar over his desk. Not like him to forget even such small details. Certainly he'd organized the rest of his office in better fashion since coming to Naknek a month ago. He raised the blind to admit the rays of a sun already risen a couple of hours. He enjoyed it whenever such sun appeared through gray clouds. The rays, separated by their passage through the tops of fir trees, glanced off the bills of lading he'd piled on the desk by category before locking up last night sometime past midnight. By the 7:00 a.m. opening of the office he'd strode through each building of the plant, from loading dock and canning floor, to blacksmith and carpenter shops, to net loft and boat storage, to bunkhouse and cafeteria. When the red salmon arrived at last, all would function correctly. All of it, this season finally in his care! Those watching his performance from Ketchikan and Seattle would see that their trust had not been misplaced. And that he wouldn't allow any of the infiltration they seemed to fear. The picketing yesterday was a little disturbing, of course—a nuisance perhaps, but nothing in the long run. A few, always and anywhere, needed to make a show. His own workers unloaded around the pickets, who soon realized they were making noise to no purpose. At opening hour, right down to the minute, his main foremen appeared at the door for briefing.

"Those twenty hundred flats we couldn't find, were they in the unmarked boxes, then?" Swede asked Thompson from the dock.

"Nope. Checked all cartons three times." The man didn't add "sir" as of course he would have done in Scandinavia. Get used to such as this, Swede told himself as he exclaimed, "Devil. Didn't come! Don't these people know how to count? Ja then." Automatically, he corrected to "Okay, I see" and hoped that nobody had noticed. He confirmed with one head man that the Filipino workers who had assembled in Seattle were to be met that afternoon by the cannery bus at King Salmon airport, then from another that all bunkhouse spaces were ready for them. "These foreigners. They need to be watched. Not to wander from the places provided for them. They might get lost. They might steal."

"Same ones come every year since that law stopped the chinks coming," said Hostetler, the canning line foreman, drily. "People who work hard, eat their Jap noodles, don't get lost, keep to themselves, don't steal. Hell of a sight steadier than the Natives we've hired—the ones that quit when they please for what they call sustenance fishing when the reds start running good. You've seen it yourself in other years, Swede, before you got put in charge of everything, so relax."

Swede suppressed a frown. The man's tone wasn't respectful. Yet, this was how they spoke in America. He turned to ask the machinist about a disassembled conveyor and was assured it would be functioning by day's end, noted to the boathouse foreman that poisons should be set for rodents that had winter-nested in the vessels, and told the foreman supervising the bunkhouses that two of the toilets he'd tested that morning had overflowed. There was, by design, at least one item on his clipboard for each man to answer for.

"Ja. Yes, okay." Time to dismiss everyone back to work. Swede considered, decided that he had to speak on the record, and cleared his throat to gain their attention. "But now! A caution from the company main office in Seattle, so please pay attention. They direct us to watch for strangers among our workers. Especially anyone with the pamphlets they give out. Pamphlets were handed out by the men from this new union, picketing beside our supply ship. I didn't wish to be seen taking such papers. But I instructed a man of ours to take one for me. I saw no others of our people take one."

"Least not while you were watching," said Hostetler. The other foremen laughed. Swede considered a moment, then chuckled himself. Best to join them.

"They call the new union a co-op," Hostetler continued. "Even got its own store outside of the cannery. Sells hip boots a dollar and fifty cents cheaper than our company store here. That's what I hear. Work gloves fifty cents cheaper. Popsicles eight cents, I hear."

"Shows right there somebody outside's footing the bill," growled Smith, the loading-dock foreman. "So I'll call it commie if you won't. Next thing it's that strike being called by the bunch up north. That'll show everybody. Boats don't fish, fish go free up the river, nothing loads or unloads, no work, everybody's fucked. Just what the commies want to happen. Then they can move in and take over. You saw what they tried in Berlin before we did that airlift. And now like they're doing in that Korea shithole? You can count on it."

"And with such a small run of fish predicted . . ." Swede began. He shrugged and decided not to speak further. Rumors without proof had been a tool of the Nazi bastards. This wasn't the year for anyone to start trouble. The biologists had already announced a possible closing of the waters to fishing boats in the middle of each week to allow full escapement. "So. We shall all be ready on time for the fishing to start next week—with no foolish strike—and then the processing, eh? Please spend a productive day, gentlemen. Good-bye."

After they left and before calling Mrs. Lacey in for dictation, Swede took pencil to paper with an English language dictionary and a thesaurus for reference. It was daily work to improve his English so that no one would mistake him for a foreigner. Thus, he wrote and corrected before finally copying in ink:

To Personnel Director Horace Stevens, Seattle.

> Sir,
> In the matter of new unions among our fishermen, it is difficult to be accurate. The new union has held meetings here, but my reports say few have attended. Only two of our people, of lower level, have been seen, so I do not recommend firing them, which would draw attention. To be frank, I cannot confirm, or disprove, that Communists are in charge.

He wrote and then rewrote the next paragraph, checking practically every word as he bit into his pencil. Once, he tore it in half, then reconsidered and placed the two halves of paper back together. *I'll say it, for my father and all whom the German bastards murdered,* he decided. Even if they discharge me!

> You will forgive me, even when this is your valued suggestion.
> But I do not find it American to send a spy to these meetings,

even if I could find a man we could trust. Forgive me again, but this is not an American way of doing. The United States is a nation where everybody speaks what he is thinking at the moment. Thus, any words that fishermen who are contracted to us may say at these meetings are justified, as they exercise their right to talk freely without fear of penalty.

He wrote the rest of the letter with greater confidence.

As you know, some of the fishermen contracted to us this year now own power boats that we do not control. But still loyal fishermen, committed to delivering exclusively to us. Since fishing boats under engine power will make fishermen more independent if they assume private ownership, I suggest urgently that the company purchase engine boats of which they retain ownership. This is perhaps the only means to retain the loyalty and dependence of many fishermen who fish for us. This year in Bristol Bay the government biologists predict a run of fish as poor as last year. With so much changing up here, such scarce catches might attract fishermen to sell to other canneries if such canneries raise the price they pay for fish. This, I think, does not mean that fishermen have listened to Communists but that they have acted like Americans who are by their nature competitive. Therefore, nevertheless, please understand that I *shall* be alert to what knowledge I can gain of competitive pricing. I shall learn this from the crewmen aboard our collector vessels, and I will report to you immediately on this matter. Will report at once by telephone, no matter how long it is necessary to wait for the connection, which is often difficult in this place far from good telephone lines.

To summarize in answer to your special question—I do not think that any of our fishermen are members of the Communist Party.

Respectfully yours,
A.S. Scorden

Swede sealed the letter, taped the envelope at the edges where the glue might not hold, then marked it "confidential" and sealed it in a larger envelope also marked "confidential." He tore the pencil drafts into pieces and stuffed half of the scraps into his pockets to distribute into other waste cans. He put the well-thumbed dictionary and the thesaurus back on the shelf. So many words that he had taught himself in English, and yet there were always more. It almost made him wish that, when his GI loan had finally come through, he had taken a language class or two in Seattle. Instead he had spent those summers—in between seasons at the cannery—studying adamantly for the Business Administration degree Miles Jackson had encouraged him to get. It might be wise now, since he was determined to become a proper American, to take a night class at some school or college.

"Come in now, Mrs. Lacey. Bring a notebook, please," he called to his secretary. She appeared quickly. Their relationship had cemented in the five years since he'd been accepted into management. Perhaps, since she had lost a son in the war, she regarded him as her own charge, even though they always remained businesslike. At the beginning she had occasionally counseled him, even covered for him, whether he needed it or no. He, in turn a year ago, had insisted she not be retired against her will when the Seattle management tried to streamline its personnel, citing complaints that she'd become snappish. Had, in fact, risked his own position with Seattle management in the process, Had even used his growing authority to ensure that she'd return to Bristol Bay when he learned that she looked forward to it each year. Otherwise he'd have chosen someone younger and prettier from among the available secretaries. At least his Mary wouldn't have an excuse to be jealous. Out of the question for a man's wife to join him here for two months, whatever she said, when there were young children to care for and one of them not yet out of diapers. That was one American notion he need not embrace.

"Now, my number one message, Mrs. Lacey. To John Nielsen at Industrial Supply in Seattle. Try first as usual, if the telephone line is open, to read it to him. Otherwise send a telegram. Copy down, please: 'Shipment of cans is short by twenty-hundred number ten flats. We shall need same by two weeks from this date. Best it comes sooner.'"

"You'd better say 'must have' if you want it on time."

"Yes, good, okay, 'must have,' please. Continue then, so-and-so, eh? Now, second message, same thing, phone or telegraph this to Henry Sollers of Marine Grocery in Seattle. Copy down, please: 'You have sent me short by thirty-six dozen eggs, also by one hundred and sixty jars of peanut butter, both ordered with other items two months ago but missing from shipment received last night on vessel *Haida*. We shall—must have—same no later than' . . . so-and-so, eh?"

She nodded without looking up. Yes, as his wife had suggested once after meeting her, Mrs. Lacey probably dyed her hair a little bit—he could see strong gray at the roots. It made this bony, brusque, capable woman seem more human, even if she persisted in doing things her own way despite the fact that he was now the boss.

"Then continue please the letter Mrs. Lacey: 'Furthermore, you have sent me one hundred and twenty more boxes of oatmeal than I have ordered. Will accept this extra oatmeal only at two-thirds original price . . .'" He allowed himself a smile, hoping to be thought agreeable. "Yes. Ha. '. . . since the rats will probably eat half of it in the place where it must be stored.'"

Her slight laugh rewarded him. No harm to make a joke when you could. Although the rats, of course, were real enough. He leaned back, more relaxed. "Now please, Mrs. Lacey, read back to me those letters."

He listened carefully, twice changed the wording to make it sound more American, and felt a pleased sense of relief when she read, corrected, and left, all in good humor. Every day he improved himself. He'd even begun to swear like an American, although not yet without thinking the words through first. Even the family name change from Skovkus to Scorden was now properly recorded, although his first name remained Arnie for any official who needed to know.

Earlier, he had brewed the first coffee of the morning, making it stronger by far than he had yet persuaded Mrs. Lacey to do during the rest of the day. Now, he paused over a third or fourth cup as he stood on the porch of the building that housed both the office and the company store. From here he faced the assemblage of wood sidings and corrugated roofs that were now his charge. The buildings formed their own community, fronting the tidal Naknek River that led from the Bay, but otherwise it was surrounded by the wilderness of stunted northern trees and undergrowth where bears roamed freely. Each cannery along the river was a similar colony for seasonal occupants who, for three months a year, worked, ate, and slept within its compound, only driving to the actual village miles away for the rare necessity. A little kingdom wrested from the bears, May through July. Left to his care to keep it functioning and productive. And do it he would.

From his porch (*yes, mine!*) he gazed down the wide-paved ramp that led past the fronts of buildings to the wharf. From here he could see any cargo ship that docked, but not the company fishing boats clustered along the piers behind the buildings. Forklifts carried crates or boxes, and men in coveralls walked with purpose from one building to another. A pickup truck drove down the ramp and turned from view. Two men in the back stood amongst gear and a pile of nets. Wasn't one of them—the one with the cap pulled close to his eyes, standing straight without bracing himself as did the other—his old friend Jones Henry the fisherman? Certainly possible, since Jones delivered to the company in Ketchikan. They had seen each other less and less except for business, since he himself had left Cousin Nels's boat to work ashore. Certainly there had long since been no more meetings at Creek Street, though the brothel district had indeed survived. Old visits that he'd never admit to Mary. What would Jones have told his own wife? Adele, was that her name? Yes. He had attended Jones's wedding—been a groomsman, even—and Jones had returned the favor at Swede's own union to Mary. Should invite them over some time, even though management and dockside didn't share views. Didn't in the old country at least. One more thing to change in himself.

Swede informed Mrs. Lacey of where he was going—a manager should never be out of reach—and followed the truck. His course took him down the causeway and along the docks. The cargo ship that had come with supplies from Seattle had left hours before on high water. All had been delivered properly, despite the annoying picket line that his workers had been instructed by their own union to ignore. The tide, now low again, exposed strips of mud that the screaming gulls encircled. At such low water the whole complex of piers, set atop barnacled pilings, now stretched up twenty feet. A few boats were already afloat below, and men in them stowed their sails and gillnets in preparation. Swede paused to take in the sight. The gang on the beach bustled and shouted. Vehicles puffed black exhaust. From the boat warehouse came the thump of big chains on blocks and the clatter of skiffs being lowered from their racks. Men pushed handcarts, shouldered gear, drove forklifts piled with cartons. Some lifted the double-ended skiffs from dollies, and others rigged them for lowering into the water. A good manager knew all his people. In past years as an assistant manager in whatever assignment, he'd memorized scores of names and faces that he now recognized—but there were inevitably some newcomers. At least those in the rubber boots would be the fishermen.

Despite the activity, things still felt suspended, awaiting the explosion of activity that would happen when the fish arrived. Swede remembered such expectation from his father's plant in the old country. Thrived on it! Bins, scrubbed and stored nearly a year before, waited empty outside the high-sliding doors that opened onto the cannery floor. The boats—empty shells now—would soon ride weighted under piles of fish. For the present, the area smelled of oils and of wood dried by winter blows and rain. In another few days, the odors of fish would obliterate all else—from the gurry that slithered out of the brailers that lifted the catch from the scows, to the heavy steam clouding inside the factory. All familiar, but here on a scale much grander. And he in charge!

In one of the previous years, Swede had helped supervise the breaking out and assignment of company boats—a promotion from being merely a management novice. One among many others. Now he could watch his own former aide do the job, while he himself assumed a critical frown learned from his own mentor—one that said he knew all the tricks and unspoken agreements. It was important to stay above fishermen's petty tricks to get assigned the best boats, while of course giving priority to the old timers who remained faithful to the cannery. You especially favored those who fished hard, stayed the whole season, and delivered only to company scows when the fish runs turned scarce. It meant that a good manager had to make notes and records and documents year by year, both on paper and in his head. In his nearly five years as a company man he'd already assembled a vast memory. Not a job to be learned in a month, or even a season. A career. A calling.

Yes, there was Jones Henry on the dock. Scorden watched as he received a net, then a small primus stove from the older man standing on the bed of the truck, and as he carried them to the boat lettered with a black *G-32* on the bow. Older boat, if memory served. Not one of the best. Boat whose days were numbered, to use an American expression. The twenty-nine footer routinely had small leaks that were never quite reached by caulking and a mast never firmly seated without wedges. He'd made it his business to evaluate the vessels of the company's fleet by interviewing fishermen at the end of the season—even though fishermen were born complainers. Next season or the one after, canneries would finally need to give in to pressures and modernize the Bristol Bay salmon fishery. When engines inevitably replaced the compulsory sailboat on Bristol Bay, fishing boats would change. Lengths still locked at thirty-two feet, perhaps, but it was rumored that no restrictions applied to beam width nor hull construction. Steel hulls would be permitted. Such aged wooden sailboats as this *G-32* vessel would quickly be consigned to firewood.

Had Swede been in charge of boat distribution he'd have found a way to assign Jones a newer boat for camaraderie's sake, newcomer or not. Should he interfere now? Why not?—the authority was his. Swede approached Jones Henry.

"Nice that the sun is shining today," he ventured pleasantly.

Jones barely paused to grunt "Oh. You. Up here now, eh?" He called over to the man still in the truck: "Dad! Don't forget them cans of peanut butter and coffee, and that sack with the wrench and pliers. Nothing else I can think of we got left up there. Oh, that belt roll of woolens and long johns—don't forget them over in the corner. Then you can tell the driver we're unloaded this trip."

"Ah . . . Jones. So you're new this year to fishing salmon here in Bristol Bay?"

Jones Henry stopped long enough to push up the cap that nearly covered his eyes. "New to this pier, mebbe. New if you don't count three seasons with my old man before the war. Used to deliver up to Dillingham—though that's all gone Native now." He cocked his head and gave the closest stretch of his mouth to a grin that Swede had ever seen from him. "Back before you ever came to this country. This thing didn't start yesterday, you know."

Swede grabbed the opening, glad for a subject to relieve the awkwardness. "Ho, I do know! Even boys in my country know of Bristol Bay. Before the war, fathers and grandfathers would come to fish here every July. So it's a famous history, Bristol Bay. Everybody knows about the famous runs of sockeye salmon here. Everybody who fishes."

"Question, then—since I'm talking to the big office, and fishermen never get told what goes on—you talk all the time to fancy government biologists, right? They're saying them fish-counters don't expect a good run. That right?"

"Coming little, I fear they say. Let's wait and see, eh? The salmon have already appeared at False Pass. So we know they're coming. Perhaps the biologists made a mistake. An announcement very soon, but I'm glad to tell you now. Today is Thursday, yes? Expect fish into the Kvichak here by next week. So you must be on the water and towed into position."

"What's this I hear about some guys going on strike? Not fishing?"

Swede considered, then said casually, "A few up in Dillingham, perhaps. Making unreasonable demands with a new union that nobody recognizes."

"That the one I hear picketed your ship's unloading?"

"A little. A little. A new union of people who wish to disrupt."

Jones in his turn appeared to consider. Finally: "Yeah. Okay. Ain't my concern. You tow us out and we'll be there."

"Good! And so, Jones. You're fishing this season here then with my company?"

"You got it." Jones's eyes narrowed. "Your company? I knew you're busy making out. But you've bought this outfit?" Any vestige of a smile vanished. "You ain't one of them commies, are you? Taking over?"

"Never!" Swede controlled his outrage at the idea. Started to add that he was indeed now the boss of this cannery and no damned Russian Communist would ever infiltrate here, but checked himself. If Jones didn't know yet, he'd find out soon enough. And it made no difference between them. As for the boat assignment—new or old—a good manager didn't intercede to give his friend a better boat. That way led to the end of order.

A car drove up. It nosed among the boats scattered on the pier before stopping. Not a company vehicle, Swede noted in annoyance. Visitors should have checked in at the office and not been allowed to roam wild, possibly to interfere with operations. The driver-side door opened, and a government official got out. So nothing to be done but to be polite.

"Yes. Hello." Swede shook the official's hand while trying to remember his name. "You see we are busy preparing." Big fellow gone heavy, a politician. Not truly of the fishing business. He'd seen the man only once before, at a meeting in Seattle when the company had sent him to sit on the sidelines and furnish production data when necessary. The fellow had brought a pile of books to the table, had read from them to make some point of no importance while sweat made his glasses slip.

"Mr. Sorman or something, right? How are you? They said at the office you'd be down here. John Goss, Department of Commerce in DC. Just flown into Naknek here today. Got an important visitor I'm showing around."

"Scorden, sir." Swede disliked the man immediately.

"Right." Goss held open the passenger door and a Japanese man stepped out. He wore a dark suit and a striped silk tie. He peered around with interest, then with a slight bow proffered his hand. Swede accepted the hand for a brief shake. The grip was firm at first, but then lost its tension. At least, thought Swede, better than the limp-at-the-start handshakes of the few other Orientals he'd encountered.

"Mr. Sorman, meet Mr. Surafurie," said Goss. "He's come over from Japan to talk about re-opening the sales of fish and fish products to his country. Our office in DC is giving it some priority. Call it a directive from the top. Way top." He raised an eyebrow and paused for effect, before resuming. "Now that Japan's a base for our armed forces going to Korea, there's a lot of business opportunity opening there. Do all we can to help, right? Thought we might show Mr. Surafurie around a bit here."

"I am Kiyoshi Tsurifune," the Japanese said mildly and added in reasonable English, "I am at your service, Mr. Scorden."

At least the Japanese fellow pays attention, Swede decided. What could he take the man to see that would not violate what might be considered company secrets, which he could then be called to answer for? (Could this man, in fact, be a Communist creeping in from the other side of the world? The careless Mr. Goss would hardly know the difference.) Should have been given time to make a phone call to the Seattle main office, or at least to Ketchikan.

"*Desverre* . . . uh, unfortunately, I do not speak Japanese," Scorden said to gain time.

The Japanese declared at once, "This makes no problem, sir. Not best, I apologize, but I have studied English very hard, and can understand. It will be very kind of you to show me your factory." He looked around. "Very small boats for the fishing, I see. And are there no engines, only equipment for sail? Therefore must I ask. Are such vessels efficient?"

Goss pulled himself to a full height and smiled benignly. "Interesting point there. Our government, just this year—1951—has changed regulations in Bristol Bay to allow fishing with an engine. Not in time for a lot of conversions this season, though I hear there are a few engine boats around already. I'm told the boatyards are booming with orders, though. Anyhow. Let's go look at your catch and sales projections for the year, okay? See where we might accommodate this Mr. Surafurie."

The United States government surely understood what it was doing, Swede decided. Despite sending a representative so clumsy with names.

"Follow, please," Swede ordered.

This Mr. Scorden was an appropriate American headman, Kiyoshi noted. Acted with authority without needing to wear either jacket or tie. His own dark suit and silk tie again seemed out of place. Mr. Scorden's smile was studied and not necessarily cordial. Businesslike. Appropriately. He had a chin that was clean-shaven and boxlike, with blond hair combed neatly— very Western. Kiyoshi had met the man's coolly appraising eyes with a smile he hoped was confident and polite. He'd controlled the impulse to bow and had instead offered his hand, preparing to tighten his grip. Indeed, he'd needed to grip hard when they shook hands, although, unaccustomed to such pressure, his hand soon lost tension.

"Long flight, eh?" Mr. Scorden said it almost as a challenge. The man's eyes seemed to add: *and what did you do as a Japanese in the war?*

"Yes. Yes. Long flight. Thank you."

"We are now busy here in Bristol Bay, you see. Today the fishermen are launching their boats. You wish to watch?"

"Very interesting. Yes, thank you." To himself, Kiyoshi noted that this Scorden did not exactly have the American accent. Or was this merely another way of placing words in English than the one he had studied?

Mr. Goss coughed to draw their attention. "First, instead of that . . . I told Mr. Surafurie he could see some of your canned or frozen stuff right away. Test their good quality, you know. See how good our American quality is."

"Not possible. The fish have not yet been caught. As you can see, the boats are just being placed into the water."

Goss frowned. "Somebody might have told me before I came all this way. Before I brought this Mr.—uh—Surafurie."

Mr. Scorden suddenly turned impatient. Annoyed, even. "There is never red salmon at the plant before the boats catch them, sir. This is easily found in all the writings available."

Kiyoshi liked this man. He was not a fool.

"What country's your home?" Mr. Goss asked suddenly.

"America."

"No, I mean, your accent. It's not from the USA."

Mr. Scorden took a while to answer. "Sweden, then Norway, sir. But I am a citizen and I have declared the oath of loyalty to the United States."

"Well, good for you. But I could tell right off that you weren't born here."

"So. I must work harder to speak." Mr. Scorden did not seem pleased.

Kiyoshi watched the open boats—obviously fishing vessels—that workmen were bringing out from a warehouse. Other boats had already been placed on the wide dock and were being readied for sea. A crane lowered one vessel into the water far below the pier. Yes, he had read that tides in Bristol Bay were extreme. It pleased him to see actual evidence of his research.

"Didn't know you had such low tides," said Mr. Goss. Mr. Scorden merely shrugged.

"The low tides of Bristol Bay are famous," Kiyoshi declared. "This is a famous fact." He controlled adding further that this was a fact known to all the world; he was rewarded enough when the fish plant manager gave him half a smile.

—★—

15

MUG-UP

For Jones, it was like a drink of cool water to arrive again in Bristol Bay and find how little had changed in the past decade. Japs had torn apart other places in the world since he'd last come to Bristol Bay as a kid boat-puller for his dad, but they'd shitted on nothing here. In Naknek village were the same weather-beaten buildings and neat onion-domed Russian church, surrounded by the same bare landscape—all of it precious for having stayed the same. For not changing with the times. And at the cannery were the same oak and cedar double-ender fishing boats stored in the warehouse, the same ferocious tides that lapped up and down against barnacled pilings. Inside, the same clank of the iron chink machine on the processing floor, ready to head and gut salmon when the time came, and the same leathery smells of tons of fish that had long since been scrubbed from wood and concrete.

Old times. Nothing had changed. Launching and stepping into the boats was the last thing between Jones and being on the water. A week earlier, when he and his dad had arrived in Naknek on a company charter plane, their first job—along with all the other fishermen whose boats were owned and stored by the canneries—had been to help set up for the season. The hundred dollars offered for this work was entered against each man's name at the office. A similar guaranteed sum would go on their settlement books at season's end in late July, if, as the cannery expected, they stayed to help load the salmon pack onto ships and to close down the buildings. Whatever their deliveries on the water yielded in between, men coming to fish Bristol Bay could count on this run money. Like the old times before the war. No enemies but wind and tide, no Jap waiting behind a rock like a poisonous snake. You worked with every muscle, you were fit enough to take the weather in an open boat, and you did it all like a man in the rough company of other good men.

But then, while breaking out the boats after talking with Swede, now puffed up with his new responsibility: "Damn if that ain't a Jap he's shaking hands with!" Here in Bristol Bay!

"Not your worry, boy," said his father. Jones shrugged and decided to put it from his mind. Management shouldn't be his business when there were fish to be caught.

"This ain't much of a boat they give us," Buck commented. No question the double-ender assigned them was old and beat-up. But she looked sturdy. He kicked at one of the oak ribs, then banged his knuckles against the ironbark sternpost. Yes. Sturdy! Everything about her pleased him. Sail. No engine noise. Just you and the water. Like the old days when Japs were only something you read about.

That Jap now. Made a half-assed little bow to Swede. Now that he didn't have a gun to blow off somebody's face. Jones searched for the boat plug, found it lashed to a cleat, and wormed it into the bunghole. Tight fit, even before swelling in the water. She'd hold. As for the Jap. Looked somehow familiar from a distance. But who could tell one from the other?

"Piece of shit, this boat," growled Buck Henry, as he brushed one of the sides with his boot. "We shouldn't still have to fish here under sail, what with engines everywhere else."

"It'll suit," Jones replied. "Likely enough them pieces gouged out along the rails will lighten her by a pound or two." The whole place bustling with activity made him feel easy. "You still ain't pulling the oars, far as I know," he added in good humor. "So you don't need to bother about weight any more than before."

Buck Henry accepted the light-hearted tone. "No other reason to bring you along."

The men on the dock, when Jones thought about it, were divided into two generations. There were those like his father, robust still but deliberate, moving in straight lines. If their caps happened to blow off you wouldn't see much hair, and what they had was graying and plastered tight against their heads with sweat. Then there were the younger guys in their mid twenties, like Jones himself, with strands of hair popping like weeds from their caps, and legs that bore them in easy leaps from pier to boat—even with shoulders loaded. Tattoos showed on some of their arms when their sleeves were rolled back. Eyes cool, less merry than those of their seniors. War stories in the back of those eyes. Yet during mug-ups in the cannery mess hall, any talk of war came from the older men. From the ones who weren't in danger of being called up again if this shit in Korea didn't stop.

Jones climbed into the boat and stomped on the deck boards to test their firmness. Sturdy. No machinery to break down here. The thought relaxed him, but for form's sake he muttered, "Don't know why I left my troller for five–six weeks of this."

"Money don't hurt in a good season. And, for starters, no radio calls from your lady every few minutes."

Jones faced his dad. "Adele's a good woman."

"Who ever said she wasn't?"

"Calls too much, but she's a good woman."

"I never meant . . ." His father considered, then said carefully, "Not like she's still got a kid to keep her busy. Your ma and I keep hoping you've started on another one. It breaks our hearts, son, but your little Amy's not coming back."

Jones busied himself test-rapping the boat's cedar planks with his knuckles. Finally: "Adele and I keep trying. I've told you that before. I'm going to get the mast."

"I'm right behind you."

"Only if you leave off about kids. Otherwise I can do it by myself."

"You forget how heavy that mast is. Won't speak of the other again, boy."

"Some likely!"

A whistle tooted from one of the buildings. Others around them stopped working. Jones welcomed the interruption. Bristol Bay was supposed to be a breather from the fights and sorrows back home. He stretched, feeling the pull of his muscles. "Mug-up first suits me." He and his dad joined the rest making their way toward the mess hall.

On the road they crossed paths with Swede Scorden. He was accompanied by the Jap and the American who'd come in the automobile. Jones stopped short and pushed back his cap for a clearer view. Japs did all look alike. But hadn't he seen this one before? Not in a suit of course. Jap now playing a big shot, when all that any of them deserved was a bullet.

The Jap returned his gaze, paused, then made a little bow like they all were wont to do before pulling a knife. Jones narrowed his eyes, the most acknowledgement he was willing to give, before continuing in a straight line to the mess hall.

"Looks like he knows you," said Buck Henry.

"Not likely. All Japs act that way."

In the mess hall, they filled thick mugs from the coffee urn, took fistfuls of fresh baked donuts from an array of plates, and elbowed onto benches at the long tables. Jones glanced at the others around him. Some had ridden aboard the company plane coming north. He'd probably know them all before season's end, boat to boat on the water. Even get pissed at one or the other if their nets got snagged. Or grateful for help in trouble. Jones stretched and settled in, comfortable at once. These fishermen were a bunch apart from the Italians and Norwegians who sat at other tables, talking in foreign languages—as if this wasn't America. Young and old, like him and his dad, the men around him all wore some variety of smudged woolens. Some, like himself, had red long john sleeves peering from underneath shirts that had been cut above the elbow. Their black or red caps all had logos from some fish gear or engine company. A few days of stubble grew on most of their chins, the telling sign that there were no wives here to boss them around. This was where he belonged. Not in some kitchen like the one Adele kept, with frilly curtains and artificial flowers on a damn bumpy embroidered tablecloth.

The man at Buck Henry's side turned at once. "Okay, Buck. What do you and your boy think? This new union. A strike make any sense to you?"

"You kidding, Russ?" Buck pulled the damp stub of a half-smoked cigar from his pocket and, after a couple of tries succeeded in lighting it. "Stay dry, with the fish about to run?"

"I say that too. We came up here to catch fish. You think the cannery's going to open for mug-ups and dinners if we don't give 'em fish?"

Buck wrapped his thick fingers around his mug and leaned back to blow out a cloud of blue smoke. "You tell me who's ever made out alright with a strike up here—except maybe the cannery people—with us so far from everything."

"Yeah!"

From across the table, someone said, "Let those new union fellows bitch all they want. We've already got our union getting us the best it can."

"I'd expect you to say that, Jack," drawled the man named Russ. "You're a Seattle union man all the way."

"And talking sense."

"Yup. And talking sense. This time, at least." Others joined him with a laugh.

Jones had paid little attention to the talk of a new, rival union and their threat of a strike. All he wanted from Bristol Bay was a time like before the war. "Seems to me—" he began, but someone else spoke over him.

"Yeah, but forty cents a fish and no more? They ought to do better than that for us."

"If our own big union under part of the CIO in Seattle can't do better by us, what do you think some local start-up's going to get?"

"But they say the big AFL's behind this new one."

"AFLs now commie-run I hear. Need I say more?"

Somebody tapped Jones on the shoulder. "Slide down, buddy." It was Gus Rosvic. He wore a yellow cap with an embroidered red fish instead of an advertisement. Jones made room gladly. "You here? Didn't see you before this," Jones said, happy to make conversation that wasn't about some damn union. "If you ain't got your boat assigned yet, better get down there."

"Came north with our own boat, man. On the steamer. New engine boat." Everybody at the table turned his way. Gus looked around, saw their attention, and tipped his cap at a jaunty angle. "That's right. Brand new boat. Thirty-two footer. Ninety-five horsepower engine, drives through a two-to-one reduction. Hydraulic power roller. Don't have to yank your guts out to pull 'em aboard."

The sounds of chatter from other tables emphasized the silent attention at their own. Gus leaned back and drank some of his coffee. Nobody spoke, but no one turned away. He stretched and continued. "Yep. Picked her up right from the Seattle boatyard. That hydraulic roller, now, you can put her either astern or amidships, or even close to the bow if you figure on bow picking—all three positions. Little wheelhouse with a roof where you can sleep dry. Port and starboard, there're seventy-some gallon tanks for the gas—keep you going for days. Fish hold capacity: forty-five hundred sockeyes. Yep. Come off picking nets and go sleep dry in that cabin. Tell you, it beats sail and oars."

After a silence all around, Russ cleared his throat. "You're John Rosvic's boy, right? Your dad with you on this engine boat?"

"Just still squaring away at the bunkhouse."

"You came in your own boat, and the cannery's going to put you up?"

"Wave of the future, sir. Sure they are. Who's going to deliver to them after everybody gets their engine boats, if they don't put us up?"

"Huh." Buck Jones finally broke the silence that followed. "Well, Gus, that's nice," he said slowly. "But what bothers me just now is, I don't think much of some boats staying ashore while the rest of us go out. Should be that all of us in the boats stick together."

His comment snapped them back to the original subject. "That's their problem," said Russ brusquely. "Lot of those guys in that new union are Natives. Want to have their say. I can understand that, since they live here, but just the same they're dumb heads being told by outsiders what to do."

"Maybe I'm the dumb head," said another man. "But damn if I can keep all this strike and union shit straight."

"From the little I understand," Russ continued, "This new union's made of two parts that keeps fishermen and cannery workers separate. That right? Now in the old days—into the early '30s—it was the chinks from I guess China that come over every year to work the lines, and one white man just answered for them all. Had no trouble anywhere, according to my old man. Now, though, it's not only Natives with their own new union, but mostly gook Filipinos on the slime line, and I hear even *they* have their whole other union. And then some Natives in the boats with their union. Everybody thinks he's got a say."

Buck growled, "I don't say these locals shouldn't have a piece of things. But if we go tie up our boats on strike, the fish will pass through, and who will make out? You tell me now, who'll make out? Somebody with a Russian accent, ten to one."

"You're making this mess as clear as anybody, Russ," said another man. "Still confusing. It's the commies running these new unions. That's what they say. Even our old one, some say. Suits 'em fine if we all go broke. That way they can take over. So! Last thing I plan to do is follow what some seat-of-the-ass union tells me to do. When the season opens at six next Monday morning, nobody try to stop me putting my nets in the water!"

Buck Henry turned to his son. "Now, here, fellows. My boy Jones. Marine come from fighting the Japs. Couldn't anything better than that earn him his right for a say here. What do you think about all this new union stuff, boy?"

They gave him their attention. Jones took no time to consider beyond what had been his intention all along: "I came up here to catch fish. Next Monday, whoever else goes out and fishes, that's what I plan to be doing!"

"Now that says it!" declared Russ. "How do you say it any clearer than that!"

Buck Henry looked around proudly as he rose. "Anybody who cares to stay dry next week, that's his business. Guess me and my boy had better get back to work. Got a mast to step. Then some oars, for a marine strong enough to handle anything. See you out on the water!"

"Goes for me too," said Gus. "Got to work that new engine to make payments."

Several at the table remained seated, their eyes back on Gus. As Jones left with his dad, Russ was saying, "Now just how much did that new engine boat set you back, if you don't mind my asking."

The twenty-five-foot mast was indeed heavy, even though Buck and Jones first lifted several to find the lightest available. With two sets of shoulders they didn't need to wait for a dolly to wheel it. But when Jones started to raise the foot of the mast into its collar, his father called: "Hold it. You forget something?"

"You don't still do that?" laughed Jones.

Buck Henry rummaged in his hip pocket and pulled out a coin. "Not that it matters. But I polished this penny to a shine before we left home. Inspected it first to make sure Abe Lincoln's face wasn't scratched." He placed it carefully at the bottom of the cradle. "Face up, Mr. Abe. Watch out for us, now. Along with them three pennies from other seasons I see down there alongside."

Part of Jones wanted to scoff. But a larger part of him felt a rush of pleasure. Anything that hadn't changed was good. Anything that hadn't been fucked by the war. His father might have begun to grumble that, but for the canneries holding on to an outdated law, they'd have a boat with an engine and a small cabin. But what about fishing under sail wasn't like play after fighting the Japs?

The work of stepping the mast firmly into place took an unexpected length of time. Indeed, the boat had been worn to death in some ways. Jones needed to cut wedges in the carpenter shop, then fit them between the mast and the sleeve before the mast rode firm in its cradle without so much as a wobble. Then to the oars. At the distribution loft, Jones accepted what the man handed him. The sixteen-foot oars all looked heavy, so there was no point in being choosy. He was man enough to pull anything. But to play the old game, he wrapped hands around one of the thick shafts and nodded toward his dad. "Now you try yourself to make sure it fits."

"Long as it fits your hands I'm okay with it, boy." Buck patted the shaft. "Fits yours right good, I'd say."

"You ain't so dumb," said the oarsman to Buck Henry. "Brought you a strong boat puller along." He had shaggy white hair and knotted hands. Probably an old timer. "Don't I remember you from nine, ten years ago when I still fished? I never forget a face. This here the kid you used to bring with you?"

"No better kid anywhere. Been a marine sergeant! Fought his way against the Japs all across the Pacific. Put the damn bastards in their place."

"Good man!"

"Listen. Give you an example—"

"Lay off, Dad," muttered Jones. His tone showed he meant it. The heavy oars rested lightly on his shoulder as he arched his back and strode off.

16

BECOMING AMERICAN

K iyoshi and Mr. Goss followed Mr. Scorden. The workmen they passed along the way moved with purpose and did not stop to bow when the director walked by as they would have done in Japan. The man who had stared at them with an unmistakable scowl lingered in Kiyoshi's mind and made him uneasy. He had been a man of about Kiyoshi's own age, tanned and vigorous—as American workmen so often were. A face vaguely familiar. But so many American faces looked the same. In Tokyo, he had grown humbly accustomed to hostile stares from some of the conquerors. They might indeed have suffered by the hands of the Japanese soldiers—only fulfilling what they thought was their duty—before the defeat. Whatever the circumstance, the man's gaze had been so steady that it was only polite to acknowledge it with a small polite bow, although he felt uncomfortable—un-American—doing so. The gesture had not been returned.

Mr. Scorden led them to an open vehicle with a seat wide enough for three. He seated himself behind the steering wheel and gestured to Kiyoshi. "We shall go to the office. Hop in, as they say. If you wish." And to Mr. Goss, abruptly: "Follow in the car, sir. Tell the driver to follow."

Mr. Goss hesitated. "Probably room in your golf cart there for the three of us so we don't get separated."

"No, no, too crowded, sir. Please take the automobile."

Kiyoshi had hoped that they would enter one of the processing buildings so that he could observe the machinery, but instead Mr. Scorden drove straight up a sloping causeway toward his office. Midway up the hill, however, he stopped the vehicle and asked curtly: "How many fish buyers in Japan do you represent, sir? For how much money?"

"Five purchasing companies, sir. I am authorized to speak for purchases that can be paid in money up to forty thousand American dollars."

"You will pardon my asking. Americans in Japan have been good for you, I think? They did not so much destroy, I understand, when Japan lost the war and they occupied your country?"

Kiyoshi frowned, not sure that he understood Mr. Scorden's meaning, and wary of where this might lead. "Hai. Americans. They were . . . okay."

"You see, I came from a country where the Germans destroyed much. Much has been rebuilt, but very slowly. Even with the great energy of everyone. Even with generous help from America." Mr. Scorden's eyes narrowed. "So. What do the Japanese think of America?"

Still on guard, Kiyoshi decided to be honest with his own feelings rather than to echo those of so many Japanese—like his father. "It was good luck, sir. Good luck for Japan that America defeated us."

The answer appeared to satisfy Mr. Scorden. He re-engaged his vehicle and drove the rest of the way to a building with a porch. Inside, they passed beyond the counter of a small store that displayed candy and clothing (*what kind of an office was this?* Kiyoshi wondered with sudden doubt) into a back room with a proper desk and filing cabinets.

"Grab a chair," Mr. Scorden said and brought one over. Mr. Goss, when he trailed in from the car, was left to find a chair for himself. The office was not elaborate, Kiyoshi noted, but still properly businesslike, with papers arranged neatly on the desk.

"Not much around here," said Mr. Goss conversationally. "What do you do for kicks?"

"Work a little bit harder, sir."

Mr. Goss laughed. "Nice answer. Might have guessed."

Mr. Scorden turned to Kiyoshi. "You wish to stay until you can inspect the fish, is that it?"

"Yes. To . . ." Kiyoshi searched for the English word that he had learned for this circumstance. Ah. "To ascertain, yes, to ascertain if the red salmon product has been prepared with Japanese quality standard."

"What's your requirement of quality, I wish to ask?"

"Good color, sir. Bright red color for red salmon product. And freshness. Having good smell, you understand? Freshness to the nose. And good appearance. Must be without cuts into the . . . uh . . . flesh."

"Well. To see this, you must remain here more than one night. A few days at least."

When Mr. Goss complained that he wasn't authorized to stay several days, it seemed to Kiyoshi that Mr. Scorden was as glad as he was himself to assure the official that he could leave next day without a problem.

Later, Mr. Scorden took them to a room in a long wooden building. It was furnished with two cots and a nightstand on bare floorboards. "For guests," he declared. "Other rooms have four or six bunks, you see. Shower baths with heated water are down the hall if you wish."

"Think I'll wait to wash myself till I get back to civilization," Mr. Goss replied.

Mr. Scorden shrugged. "Toilets there also, of course, sir. Down the same hall. If you cannot wait until civilization." The cannery manager then escorted them to what he called the mess hall. Kiyoshi found it a noisy but cheerful place, where food of uncanny variety was offered for their choice. Not all food was prepared for the finest depths of flavors, perhaps. But such abundance! And such easy waste of food ordered but not finished! Kiyoshi watched vegetables and even large pieces of meat slide off plates and into garbage cans. Happy people, to do this without a care.

That night, in the cannery's bare guest room, Mr. Goss grunted complaints about the accommodation. Kiyoshi listened restlessly. He finally excused himself with, "I must go to find the toilet, sir."

In the lavatory down the hall, he had stared into an adjacent room where pipes in the wall spouted down steaming water—a true shower compared to the ones from a half decade before in the American prison camp, where cold but clean water dribbled down from a cistern. For all the years of peace, he had bathed in tubs or communal pools of comforting hot water, never forgetting the terrible years of war and privation when often the only means of cleaning oneself—even in desperation—was with a rag dipped in a barrel of scummy water shared between dozens of men. So. American bathing!

Back in the room, he again excused himself from the grumbling Mr. Goss and walked back down the chilly corridor carrying a clean towel and the bar of soap left on the nightstand. In the steamy room he undressed and nodded shyly to other naked men already standing under the sprays of water. These men did not necessarily seem to be officials—were perhaps mere workers—but they all talked amongst themselves with a rough good humor impossible not to enjoy. By now, Kiyoshi had concluded that few Americans cared about the exciting art of Jackson Pollock or any other of the great modern artists. But American boxing and baseball were, possibly, another matter. From his concentrated reading back in Japan, he found the courage to venture, "It is now only three weeks away. In the city of Pittsburgh in state of Pennsylvania. Who shall win the boxing fight, please tell me? Mr. Jersey Joe Walcott? Or Mr. Ezzard Charles?"

"Hey," one of the men said. "Listen to this." In the friendliest manner they began a discussion of the two fighters, with laughing questions put to Kiyoshi about his own choice.

"I wish only advice, please," he said, still bashful under their attention.

"Go on, man, let's hear it. Choose!"

Kiyoshi looked from one to another. Their expressions were not hostile. Emboldened, he declared, "Mr. Ezzard champion!"

"Hey guys, hear this. You got five bucks in your pants says?"

Kiyoshi backed away. Had he been mistaken, and was now left in their power, naked and vulnerable? Or were they actually inviting him to gamble with them?

"I do not understand, sir," he said to gain time.

"Back in your pants—wherever they are—, man, your wallet. You got five dollars to bet on Ezzard Charles?"

They were inviting him! Like an equal American! Happily, he replied "Hai, hai. Yes! Back in pants, excuse me, I will go and . . . produce!"

"Relax, take your word, take your word. None of us going any place but here. Hey, what else do you people know? Ever heard of the World Series?"

"Hai. Baseball! Yankee team from New York City!"

"This man's buzzin'! So, couple months from now, who's going to win the World Series?"

Ever since his encounter with American World Series baseball outside the Tokyo train station, Kiyoshi had studied to keep up to date with the major teams each year. The effort was not difficult, since many Japanese had become enthusiastic about this fascinating game. It was also easy for him to choose his favorite team, since New York was the city he most wanted to visit and the New York Yankees had won every World Series but one since 1947. With happy confidence he declared, "Yankee team shall win again. Yogi Berra! Famous Joe DiMaggio! 'Scooter' Phil Rizzuto!"

Their laughing cheers were beyond his wildest fantasy. Yes. Even in this remote wilderness of America, surrounded by dangerous animals perhaps just near the buildings, there was American conviviality and abundance beyond the dreams of the Japanese.

Back in the room, Mr. Goss muttered, "Well, now you see how they stay clean in the boondocks. I'm sure you people have worse back in Japan, but don't take this as typical over here. I'll be glad to get back to a proper hotel."

"Yes. Yes," Kiyoshi said to be polite, hoping to avoid conversation.

When lying in bed, Kiyoshi contemplated the future of his life. Japan was his home. And his culture. However. He resolved to participate in America in every way possible. Perhaps Mr. Scorden was also so resolved. It was why they regarded each other with narrowed eyes, but, he realized, with an understanding beyond the comprehension of Mr. Goss. For Mr. Goss had never been called upon to change himself.

Three days later, now on his own in the room, someone rapped on the door at four in the morning. Kiyoshi Tsurifune was awake and dressed, although for form's sake and to hide his eagerness he pulled the covers around his neck like a child and pretended to be asleep. A worker entered and shook him. "Swede says to tell you the scow's nearly ready to take off to the grounds. Got a half hour to get down there. Guess they'll feed you breakfast aboard."

"Ah. Yes. Thank you."

Alone again in the simply furnished room in which he'd grown quite comfortable ever since Mr. Goss had left it, Kiyoshi rose and stretched. Rays of morning sunlight gleamed orange on the metal rooftops outside the

window. All he needed to do was put on and lace up the heavy leather shoes
Mr. Scorden had provided him. That soapy odor of stiff new denim clothing remained the same as aboard the American warship six years ago. Only
six years. Who might have believed at the time that the disaster wouldn't
last forever? No question any more of finding food for the next meal. How
defeated and humbled he'd felt! So close to killing himself. Imagine. Now
with American dollars possessed in abundance he'd gambled with Americans
on the outcome of a mere boxing match!

He put on the heavy jacket he had been given. They'd even given him
rough warm clothing to wear, issued new from the store without charge
at Mr. Scorden's direction. (The denim pants he needed were two or three
sizes larger at the waist than the ones now limp with washing that he'd
preserved back home! Thus here was the real proof of prosperity.) His dark
suit and silk necktie, which now appeared incongruous, hung in the safety
of Mr. Scorden's office. So also discarded, and placed beneath the suit, were
the polished shoes with thin soles. No one would bother them, he'd been
assured, since they were of no use to anyone here. All his papers, of course,
had been locked in the office safe.

Three days had passed since he'd arrived in Naknek. After the officious
Mr. Goss left, Mr. Scorden had seated him again at the office and said,
"Now, sir. Whatever you expected, it will be several days before you can see
fish being processed. I've spoken to my manager in Ketchikan who has spoken to the owners in Seattle, and it's agreed that you are here as our guest.
Clearly the Japanese market has become of interest to my company. But you
see that I'm busy and it's not convenient that I entertain you. I'll write down
the meal times. You are free to see what you wish, but don't interfere with
the work or the machinery. Understood?"

And then they had left him alone, free to observe as he chose. After he'd
tired of watching workers prepare the machinery (bowing to one mechanic,
who in the shower room had accepted his American five dollar bill to hold
against the outcome of the boxing fight) he wandered back to the waterside.
But now all of the fishing boats had been launched and the dock was empty.
Without work of his own, Kiyoshi began to feel restless.

One day Swede-san, as Kiyoshi now called him routinely, arranged for
him to ride with a company truck into the village. He walked among the few
wooden buildings—at first with the purpose of discovery and then because
there was nothing else to do until the driver had finished his business. In

the buildings that were stores he inspected the goods on all the shelves while glancing at the customers. Some appeared to be actual Eskimos, to judge by their dark skin and Asian eyes—the first he'd seen outside photographs. If people stared at him he nodded back, controlling his impulse to bow. Then, in a bar that smelled of stale beer, it was so dark that nobody paid him any attention and he could watch how ordinary Americans behaved. He even eavesdropped on their conversations. One particularly strange exchange caught his attention, although its meaning escaped him. One man had said, "What about your brothers up in Dillingham, buddy? We're together with this new union. If you guys down here joined us and stayed dry next week, you think the canneries wouldn't give in? Pay what those fish we catch out there are worth?"

And the man listening had replied, "I don't know. I don't know." They drank in silence and gave Kiyoshi no further clues as to their meaning.

After two hours of wandering, however, he knew every muddy path off the single paved road. All most interesting, although not the vital America of tall buildings and well-dressed people and bold abstract paintings that he so yearned to see. He was ready to go when they at last returned through the wilderness to the processing compound.

Thus, at dinner when Swede-san suggested that he might like to travel out on the water aboard a collection vessel, Kiyoshi was only too happy to agree. And so this early morning, still sleepy, he hurried from the bunkhouse along the boardwalks that had been built over tundra to the paved ramp and down to the water. He passed no one until he reached the docks. There, people strode purposefully and he needed to step aside for vehicles.

The only vessel at the pier was more like a huge box than a ship, ugly at best, at worst unseaworthy. Its rails and housing revealed old wood painted in some places and scuffed bare in others. The deck lay far below the top of the pier, to be reached only by a slimy metal ladder. This surely could not be the boat he was to stay aboard for two days! He stopped one of the workers who appeared to have some authority. He pulled himself together and spoke carefully: "Please, I am wishing to find collection vessel *Evelyn K.*"

"You're looking at her."

"It's okay," a man called up from a scuffed cabin above the deck. "He's expected. Not going to blow us up, far as I can tell. Just see he gets his hands on the ladder, then toss over his bag there."

Kiyoshi decided this was, after all, part of the adventure. Holding himself erect so as not to appear vulnerable, he gripped the slippery metal rungs and began to descend carefully without looking down. Below the pier boards, the pilings were a mossy green peppered with white barnacles. All of it smelled of sea rot. Thank Swede-san for his heavy shoes with soles of rubber tread. The busy manager had looked out for him after all.

Suddenly his foot stepped down into air. He steadied himself back on the final rung. Below him lay a gap of several feet to the vessel's rail. Kiyoshi felt his eyes widen as he hesitated, one leg waving free.

"Jump over, we'll catch you," said a gruff voice. Kiyoshi looked down at a face framed by black hair and black beard, a true American savage. The man stood on the rail with a hand reaching out close to Kiyoshi's leg. *American version of the Kiyomizu-dera gorge*! he thought with sudden fear. But feeling all eyes watching, with a bold "Hai!" he loosed his hold on the ladder.

Hands caught him firmly and helped him over the rail onto the deck. "Well good for you," the man laughed. "Thought for a minute we was going to need a cargo net!"

"Hai. Thank you!" Kiyoshi panted.

"No problem. Skipper's up that short ladder in the wheelhouse. Can you make it?"

"Hai, hai, thank you!" He straightened himself to stride across the deck and gripped the second ladder firmly, although with trembling hands.

"Japs not so tough I guess when they don't have a gun in your face," said a voice behind him.

"War's over, leave it alone," said the gruff man who had caught him. "Didn't he let go and drop down when I told him?"

"Sounds like you never saw Pacific duty."

"Whatever, man."

At the top of the second ladder Kiyoshi placed his feet on the deck with assurance and faced a robust man of about fifty who was sweeping with a broom. He bowed slightly. "You will please direct me to captain, sir."

"You're looking at him. They said you'd be down. What's your name?"

Kiyoshi withdrew the business card he'd placed in his shirt pocket. Before he realized, slime that covered his fingers from the ladder smudged it. He held the card, suddenly uncertain what to do.

"Give it here, then." The captain took it with hands shockingly black-ened by dirt or perhaps grease. "Mister what? Tee-surafuny?" Kiyoshi pro-nounced it correctly for him. "Right. Going to ride along for a couple of days, eh? Understand you're not to get in the way. I'll show you a corner in the wheelhouse where you can stand."

Aboard either of his company's vessels, the captain or any crewman would have stumbled over themselves to provide him with at least a com-fortable chair. And no captain would be discovered with hands so stained from common labor. So. America.

From the window alongside his post, wedged between the chart table and the bulkhead, he looked straight out at the barnacle-encrusted pilings. Only by pressing close against the window could he see down to the vessel's rail and part of a deck where the men prepared for sea.

Despite the warning that the vessel would leave soon, no one seemed in a hurry. He watched whatever activity occurred in the wheelhouse, although this was sporadic at best, since even the captain appeared to be occupied elsewhere. Well. He watched the vessel slowly rise against the pilings. Pilings in Japan were no different than these, but such tides! Like everything else in America, tides were bigger. He began to grow hungry. Best forget this, and remain obediently where he'd been told to stay.

More than two hours passed. Finally, "Oh shit, you had breakfast?" the captain demanded, facing him for the first time since he'd come aboard. "Forgot about you. Follow me." He was led down enclosed stairs to a cramped room with a single, long table where the air smelled unpleasantly of cooking grease and soap. One crewman sat drinking from a mug. The captain gestured for Kiyoshi to sit on the bench at the other end of the table and snapped, "See this man here gets something to eat. He's going to ride with us." And the captain was gone.

The crewman—it was the one who had made the hostile remark when he'd come aboard—regarded Kiyoshi for a time. At length he went into a small galley, returned with two pieces of soft white bread and an open jar of brown stuff labeled "peanut butter," and slapped them down. "Speak any English?" He took a dinner knife from a drawer and pushed it over. "Guess you people know how to use one of these—though it ain't as sharp as you're used to. Coffee's over in that pot. Cream in that can beside it. If that's what you people drink."

Kiyoshi fought to control his rising anger. "Thank you." But he left the food untouched, despite the feeling of hunger gnawing at his stomach. *My ancestors*, it roiled in his mind, *were samurai, while yours were at best common laborers. A few years ago, with an arrogant American like you as my prisoner . . .*

"Thank you," he repeated in order to keep his perspective on the present. "I am not hungry."

"Yeah. Right." The two men eyed each other, neither willing to look away.

"Well, hey, there's my man!" exclaimed a gruff voice at the doorway. It was the black-bearded crewman who had told this man to "leave it alone." Kiyoshi leapt to his feet, relieved, bumping his shins against the bench.

"Sit, man." The newcomer turned to his crewmate. "Seen to feeding our guy?"

"If you want to call it that, Vic. But I guess he's particular about not getting fish heads and rice."

"Ease off, Spike." Vic poured two mugs of coffee, came over, and pushed one toward Kiyoshi. "Riding with us, eh?"

"Hai! Yes. Coming on this vessel for . . . observation of the fishing." He gripped the handle of the mug, put its hot rim to his lips, and drank, even though the liquid burned.

"Then we'd best find you a bunk to throw your gear," Vic continued. "Going to be a busy day once we get started. You don't like peanut butter?" In answer Kiyoshi knifed a glob of the brown paste from the jar, spread it across the bread, and took a bite. He had never eaten it before. The man named Spike shrugged and left.

"From Japan, eh?" Jimmy continued. Kiyoshi nodded. The peanut butter stuck in his mouth, but he managed to say: "Yes. Japan. Coming to America first time."

"Pretty different here, eh?"

"Americans are . . . different. Hai."

17

FISH PICKERS

At high slack on Monday in 3:00 a.m. twilight, the high-powered company crafts they called "monkey boats" prepared to tow the fishing vessels in strings to the grounds. Buck Henry had checked the destination of each available tow and decided which flats of the Bay he'd work. Men in the twelve fishing boats of the tow secured their lines: bow to the stern of the double-ender ahead of them, a wrap around their mast to absorb the strain, then stern to the next bow tugging behind. With a throb of its diesel engine the monkey boat started its procession from the pier. Rope by rope the fishing boats' towlines tautened while their hemp fibers stretched and squeaked under the pull.

Their thirty-foot double-ender was third in line, close enough to the monkey's belch to blow exhaust into their faces and leave them coughing. "Next week we'll make sure to tie further down the damn row," grumbled Buck Henry.

"You got it," muttered Jones. "If we can." But he wasn't unhappy. It was all part of the action he remembered from times past when there was no war and the only blood to be spilled came from the fish. As for the boats that might stay dry as part of that new runaway union's strike . . . well, that was their business.

Their row of boats moved up the Naknek River toward the bay. Other tows pushed out from the piers of other cannery settlements along the way. Shouts rang from man to man across the water in English, Norwegian, Italian, or who-knows-what. Men aboard the boats guarding their towline or stowing for the work ahead looked up to laugh and joke back.

The monkey boat's deckhand stood by its stern and drank from a mug of coffee as he idly watched the fishermen. *Dumbass*, thought Jones without heat. *To merely pull the rest of us around and then to hustle piles of dead fish— never live ones.*

"You'll mebbe stay dry," he muttered. "But you won't be in the real part of it."

"Say what, boy?"

"Nothing, Dad."

Before they had traversed the length of the river and passed the right-hand shore where low, weathered roofs and the little Russian church of Naknek rose above the scrub, the tide had begun to ebb. It pulled them out. When they entered the open Bay, the towboat headed north into the flow. Swells passed from boat to boat, creaking their sternpost and slapping bursts of spray into their faces.

Jones licked the salty water from his lips. He'd forgotten, trolling alone, that fishing in company had its good points. Not like soldiers stuffed butt-to-butt and no relief. Adele, at home, was a fine girl, and he'd done right to marry her. But not much company anymore when closures or bad weather kept him at home. She wasn't near as lively as when they'd courted just five years ago. Let the baby's death get further behind them and then see. He himself wasn't so good at making people laugh if they weren't already prepared to have a good time. Seen too much killing maybe. In truth, even as a kid, he'd enjoyed having tricks played on him and would return them with satisfaction, even glee, but he was never much of an outright laugher himself. Adele would have to restore the laughs. When she was ready again. Whenever she'd stop crying the minute she stopped the constant, almost hysterical, chatter. No wonder the company of men suited him best.

He watched his dad. Also serious, not much of a laugher either, unless Mom started it and pulled him along. Bones wide and tough. Hands big enough to grip anything. More squint lines around his eyes than a few years before, but nothing had changed the clear cool stare of those eyes.

Nothing changed there. Hair full and curling from want of a trim—since it looked like mother hadn't corralled him to sit for her scissors recently—but graying. Didn't like that. Call him "the old man" for fun, but not to his face.

Oh shit. Don't let things change.

As if in reply, straight in his face, an engine boat their own size eased alongside the tow, and Gus Rosvic himself shouted over, "Hey man!" Gus's dad stood grinning at them from the little enclosed wheelhouse while Gus hefted a gillnet on deck and grinned even worse. "Need an extra push, man?" From inside, John Rosvic senior pushed a throttle. With a sputter, white smoke puffed from their exhaust pipe astern. The engine boat gunned ahead, then drifted back alongside.

"Just let that put-put of yours foul and you'll be on the sands," called Jones in equal good cheer. If only Gus had come along when they were free of the tow and in control under sail! "Let that ol' engine stink up your day? Of course, only an expert can do it under canvas."

"Dinosaur, man. Don't you know that's what a sailboat is here, now the law's changed? Don't have to fish Bristol Bay under sail no more. Finally. Vets like me bucked the cannery bosses. Put enough screws on the bureaucrats in Washington to change the fuckin' law. Where were you?"

"Sail suits me fine. No need to change what a man's good enough to do by himself."

"Yeah? And what about this new union? Time we stopped jerkin' off the cannery bosses in Seattle. You fought the war. Now you're going back to taking their shit?"

John called sharply that they needed to go. Gus shrugged. "Later, man. See you around!" And with engine in gear the Rosvics' boat roared away.

"Son of a bitch," muttered Buck Henry. "Law's been changed, and here we are still being towed and jerked around."

"Wait till we've squared our fish aboard, and there's the Rosvics with nets still in the water while they worry over oil pan slop or some leaky carburetor."

"Wonder how much that new boat of Rosvic's cost him?"

"Two years of fishing, likely. We settle free at end of season." Jones considered, then added, "Okay. Gus told me. Seven thousand five hundred."

"I figured she didn't come cheap. Even got a little cabin aft there to keep off the rain while you sleep warm." Jones found no answer for that one. At least they had no discussions or disagreements about a new union or about commies taking over. But now that the authorities had finally caved to allow engines after all the years of making sail compulsory, everything would change. He'd need to change with it or get out. Strange that he should be the one resisting rather than the old man.

The monkey boat towed them to the traditional Salmon Flats in north Kvichak Bay, in sight of Copenhagen Creek off the west bank. One by one the boats freed themselves from the towline. Some put out oars to maneuver for position, while the men on others broke out their sail at once.

"Your call," said Jones to his father. Buck Henry immediately turned alert, his yearning for motor power forgotten.

"Mud flats of Halfmoon Bay are too close from here. We should set further east." He raised a bushy eyebrow. "Ha, boy. What else we got them paddles for?"

"You got it." In good humor Jones unlashed two of the oars provided them, fitted their thick shafts into the oarlocks, and bent their blades into the water. He stood with legs braced and pushed with arms and back, feeling the water's resistance. Good clean feel. His muscles locked into place stroke by stroke. The heavy wooden bow cut through the rips of an increasing ebb, driven alone by Jones Henry, man and fisherman on top of it all.

A few hours later, fish had entered the Kvichak system on the flood and Buck and Jones Henry were in the thick of it. Six-pound sockeyes stormed their gillnet. A sparse run had been predicted for 1951, but the water around them sometimes boiled with fish so packed that the glistening bodies broke the surface. So much for know-nothing biologists at their desks. For good or bad, before they'd finished picking fish from one shackle of net filled on the flood and brought aboard, the other shackle left to soak had filled again. No rest possible here.

Regulations allowed each boat only nine hundred feet of gillnet—or one hundred fifty fathoms, in the biologist fancy-talk that Jones scorned. Stretching astern with corks holding it to the surface every twenty-five fathoms, as required by law, it didn't seem to Jones like that much net—except when it snagged with that of another boat. He hadn't remembered! Now, fish snouts clogged into the five and one-half inch spread of the gillnet meshes. He judged it likely that at any given moment he and his dad were pulling a hundred and fifty-some pounds of flapping sockeyes up from the sea and lumping them over the roller. Just as good the fish-diddlers hadn't regulated a longer net.

"Bet those engine boats have a power takeoff that helps turn their roller," panted Buck Henry.

"Who needs it?" muttered Jones. He tried to shake sweat from his eyes without removing his grip on the web. If they stopped pulling it would require an extra yank to start again. A little engine boost wouldn't hurt, he had to admit to himself. Jones surreptitiously glanced at his dad, who was kneading his right shoulder between pulls. Not what he liked to see in a man heretofore capable of any work. The man who had pulled dory oars in the days of cod in the Bering Sea, who only a few years back he'd watch lift a hundred-pound sack or piece of gear on his shoulder and carry it across a gangway.

The fat salmon squeezed in steady clusters over the roller. Each knot of the slippery silver bodies required an extra tug with arms and back while maintaining a rhythm. Heavy! The cork floats had already begun to absorb seawater, giving the nets even more added weight. *But okay, I'm fit for this,* Jones told himself, even when his breath ran short. *This is my time, my place.* He pulled harder, beyond an enjoyable stretch of muscles, to make it easier for the old man.

Jones soon came to remember the old landmarks of the Kvichak River, even though much of his earlier fishing had centered to the north in the Nushagak. The Deadman Sands lay south of Halfmoon Bay along the west bank, invisible until the tide fell, to appear first in warning ripples and finally in fingers of muddy ground. Keep them far to the west and row like hell if an easterly started to edge you toward them.

By mid week they had fished from flats off Copenhagen Creek on the west to Pederson Point on the east. To harvest the salmon that they'd grunted aboard, they settled cross-legged on opposite sides of the net that lay heaped on deck. They'd isolated each shackle or segment of net as best as possible.

"In case you don't remember, Marine," Buck explained. "This way, if we're into fish, we just untie emptied shackles and set them back astern to start catching again."

"Haven't forgotten," returned Jones comfortably.

Removing fish clotted in gillnets was a different kind of skill than to just shake them loose from a trolling hook. Jones had done it before the war, up here with the old man, but he had to admit to himself that that kind of patience and concentration took some relearning. His pick tool soon became even more bloody and slime-handled than Buck's. It was easy enough to free a fish snagged just by the gills. All this took was a snap of the wrist. However, strands of web wrapped most of them tight, since they tended to start thrashing after finding themselves trapped. Some were so enmeshed in the net that their freed bodies bore blackening crisscross marks. Worst were those with tangles around their heads. Sometimes Jones had to cut a strand or two of the cotton web to free both snout and sharp-edged, flapping gills, but such cuts enlarged the mesh opening and formed an escape hole that could be used during future sets. Better in these cases to bloody the fish head, so long as the meat of the body stayed unharmed.

Many of the fish still gasped as he worked to free them. All part of being a fish, Jones knew, but he'd still smack them dead with his gaff when convenient. Within the tangle, Buck Henry grabbed and freed a salmon almost double the size of any other. He picked off the net around its head with care, so that it was not bloodied. The fish still flapped sluggishly.

"Oh, but you're a beaut!" he exclaimed and threw it back into the water. The creature stayed inert for moments, then swam from sight.

"Thought we were catching them," Jones growled.

"You ain't so smart after all. Pay by the pound, you'll see how fast that big fish goes into the hold. But pay by the fish like the canneries do, he takes up too much space. Got to change the rules. That's one of the things that union they're trying to organize is demanding—why people call 'em commies. Another's to let a fisherman sell to canneries other than the one he's signed to."

"You don't know how commies infiltrate everywhere, Dad. There's talk of drafting me back to Korea because of them. Shouldn't meddle with stuff that's worked all along."

"You're young, but sometimes you sure talk old. Not like some other vets your age."

Jones shrugged, annoyed and unsure why. They tossed the freed fish forward toward the hatch, then at intervals stopped to store them below. Now and then with a shrug, they'd throw other big ones back, if only to spite the cannery. As Jones gained his stride, he and the old man competed to stack the highest pile of fish, although neither called it such. By the end of each set they took turns sloshing each other with buckets of seawater. Fish blood and slime plopped from their oilskins in globs, and they happily insulted each other about who had left the biggest mess.

After fishing for eighteen hours straight, with the rain turned steady, Buck Henry declared, "Maybe take a little break for sack time. Okay, boy?"

By now, Jones was working on automatic, but offered: "If it suits you." He removed the rubber gloves that had grown soggy with fish blood and slime, dried his hands on the flannel shirt under layers of wool and oilskin, and reached into the canopy space that was their only shelter. Groping about, he found the dollar clock they'd wound in a piece of rubber to keep off the salt water. The radium dials showed through the darkness that the time was just past midnight. Start of the third day. Jones made a pencil notation in the little notebook they had also wrapped up against the weather. They were about halfway through this opening before a tow back to the cannery and a dry bunk for at least a night. Hardly seemed worth stopping.

They eased stiffly, headfirst like parallel logs, under the canvas covering the bow. Then they pulled an old bearskin Buck had brought as high over their chins as they could while still covering the open tops of their boots, sticking into the weather. The long johns pressing against his skin warmed and began to dry. The boat rocked comfortably. *Well*, Jones decided, *a little rest won't hurt*.

"You know what, boy?"

"What, Dad?"

"I figured it out. It's not but fifteen thousand fish we'd have to catch to make up seven thousand five hundred dollars."

"No way. You added wrong." Jones tried to calculate in his head. "That's if we got fifty cents a fish, not forty. I think."

"Oh. Well, still."

"And then, if you spend it all on a boat, what'll you live on? What's left to buy the gas, much less chow and things?"

After a long pause, just as Jones started to drift off. "Boy? Don't the government give discharged Marines what they call a GI loan? So you don't have to pay everything at once?"

"Go to sleep, Dad."

Jones woke after a short period to knots throbbing in his arms. He massaged them surreptitiously, as Dad had his shoulder during haul-ins over the roller, but since they were now lying hip to hip it was hard not to draw attention. Rain pattered on the canvas tented above them. Only one drip fell, from some little hole they hadn't yet found and patched. Jones wore enough heavy clothing, sweated outward from long johns and screened inward by a wool shirt, that rain made no difference except on his face—which, naturally, is where the drip landed. Straight to the nose or the cheek depending on the way he shifted his head. He tried to alter position while still kneading his arm.

"Stay on your own side," growled Buck Henry without heat. "What's wrong? Tendons from rowing got you?"

"Nothing to speak of."

"Guess I might have just let the wind take us with the others toward the Copenhagen, instead of making you row us the other direction."

"No complaints. But now, just give me two more inches over your way to duck this water, and stop bitching. Alarm set?"

"For three hours like I said."

"Then shut up and good night, Dad."

He woke only once more to the pain in his arms. Under the canvas, the smells of fish and wet wool, and whatever else had accumulated were as thick as taffy. He attempted another massage, holding each arm straight up to allay the pain, and then slept.

When the alarm jangled, he was glad to let Buck uncover first and start the primus under coffee water, before stretching out full and kneading his arms again. During their brief night, the drip had accumulated into a puddle beside his neck, where it did no harm.

"Good sleep, boy?"

"Finest."

"Then shake it out of there and go check the net."

The rain had stopped and the sun rising low on the horizon now shone straight through the dark overcast into his eyes. On impulse Jones removed his hip boots and socks and padded forward on bare feet. Dry socks waited in the little waterproof bag he'd been smart enough to pack. He wriggled his toes in the chilly puddles on the way, but balanced carefully in case they had missed some patch of slime during sloshdown. The net stretched behind in a line of corks. It was calm. Other boats bobbed nearby. Most also had their nets out, all aligned with the current. Jones took a leak over the side and breathed the fresh air. The ache in his arms had subsided. Sun beams caught sparkles and shadows all along the water. No sounds except low voices from other men also rising and the lap of water against their hull. Somebody's tin pot gave a clang. But no engines. No rifle cracks or bombs. Nothing that threatened the peace.

Back under the canvas he picked out his waterproof bag. Bilge water had seeped into the opening, and his spare socks were sopping wet. So what. He wrung them out and put them on. They were on to the fish. What else had they come for?

He didn't want change! Let there be at least something that stayed the same—even if it was hard to do and sometimes hurt.

By Thursday morning around eight, with only a few more hours of sleep in between, they had picked the final net they'd left to soak. Not as many fish as the day before. Morning light filled the sky after a steady rain. Buck Henry looked down into the hold. Despite the taper in the quantity, there was still a satisfying mass of thick-bellied sockeyes. The silver of their scales had dulled, and dried blood clotted the black-rimmed mouths of some, but: "There's a pretty sight, boy. Could stand looking all day."

"I don't disagree."

"Hold's about full. Some seasons she'd have been full a whole day earlier. Anyhow, time to make market." Work had taken them a few miles from the tally scow. But, with some five hundred six-pound fish in the hold as ballast and their sail filled by a four to five knot easterly, they pushed a straight and steady line through the water. Behind them swirled a dovetail of water that proved it. Their net now lay heaped astern, powdered with salt to keep it from rotting. Jones peeled off his oilskin coat and the sweated woolens beneath, then his boots and socks. He stretched bare-chested, balancing atop the spongy net, and savored the easing of the muscles in his legs and arms. Other full sails could be spotted on the horizon—some within shouting distance. The air smelled fresh and good.

"Watch yourself, boy," called his dad at the tiller. "Stand clear. Don't cut my wind there."

"Plenty of wind for both of us." In answer, Buck touched the tiller just enough to alter its direction a few degrees. He laughed when the sprit bumped Jones's leg. "Hop when I tell you! Can't you see I'm racing Nick Sandstol's boat off our starboard?"

"No. Didn't."

"That what the Marines taught you? To lollygag and smell the flowers?"

"Taught me to grab any little good thing when it comes!"

"We gonna let Nick grab a place ahead of us delivering, just because you help yourself to feeling good?"

"So what?"

"So that's the hell kind of kid I raised?" With equal vigor Buck called to the boat now obviously racing them: "Loser foots a jug of best bootleg at the cannery this Saturday!"

"Pity to see you waste that kind of money, Buck. But that's how she's going to be!" Buck Henry tightened sail. So did Nick. Their two boats chopped across the water neck and neck.

The tally scow squatted in the water ahead of them. Its hundred-some-foot length and square wooden housing made it seem more a creature of the shore, a bump of land alongside the agile sail crafts that maneuvered around it to dock and make delivery. Three boats already bobbed against the scow's rail, while another approached under oars.

"Current's pulling four–five knots I judge," muttered Buck Henry at the tiller. His right hand controlled the line of a choker on the boom. "Judge the breeze blowing against us to be about the same." On the Sandstol boat, Luke the boat puller was setting up his oars while skipper Nick began to lower sail. Jones kicked one of the sixteen-foot oars lashed along their own rail. "Reckon you'll need me at these buggers to get us in. Figure that's what I'm along for, so I might as well—"

"Leave 'em be, boy. Quick, ready a line you'll heave to starboard. When I slack the rings, you go ease the sail down halfway—no more. Then stand by and just do what I tell you. When I say it!"

"Yo, Captain!" Jones felt himself grinning in his hustle, remembering old times. He secured a line to one of their cleats and looped it for either heaving or letting out, then took his place by the sail. At Buck's yell, Jones lowered the triangular canvas to half its span as the big wooden rings clattered in his hands.

At a point just ahead of the scow—the wind and tide shooting them forward, so that they would pass the larger vessel within seconds—Buck turned the tiller hard to port and barked, "Drop sail all the way!"

With the strength of his whole body, Jones bunched the remaining canvas and rings straight down. Under Buck's coolheaded control, their boat made a 180-degree turn that lodged them exactly to the portside rail of the scow. Just barely bumped the last boat tied to deliver. Jones leaned out with his looped rope, ready to grab the end boat's rail or to jump aboard her, but a crewman on the scow shouted out and caught the line Jones quickly heaved. With a soft bump the current drifted them into the string of boats waiting to deliver.

Nick Sandstol's boat, working in more slowly under oars instead of sail, was forced to tie astern of them.

"And oh my, how I'm a-sudden thirsty!" called Buck.

When their turn came to deliver, Buck jumped to a ladder against the scow and called back heartily to his son, "Skipper does the counts. Don't need to tell you what the boat puller does."

"Then it's skipper's ass if he screws the tally!" returned Jones in equal humor. He grabbed one of their pronged poles, pulled his hip boots to the top, and waded in among their fish. The catch of three days had an odor now less like silver and more like brass. He drove the prong into the head of a fish and swung its carcass over the boat's rail. With a flick of his pole, the fish thumped free onto the scow's deck.

18

DELIVERY BY PEW

It turned out that the captain of the *Evelyn K* had expected Kiyoshi to stand in the corner only while in the wheelhouse. Inside the rest of the vessel, he was free to wander as he pleased. Although that was soon amended: "Just don't interfere with the work. Stay off deck."

The bed that Vic the bearded crewman had taken him to was a top bunk in the dark, stuffy room where the crewmen slept. Several boxes, one of them slippery with grease, were piled atop the bunk. Vic handed them off without ceremony and directed Kiyoshi to stack them in the corner. "Didn't send a sleeping bag with you, eh? I'll find you a blanket. Lot of times we just sack out in our clothes since we're up and down all night out here. Okay?"

"Hai. Yes." It was a doubtful reassurance. How long before he could return to the bed ashore? It suddenly seemed a luxury.

"Now this bunk right below you—Spike sleeps there. Mind you don't kick him in the nose or step on him when you climb up, eh? That'll just start things all over again. Understand?"

"Very careful. Yes."

For the next few hours, Kiyoshi looked on at the men below from his corner in the wheelhouse. The cold rain, after all, came down hard outside. He watched it glisten down the waterproof coats of the workers. Preferable, of course, to stay dry—as befitted the owner of a Japanese company who had come to inspect and buy product. From the window he could see the open fishing vessels move in, but they disappeared beneath the scow's rail so that whatever the fishermen did to deliver their catch remained hidden to him. Nor could he see the full deck without moving from his assigned corner to the front windows of the wheelhouse, where the captain had not given him permission to go.

The sky remained dark all day and outside lights illuminated both the vessel and the nearby water, yet daylight never seemed to end. No one objected when he left the corner to wander to the galley and spread more peanut butter on bread. Nor when he climbed into the bunk assigned him to take a nap. By true nightfall, when the sky turned black at last, Kiyoshi had grown restless with boredom. Finally, risking the embarrassment of a reprimand (a bold risk that would be unthinkable back home) he ventured out to the open deck, but stayed in the shadows close to the bulkhead. Even in the half-shelter, the cold rain seeped into his clothes. Suddenly the captain, in passing, slapped him on the shoulder with American familiarity.

"You're wet. Didn't you bring foul weather gear?" He called to the dark figures working under the deck lights. "One of you guys get our friend here some oilskins." When no one turned: "Ahh never mind, follow me." The captain led the way to the small cabin where he slept, opened a drawer beneath his bunk, and pulled out a folded suit of green oilskin clothing. "Here, pull into these. Little wide for you, maybe, but they'll do."

"It is with permission that I come on the deck, then?"

"Yeah, yeah. Just stay out of the way." Kiyoshi tried not to sound overly grateful. He thanked the captain only twice while maintaining his dignity.

By the next morning, when the sun had risen on the horizon in a vivid red ball and disappeared for the day behind low gray clouds, Kiyoshi had settled in.

"Long as you don't touch any handles or levers," explained Vic. Kiyoshi stood with him in the cramped bay above deck. From here Vic operated the controls that seated the cargo boom after it had lifted crates of supplies from another scow. An overhang from the wheelhouse sheltered them partially from the rain.

Kiyoshi licked refreshing raindrops from his lips and acknowledged, "Yes!" From his vantage point above the main deck, he could watch the fishing vessels that moved alongside by sail or tow. The vigorous fishermen aboard them had faces unseen beneath caps and hoods, but he could see clearly the sockeye salmon that they pitched from their holds. The glistening fish tumbled and slapped against each other onto the pile below. Splendid creatures! Meat from such fish, cut properly, would make a glowing presentation on a platter amidst various greens and thin-sliced radish.

Kiyoshi followed gladly when Vic traded positions with Spike, the hostile crewman. They moved down on deck to count the fish coming aboard. By now he'd been loaned rubber boots. When fish inevitably slid against the housing rather than into the hold, "Just kick her in," Jimmy kept telling him. But the size and fatness of the salmon impressed Kiyoshi too much for that. With an apologetic shrug, he picked each one up and carried it to the hold in the crook of his arms, enjoying its weight and clean brassy odor. Slime soon covered his oilskin coat and even crept under his sleeves. In Japan, it would have embarrassed him, now the head of a fishing boat company, to be seen acting like a worker. Here it made no difference. And the banter!

"Look sharp there, boy. You pew like an old lady," said a gray haired fisherman who had come aboard from his boat to check the count.

"Get your ass down here then and show me, hotshot." The younger man in the fishing vessel speared two fish together and sent them flying straight into the chest of the man addressing him aboard the scow. Both laughed, as did Vic, who didn't break from counting, as one of the fish skidded far from the hold.

"See that? Kid of mine there. Never was much use. Went off and joined the Marines first chance he got. Hope he shot a gun better than that." More laughs. Father and son? Kiyoshi wondered. How inappropriate such a relationship would be with his own father. Yet here in Alaska it seemed natural. Feeling lighthearted himself, Kiyoshi smiled as he went to retrieve the fish.

The carcass he lifted had been pronged in the body. Instead of a bleeding head, which made no difference, the cut left the sleek body torn through the skin and into the meat. Such a fish had been ruined for the Japanese market! He brought the fish in his arms to Vic.

"No good. I cannot purchase such a fish for Japan."

"Hey," called Vic to the fisherman beside him. "My friend here says your boy down there's fucking up his fish. Looka there."

"After you slap 'em into a can, what's the difference?"

"Just telling you, man. The Jap market's different."

"Hey, Jones, boy. Keep your hook out of the body, okay? We're getting particular up here."

"Who says?"

"Man up here who's buying."

"Yeah? Tell him when he buys by the pound instead of the fish we'll take notice." And suddenly: "Oh, shit now! You see how head-spearing goes!" One of the fish had slipped off the prong and splashed into the water. On the scow Jimmy and gray haired man each grabbed a net and leaned over the rail. By the time they did it, the current had carried the fish down the line of other boats waiting to deliver. A fisherman two boats away dipped it aboard and called the news. Vic laughed. When the gray haired man joined him, Kiyoshi laughed also. Whoever now owned the creature was irrelevant, and Americans were so prosperous they could joke about the waste. But, "shit!" again declared the man responsible for losing the fish. Kiyoshi looked up from the rail and the two men's gazes met. Kiyoshi attempted a friendly smile.

"What the hell you grinnin' at?"

Kiyoshi straightened and turned away, startled. Familiar hostility! Familiar face, even? No, too much coincidence. Just another American who hated Japanese—not the one he couldn't forget, who had faced him outside the Tokyo train station so many years ago, while American baseball played on the loudspeakers.

What could any Japanese have done back then but obey his Emperor when arrogant Westerners tried to destroy their nation? *Yet, if we had won, would we have been so generous to you?* He turned away. There was no way to explain. Why risk confrontation?

Kiyoshi left the deck and returned to his corner in the wheelhouse. Perhaps best he should dress again in the dark suit and necktie hung in the safety of Mr. Scorden's office.

A Jap! Jones narrowed his eyes and glared at the man's retreating figure. *Yeah just keep walking. Better for you never to come back.* Was it the one who had come in the car all dressed up a few days ago? Or was this another? What kind of game was Swede Scorden pulling at the cannery?

Before Jones had time to think any further: "Just keep 'em coming, Jones boy!" Nick Sandstol called from one of the two boats behind them still waiting to deliver. Nick held up a gaff with Jones's lost fish swinging from it.

"Shit!" Jones muttered, while his dad bantered merrily with Nick over the way some men needed to make their catch. He returned to pronging only two fish at a time, and the bigger ones just one by one. Most times in the head, but not when inconvenient, until he had time to worry about it further. At least, up on the scow's deck, the nosey Jap had disappeared.

By the time he had pewed fish number one hundred and ninety, he was sweating heavily but his body had entered a satisfying rhythm. However, *These fish should fucking-A be paid for by the pound*! Again he thought of Swede at the cannery. That guy wasn't the shydeck hand just over from Norway any more. No longer the one he'd set up with the Creek Street whores and who'd later danced at his wedding with his own Adele. The guy had become management, sucking around with Japs, screwing the fishermen wherever he could.

In the end, with sweat now running into his eyes and thoughts of satisfaction long passed, Jones needed to drop into the tight hold to collect the few final fish. One creature still wriggled when he gripped its firm body, although its skin had already begun to slime. Jones considered, then picked up a gaff secured on the bulkhead and whacked the fish's head with the wooden handle until it lay still. Only a dumb fish. But just the same. The action calmed him. Out on the water he called the shots.

After delivery and wash down with the power hose provided, they moored on the scow's opposite side and climbed aboard. Jones stretched and stretched after the cramp of the boat. Hot soup, as well as coffee and donuts, waited in the scow's galley. They took turns on a toilet enclosed in the housing aft. By the time they had used up all excuses to linger, with other boats crowding the rail, Nick Sandstol and young Luke had joined them.

"Kept lookin' for more gifts from you, Jones," said Nick easily, clapping him on the back. "But you got stingy."

As Jones tried to think of a suitably light reply, his dad said, "Well, we asked each fish as it came pewed from the hold, and they all said they liked our boat better. Fish got better judgment than you'd think."

Luke the boat puller faced Buck respectfully. "You're some pisser with that sail, sir." He was a husky kid in his late teens. Buck shrugged, pleased.

"That's nothing but a thick head and strong arms," joked Nick.

Jones was glad for the chance to speak for his dad. "Comes from dory-hooking cod under sail in the Bering Sea before you were born. Almost before I was born." Buck shrugged again.

At the ladder back down to their boat came a, "Heeey man!" Jones turned to face Gus Rosvic, just arrived with his dad in their engine boat. "Still got that canvas, I see. Looks like the Middle Ages," Gus continued. "When're you guys going to enter the twentieth century?"

"Doing good like we are," Jones retorted. He couldn't help noticing how clean Gus's clothes were. Able to carry dry spares on the engine boat, apparently.

"Well, we were fishing way down near Egegik when we heard the fish were runnin' better up here. Wind was against us of course, but we just throttled the engine and scooted up to have a look." Gus turned serious. "Need to talk back at the cannery, man. Private." He lowered his voice. "About this strike."

Jones suddenly didn't want to banter anymore. He glanced at where his dad was talking to John Rosvic. The old man seemed equally restless. Little more than an hour after tying to the scow's rail they were back on the water, with other boats claiming their place. All the other craft around the tally scow had either rowed in or motored into position rather than scooting in under canvas, Jones noted with pride. But, long after the Rosvic boat had delivered and then disappeared by sputtering engine back to the grounds, he was again pushing oars against the wind toward the same location.

19

THE OUTSIDER

At week's end, Jones Henry and his dad were glad enough to tie up anywhere on the tow for a ride back along the river to the cannery. A hard easterly blew. The scow, rather than expecting them to sail or row to a central point, came around to pick them up like little ducklings. In the boats, men bailed water from around their boots while spray slapped them thickly and rain pelted from above. Though rain washed over the nine hundred feet of gillnet piled aft, Buck and Jones opted to hold off on salting the net in favor a few hours of rest. But as soon as they were finally tied rail to rail at the company pier, with the tide already far enough ebbed that their keels scraped the mud, their first job was to horse the net deck over deck and up the ladder into the tub of stuff people called "bluestone." Each boat did the same. If the nets were not leached of seawater by the copper sulphate solution the cannery provided, the linen strings of the net would rot away before the season ended.

"Hear the latest about the Japs?" asked one of the dock gang. Jones grew alert at once.

"Yeah," he replied. "Bitched about how we pew our fish. Jap who's probably never pitched a fish in his life."

"Worse, man! Bigger!"

"What? Joined the fuckin' North Koreans against us? That's their style of treachery."

"You wish. We could handle that. Just bomb them to hell again. No. Weaseling with Washington bureaucrats to get back onto our fishing grounds. Right as we speak. Damn if some high Jap didn't pass through here on his way, I guess, to a US Congress man or Truman himself, talking about exactly that."

"President Truman ain't that stupid!" Jones forced a laugh to hide his outrage.

At the wooden vats containing the bluestone, others were pulling their linen nets from the solution and draping them in racks to dry. Jones and his dad, still waiting for their turn, had not yet shucked their oilskins. Gus Rosvic and his dad walked by in clean shore clothes, trailed by another crew of equally clean men.

"Jones my man! Engine sure gets us in ahead of the line. And with our new nylon net, that bluestone shit's history. They developed nylon during the war. At least it gave us something good. Might as well take advantage."

"Can't argue with that, Gus. By next year, if the cannery don't supply it, we ought to find the money to change ourselves."

"Cannery spend money if they don't have to? Fat day in Hell! All my new stuff is on a GI loan. The cannery don't own my boat or my net. Government does until I pay it off. You see, I'm still delivering to the cannery anyhow." Gus lowered his voice, "Yo now, Jones. New union's having their meeting tonight at the Vet's. You know where that is? Up the road toward town a mile. All the canneries here in Naknek say they won't pay more than forty cents a fish—that's about seven cents a fuckin' pound. Everywhere else in Alaska's getting more. Sixty-six a fish offered in Cook Inlet. And just past in Kodiak they paid sixty-four to company boats. Independents get twenty more, they say. We're demanding sixty. Maybe going to strike for it."

"I don't quite know, Gus . . . you strike and don't catch fish, who pays for that new boat and net?"

Beside Jones, Buck Henry growled just as quietly, "Everywhere in Alaska's not here. Out here they've got to supply you with food and gear. Stuff you can't just go out and buy that they've got to ship in. And where you going to sleep on days off-season? In that open boat? Your dad beside you knows that, even if you don't! Be careful how you challenge the canneries when here's the fish and nobody else to buy them."

"Things gotta change, sir. We didn't go fight Japs and Krauts for four years to come back and let the cannery bosses in Seattle run over us like in the past."

"You strike and you'll let the big run here go by. These Bristol Bay reds peak and then disappear in two–three weeks tops. Then its scratch and nobody wins. Then how you going to pay for that engine boat?"

The senior Rosvic leaned over to mutter, "Buck, I don't know. I just hope it ain't the commies behind all this union stuff, like the canneries keep saying it is."

"Jones man! See you inside later, eh?" said Gus, and he sauntered off with the fishermen his own age from the new engine boats.

By Saturday evening Jones and his dad had staked out beds in the cannery bunkhouse and had showered and changed into the clean clothes stored in their locker ashore. They joined Nick and the others queued in the rain outside the mess building for a proper dinner. The very smell of meat frying in the galley had Jones salivating long before they entered the big warm hall.

Around them in line were fishermen paired off in groups, talking and gesturing in their various Italian, Norwegian, or whatever, lingos. Buck Henry slipped back to a bunch from Monterey to exchange greetings and a hearty joke, almost as if he were a wop himself.

In the hall Gus Rosvic was already seated and eating with his new friends. By his elbow were men his and Jones's own age, with whom Gus laughed buddy-style, slapping their backs. Guys who had chugged past in their engine boats without even a nod to the fishermen under sail. Probably veterans like himself and Gus. Was Jones Henry the only one against change?

As they waited, Swede Scorden strode past the fishermen's line with that same Jap: the one on the scow who'd complained about American-style delivery, who'd been spying atop the pier a few days before while the men launched their boats. That Jap still looked somehow familiar. He might have tried to blend in with his dungarees, but anybody could see that they were so stiff and new they hadn't seen a lick of work. Fooled nobody. At least fooled nobody who'd ever seen a Jap's slanty eyes staring, concentrated, from behind a gun.

Swede nodded absently to Jones, but he didn't stop. The Jap himself paused a moment to glance at Jones and nodded with a half-assed grin. Without lining up, the pair continued past the long mess hall tables to a round table set for the managers. They glanced at menus and a woman jotted their orders on a notepad, just as if they were in a fancy restaurant.

"That's the boss all right," muttered Nick. "You'd think he was King Boss the way he's been strutting around this year. Just last year he wasn't half that important. But back then already a hard ticket if you had to get something off him."

"Way I see it," muttered Jones, "What's new about him is what he's sucking up to."

"Well, if the Japs want to buy our fish that's good. Raise the price to fishermen!"

"Don't count on it. They have more ways than you can imagine to screw you over anything that suits 'em." The chow line finally reached the food tables. At the sight, Jones forgot his burn for the moment. Besides all kinds of peas and string beans and baked beans in big pots, there was fried chicken, hamburgers smothered in onions, pork chops in a thick brown gravy, and fish in some kind of tomato glop with rice and peppers. It all looked good.

"Some of each?" ventured Jones, expecting to be told he could have a single choice. Without question, the serving woman piled his dish so high that the gravies pooled together on his tray.

At the end of the line waited cupcakes with thick white icing, along with blocks of harlequin ice cream in a container of smoking dry ice. Jones glanced at the long line behind him, decided he'd better not risk coming back, and piled both cake and ice cream on the edge of his tray.

"Your boy's got some kind of appetite," observed Nick.

"Not surprising," said Buck Henry loud enough for others to hear. "Marine all through the Pacific War, guess he knows how to pack it in." Jones felt their approving eyes on him. He was stuffed by the time he'd eaten all but the dessert and would have gladly stopped, but now he had a reputation to uphold. He spooned the last of the ice cream—now melted—and forced it down, then muttered loud enough to be heard, "That all?"

"Go get back in line, boy. Ain't nobody going to skimp you around here."

"Guess I'll leave a little for somebody else."

"That's the Marines for you. Always look after your buddy. That's their rule, you know." Jones shrugged, finally restless at so much attention. Time to move on. He glanced around. Along with the old-timers like his dad and Pete, there were plenty of younger guys. Probably also vets still putting it back together. In the rush to ready the boat and then to fish, he'd only talked to a couple of them. All of them, including himself, were wary of letting down their defenses. Were they the ones that pushed the government to allow engines on Bristol Bay so that anybody could fish here, not just skilled sailors? Guys should have thought it through better.

Buck Henry had been carrying a copy of *Pacific Fisherman.* "Look at this ad now, boy. Seattle Boatyard." He read from the paper, "Boatyard says: 'Economy, Durability, Dependability, and Safety.' Their new thirty-two-foot Bristol Bay Gillnetter they call it. Has a 95-hp engine with two to one reduction gear. Look at this picture. Hydraulic roller, even has a little cabin. Down at the bottom says capacity for 4,500 red salmon. Price $7,500. Think the government would give you a GI loan for that?"

"And just let the engine break down for five minutes, wind blows us onto Deadman Sands. You thinking?"

"Pah!" Yet there was Gus Rosvic, finished with his meal and rising from the table. Gus with new friends and Jones Henry left behind with the sailboats. Gus and the two others walked their trays to the collection niche by the kitchen, talking all the time while they bumped their trays clean against the garbage can. Out they walked, laughing together now at some shared joke. As Gus passed, he paused by Jones and tilted his head in the direction of the door. "Like I said, the vet's hall is up the road about a mile. Got a truck taking us up in fifteen minutes. By the bunkhouse. Coming?"

Jones glanced at his dad, who looked away. "Don't know, Gus. Mebbe, mebbe not." Had any of them seen that Jap sitting at the managers' table? Any of them care? Jap sitting at the table like he belonged! But the one who didn't belong, he realized, might be Jones Henry himself. The one who didn't want things to change. But still, no harm in going.

A hand patted his shoulder. "Uh, yes, Jones? And your father Buck, is it?" It was Swede, passing by behind them. "Time for a visit, eh? Please, you'll come to the office now for a little drink." The tone was less an invitation than a command.

"We'll be there," declared Buck. Jones shrugged. A union wasn't going to change things anyhow. Time for a visit with management and then some! Time to find out if the Japs were jerking around this new cannery manager, or just jerking the fishermen. Let the unions talk on without him.

Jones might have expected something fancier for a cannery boss. The office had plenty of radios and microphones surrounding the desk, but it was crowded into a niche of the warehouse behind the company store. Swede stood waiting, his necktie knotted tight. At dinner it had been hanging loose around his neck, Jones remembered wryly. Swede gestured toward a set of chairs in front of his desk. Without bothering to ask, he produced a bottle from his desk drawer and poured out three small glassfuls of a clear liquid.

"Come. Aquavit, after a long day of fishing and of the delivering of fish. Let us drink to the good quality of the salmon. *Skoal*."

Both Jones and his dad were glad enough for the drink. A good way to start off a night that would likely continue back in the bunkhouse with a bottle of lesser stuff. It burned smooth, the way a shot of high-class alcohol should.

Swede returned the bottle to its drawer. "I see you not so often in Ketchikan anymore, Jones. I hope that you and your wife Adele have good health?"

"Just fine. Hope the same with you and Mary?"

"Yes. Yes. All good. Starting our family. Kids, kids. Oh! Ah . . ." Swede caught himself. Jones wondered grimly if Swede just remembered that the Henrys' only child had died of meningitis. Jones, too, wanted to change the subject. After their respective weddings, there had been little socializing. Then, when Swede had advanced into management, he'd turned dignified and became so damn full of himself. A kick at him wouldn't hurt, Jones decided. He turned to his dad.

"Took this man here to his first piece of ass on Creek Street." The statement had the effect he'd anticipated. Instantly, the cannery manager frowned uneasily.

Buck Henry laughed and joined in the game. "Don't say? Not Miss Eva I hope?"

"Better ask Miss Eva that one."

"This was long time ago, Jones. Not to speak of any more, I think. The whorehouses are not good for Ketchikan. My wife Mary says this strongly and I must agree. Surely, Jones, you do not go to such a street anymore!"

Jones winked at Buck, who shrugged. Swede opened the drawer and produced his bottle again.

"So, yes?"

Jones was enjoying himself, and he held out his glass for a refill. "'Night's young' as they say."

"Now, Jones and Buck, please, I must make a thing clear. Drink first. Drink. *Skoal*, ja?" Swede raised his own glass and held it until they too raised theirs and drank. "So, Buck and Jones . . . good fishing? Not such heavy runs of salmon this year in Bristol Bay. Or last year. Like the biologists predicted. So. Every fish delivered must have good quality, eh? For example, no hole in the side."

Jones laughed harshly. "Thought you'd get to that. The little Jap complained, didn't he? Tells me how to run my boat like I'm back taking orders from some officer!"

"In Norway and Sweden, Jones, the condition of fish is of great importance. The presentation. So also for other markets."

Jones made a show of looking to his left and right. "We still part of the United States here in this building? Since when is it a big deal to toss a dead fish any way but what's convenient? Going to be stuffed into a can however you do it! You ever tossed a few hundred big fish one after another?"

"Yes, Jones. A little." Swede lightened it with a trace of smile. "However, sometimes only. Not so much as you."

"I'd say so!"

"Go easy there, boy," Buck muttered. Swede rocked back in his swivel chair and steepled his fingers together.

"Other markets, Jones. You must understand this."

Like a damn banker, Jones thought. Like any puffed-up fellow who thinks he's in charge. That union in Naknek organizing against the canneries had it right after all. Without men to catch the fish, what were the canneries going to do? "Mebbe you fellows want to go put a moose in the can for them other markets."

"Yes. Ha. Good joke. But you see, Jones. Freezing the fish whole will soon be a product. We have a freezer boat already at sea to experiment with such technology. Modern times." Swede considered, then proffered his bottle again.

Jones started to hold out his glass, then shoved it aside on the table. "That Jap who's nosing around here. You kissing his ass? He telling you what to say?"

Buck Henry touched his son's sleeve. "Easy there. I don't mind pitching some fish. We'll take turns."

"That ain't the problem here, Dad. Problem here's who calls the shots."

Swede shook his head. "It's business we're talking here, Jones. You must understand."

"Guess you never crawled into a foxhole to save this country from people what wanted to tear us apart. Never seen what Japs do to you when they get the chance!" In the silence that followed, Swede's face reddened and Jones decided that he had made his point. "Mebbe I'll do what I can to keep holes outta your damn fish. But not to make some Jap happy."

Swede rose. His face was still flushed and his expression had lost its look of comfort. The tightening around his mouth increased the outline of a scar on his cheek. "Your father sits here beside you. Do you understand such good fortune? My father is dead from whips wielded by the hands of the German bastards. I also have hatred that will not forgive. So, when I speak to you of reality in the market, understand that I am not . . . fooling around. Eh?"

After a silence, Buck Henry spoke up. "That's a bad thing to hear now, Swede," he said. "Tell you what. We'll see your fish come through right. Come on, boy, let's go back to the boat."

Jones lowered his eyes so as not to meet Swede's. Shook his head. "Sorry," he muttered. Then, crossing his arms over his chest, he looked up with a glare of determination. "But it ain't the Krauts coming over here now to say how you run your business. It's the other ones, from my side of the war."

The door connecting the office to the store opened, and in walked the Jap in the suit. When Jones scowled at him, the man started to make his way back out.

"No. Come," snapped Swede. "Maybe settle something. We're all here together talking fish."

"Yeah, come in," growled Jones. "Let's look at you up close."

The Jap put his hand on the door knob. "Forgive me. I will come to talk later, Mr. Swede."

Instead, Jones advanced on him. "Man here says you don't like it, to see a little hole in your fish. Think that makes air space in your can? They stuff them cans full by weight."

Kiyoshi continued to shift away. "I will come later."

Jones walked over to face him. "Last time I heard, we beat your ass. Did it with blood from my buddies. My blood! And now what's this they say?

You people want to push us to let you come fish right here in Alaska? Some shit about doing it before the war?" The Jap looked down. He seemed to grow smaller. To Jones, it confirmed that he was right. "Try to push boats like mine right off the water! That ain't going to happen, you hear?"

Jones's energy had pushed the man up against the door so that he couldn't get it open. At first he tried to look away, then looked Jones square in the face.

"Sir. Japanese people . . . live on fish from the sea," he said mildly.

"Then catch your own fuckin' fish, not ours."

"Japanese are good friends now. Are hungry and need fish. Not enough off Japan because of the war. The great General Douglas MacArthur has said this himself. We have many vessels. And many men who must work at being in peace, not war. The seas have many fish for all."

"Many, many! You've sure learned our language fast. Well, get this. These are *our* fish in Alaska. And we'll catch 'em the way that's best for us. Go catch yours in your own water and do with them what you want. Got it? Our government ain't going to sell us down the river to you people what attacked us and started a war. Understand?"

"Hai, hai."

Jones thrust his face, eyes narrowed and chin blackened with a few days' growth of beard, into the Jap's face. "Say. I *have* seen you before. Long time ago. In Japan. Am I right?"

The Japanese fumbled with the door and managed to open it wide enough to allow for escape. "Forgive me, I must—" And he was gone.

"Now Jones," said Swede. "You don't notice some things, I think. These people do not like confrontation."

"Nice way of saying they won't look you in the eye!"

Buck Henry laughed uneasily. "If he's the one buying, don't think it means he won't have his say when the time comes, boy. I remember once before the war, some Oriental—I guess Jap—came to Ketchikan to buy fish for his company. Made for the nearest exit if anybody raised his voice to argue. But it made no difference when it came to paying money. They got their way."

"Then they'd better learn to change. Because I ain't changing, and we won the war."

"Please be calm, Jones," said Swede. "Here's the truth. The one with the money to pay is the winner. I pay you, so therefore I'm right when I say there must be no holes cut in the side of the fish I buy from you. And the Japanese is right if he pays me only for the fish that have not been cut. A famous rule. The customer is right. Always."

"Yeah? Well, without me you haven't got any fish to sell. The workers you've shipped up wouldn't have much to do, but you'd still be stuck feeding 'em. Then I'd have you by the balls."

"Please count the boats out there, Jones. If you don't bring me fish, fifty other vessels will. And they must follow company rules or they go home without money."

"He's right, boy," said Buck. "We came up here to fish because that's how we earn our living."

Jones considered, chewing his lip while he cleared his head. He leapt up so suddenly that the chair clattered behind him. "Got a truck or something to catch. Good night."

Outside, he turned toward the bunkhouse and began to run. Rain slicked the walkways and blackening sky reflected a pool of lights. The truck had already left. He continued at a sprint through heavy bush to the main road, then on toward the village and the Vet's hall—wherever it was. Didn't like the way his own dad had spoken. Everything was screwed. The old ways. Everything!

20

STRIKERS

How good it felt to run! All that arm and shoulder exercise on the boat left nothing for the legs to do except brace against the motion and bend to carry weight. Even at his pace, hungry mosquitoes were attracted by his sweat and locked onto his skin. He smeared them from his forehead without slackening speed. It was easy to spot the hall—it was surrounded by parked pickup trucks. A few men were straggling on the steps, but amplified voices told of the action inside. A man stood at the entrance, taking notes. "You boat or cannery, buddy?" he asked with half a glance.

"What the fuck do I look like?" growled Jones as he pushed past. The idea of being mistaken for some cannery monkey outraged him. Another man demanded, "You AFL or CIO?"

Jones stopped to consider. "Fisherman's Union, what do you think? What else you got?" He pressed on to avoid further conversation. The man called after, "Seattle CIO or local AFL. Don't you know the difference by now?"

Inside, the air was white with cigarette smoke, despite a hand-lettered sign that read NO SMOKING. Fishermen filled rows of folding chairs and those left standing were filled in so deep that they shouldered each other against the walls.

"I'm trying to get it straight," said a voice from the audience. A graying man in a checked wool shirt addressed the lectern. The man standing behind it was in his twenties, set-faced, with black hair strung to sideburns. He exuded energy from his keen gaze and squared chin, to the width of his shoulders beneath a faded army jacket.

"Okay, buddy. What don't you understand, then?"

"You say you're from around here but used to belong to our Alaska Fishermen's Union? Which I've belonged to since maybe before you were born. So who the hell are you? Telling us now we should break away from our old union because they've gone commie. That's what you're telling us?"

"My name's Ed Torgersen. Father came from Norway long time ago, married local. Fished all his life right here."

"Means he's part Native," muttered somebody close to Jones.

Ed Torgersen gripped the sides of the lectern and leaned forward. "I'm American! Fought all through Germany, buddy, so I saw plenty of Russians, and what I'm saying is: Red infiltration! You've watched it happen yourself. Just look at Berlin if you don't believe me. And Korea on the other side! Russia's almost as close to us here in Bristol Bay as Seattle."

"And the Japs moving in from the other side," growled someone. "Saw it today right down the road here!"

"Now you got it!" Jones nodded vigorously as he craned to see who had spoken.

"Okay. Okay!" The man named Ed cleared his throat to regain their attention. "Let's get it straight." He glanced down at a paper. "That AFU you think's looking out for you is part of the ILWU, which is part of the CIO. Don't matter that IFAWA linked up there and then got thrown out of CIO for red infiltration—CIO's still gone commie right up at the top!" He looked again at the paper. "IFAWA. That's International Fishermen and Allied Workers of America, like everybody here knows. And CIO . . . everybody knows that big overall union so I don't need to—. The big point is, the old union's gone commie and don't represent us anyhow. So we've started our own local union. The National . . ." Finally, he held the paper up and read from it directly. "Listen. The American Federation of Labor—that's the AFL—through its branch the Seaman's International Union—which is the SIU—has recognized us. I'm here to get you to join us. Join us in brotherhood. Against the capitalists."

Several in the audience muttered. One man pushed back his chair with a clatter. "All we ever had going for us is sticking together. We split into two unions, just watch the canneries eat us for breakfast." He stormed out of the vet's hall.

"Listen!" Ed persisted, gripping at the lectern with his free hand. "Ever hear of reunited? Our new Bering Sea Fishermen's Union ain't going along with that CIO shit. Everybody's gotta make the switch together! We're new, but SIU—which is part of AFL!—is taking us in. Taking us in right up here, not down in Seattle where other people run it!"

A hand slapped Jones on the shoulder. He turned to face Gus Rosvic. For once, Jones's fishing rival and old wartime buddy wasn't grinning. "Anybody follow you here?"

"Didn't think to notice. You afraid of something?"

"Shit no! But some things you can't tell, you know?" Gus gestured toward the lectern. "That guy up there talks sense. I ran into him a few nights ago up here in that bar Pioneer's. Had a drink together. Ed-something. Norwegian from his dad but his mother's Native. Lives in Dillingham, but used his GI Bill for a couple years of college in Seattle before he said fuck it. Asked me to come tonight. Talks a good line up there, don't you think?"

"Quiet!" somebody called. "We're trying to get answers from this guy."

"Yeah, yeah, sorry," said Gus. He took Jones by the elbow and steered him toward a corner. Gus put his mouth close to Jones's ear so that he could speak quietly. "Been going on like this since it started a couple hours ago. But I dunno. Makes sense. Times change. Got to stand up and stop taking shit. Get paid more. For our new boats if nothing else."

"Nobody made you buy that new boat," Jones muttered.

"What say? Noisy in here."

"I think you heard me."

"Okay, listen," Ed pressed on. "Some of us veterans from around here have set up in Dillingham for good. Getting organized. We've finally got ourselves a fire department. Started a newspaper to go with it. Guys back from the war who expect more than just bartering and to catch only the fish they eat. Just as I speak, we're starting our own store so as not to be beholden to any cannery store. No more of that PAF—those cheatin' 'Pay After Fishing' stores that the canneries run. That's why we picketed here when the supply ship from Seattle that was allied with commie CIO came up here to unload. Even though goons crossed our picket line and unloaded anyhow. You follow?"

"Follow?" called a voice. "That did a lot of good. They just walked around us!"

"Follow who, buddy?" cried another. "Everything's screwed when some boats go out fishing and you tell the rest of us to stay dry."

"Yeah, who's following? Those of us who went along with you and stayed dry last week? What did it fetch us except losses?"

"Show some guts here!" barked Ed suddenly. "Like we just finished doing in the war with the Krauts and Japs. They're not paying enough for our fish. And it's up to us to make sure they don't keep walking all over us— and around us, like that picket line."

"Yeah," muttered voices from the audience.

The speaker resumed in a more reasonable voice. "And that's why we're holding out against the canneries—the greedy canneries!—for more than just forty cents a whole red salmon. You know that comes to a whopping seven cents a pound, and that much only if you're lucky enough to catch just little fish. You following now?"

"I sure follow that we ought to get more for each fish. Or get paid by the pound. I sure follow that. But look what's happened. Seattle boats went ahead fishing last week anyway. And you're still telling us to stay ashore with our thumbs up our asses."

"Then do I need to tell you?" At the lectern, Ed shuffled through his papers. "Canneries here offer us forty cents? Get this. Prince William Sound fishermen, just like you, get fifty-five cents for their reds, Kodiak gets sixty-four cents, and Cook Inlet gets a few cents more than Kodiak! We don't roll over, and when the canneries see we don't, they'll give in. And the higher price we demand's going to make up for that loss of a few days' fishing."

Another man stood up. "They say Bristol Bay's so far away it costs the canneries more up here to operate. That they can't afford to pay us more. Got anything to say about that?"

"I say it don't cost *that* much more. That's what I'm saying."

"Then what about this? One cannery's already started shipping their Native workers back home since there's no work for them. Cannery at Pederson Point, I hear. Don't matter one bit to any Seattle outfit that's got canneries everywhere else."

"Come on! With Bristol Bay's the biggest red salmon run in the world, probably? Bigger runs most years than even the Fraser? Don't kid yourself. Up here, canneries get rich!" Ed turned back to the first questioner. "Then okay, buddy. My point. Listen now: any of you here who last week went fishing and didn't go with our strike call—strike call from your brothers on the water. If we strike together now, lose a few fish up the rivers, we'll quick make it up in price when the canneries have got to cave. Then we get paid what we're worth in years to come. Any more questions?"

"I guess not. It's just that, the fish are running now. Not that many this year either, they say. I come up here to make pay. Not to sit on my ass and watch fish get away. Or watch other guys catch them." The man sat down slowly.

Gus nodded toward the door. He and Jones slid outside, slapping mosquitoes from their faces. "Maybe about time we wised up and joined 'em. This strike won't last more than a day or two more if we pull together. Time to bring the canneries to their knees."

"Well, I finally see it clear!" exclaimed Jones. "Now I know what that Jap back there's waiting for. Same thing as the commies. Fight our old union with a new one. Make everything here go broke and then come take over. Gus, things are working just fine as they are. And the fish ain't going to wait for us to change things. If some of these guys want to stay out, I say let 'em."

"Oh, Jones buddy, you're behind the times! You think the canneries can pack fish without fishermen to catch and deliver? This new union's going to crack things wide open. We hang together and the canneries have to go along. I didn't fight Japs for four years to come home and get fucked by Seattle fat asses. Look, we finally got the politicians back in DC to break the cannery hold up here against power boats. You wait. Next year or year after that at the latest, you won't see a single double-ender sailboat like yours this season banging on the reds here. Except in a museum. Give it a year and you'll switch over. Get a good price with this strike, and in one season instead of two your boat's paid for. Your own boat with an engine, not a cannery handout. Canneries won't hold us by the balls no more. We'll tell them, instead of them telling us, what price they'll pay."

"You've got it wrong!" Jones declared. "You break up our Seattle union, and you leave the canneries free to fuck you in any way they please. I'm outta here."

"Come back inside. Come on. Just to listen, okay?"

Suddenly the room inside turned noisy with shouts. No one guarded the entrance now, and they went back in unchallenged. A man in the audience was shouting at the speaker Ed. "You're good at pulling that army service crap. But if I look in your wallet, you so sure I won't find a Communist Party card in it? Because half of what you're spouting up there—"

"You're calling me what?" Ed left his lectern and strode straight through the sea of people toward the man who called him commie. "Want to say that to my face, buddy? Got the guts for that?"

"Afraid to show all your cards, pal?" Others intervened before the men reached each other. The crowd formed separate knots around each aggressor. In the commotion, another man took the place at the lectern and pounded on it with a metal ashtray. "Order! Knock this bullshit off! They'll screw us if we don't stick together."

Gus could now speak as loud as he pleased. "The fishermen's union down in Seattle gets jerked around by the canneries and the commies because they're all in it together. Your old cannery union down there's signed a buddy agreement to deliver for forty cents a fish. That's how they've sold us out! This new union's demanding sixty. Demanding! And if we stick together we'll get it. Sixty cents a fish. Maybe we'll come down to, say, fifty-six or seven. Whatever—canneries can pay it. Hell, even the US military buys the salmon canned here. Make the army pay a couple cents more if that's what it takes. Don't they owe us that much after all we went through?"

The masses in the Vet's Hall held a vote to support the strike. Men lined up to sign their names in a notebook at a table beneath the lectern.

"You with us?" Gus demanded as he stepped into line. Jones shook his head and left the hall.

21

ENCOUNTERS

The late June sky in Naknek never darkened completely. The night was merely a dingy gray as Jones made the trek back to the cannery compound. He walked the deserted road, idly slapping mosquitoes. He stepped off into the brush when the occasional truck rumbled by, debating whether to turn back, but he kept going. By the time he'd reached the road to the compound—bounded by dark shadows and the threat of lurking bears—he had no doubts left. He burst into a run.

Between the darkness and the speed, Jones nearly collided someone. "Watch where you're going," he muttered without apology.

"Very sorry, sir. Not looking."

Jones peered through the half light. It was the Jap. "Yeah. Don't hurt to watch where you're going." After reflection he added, "You might get hurt."

The man started away. "Very sorry. Good night, sir."

"We ever met?" Jones demanded, overwhelmed by the feeling he'd been getting lately that he had really seen this man before. Best to make sure.

"In office, sir. Three hours ago. Before, the time from delivery vessel at sea. Before, by vessels making ready for sea."

"You know what I mean. Not just here. Somewhere in Jap-land mebbe. Few years ago?"

"All Americans of same age look the same, sir."

"You can sure say that about all Japs. I guess you was in that war that we beat you in?"

There was a pause. "Hai. In war. All Japanese in war, sir."

"And now you're here, acting like you own the place. Think to tell me how I pew fish. You got no right here. Should kick your ass back to where you come from."

"You are . . . violent, sir."

"Yeah? What would you do back there in Jap-land? If half the boats went on strike while your half was busy fishing?"

The Jap straightened suddenly, and the subservience in his voice dropped away at once. "Sir! I do not understand. However, sir. Everyone must . . . cooperate."

"Cooperate how? Go on strike? When we close down the cannery, you and your people will come and take over."

"All must make agreement good for everybody. American and Japanese together for the resource!"

"That ain't what I was saying. Don't know why I bothered." Jones stared into the man's face again. "I don't see that kind of straight-in-the eye look from a Jap every day." Jones's eyes narrowed suspiciously as he regarded the man in front of him. "Say! A few years ago . . . You wouldn't have been on Okinawa in a prison camp. Right after the Japs surrendered?"

After a short pause, the Jap muttered curtly, "Do not understand, sir."

"Only seen one other of you people look me in the eye like that. Some fellow, an officer mebbe. Hard to tell with a uniform full of holes. Just before he keeled over. Never thought of it much but as I remember, I got him a medic because of that look. Later tossed him an old ground cloth. Mebbe because he'd started walking around like a man, not some dead fish. Not like the rest of you people always bowin' and lickin'."

Jones heard the sharp intake of breath, before the Jap, soft voiced again said, "Forgive me. I must go." *Well,* Jones concluded. *It was a mistake back then being nice to a Jap. Mistake again now.*

—★—

On Sunday morning, as rain poured down outside, Jones stayed buried under his covers. He had the upper berth above his dad at the cannery bunk room assigned to their boat and Nick Sandstol's.

"Where'd you go last night, boy?" Buck Henry demanded once. "After you spouted off at that poor Jap, you just disappeared. Didn't see him again either."

"Humph."

"That fellow Swede invited me to stay and we played crib. Nice to sit at a table with legs on the floor, not rocking on some boat. Lamp with a shade. Elbow room. All dry. Don't appreciate those things until you've gone without them a few days." Jones made no answer. "Swede's a nice fellow. Wasn't he at your wedding?"

"Long time ago, Dad." Jones pulled a blanket over his head and rolled toward the wall.

Later, Buck made another incursion: "Lunchtime here's mainday dinner, boy. You skipping that?" he asked.

"Alarm goes off at three tomorrow morning, Dad. Till then, it's warm under the covers. Leave me sleep."

"That what the Marines taught you? I hear it's steak and ice cream. You expect me to bring you some?"

Jones groaned. A few minutes later he crawled from the bunk, stretched, and stepped into the dungarees he'd tossed over the back of a wooden folding chair.

In the mess hall, fishermen and cannery workers had divided into separate tables almost automatically. The benches on one side were occupied by people from the cannery floor on changing shifts. A few of them, white and Native women alike, still wore the waterproof hair caps from the lines. Some of the men wore smaller paper caps atop shorter hair. All of them working today, Jones noted. He'd forgotten that cannery was routine, still processing Saturday's delivery. Then they would have their own Sockeye Sunday on Monday while the boats caught new fish.

In walked boss Swede with the Jap following beside him. Both were wearing suits. They went to the table reserved for management, where a woman took their orders.

Thick as thieves, Jones thought. *Even if I joined that strike tomorrow, they'd still get all dressed up and get rich.*

Gus Rosvic edged in beside him at the long table. "Maybe the last chow I'll get here," he muttered. "The old man's not happy about it, but I told him. We stay dry tomorrow. Going to support that strike. The canneries are cheating us with what they pay. What about you?"

Jones didn't need to consider any longer. "A strike's just what the commies want. Wouldn't be surprised if that's what the Japs want too. If everything falls apart, they take control. So no. We're fishing."

"You still don't get it." Gus took up his tray and moved to another table.

As on the week before, the monkey boat waited at 3:00 a.m. The boats rowed to it and tied in line for a tow to the river and the fishing grounds. This time Buck made sure their boat was placed at the tail of the line, so they didn't have to swallow exhaust or bear the strain of a long tow behind them.

Jones counted boats around him. Maybe one or two fewer than last week. Some might have fastened to another tow. No big difference if any had decided to stay dry and support the strike. And out on the water it made little difference what the Japs were trying to do. Truman wasn't going to give away Alaskan fishing grounds to the Japs just because they'd weaseled into them before the war. Any more than the Seattle union was going to give up their hold in Bristol Bay just because the commies were infiltrating everywhere. That breakaway union business had been all talk.

They worked the Bay principally from north of the Halfmoon Bay mud flats to further south off the Deadman Sands. Buck Henry may have complained that he lacked the advantage of an engine, but when they needed to move under sail, he worked with cool precision whatever winds or gusts might blow. He could drive the boat on a lick of breeze or heel it under a steady easterly. At those times, Jones gladly jumped to his commands as in the old days. *Okay*, Jones admitted, in a rare moment of enjoyment. *Maybe I can kill Japs better than he'll ever imagine, and maybe duck being shot myself, but the old man still has things to teach me. Things worth knowing. That we wouldn't be doing if we had an engine. Or if I hadn't helped beat Jap ass in Okinawa. Good feeling. Old man's still got it.*

But he missed the rumble of an engine and breezy, grinning Gus Rosvic motoring by to bug him.

Then, some time midweek, Jones and Buck moved under sail to a spot where several boats were grouped off the sands. There bobbed the Rosvic boat with Gus and his dad working their net.

"Changed your mind?" called Jones. Gus pulled a few feet more web over his roller before acknowledging. He looked up only to say: "Union caved. Not enough boats to support us. Couldn't hold out. Price stays at forty cents a fish. You happy?" He returned to gripping web.

Jones felt both relieved and sorry. Maybe he should have joined them after all. But the failed strike did change one thing—Gus stopped pestering him with friendly insults and challenges. Even when their two boats fished the same water, Gus Rosvic kept to himself.

Most of the boats fished in groups of their own nationality. That way, if nets tangled, you could straighten things back and forth in your right language instead of some gobble in half-Italian or Slav or Native. Their boat now fished regular buddy with Nick Sandstol's. One day a few birds began to squawk a few hundred feet ahead, where Nick and his puller Luke were hauling in. Netted fish lay around them on deck. But bad sign: the portion of net in their hands was clotted with twigs rather than fish, while from the way they tugged and the web stretched without moving it was clear they'd snagged. This was no time to yell over a joke. Jones watched them strain, then with apprehension went aft to check his own net. Half the corks had sunk out of sight. The current flowed in ripples around their boat. There was no way to tell whether the sunken part of his net lay free or snagged unless they started to haul.

Buck, who had wrapped himself in the bearskin rug to nap between sets, rose at his call to assess the problem. "Best get out them oars. Try to pull us into deeper water and break that snag."

Just then, three boats under engine power rode past a few hundred feet away. Gus Rosvic waved from one of them but didn't bother to call over. He now fished, and even delivered, in a different pack, more and more removed from fishermen under sail.

"Yep," said Buck. "An engine sure could free us from this snag easy."

"Unless you snagged the screw itself!" snapped Jones.

But the old man was right. A propeller snag was remote, while the oars promised a hard pull that might or might not do the job until high tide freed them. And why would you spike a fish in the side if you could help it? Common sense to leave him whole the way you'd caught him, if only from respect. Right and wrong had been easier to see, back in Okinawa.

22

SOUTHEASTER

A day later it was so calm that a westerly puff from shore—although it wafted in a few mosquitoes—barely lifted a streamer tied to their mast. In company with Nick Sandstol, Buck and Jones were fishing a channel familiar to the older man. It cut between the land-based mud flats of a creek and a range of offshore shallows, both of which watered over at rising tide. The two boats had filled their nets reasonably on the flood. With sails dropped and under oars, they first maneuvered to throwing distance so Buck could trade Nick two hardboiled eggs for a chocolate bar. Then they anchored far enough apart to keep their nets separated, but still close enough to call cheerful insults to each other as they picked the fish from their nets.

With the fish stowed and the net itself hosed and salted against temporary rot, Buck called over, "Wind's down. Might as well go beached here for the ebb. I couldn't tell you a better place. We'll lay in deep water just off the edge of this bar, then slide the boats free again when the tide lifts if we need to."

"Good plan," called Nick. "Finest!"

"Makes no sense to row somewhere else when your spot's just laid out for you like this," Buck added comfortably to his son. He kicked the anchor line to make sure it held. The anchor's shaft already showed as the water receded. "Keeps us steady when the tide comes back in. Low tide might ground us for a while. But the new tide'll just float us anchored in the same place, all set to keep fishing this channel if it suits."

Jones nodded in agreement. The old man knew what he was doing. When his dad spat a mouthful of red tobacco juice over the side and offered over a plug, Jones took it gratefully. Old-timer stuff. Part of tradition, in open water when neither cigars nor cigarettes stay lighted. The hard tobacco taste filled a gap, after a steady supply of beans and meat eaten cold from a can—or scorched and lukewarm from the little primus—and nothing hot but coffee. Let it all stay the same!

Just as the flooding current had pulled their gillnet northward, the ebb would push their next set south. The boats floated firm, anchored in the shallows while the water depth continued to lower around them.

Suddenly from the deep water on the far seaward side of the bar, the Rosvics' engine rumbled to within shouting distance. On deck, John called over to Buck, "Thought we ought to tell you, since we have this sideband what come with the new boat—picks up news. Southeaster expected. Heavy blow coming. My boy says suit yourself how you handle it. He and Jones ain't talking. But he thought you guys without radio ought to know."

"Thank you," Buck called back. He had watched the conflict between their sons and, like John, had declared he'd stay out of it. "Those two boys went to war for their country and earned the right to act on their opinions," he'd said back at the cannery, and John Rosvic had shrugged agreement. "Guess you heard that, boy?" Buck said to Jones, who was heating coffee water under the forepeak canvas.

"I heard. Wouldn't put it past him now to fool us away from a place where there's fish."

Buck shouted the weather warning over to Nick. Their message delivered, the Rosvics' engine boat had roared off toward the more sheltered windward shore opposite theirs. As the ebb increased, the lowering water made a sucking sound across the sand. Their boat grounded and stopped rocking. Gradually the sand itself surfaced around them as the water line receded. Puddles remained. One held a stranded fish. *I'll jump down and get him when the ground drains more*, Jones decided. But as he watched, a seagull landed and pecked at the fish's eyes. Jones found a piece of broken float on deck and he heaved it squarely into the gull's side. With a screech the bird lifted from the fish—the eye still in its beak, trailing slime—then settled back down to pecking out the other eye.

"Son of a bitchin' gull," Jones muttered. He threw another piece of float straight at the bird's head. It missed and instead smacked into the creature's wing with a shattering crack. The fish's eye still dangled in its beak as the bird started to limp in circles, its wing dragging a line in the sand. Two other gulls swooped down and started pecking at the forgotten bounty. The fish flapped helplessly in its dying throes. The gull with the broken wing moaned, tried to flap away, then trotted instead in helpless, aimless circles.

"Son of a bitch anyhow!"

"Stop fooling around! That bird you hit's a goner now, boy. Check the anchor line we laid out, if you've got nothing better to do."

One less eye-picking scavenger suits me, Jones concluded. But he had to force himself to look away.

Buck looked out over the line of corks that marked their net. It was now set on the ebb in the channel just beyond. Some of the floating corks dipped vigorously with newly snagged fish. A few silvery bodies flapped sluggishly in a piece of net beached by the falling tide.

"There's fish here." Buck commented, considering. "Still, we might want to pull her in early and stay loose if a real blow's coming."

Buck repeated the weather warning to Nick, who shouted back: "You kidding? With best ebb haul this week?"

"Southeaster's just going to blow us into the channel," Buck reasoned. "Long as we don't slip anchor and let it take us onto the opposite shoal by the land there, we're okay." A few minutes later, however, he added, "Still, wouldn't hurt to get out from between these two flats and to open water if we have time. Don't want to homestead here if we can help it."

Jones spat tobacco juice to clear his throat. A sudden gust carried the drops several feet across the water before they dropped. "Your call. But look at that."

A second gust lasted long enough to kick up small whitecaps. Buck studied the sight, then snapped, "We're hauling now."

The net had soaked barely an hour but it was already weighted with fish. The sleek bodies, still twisting with vigorous life, lumped over the roller slowly no matter how hard they were pulled. By now the wind was steady and increasing.

"Leave it to have a big haul just when the weather comes down," grunted Buck. "Pull boy. Like you was a marine again!"

"Don't waste your breath." They kept kicking the net forward as they brought it in, but in their haste the web and fish tangled around their hip boots. They had barely started hauling the second shackle when Jones pointed, shouting, "Look there!"

Whitecaps tumbled toward them over the open water, higher than the sea beneath them. "Water wall! Go!" Buck shouted across the water to Nick. He kicked free of the net underfoot. "Getting out of here, boy. Help me pull anchor."

"Half that shackle's still in water."

"Cut it! No, leave her. She'll help steady us maybe. But keep your knife handy!" They had barely begun pulling in the anchor line when the wind hit with such force that Jones felt the edges of his mouth blow wide. With a thud, their boat's keel bumped ground as the incoming water swept out beneath them. They faced bared sand again, with the wall of water building their way.

Buck tossed back the anchor line. "Too late. Quick with me, boy. Second hook." He was already freeing the spare anchor. He threw it over to place its line at nearly right angles to the first anchor line, while he snapped, "Do as I say. Lay our boom down the center of the boat. Then come help me with the mast."

Jones obeyed without question. Buck wrapped his arms around the mast. "Now grab here and help lift it free." With Jones balancing, they unseated it. "Now pull off rings and sail. Wrap off the sail down there across the boom—watch your legs, that's it! Now help turn the whole mast across the gunnels. Steady it while I lash down." In minutes they had secured the twenty-five-foot mast amidships at right angles to the boat so that several feet of it protruded on each side. "Maybe keep us from rolling over," Buck declared. "Should!"

Jones centered the boom down the length of the boat. It left them only tight passage on either side. "Now quick," Buck continued. "Smooth out the sail all along the boom." Buck fumbled a hammer and nails from the tool kit, wriggled forward over the canvas-covered boom, and nailed one end of the sail to cover the bow as he called back, "Weight the canvas by your feet however you can. Keeps water from our gear under the bow."

Jones was already doing this. "Got it!" Their bow, now roughly covered by the sail, faced the wind. The section of net they hadn't been able to recover continued capturing fish astern. Across the exposed shallows no more than two hundred feet away, Nick Sandstol and his boat puller Luke continued to bring in their net. Their backs were turned to the growing wind and they were oblivious to the water tumbling toward them.

"Turn around! Look behind you!" Buck shouted. Nick lifted his head up to indicate a brace of fish bunched at the top of their roller. He glanced over his shoulder, cried out, and raced toward his mast. Buck and Jones didn't have time to watch further. The wall of water glistened under gray sky. It approached like a living creature through a base of froth. Jones braced himself as Buck shouted, "Hang on to something!"

The water hit. Their bow reared high. The boat shuddered up against its anchor lines, bounced twice against the sand, then steadied, bobbing afloat. The ends of the mast lashed across their rails, plunging first into the water on one side, and then as the boat rolled, deep into the water on the other side, had kept them from capsizing. Jones and Buck staggered but were still standing, clutching tight to anything firm. As the water caught their net astern, it pulled emptied web back off the roller while the attached floats thumped across deck and back into the waves.

"You okay there, boy?"

Jones laughed. "Steady! You?"

"Steady. Anchor's held. We'll ride it okay now. First haul back that net. Don't need to cut it, but it's no use letting it pull us. Then we'll step back the mast, make sail, get to deeper water, and ride this out. You might want to start bailing when you get your legs."

Jones was the first to look toward the Sandstol boat. At his sharp cry, Buck looked up too. Nick's boat had capsized. Its net, outlined by corks, was dragging astern, slowly drifting past them. Nick and Luke clung to the slick bottom, gripping the only handhold in the slot that seated the centerboard.

"Shove out the mast!" Buck cried. Jones had already grabbed his knife and was slicing the cords that held the mast across their rails. They nearly capsized themselves as they maneuvered the tip of the cumbersome pole out toward Nick's boat.

"My fingers!" screamed Luke from the capsized hull.

"Hold on anyhow, kid!" Nick bellowed back. A streak of blood trickled from the slot where the centerboard ground up and down on their hands.

A wave over the hull splashed blood away and another streak started. The mast end came up a dozen feet short. In the upturned boat, Nick flailed one bloody hand to try and reach it while clinging to the slot with his other.

"My fingers, ohhh!"

"I tell you—hold on, Luke!" But with a shout, the kid let go. As he slid off the slippery hull, Nick grabbed at his arm. The kid slipped free. His head disappeared first into the water, then his outstretched arms still thrashing for a hold, then his mangled hands. The hull continued its course downstream—pulled by the strength of the current—leaving whirls of empty water where the kid had dropped.

"He's gone, Nick," Buck cried. "Grab hold of the mast!" Nick pushed himself free of the hull. He swam toward their mast end, but his arms were constricted by the oilskins. His first strokes were focused. Then they became disjointed. Buck had by now lashed a line to a buoy. He heaved it in front of Nick. The wind buckled the line and veered the buoy far from target. The current wove Nick away from both handholds. He raised one arm toward them. Then the water sucked him under.

Jones had peeled off his oilskin coat and was tugging at his boots.

"No you don't," barked Buck. "Current'll take you too!"

"I'm strong!" Jones gripped the rail with one boot off, preparing to jump. Buck knocked him back into the boat with such sudden force that Jones splayed flat on his back. Bilge water stung his eyes, but he scrambled up dripping, ready to fight.

Neither Luke nor Nick had surfaced. The bare hull had moved further over empty water. A streak of red still stained the centerboard, grinding up and down in its slot until a wave washed it clean.

"It's done, boy. We couldn't do more than we did. Wasn't going to lose you too. Go make us coffee." Jones had seen enough death to understand. He ducked his head under the dripping canvas sail and groped for the little primus stove. Marines saw everything bad there was to see, he told himself. Marines don't cry. ·

23

GOOD RYE WHISKEY

During the following day they worked their nets by rote, speaking only as necessary, treating each other with caution. Buck sought grounds with a fleet of other boats in deeper water. They stayed at the cusp of the group, but still within sight of it.

No set came close in abundance to the one they had risked by going dry, but they spent more effort fish by fish to grunt each one aboard and stow it. Neither man wanted to be left idle.

Next evening, safely anchored in more open water than before and with their net laid to soak, Jones watched ripples reflecting the gray sky. Without a word, the old man had already covered himself and hunched under the bow for a few hours' sleep between sets. The setting sun, as it dipped below clouds at the horizon, penciled a shaft of red light on the water. The night sky closed around them. Boat lights blinked on—the men aboard wouldn't have a care but for their next haul of fish.

The old man might have been right to stop him like that. But what if he'd swum it—strong as he was—and saved Nick? Even found the kid and pulled him out alive? They'd all be laughing about it now. Soberly, of course, and tied to the scow with the rescued men under blankets. But then, what if he'd drowned? What of Adele? Jones supposed she'd wail a bit, then marry again. No kids, young widow alone. What difference would it have made after a couple of years? Even to a buddy like Gus? To Dad and his mom, it'd be different, of course. But no different than if he'd been killed with his buddies in the war. They were half-forgotten now too.

Finally he peeled his hip boots halfway to let air inside and crawled under the bearskin to catch his own forty winks. After the fresh air, the smell was stuffy with traces of wet wool and coffee grounds, but it was warm, comfortable.

After some time, Jones heard: "You awake, boy?"

"Awake."

"Hope I didn't hurt anything when I hit you."

"You didn't."

"Always figured your head was too hard for anything to hurt it other than maybe a sledge hammer."

Jones's eyes filled with tears in spite of himself. "Been hit by worse."

There followed a silence long enough that Jones assumed his dad had fallen asleep. But then: "Boy? Everything okay between you and Adele?"

"Why wouldn't it be?" Jones replied automatically. Considered. "Well. Nothing makes that girl happy any more, since you ask. I don't think even she herself knows why. Since the baby died."

"I guess we've sensed that. Your mom especially. You know, when you and Adele first married, she was such a bright thing. Always ready for anything. Glad to laugh. When you and me'd be out fishing on our boats, they'd have dinner together. Even meet during Adele's lunch break at the bank to go shopping. First just for stuff women like to get, then for baby clothes. Then that sweet little Amy when she came." Silence reigned for a time. Buck's voice turned husky when he resumed. "You think we didn't grieve too when Amy left us? Like the sunshine died with her."

"Sure changed everything. Adele won't let it go, either."

"Give her time."

"Been a year and a half. Ain't that time enough?"

"Ever think of having another?"

"Thought about it. Hasn't happened yet." Jones tried to seem gruff, make it sound like he wanted to drop the subject.

"I hate to say this, but your mom and I've talked about it more than once. We think that maybe Ketchikan's too much of a reminder. That you ought to move."

"Leave you folks?"

"We're not your duty, boy. Don't mean we couldn't visit back and forth—I'm not saying you should move to Japan."

"She sometimes talks about packing it down to the States, where her parents are retired. But leave the boats? Not a chance I'd do that." Jones stopped. "Guess we ought to get some sleep."

"Then don't crowd me out, boy," Buck said almost merrily. "Stay on your side."

"Shove over a little yourself, Dad."

Jones and Buck had finished their delivery. Around the scow's mug-up table, although they now talked easily again between themselves, they remained taciturn when others tried to start conversations. But the scow's deckhand came down to address Jones. "Swede's on the radio topside. Asked if you were aboard to talk." Jones went up in silence.

In the radio room, Swede's voice crackled over the airwaves, "Are you and your father okay, I hope, Jones?"

"Managing."

"Then, Jones. I think that my plane has located something off Egegik that has been left by the tide. Near a beach camp. If I stop the plane now by the scow, will you come with me to investigate?" Jones hesitated. He asked Swede to hold a minute and went below to consult his old man. Buck told him he should go. "I'll tie astern here and wait for you to come back. Won't mind a sleep. Don't worry, boy, I won't go fishing without you."

Far down the bay in a marsh near the camp, two bodies had washed ashore at low tide. "Not what you want to see," warned one of the beach fishermen as he lifted the tarp that someone had used to cover the bloated forms.

Jones nodded without emotion. No mistaking Nick and Luke, although their cheeks had been chewed out by some sea predator. "At least you got 'em before the fuckin' gulls pecked their eyes."

"Probably because they washed up face down. Everything feeds on something, don't it?"

No worse than seeing buddies what have been blown apart, Jones kept telling himself. No worse. He took the canvas to cover their faces himself and nodded affirmation to Swede.

"I'll send instructions by radio," said Swede. "Fly down two employees to wrap the bodies and transport them back to the cannery to be shipped home."

"Do it myself. Now."

Swede considered. "Okay then, Jones. They're ours. We'll do it together."

In the week that followed that of the failed strike and the drownings, Gus Rosvic continued to pass Jones Henry by without so much as a word. The Rosvics fished their engine boat somewhere else in the Bay system, and back at the cannery they kept to a quiet group of other would-be strikers in a far corner of the mess hall. A relief. No more goading and grinning. And with it, no hints that an engine boat and the different keel that came with it might have kept a certain boat from capsizing. But now Jones would have welcomed banter—even the kind that drove him nuts with frustration and annoyance—from someone who had shared in war and death. During one meal, Jones watched Swede walk over and speak in a friendly fashion to the failed strikers. Jones himself kept away. *Fuck it.* Let Gus get over his burn and make the move if he wanted to.

Jones and his dad didn't make the return to the bar and channel where they had watched the Sandstol boat and its two men get swept away. "Other water to fish," muttered Buck, but Jones needed no rationalization. The next Saturday at the cannery mess hall, Gus, at last, walked over from his distant table. "Was them, huh?"

Jones looked up cautiously. "Yup."

"Bummer."

"Yup."

After a pause, Gus offered, "Got a bottle. Want to help drink it?"

Jones rose, relieved. "Suits me." Without further talk they walked outside into the rain. At the end of a long building that faced only scrub, they kicked

aside the weeds that had grown under the overhang of corrugated roof and settled in. Water dripped only on their outstretched brogans. Beyond observation.
Gus unscrewed the cap on the whiskey, took a swig, then passed it to Jones.

They shared the burning liquid back and forth as the bottle emptied.
Neither spoke while their thoughts blurred. Both wept, but with enough
self-control not to show it, even through their swimming minds. Eventually
Gus cleared his throat and ventured, "Kodiak. You been there?"

"What for?"

"Action. All kinds of stuff. Big crabs even. Especially big crabs. They
say." Jones took a moment to absorb this. A mosquito whined by his ear. He
slapped at the side of his head—under the relaxing influence of the whiskey,
he was too slow each time to hit his ear just right and get the bugger. Soon,
anyhow, more mosquitoes nipped than he could slap.

"Like I said, man. Kodiak's got action."

"Got action enough in Ketchikan. Adele crying all the time. Now my
dad on my tail."

"That Adele's a good woman."

"Did I say different? Just don't know what she wants. Ever since the poor
baby died. Move to another place, mebbe? Think that'll change things?"

"Change for both of you, asshole!"

"Adele says . . . California. But not for me."

"Like a woman! But Kodiak's got fish! More fish than . . . Bigger fish.
Soaker halibut! Big crabs, I don't know man! Everything action out there."

"I dunno."

"Tell you what. Screw that company plane what expects to take us home
to Ketchikan. Instead, we take a plane home by way of Kodiak."

"What for, say again?" Through the haze, Jones tried to give it some
thought. "Oh. Mebbe. Why not? Got more of that stuff?"

Gus laughed with some of his usual good nature. "Not for you. We got
our money's worth." He held up the empty glass bottle that held only the
dregs and tossed it into the rain.

PART THREE

24

JACKSON POLLOCK IN TOKYO

JULY 1951

"Your trip beyond Anchorage was not authorized," Itaru Sasaki snapped, after he'd recovered from the sight of a respectful, but grinning, Kiyoshi Tsurifune. Kiyoshi had overtaken him at the Chicago airport. Both now waited for the connecting flight home to Tokyo via Seattle. "Our company had no concerns in New York. I am your senior—how am I to explain it? Don't expect your sponsors or your government to pay for your vacation."

"I understand."

"What an extravagance. You must be wealthy."

"It was my personal expense."

"For two days, three days? No way to understand why you'd go to that place when I was already here in Washington dealing with these people. Why didn't you stay in Alaska where you'd been sent?"

"My work there was accomplished."

"Work is never finished. And what's that you're carrying?" Indeed, Kiyoshi was cradling a large, flat parcel, and he gripped it nonchalantly at Sasaki-san's inquiry. It sounded almost like an accusation.

"A painting."

"Pictures enough to be had in Tokyo for anyone so foolish as to pay money for them!" Kiyoshi knew he had overstepped his mission and would probably be called to account. There was no need to make this worse than it was. Yet in spite of himself he said, "Original abstract expressionist paint-ing by the famous artist Willem de Kooning! Original! No other like it, you see. There would be nothing like it in Tokyo." He didn't bother to add that any work by Jackson Pollock had now become too expensive for his limited means. Nor that the newly-popular de Kooning—while only part American—had, by his presence in New York, helped make this city the hub of the art world.

"Ah. So, cleverly, you'll sell this picture in Japan for a high price?"

"I'll keep it for my own pleasure."

"You were sent to America—at great expense—to examine and arrange for the purchase of fish in Alaska. Certainly not for pictures in New York City."

"But, however!" Kiyoshi had begun to understand how often consent rested on persuasion, and he'd rehearsed his words for days. "We're forced to understand Americans in order to make them willing to do business with us. Not only with fish. I was exploring other ways into the strange American understanding. When I meet with Americans, I'll now have one of their famous artists to talk about in addition to fish."

"Hah!"

"As, also, knowledge of their New York City. I can speak of the Empire State Building. And the Statue of Liberty, which is of great importance to Americans." Kiyoshi decided not to mention the Museum of Modern Art that he had visited twice in as many days. But, with Sasaki's "Well . . ." he knew he had the man's grudging attention.

"It is many hours before our connecting flight to Seattle and then Tokyo. Could I suggest that, for informational purposes again, I take a taxicab to now observe some of the streets of Chicago? Every great city has famous sights. It will provide much conversation when we meet with Americans." He tried not to sound at all eager. "I can do this without inconvenience to you and report back all details."

Mr. Sasaki made a show of considering before he spoke. "Well . . . then I too shall go! We won't leave the taxicab for any reason and shall return here quickly. This Chicago is famous all over the world for gangsters. It will be interesting to see safely from a vehicle."

Gone was the chance to rush into the famous Chicago Art Museum for a few minutes! But still, Kiyoshi realized, even a glimpse of the city was better than nothing. And indeed, perhaps they might see Chicago gangsters as in American movies with the famous Edward G. Robinson!

By now, Kiyoshi had become accustomed to the sight of great American cities untouched by destruction. Chicago turned out to be a metropolis almost as lordly as New York. It was bordered by a great circle of waterfront. Nothing they saw suggested crime or even destruction. Sunlight gleamed over the vast water and reflected on windows in tall, handsome buildings.

"They stayed safe enough, you see," muttered Sasaki. "No atomic bombs fell here."

"Yes, I see," said Kiyoshi respectfully. To himself he remembered the promises made in the name of the Emperor. Made with true conviction, made from his own lips and those of soldiers under him as they survived jungle rot and the filth of a cave. Promises that the downtrodden cities of the weak, decadent Americans would be leveled in punishment. They would retaliate against the Americans' arrogant opposition to Japan's march toward destiny. So far in the past!

For the Japanese soldier, the promise of that destiny had meant sacrifice after sacrifice, while they ate food crawling with insects and diluted with sawdust. Without first American science and then the victor's generosity, Kiyoshi would still be living on sawdust, or maimed or dead. His parents would be destitute. You too, Sasaki-san. You'd also be dead or still picking lice, rather than dressed cleanly and waiting for our next meal to be served on washed dishes. But for those two terrible bombs. And now, thanks to the power of the Americans who needed Japan in the fight against the Communists in Korea, wasn't Japan becoming stronger again by the day? Sasaki wasn't thinking.

At the Seattle airport they waited for the long flight home across the ocean. Kiyoshi feasted his eyes on the men and women who walked past down the long, pristine hallways. Some seemed to be gentlemen and were dressed prosperously—others looked more rugged, carrying heavy knapsacks and lining up for voyages to places bearing names unpronounceable. No place in America seemed ordinary!

"Don't wander," Sasaki warned. "Our plane might decide to leave early."
He kept his eyes fixed on a sign behind the checkout counter that read:
SEATTLE-HONOLULU-TOKYO: ON TIME.

"We have more than two hours before we must go aboard." Sasaki shook
his head.

"No time is soon enough." He glanced around and switched to speaking
Japanese. Still, he lowered his voice until it was nearly inaudible. "Keepers
of world-famous fishing grounds that they refuse to share—even though all
they eat is beefsteak while Japanese starve for seafood!" His jowls quivered.
"Their greasy food has given me indigestion for days!"

Kiyoshi found his attention drifting from Sasaki-san's diatribe. Suddenly,
he remembered the caresses that awaited him from his wife Miki—at home,
after their initial formal greeting. Perhaps a spontaneous hug from his little
son Shoji. "Do not worry," he said, firmly. "We won't miss that plane."

At the Tokyo airport, a car with a driver and two senior officials, who
Kiyoshi knew as Yoshihide Namamura and Hajimi Itai, waited to take
Sasaki-san and Kiyoshi into the city as soon as they cleared customs.
Kiyoshi held onto his wrapped painting while the driver thumped their
bags into the rear, before resting it carefully himself atop their suitcases with the admonition that the object was fragile. He spoke with
such straight-backed authority that the driver saluted automatically.
Then Kiyoshi took his place inside the car, with suitable deference to the
senior men around him.

After they had settled in, Namamura, who sat in the front passenger
seat, turned around and demanded, "Well. We're anxious for your news, so
we decided to meet you ourselves rather than wait for the formal briefing."
His bald head glistened, and with his dark suit, he was grave enough in bearing to take charge even without his apparent seniority.

Sasaki settled back. "Willfulness unchecked, sir, as with all Americans.
And their food, mostly grease and raw flavors."

"Yes, yes, we know all that. Not what you went for."

Sasaki continued, "But they need us. People at their State Department
assure me that enough members of their Congress have agreed. Aleutian
fishing waters will be reopened to Japan."

"We assumed this would happen eventually, since they need us in Korea. What we hoped for was to speed up the process. Our vessels with nets for salmon are ready to leave immediately. I've seen to it that the fishery's organized for maximum productivity."

"Americans are slow, sir, when it comes to their selfish interests. As I understand it, with their process we can't expect to have Japanese fishing vessels back in Aleutian waters before next June."

"Bah!"

Kiyoshi listened with mixed feelings. Americans had so many facets. So many interests. Perhaps the delay would provide an excuse for Kiyoshi to be sent back—if he kept the trust and goodwill of the men in the car. Thus, he reacted audibly with the rest.

"All right, now. And you, Kiyoshi Tsurifune?"

Kiyoshi told them, making it sound as positive as possible, that the famous red salmon of Bristol Bay were in short abundance this year, as they had been in the year previous. Also the entire fishery was in transition, with boats converting from sail to engine while the labor unions called strikes and caused discontent.

"With respect, then, this is a year of commotion in Bristol Bay. We should proceed with caution until they settle their own problems, so that they don't direct their outbursts of anger toward us. Out on the water, however, some vessels now freeze salmon for shipment to canneries further south. Cannery people do not appear hostile to selling Japan such products—if we can pay and provide a market."

"Good. Good."

Kiyoshi considered, then added—hoping it would sound positive: "Some fishermen themselves don't appear happy to see Japanese. However . . ." He decided to keep to himself the sense that American fishermen, like other Americans, were aggressive and sometimes violent in their independence. "However, I myself, speaking English, found many fishermen friendly. They need more contact with us, to understand our need. This is one of the reasons I've worked hard to learn English. On my part, I—"

"Pah! Fishermen don't matter," Namamura snapped. "They'll do as they're told, like common workers."

"That is certainly true," said Sasaki automatically.

"No no no. Not necessarily," said Hajimi Itai, seated beside Kiyoshi in the back of the car. He was lean, with a full head of hair. The glasses that made him appear studious also made him seem more thoughtful than his colleagues. "We should try to gain the good opinion of even common Americans, because they too vote and sometimes their leaders listen to them. I've made it my business to study this. You started to say something further, Tsurifune-san?"

Kiyoshi turned to address the astute Itai-san specifically. "It would be wise for us to know Americans and their culture. Thus, as I've said, I've worked to learn and speak English. While Sasaki-san was dealing with officials in the great capital of Washington, DC, and wisely examining their culture and monuments . . ." He glanced at Sasaki on his other side and was rewarded with a cautious nod. "I myself traveled to their largest city of New York, second in influence to Washington, DC, to observe another part of America's culture. Their Statue of Liberty, the famous Broadway, the notorious Wall Street. Even," Kiyoshi paused, embarrassed, "even their Museum of Modern Art. To increase our ability to understand Americans."

"Did I hear correctly?" growled Namamura in the front seat. "This was not part of your mission. Sasaki-san, you are the senior. Why did you allow it?"

"Questionable initiative," interrupted Itai. "But interesting. Perhaps going to New York for perspective was a good idea."

"Huh. Only perhaps," Namamura grunted.

"I did not—" began Sasaki. He turned from Namamura to Itai, blinked, and caught himself. "Yes. Yes, interesting. I . . . felt that . . . since Tsurifune-san spoke English and appears to be a good observer . . . since he had gathered all pertinent information in Bristol Bay . . . and was willing to pay his own expenses." He glanced sharply at Kiyoshi, who nodded him on. "Thus, in order to gain extra knowledge—perhaps useful in negotiation, without extra expense . . ."

"Still far from the mission," Namamura snapped.

"But interesting. Interesting," Itai repeated.

Itai-san's comment gave Kiyoshi the impetus to continue. "Then, as Mr. Sasaki and I were returning home, we together made a rapid taxi ride through their great central metropolis of Chicago. For impressions. In time otherwise wasted—as we would have been waiting in the airport between plane flights. Again to better engage in future negotiation."

Itai nodded. "Not planned, but perhaps it could prove useful."

"We felt so." Sasaki nodded relieved approval across at Kiyoshi.

"But you were not sent to gather impressions," Namamura insisted. "Did you collect any facts that we could not have found by reading a book?"

Itai shrugged. "In the West, I understand that impressions sometimes matter more than facts. And that interesting flat package you brought with you from America, Tsurifune-san. Am I to hope perhaps that those are Alaska charts with sea-depths for our edification?"

Why did that not occur to me! Kiyoshi chastised himself. Aloud, he said meekly, "No, sir. Only a modern American painting. I had hoped it might give me something to speak with Americans about."

"Bought with his own money," interjected Sasaki.

"The true insubordination here, Sasaki-san," said Namamura, "is that you allowed Tsurifune-san to go outside his mission without authority from Tokyo."

Mr. Itai intervened again. "Too bad. Not one hundred percent on the mission. But Tsurifune-san's actions may indeed prove useful. And at his own expense. So let us forget it." They drove for a while in silence. Kiyoshi, stuck in the middle seat between Sasaki and Itai, stared out the window on Itai's side. He was relieved, but avoided looking at Sasaki.

Rice stalks and hedgerows hemming the wetted fields were all in green, as were the trees in leaf, and the farm houses alongside showed fresh paint and red tile roofs—intact—that gleamed under the sun. Little remained of the desolation he had witnessed on the trains back from the war only half a dozen years before. Even the farmers who bent over the green shoots in one of the paddies seemed to be wearing brighter clothes. But for the quick ending of that war—by whatever means—the fields and houses he watched might still be a battleground, with Kiyoshi himself crouched somewhere in that mud.

"American painting eh?" Mr. Itai turned to face him again. He appeared both brusque and amused. "Of fishing vessels? Skyscrapers? Prostitutes? Their gangsters?"

"Abstract, sir. Nothing specific," Kiyoshi replied, then continued with fervor, "Shapes and colors that lead the viewer to his own impressions. By a famous artist in a new style influenced by American energy."

"Interesting. You'll show it to us please, when we arrive. Perhaps we'll learn something useful from it. The world's changing. Young people have grown bolder—even in Japan. Perhaps they need to if they must deal with people outside of their own country."

Kiyoshi spent the rest of the drive into Tokyo concentrating on what more he could say to this official who had the flexibility to grasp matters beyond his indoctrination. He himself began to believe that he had traveled to acquire the exciting and vital new American art as a part of his mission.

Back in his home town at last, Kiyoshi's greeting upon entering his house was all he could have wished for. Little Shoji ran forward and clutched his legs. And Miki, although now the modern woman who managed the Tsurifune company office, greeted him with a smiling low bow while dressed in a traditional flowered silk kimono. Kiyoshi's own eyes filled with emotion and happiness at his return.

Later, a few houses away, his welcome was far more mixed. His mother bowed while she wept happily. And at first Father—seated on the tatami but with legs now too weak to rise without effort—stretched out his arms. Kiyoshi had been absent only a few weeks, including the preliminary conference time in Tokyo, but he had indeed crossed the greatest ocean and traveled where none of his family had ever so much as considered going before.

But then his father straightened and frowned. "What is this I've just learned from Tokyo? Without agreement, it appears that you left Alaska to travel to New York—across the country. Without agreement you abandoned your mission. Have you become so influenced by American ways that, without permission from those who sent you, you acted on your own?"

"At my own expense, Father. Money I've saved year by year."

"Irrelevant! How am I to justify this to the others?"

Kiyoshi considered, debated with himself, then declared with a boldness that he had never before used with his father, "I did no harm. You can say that in America I acted like an American would have done." Mother clapped a hand to her mouth. "To better understand Americans with whom we wish to do business, Father," Kiyoshi added, suddenly anxious in spite of himself.

After a silence, his father said in a quiet voice, "The owners are all waiting to hear of your mission. We'll meet today, at once."

Kiyoshi felt relief, followed by a surge of confidence. "Let me first collect my thoughts, Father. Forgive me. Let us meet tomorrow."

Next day the assembled vessel owners listened gravely to Kiyoshi's report of the information he had gained regarding American red salmon fishing in Bristol Bay, Alaska. Some of the six nodded in support—even now his father, who held authority as the oldest among them, and his father-in-law Munio Nitta who fumbled with his cane. Others, especially the aggressive Mr. Susumu Nojiri, were overtly impatient. Nojiri glowered and shook his head as Kiyoshi went on to explain—picking his words from what Mr. Sasaki of the Japan foreign office had told him on the plane ride home—that only after another year of high level negotiation could they expect Japanese fishing vessels to be permitted again in American waters off Alaska.

"The American State Department wishes it," Kiyoshi explained. "However, many citizens do not. Sasaki-san tells me he'll say this in his formal report. Many citizens were soldiers and have not forgotten the war. An example. A former soldier whom I encountered, now a respected fisherman—"

Susumu Nojiri contained himself no longer. "Facts, facts, young Tsurifune—not impressions!" Nojiri was a big man—once fuller-bodied, but now the shoulders of his jacket slumped. As a former trawlerman in American waters and a man of samurai descent, he considered himself the greatest authority in the group. "Oh yes. We saw their soldiers during the occupation." He glared. "I am speaking among colleagues or I wouldn't be so blunt. American soldiers who ate-ate-ate while we watched them hungrily. Well. So now they leave us to starve another year! Not enough sea product off Japan to feed us, but that makes no difference to the Americans. I've heard they even object to eating whales for nourishment. They feast on cow and pig. How would they understand?"

Munio Nitta cleared his throat for attention. "Then allow me also to be blunt among colleagues. We might have gone hungry for a time. But after a few months, they did not let us starve. Let us recognize that." Kiyoshi

knew that his respected father-in-law, sometimes acerbic in his own home—
perhaps from the loss of his oldest daughter from wartime privation—now
strove to be reasonable when no one inflamed him. Father Nitta had regained
enough flesh in the six years since the war to have a face now rounded and
a disposition no longer despairing, although a cane remained by his side.
"Remember that after the first terrible months they let our vessels fish again
in water close to Japan." Nitta glanced around hastily. "Not that Americans
understand us."

"How could they?" Shoichi Hosono snapped. "But you're correct, Nitta-
san." He was bony and shrewd-eyed, in control except that his lip twitched
when he became too excited and had more to say than he could get out
in time. "Yes, yes. Only logical. Therefore yes! No! Therefore, no indeed!
The truth was, at last, they did not want the burden of too many starving.
Therefore, they were only being logical, to open a few fishing waters that
mattered to them not at all."

Hitoshi Uchimura, the former clerk turned vessel owner, rose to inter-
rupt. "Please face the truth, gentlemen." He looked around cautiously.
"Forgive my observation, but we're dealing with the victors." After a silence,
Nojiri made a gesture of annoyed dismissal, while bony Hosono's lip twitched
even more under a face that otherwise went blank. Compared against the
lean frames of the others, Uchimura was fat, but he moved with alacrity
despite his girth. During the years since the war he had gained confidence
despite the disgrace of once being caught selling village food—the best fish
in the village set net—on the black market.

"My colleagues! We'll survive only by being realistic." Uchimura's
tone commanded the others' attention. "First accept the truth. If we were
weak enough to lose, our leaders should never have made an attack on
Americans. They failed to understand this." He looked around hastily. "Not
the fault of our Emperor, of course. But nevertheless. We must now deal
with Americans on their own terms. Although perhaps not forever."

Tsurifune senior stroked his mustache—still modeled after the
Emperor's—and looked down at the table. Since Uchimura's disgrace,
Father had dealt with the man only at a distance. Of course, such a man
might now disparage Japan's failed heroic effort to deliver Asia from the
Western armies. The others stayed silent. "Thus," Uchimura declared,
"Making such war was immoral since we failed to win it. Our leaders

lied. That's the truth we must accept." Father shook his head, while Nojiri snapped, "Not to be spoken!"

"Not the fault of our Emperor, of course," Uchimura repeated hastily. "But we must face it. Our leaders led us on, then humiliated us. Thus, we must now make terms with the enemy as best we can."

Nojiri rapped a fist on the table. "Don't talk of this further," he muttered.

Tsurifune Senior looked up suddenly. "As you know, one of my sons died heroically, fighting this enemy we now call friend. But Americans have been generous."

"I agree." The forty-year-old Muritaka Tamai, who had served as an officer in Manchuria, broke his usual brooding silence. "And not your son alone, Yuichiro-san. Even the youngest here have carried ashes in sorrow and humiliation. As you know, I myself survived the war to find that my honored father had been taken by police, never to be seen again. Our Emperor wouldn't have permitted such a thing if the military hadn't stolen his power."

They all fell silent once more. Uchimura allowed time for his colleagues to regain their composure. "The past is over. Let us plan. This is why we're here. We sent young Tsurifune to observe for us, so we'll hear what he has to tell us. Never fear." He nodded meaningfully to them all. "When we're finally let back into American waters we'll make up for lost time."

"Well, at least you're thinking ahead instead of toward the past," conceded Hosono. "Wisely. Good. We must think ahead."

Uchimura rubbed the sides of his jacket, smoothing wrinkles to reveal his girth. "All the Americans care about is salmon and halibut. This is common knowledge, eh? They don't care for crab except what comes from a can, or for the smaller fish in their waters that can make more common food or fish paste. There lies our fortune and future."

"Concerning crabs, I must tell you," Kiyoshi began. "I overheard—"

Nojiri interrupted. "So long as they don't disturb a Bering Sea ground that one of my boats discovered before the war. It had great mountains of those big crabs. One of my colleagues in Tokyo now has a vessel allowed to catch them in the Sea of Okhotsk alongside the Russians. He puts the meat into those cans you speak of. Sells it around the world under the clever label 'Geisha' and calls it 'King Crab.'" He shared an appreciative chuckle with Uchimura for its aptness to attract buyers in the West. Kiyoshi ventured again to speak of the new American interest in such king crabs that he had heard of toward the end of his stay.

Uchimura spoke over him. "Let me finish, young Tsurifune. If, I say, we leave them their salmon and halibut—we'll buy their red salmon from Bristol Bay out of necessity, for a while at least—but if we leave the Americans those two species alone, then we'll have all the rest. Don't you understand? The crabs and the bottom fish I mean, of course." Some of the others grunted their approval.

"Their fish trawlers are of negligible size," Uchimura continued. "And Americans have no experience in the successful canning of crab meat. It doesn't interest them. Our Geisha brand is world famous for its taste and quality and so Japan will control that market again. And where are these vast schools of smaller fish and those big crabs for future harvest? In the American Bering Sea, ignored! Waiting for the day when they let us back into those waters."

"Waters that my vessels are now impatient to enter!" declared Nojiri.

Uchimura nodded assent. "Therefore, you see, Nojiri-san and others here, we must keep urging our diplomats further and be patient. The Americans have lost themselves in a new war with our Korean neighbor and they need Japan's landing fields. They need our goodwill and support. We'll have their waters back soon if we don't upset them by appearing too urgent. Eh?"

Tsurifune senior rapped on the table to gain their attention. Uchimura deferred to him and concluded his message with: "So. Thus my . . . respectful urgings."

"My colleagues," began Tsurifune senior. As the eldest and most composed of the council, he was able to take his time without worry of interruption. He removed his thick glasses, wiped them, and replaced them, holding their attention despite his trembling hands. "My son Kiyoshi traveled to America to represent our interests. From our conversations since his return, I wish to inform you, he's not only talked to the people of the fisheries but has absorbed much information about American tastes and character that we may in future put to use." He looked around, almost defiantly. "Information. Not mere impressions."

Munio Nitta had stirred in silence since venturing a positive word for the American occupation. Yet suddenly he grasped his cane and faced his son-in-law. "Everybody knows Americans gobble beef, not fish. I'm surprised you didn't notice that. Instead of running off to buy a picture that doesn't make sense. Oh yes—your wife, my daughter, showed it to me. Yet, being a faithful wife to her husband, she tried to tell me what a good picture it was despite the truth before my very eyes."

"Let us stick to the point," snapped Nojiri. The aggressive former fisherman hunched over a paper in his hand. "I have here harvest statistics. And I must disagree with Uchimura-san when he suggests that we leave red salmon to the Americans. Perhaps leave them local Native catching and initial processing if we can then buy the product from them cheaply, but not the market. Yuichiro Tsurifune, your son went to inquire about the Japanese purchase of red salmon caught by Americans. Clearly we should find a way into this prosperous fishery. And I wish to hear what he has to tell us."

"No, no," persisted Nitta. "Now that I've started let me finish. Kiyoshi-kun, young man. You're my respected son-in-law but, however! My daughter has told me." He turned to the father. "Yuichiro Tsurifune, I spoke earlier today with Mr. Itaru Sasaki, whom your son accompanied. Oh yes, I spoke to him in Tokyo by telephone. Your son is entranced by American paintings that don't even look like living creatures. Do you call that the American understanding, young man? Perhaps they've been so much affected by bodies dismembered by their atomic bombs that they can't even look and see a complete human being anymore! As for me, please give me something comprehensible to see, even if it is only a humble fish or crab!"

Kiyoshi bowed his head, uncertain how to reply. Indeed, as he reflected, Miki had at first nodded gravely at the splendid de Kooning painting, but had then sucked in her breath—a hand clapped to her mouth—when she learned that the price he'd paid for it had taken much of their savings. Before Kiyoshi could answer for himself, Uchimura declared: "Yes, yes, Nitta-san, interesting. But we've met to discuss other matters. Let us hear from young Tsurifune about the Americans, since he went there on our behalf. To start, tell me, young man. What are Americans like in their homeland? Eh?"

Relieved, Kiyoshi bowed and began his narrative. "Americans may be strange to us in many ways. But I found most of them generous." He thought of the hostile man named Jones Henry, who had been his savior on distant Okinawa. "Although sometimes they can be angry. Rough even—at least among workmen, who are, incidentally, not ignorant and stupid like our own." He looked from one to another. They did not seem impressed. "But please listen. I believe that they're now investigating those large crabs! I heard talk of this."

"Exactly what I was urging you to hear from my son," Tsurifune Senior declared. Another silence. Again, Uchimura took the initiative.

"Bad news. Well. We cannot control their encroaching on grounds that we once fished exclusively. These are American waters, after all. But before our negotiators win us the right to fish off Alaska once more, we should know the extent of these operations."

Nojiri pounded his fist on the table. "Tell them that historically it was the Japanese who have processed these crabs into canned meat, and it should be left to us!"

"With respect, sir. That would make Americans all the more eager to learn the process and do it themselves!" Kiyoshi's sudden boldness astonished both himself and the others. Even more surprising, the seniors at the table didn't challenge his right to speak.

Uchimura raised a hand for attention. "Young Tsurifune may understand Americans better than some of us." He considered. "Perhaps our best chance is to prove we can do it better than they can. And thus keep their good will and keep the crab market for as long as possible." He paused. "Then, as it will probably happen, once the Americans learn to find and process the crabs that were once ours, we will still retain our rightful share of the market." Another pause. "In all matters be realistic. We're in a world that changes year by year, my colleagues. To survive, we must be friendly and understanding—like young Tsurifune has been trying to say—to keep all that we can." He surveyed their grave faces. "Control by military conquest is no longer our option."

After a silence, Tsurifune Senior said, "Very well. Then give us your frank opinion, Uchimura."

Uchimura acknowledged with a nod. "All the more reason to be friendly to them, then. Friendly and generous may also suggest that they are easy to persuade. We need their fishing waters. And, worst case, at least their markets to buy and sell. So we'd better forget our memories of American

Imperialism and concentrate on this generosity that our young Tsurifune has spoken of. I, for one, would be willing to send him again to America on our behalf. We must learn more about their interest in crab and whether or not it truly grows." He looked around in challenge.

Both Nojiri and Hosono signaled assent, while Tsurifune Senior inclined his head to acknowledge his son's endorsement.

Kiyoshi could not conceal his surprise. At last, the words he had not dared to hope for!

Uchimura turned to Kiyoshi. "Now, perhaps, you would show me this American painting Nitta-san speaks of. Yes, gentlemen," he continued, with a hint of a smile. "Do not suppose I am uncultured because I deal in fish."

25

PROSPECTING KODIAK

JULY 1951

As July drew to a close, Jones and Buck Henry did their part to help in the shutdown of the Bristol Bay cannery for the season. *Bum year all around*, Jones thought. At least their run money for setting up and closing down was guaranteed. Their gang moved crates of canned fish from the storeroom to the cargo ship. Gus and some of the others with engine boats worked another part of the shutdown. Swede had kept them on with no hard feelings.

"We could stay a while longer and fish for silvers," ventured Buck Henry. "Course I'm getting to miss your mother, and there's Adele waiting for you."

"Adele's always waiting these days. Hard even to catch your breath around her."

Buck turned grave. "She's your lady, boy. Yours however she acts. Remember what we talked about?"

"Well, Gus is on me to go look further west. Like Kodiak. Might be opportunity, if you come too."

"Me? I'm settled. But they say Kodiak's where the action is, for a young guy like yourself. And for a wife who needs to meet new people who don't remind her of things.

"Don't want to leave you and Mom behind."

Buck grunted as he heaved a crate from the floor. "Way it has to be, I suppose. It's Alaska, at any rate. Unless you want her to drag you down to California where her folks are retired." He raised an eyebrow at Jones. "Yeah, that got your attention, didn't it?"

Jones Henry looked around him at the busy Kodiak airport. There were men with cased rifles, others with hip boots strapped across their rucksacks, many in navy uniform, and even some fellows in suits and ties. There were few women.

"Fleet must be in town," Jones observed.

"You sure are ignorant," Gus laughed, his sly grin back in place. "There's a big naval base on Kodiak Island—just a few miles down the road. Kodiak town's in the other direction, where we're headed. Of course, since I was in the navy, I pay attention to such things." He puffed out his chest. "Looked it up. You Marines just went where they sent you."

"We went ashore and took care of things, while you navy goldbricks waited in clean bunks for the all clear."

"Waited close in to give you cover. Dodged shore barrage. Some of us got sunk."

Jones shrugged. "At least you sunk in water, not fuckin' mud."

The airport shuttle to town followed a paved road. Mountain slopes rose on one side and open water lay on the other. Unlike the tree-bordered waterways around Ketchikan, sheltered bays here stretched beyond land points into the open sea, where sun sparkled on ripples. The light silhouetted an array of boats pitching on various courses.

"Whole fleets for all kinds of fish and crabs you don't get down south," muttered Gus. "They say."

"Guess we're free to look. Stop crowding."

"Then shift and give me the window."

"Not with your head, all that hair in the way," Jones shot back. Then, "Some of them boats are longer by a length than ours in Ketchikan."

"For halibut longline. Mostly run by Squareheads from Seattle, I hear."

"You sure know a lot about this place."

Gus tapped one of his sideburns. "I talk to people. Don't just keep myself company."

"Bar time, you mean. Don't have a wife who expects you home."

"For good or bad, buddy." The shuttle deposited them on a paved street beyond the piers.

"Come on," Jones said, trying to keep the eagerness out of his voice. "Let's walk back to the boats."

"Easy, Jones. Let's check out the burg a minute first."

Jones trailed grudgingly. Kodiak appeared less of a *place* than Ketchikan, but it beat Naknek. Level ground stretched far enough beyond the main street to allow for a couple of parallel avenues before the land rose toward a steep hill. Gus and Jones strode past the usual supply shops, rugged clothing stores, and bars. But also, through a large salt-crusted window, they peered at an actual tablecloth restaurant—the sort Adele would jump for. If it didn't cost to the sky. Remember the place, if he decided this is where they'd want to settle—a place to argue against California. He examined the menu pasted on the glass. Prices about double that of a regular restaurant—one with counters. Worse than the fanciest place in Ketchikan. But if going fancy couldn't be avoided, at least they served a reliable choice of steaks and salmon with salad thrown in for the same price. And other things. "Something called 'Crab Louis.'" Jones pronounced it with a hard "s." "Ever hear of that?"

"You poor dumb-ass," Gus sneered good-naturedly. "They call that 'Crab Loo-ie.' It's French. Crab with a fancy pink kind-of sauce. I had it once, down in Seattle. Not so bad."

"She'd go for that, however it tasted." Jones looked up and down. "Likes fancy things." He turned from the window to stare down the street, his arm clapped over his forehead to block out the sun. "Buildings newer than in Ketchikan, mebbe. Not as many. I don't know. One thing that woman likes is stores."

"Does she cook you a good dinner?"

"Now and then."

"Then stop bitching."

Jones turned restless. "Why're we here instead of looking at the stuff that matters? Come on."

"Okay, okay. But you'd better look hard at this city stuff if you ever think that fine woman's going to follow you here."

Jones stopped to consider. "You're right. She's got to be happy some place." *Got to stop crying and forget our dead baby.*

The day had started out overcast, but by now the sun was blazing in a blue sky. Jones pointed through an alley toward a range of frame buildings. Above corrugated roofs, poked masts that glistened in the light. "That way now."

Back toward the airport and naval base stretched the gravel road they had passed coming into the town. It led to the wharves and fish plants. Jones steered them down among the buildings, ignoring an open bay where women in yellow aprons bunched around a long table heaped with fish. He turned in toward the water, relieved to be with boats—something he could understand. Even a quick glance showed that these were heavier boats than all but the best of those in Ketchikan. Built stronger to carry a heavier engine, most likely. They were even more weathered on the wooden surfaces where paint would have been scuffed and painted again. Their straking might be of thicker oak than the boats of Ketchikan too. Also their rails. But the rails were worn to the grain, a sign of heavier gear that was pulled in over them. The wheelhouses, too, seemed of more solid construction. Their seaward windows had thicker caulking—none of it cracked from age. Maintenance. Nothing careless and nothing left to chance.

Jones had a swift sickening vision of Nick Sandstol's double-ender floating empty, bottom-up. Of Nick's head bobbing up, then gone with the kid's. Needed a boat built to take it. And the right engine. Then bad weather wouldn't matter. Then let the worst come.

He looked across at a boat deck just below the pier planks. A man sat cross-legged, mending web. A wool watchcap was pulled to his ears, but he worked bare-chested under the sun. His right arm, half turned, showed part of a tattoo that looked like a Marine globe and insignia. *A man worth talking to*, Jones decided. *But don't spill over him all at once.*

The bunched net around the man appeared to be part of a bottom trawl rather than a seine, since it had bobbins and fatter leads. Tighter mesh than a purse seine and heavier than he himself had ever worked. Jones cleared his throat.

"Call that about a number ten twine, I'd judge," he ventured.

"You'd judge right." The man spoke around a cigar that dangled from his mouth, untouched by the hands working the net. His chin had several days' growth, enough to be black. An oilskin jacket and plaid shirt lay bunched beside him.

"Sun feels good, eh?" Jones continued.

"When it comes."

"Down where I fish in Ketchikan, it rains most of the time. Except mebbe August."

"Rained here this morning."

"That so?" After a silence, "Down there we don't need that thick of a twine." The man nodded without answering. Jones, usually taciturn himself, suddenly wanted information. Maybe Kodiak was the place for him after all. He realized that it was up to him to pump for it. "Down in Chatham Strait, we get pretty good blows. Mebbe forty–fifty knots, times."

The man spat out the remaining stub of his cigar, slowly licked his lips, then said, "Mister, out on the Albatross here, Albatross Bank, we'd call that a Sunday school blow."

Gus stood watching, and laughed. "Guess that says it! I'm going to look around." He sauntered off to peer through the open sliding door of a building adjacent to the pier.

Jones watched the net-mender for a time, then ventured, "We seined for reds up in Naknek just now. They run by here yet?"

"Red salmon come and gone over a month ago, out at Igvak. I'd be on to the pinks and silvers here now. If that's what I was doing."

Jones glanced at the reinforced wooden panels of the boat, lashed near the stern at each side. "Guess you're dragging."

"What it looks like, don't it?"

"Need a heavier engine than for seining, I judge. What power and make you got? And for what kind of fish?"

The man looked up. "You some kind of spy?"

Jones turned away, resentful, but embarrassed at his own boldness. "I'm a fuckin' fisherman like yourself. Was Marines too if you want to know. You can go to hell."

The man went back to his mending. He appeared to think it over, then called, "If you want, go see that live-box built into the water. Further down the dock. Go take a look if you want." Jones considered, then altered course to go where the man pointed.

He lifted a wire mesh lid fitted over weathered boards. At first all he saw was a surface of water reflecting sky. Then, dimly, a few inches down, he saw a round creature the size of a saucer. A thick bumpy arm ended in a claw. The creature circled in an easy motion and then disappeared into deeper water below.

"They teach you about them in Marine camp?"

"No place has crabs that big," Jones muttered. "So I don't know what I saw."

"Go grab one! Stop! Just kidding. Take that big net lying there, and dip way down to bring one of 'em up." Jones did as he was told. The net's metal rim scraped against the bodies of creatures that moved sluggishly out of sight. They had hard, slick shells to judge by the feel—massive ones. He finally trapped one and felt the weight of several pounds as he raised it to the surface. It was a crab all right, but it was bigger by far than any he'd ever seen. The main shell measured nearly a foot across.

"What do you feed these buggers to make 'em grow like this?" Jones exclaimed.

"They grow like that in deep water, buddy. No help from me. I hear the Japs used to catch them around here before we kicked their ass."

"They good to eat?"

"Well, the legs shake out meat by the hunk. Tubes of it! Three–five times thicker than from one of them Seattle Dungeness crabs. Got a restaurant in town that buys from me. They give those legs some French name and serve 'em at a high price. Cover 'em with some kind of pink or red stuff I hear, then don't mind charging for it. They say. Suits me, since I charge them more by the pound than for a prime salmon."

"Ever eaten any?"

"Not with some French name on it. But we boil one on the dock here now and then. It's definitely crab, but you can't eat much all at once. Leg meat's rich like butter. One of the boys said it reminds him of lobster from back East." He glanced at Jones and shrugged. "I might have been to Iwo and places, but never to Boston where they sell lobster."

"Iwo, eh?" Jones nodded slowly. "You own that boat?"

"Me and the government."

Jones hesitated before offering: "Did the Canal and Okie, myself."

The man studied Jones for the first time. "Huh. Well, then. You look over those crabs. King crabs we call 'em. Then come aboard and maybe I'll find us a drink somewhere."

"I've got a buddy here with me. He's snooping down the pier just now, but he's with me. He was only navy. But Pacific."

"Only navy. Too bad. But he's welcome too."

Jones took one of the creature's legs to pull it from the net. Its big claw at the end of the leg opened and closed sluggishly. Claws on the other of its eight legs snagged in the net, all in slow motion. Jones bent down and started to yank free a tangled claw.

"Careful, man! Those claws might not be snappers like the Seattle crabs, but let one close slow on your hand and you'll have less fingers than ten." Jones found himself laughing. Something he hadn't done for a while.

When, not long after, Jones and Gus jumped over the rail—not soberly leg by leg, as he would have done just hours before, but with a spirited leap— he declared by way of introduction, "Name's Henry, Jones Henry. And this here's Rosvic. Gus."

The hand that gripped his was appropriately large and firm. "Hoss is name enough for me." The man had put his wool shirt back on and had shoved the flaps into his dungarees. He hung his oilskin jacket neatly on a hook by the cabin, opened the wooden door, and gestured them inside. "Two steps down. Careful with your head." On entering himself, he removed his watch cap, releasing long blond hair tied up with a strip of red cloth.

"You're sure a hoss with a tail, Hoss," joked Gus.

"Keeps it out of my eyes, buddy. I always said when they'd shave my hair to the skin back there in the Pacific, that some day I'd see how long it could grow when I didn't need to worry about lice." He gestured grandly. "Just sit where you please."

The seating choices consisted of a single bench alongside the narrow table that filled the center of the cabin. One end of the bench adjoined a platform by the steering wheel; the opposite end crowded an oil stove radiating heat. There was a small sink opposite the stove, stacked with plates and cups in even rows. Above on each side was a pair of curtained bunks. Despite the cramped quarters, no woman could have kept the cabin in better order, Jones noted. Quite the opposite of his own boat cabin—and that was smaller by a few feet.

Hoss opened a cabinet above the sink and brought out a nearly full bottle of whiskey. Strips of black tape anchored the cap to the glass. "This ain't a drinking boat, fellahs. Nobody touches the stuff at sea or even at anchor. But here in port, tied secure, with crew ashore and probably boozed by now anyhow, just a shot won't hurt." He paused. "To tell the truth, sometimes I get . . . well . . . bad dreams." Hoss glared at Jones. "Things you can't forget, especially after everybody's stopped talking and gone to sleep."

"You know it," Jones said softly.

"I figured you might."

"Don't need to explain."

Hoss brought down glasses from a cupboard and poured a measured three fingers of the amber liquid into each. "Water over there for anybody who wants it." He replaced the bottle and shut the cabinet door. "Overdoin' it ain't my style. Too easy then to . . . you know?" He raised his glass, leaned over to clink both of theirs, and drained the whiskey in two rapid gulps. Jones glanced at Gus, shrugged, and followed suit. Gus laughed and raised his glass. "Okay, down the hatch!"

Jones's eyes watered and his throat burned. At least it appeared that Gus was having the same problem. He coughed and regained his voice. "Good stuff."

"Only one life. No use to drink shit." The whiskey spread warmth to every dark corner of Jones's body. He settled back. "You keep a shipshape place here, buddy."

"You know any other way, marine?"

"Sounds like you was a real ass-buster."

"Well, one thing the Marines taught me was standards!"

Jones thought it over before declaring with a cheerfulness he hadn't felt for a long time, "Good thing, standards."

"You know it."

"So . . ." Jones glanced around and, growing increasingly relaxed, leaned back against one of the lower bunks and put his hands behind his head. "Catching these big crabs, huh?"

Hoss glanced at Gus from under thick black eyebrows leveled to a scowl. "Not sure I trust Navy here with a secret."

Gus waved his hand in good humor. "Ever heard of navy honor, buddy? Trust me. We did the Pacific, too, you know."

"Yeah," muttered Jones with continued high spirits. "With a clean bed every night."

"The fact is . . ." Hoss stopped to study them, then wiped a hand across his forehead. "Fact is . . . navy transport once . . . It was taking us from one island to the next. Got torpedoed." He forced a laugh. "At least a foxhole don't sink under you."

They fell silent. Finally Jones cleared his throat. "Those are big crabs, like I was saying."

Hoss came back to life. "Yeah. Well. You see. Before the war, the Japs knew about these king crabs. Caught 'em. Shipped 'em home. Got rich on our American resources, since those Japs eat anything. Took us what?—four hard years to put a stop to that shit. Those years taken right out of my ass and yours. Now, them crabs belong to nobody but us."

"You can say that again!" The whiskey had turned Jones mellow. It wouldn't hurt, he thought, if this new buddy broke out the bottle again. He turned toward the cabinet. The guy's glance caught his, as if the man knew what he was thinking. Eyes turned sharp with lids compressed— the look lasted just seconds, before settling back into a cool gaze. Even the lips around his unshaven chin had tightened. *Leave be*, Jones decided on the instant. *This man needs space.* Bad stuff had been out there in the Jap-land Pacific—things one drink might help make bearable, but more could make them boil over. "Crabs are ours and you're catching 'em, eh?"

Hoss resumed with less hesitation. "There's this American fellow named Wakefield. Lowell Wakefield. He's got a special-built factory ship called *Deep Sea*. Scouting where the big crabs are. Mainly in the Bering. But he's got some of us prospecting around here, too. I've leased this little dragger instead of hitting the salmon at this time, like I'd be doing in other years. Call it a gamble. I never took a chance like this before. Always depended on the salmon run to see me through, you know? But . . . only got this one life."

Jones nodded. "You can say that again."

"The fact is, after I mustered out, I wasn't sure what I wanted for a couple of years. Figured I'd do something new and fuck if it don't work out. So I crewed one winter for Lowell aboard that dragger *Deep Sea*. Back in winter of '47. Bering Sea. Weather was a bitch most of the time. Wind usually up to a gale. On deck, twelve hour shifts. You'd bat ice off your shoulders and watch it blow like ashes out into those black waves. Not that I wasn't up to anything that came. We tried for both bottomfish and king crabs at first. Then hit a real field of these crabs. Saw the future, man."

Gus rose and happily bumped his fist against the overhead for emphasis. "Right on! That's the sort of reason why I sprung for an engine in Bristol Bay, buddy. Take the chance and go for it. Now Jones here—not saying he ain't finest kind, top notch. But he only wants for nothing to change."

"Bull." Jones said it with none of the heat he'd usually feel when cold sober. "Those crabs you have out there are big buggers," he mused. "Makes a right kind of handful, each one, when you grab him."

"You know it. Then think when you've got a whole drag of 'em aboard. They try to claw right through your boots. Pick each one from the net 'til your arms hurt."

"Whoo!" Gus exclaimed. "Guess I'd need another slug to handle that kind of crab!" He glanced toward the cabinet.

"Middle of the day, you asshole?" Jones exclaimed before Hoss could reply. "No thanks from both of us. This ain't the navy. We've got stuff here in town to do." He turned quickly to Hoss. "Now me. I wouldn't mind my arms to hurt from pitching crabs like that!"

Hoss grinned. He seemed relieved. "And what you just picked up outside was nothing. This is still the wrong season for big hauls. Crabs are just finished moulting. Those buggers will be nearly twice as full of meat by October–November if we leave 'em be now."

"Then why catch them now? You just showing off?"

"No harm to scout around and be prepared. That's what I'm doing. Sure, we sell what we catch for whatever it brings—they still have meat, don't they? Get restaurants interested in the product. Lowell says the meat packs well in cans, but whole legs frozen in their shells go to fancy restaurants for a better price. I'm talking about the future!"

"I guess I wouldn't mind fishing them things. Never seen crabs like that down in Ketchikan."

Hoss sized him up, took in his muscular appearance, then nodded. "I'm one man short. A guy just quit last week to crew salmon with his brother. I'd pay you half a crew share till I saw you knew the gear and could stand up to it. Not that a Marine couldn't take anything that comes. Make it two-thirds."

To Gus's laughing amazement, Jones held out his hand to shake with Hoss. "What about your wife back home, asshole?"

"Adele's a fine girl. You tell her if she can't do without me for a little while, she can come meet me here in Kodiak."

26

CRAB DREAMS

AUGUST 1951

Harold Simmons was Hoss's proper name. Jones made a note of it as he signed the boat's log and became a crew member of the fifty-four-foot wood hulled dragger *Kodiak Star* at two-thirds provisional pay. A boat some twenty feet longer than his own troller out of Kodiak. Engine about double the size and three times the horsepower of his own, and diesel at that. Certainly more elbow room in the cabin, perhaps because anything that could be moved was tucked snugly away. Jones's own boat, shipshape by ordinary standards, suddenly seemed a mess in comparison, even though he'd occasionally sneered at the pigpens kept by other fishermen. Yet the orderliness made him feel right somehow. It didn't hurt to have standards, and maybe since he'd left the Marines, he'd let a few lapse.

Hoss patted an upper bunk with a clean, bare mattress. "Yours. Sheet and blanket down there in that cabinet. Got a sleeping bag with your gear?"

"Back on my own boat in Ketchikan. Up in Bristol Bay we just slept in blankets and a bearskin."

"I heard they lived like pigs up there."

Jones suddenly felt defensive. "Open boat. Only a half canvas for shelter!"

"Yeah." After a pause, Hoss offered, "You can borrow my extra bag for a while. Get it cleaned ashore before you give it back." Standing face to face, Jones noticed Hoss's eyes were gray, and his expression had turned impersonal, no longer vulnerable nor defensive. "I don't need to tell a marine that everything stows exact aboard here."

"Last thing you need to tell me." Jones found himself snapping it, almost adding the obligatory "sir!" He felt like he was back as a private—at most a corporal—answering to his sergeant again, back before he became one himself. In the years since the Marine Corps, he'd become accustomed to his own authority on the water and to accepting orders from his dad with a shrug toward age and experience. Maybe it was a bad decision to come aboard here, to leave Gus behind. But he remembered the heft and spiny feel of the strange new crabs. As soon as Jake, the other crewman, staggered aboard—swaying drunk—and crawled into his bunk, Hoss started the engine and announced: "We're off."

Jones stood with him by the wheel. It felt wrong not to be in charge. As soon as they had left the shelter of the harbor, the boat's bow pitched and westerly swells began to push them a few degrees off course. Behind the wheel, Hoss corrected easily, but not before they approached a red whistle buoy and Jones automatically let out: "Need to take that to portside."

"What the fuck you think I'm doing?" Hoss demanded. The course he had set skirted the buoy without issue. "Maybe what you want to do is ready the drag on deck."

"Figured first off I'd follow how you two did it, since I'm more used to line and seine gear."

"Then don't be givin' the orders."

Reeling from the sting, Jones clenched his fists. He hadn't taken officers' shit since leaving the battlefield. But in all fairness, it was better to follow new gear at least once before trying it alone. Once was all he'd need. He wouldn't screw it up.

"Think you also need help finding the ice chest topside? You'll want to get out some hamburger, cabbage, and carrots to cut up. Light up the stove there. Got coffee water to boil. Or you think I'd better show you first?"

Without replying, Jones went on deck and climbed the ladder topside. He squinted into a low sun ahead on the horizon as he pulled the provisions from the neatly ordered boxes. He barely noticing the spray plumes that cascaded from the bow, and he re-entered the cabin, dripping. Before he could search around the sink for a cloth to wipe off with, Hoss remarked, "I don't expect to slip on a wet galley deck."

Jones clenched his fists again, ready for the impending battle. Marine horseshit all over again. Then, suddenly, even in his own mind, he shrugged. *Damned if I haven't done this to myself. What the hell.* He found the cloth and hunkered down to wipe up the water he'd dripped.

It took them only a few hours from Kodiak to reach the deep water where crabs might be schooling. But, two days later, they were still scouting. Their drag brought up bagfuls of fish they didn't need except for meals, but only a stray crab or two. Skipper Hoss turned more and more demanding. Their lack of any success seemed to spur him on and he drove his two-man crew harder and harder. When the depth sounder suddenly crashed without warning, "Shit! No! We're not going back to town just to have the fucker fixed, maybe have to buy a new one," he shouted as much to himself as to the others. "Fuck no—not till we find the crab we came for! I know the fucking crab is here!"

Net-hauls gone wrong didn't mean slack. When they weren't hauling web every couple of hours to check it, Hoss had both his men on deck— rain or sun, daylight or dark—heaving hand lines to give him depth. Jones—as the junior man, he was also designated the cook—soon barely had time to render bacon in a pan and throw in slices of fresh-cut fish before he was ordered back on deck. Hoss gobbled his fried fish on the run, lapping up the grease with a handful of bread, and it was clear he expected Jake and Jones to do the same.

"Reason you got aboard here so easy," Jake muttered to Jones as they stood on either side of the boat, tossing and pulling back hand-over-hand their fathoms of dripping line. "Last guy wasn't taking any more of this shit. I'd go too but for don't feel like being on the beach. Salmon boats were all crewed for the season when I got here last month. Work on a cannery line like a gook or a girl. Or college kid? Not me!" He laughed. "After the Marines, I wasn't going to take shit no more. And now here you see me. At least it's hard shit, not soft. Familiar. Know what I mean?"

"Mebbe." Jones swiped a hand over his face to clear a shower of spray. Water in rolls higher than their rail broke across deck. But sun glistened on the wave crests. For reasons he couldn't explain, Jones was not unhappy— even though his hands ached from the cold water on the line and he'd slept only hours in the past two days.

"Look sharp now!" called Hoss from the exposed wheel topside. "Pull your lines. Make sure they're coiled proper. We'll haul again since it feels like we've got some drag."

"Yeah, yeah," muttered Jake.

"How's that?"

"Nothing, Skipper." A few minutes later, Jones and Jake stood opposite each other astern ready to grab and secure the otter boards when they surfaced. The trawl warps clattered up the ramp accompanied by water that sloshed a foot deep around their boots.

When the last strip of marker surfaced on the cable, Jones called, "Twenty-five."

"Fathom twenty-five," repeated Skipper Hoss. "Steady as she goes. Stand by."

"What's it look like we're doing," muttered Jake automatically. The wooden otter boards surfaced. Hoss slowed his winch until the boards had thumped alongside port and starboard, then stopped for his crewmen to secure them with chains. "Hustle it," he called. "Ain't got all fucking day."

"Got all fuckin' day and night," Jake hissed under his breath.

"What say out there?"

"Nothing." Jones wiped another gust of spray from his face. The water had slammed him hard enough to enter under his oilskins and creep cold down his neck. Somehow it didn't feel bad. Maybe even good. The top of the trawl bag broke the surface. Giant crab claws waved through the mesh.

"Well look there!" exclaimed Jake, and to Hoss he called: "Found 'em!"

Indeed, as the trawl bag flattened against the ramp and inched aboard, it was clear that they had located a pod of king crab. The bag undulated with the big restless creatures. It was alive with them. When the bag finally lay on deck, Hoss strode over shouting, "Don't touch it!" and he pulled the mouth open himself. The crabs spilled out on deck, crawling over each other sluggishly. When one left the central pile Hoss nudged it back gently with his boot. "Got our week's money here, boys. Maybe the fucking month's money if we can sell 'em all." He peered across the water at a distant gray strip of Kodiak Island. "What's your last sounding? I'm going down to mark us on the chart. Then you forget this location, hear? No call to have a hundred other boats dragging what we found."

Jones found himself laughing.

"You see something funny here, Marine?"

Jones returned Hoss's glare eye for eye. "Funny as hell, marine! But don't worry." He strode over and lifted one of the heavy crabs by a leg. He started waving it, enjoying the feel of its weight. "What we found here's ours!"

"Then put him back on the pile and treat him like food, marine. This ain't play, you know." Jones considered, then dropped the crab lightly back into the pile. The creature burrowed in, knocking its big-shelled mates aside.

In another hour they had hosed and stowed their load of king crab. It might have made sense to return to Kodiak, but Hoss declared, "We'll keep these alive and scout some more."

It had now turned dark for one of the few hours of Alaskan summer night. Jake straightened his back and stretched. "I'm sacking a few hours and you can sniff it. We've been up on this deck twenty-some hours—since before sunrise last morning."

Hoss glared at him, then said dryly, "Go on then, if you can't take it, just when we've hit what we came for. We'll manage the next drag without you."

Jones, too, felt bone-weary. He watched Jake peel off his oilskins and rack them carefully on a hook by the cabin. He disappeared inside. Jones, too, lingered hosing himself down. "Setting again right here, eh?"

"No. I'm scouting. Go on two or three miles, then set again. I need to see the size of this."

"Well. If you can do it, so can I." Jones started toward the cabin. "Shout when you get there and ready to set."

"I expect soundings on the way."

"Then wait a fuckin' hour." Jones opened the hatch door without removing his oilskins and started down the steps.

"Marine! You forget my rules about wet-gear inside?" Jones straightened, aching for a fight. He wore weather gear, yes, but it had now been hosed and dried by the wind. "Call me in an hour, marine."

In the warm cabin he stretched out on the bench along the table, and fell asleep before his head reached the board.

Crabs pushed against each other, crawled over their fellows. Their shells had faces. Jones recognized his own among them, but he was also outside the pile, watching them struggle, aching, in the pile. Faces of old Marine buddies. They all talked to him at once, while the mouth of his own face moved up and down. But it was warm, nice, because they were all together.

Then the fire started. One by one the faces screamed, burned, blackened, remained screaming. And Jones realized he'd already watched each one of them die at least once before. The fire flickered closer to his own face. Its scorch reached him, closing in on him, and he felt the heat just when he woke. He lay on the galley board, listening to his own breathing.

"Ready to set now," said Hoss, looking down at him. "Guess I can take the sounding myself." Jones rose. Relieved to not be burning.

"No, buddy. I'm on it."

27

SWEDE SEES CRABS

Swede followed three sealed cartons of company documents to the steamer. One of the fishermen, now crewing aboard as part of his contract, pushed the cartons up the gangplank on a dolly. On deck, Swede gripped one of the cartons himself to show that he wasn't above doing it—but it was, perhaps, the lightest—then returned to the ship's office for a final check.

"Okay, finished!" he told his assistant. "Office closed. Company's sending me west for a look at something else. Anything left is yours to care for and deliver safely."

"Got it."

Swede went to his quarters to close down there. The day at the end of August supervising the shutdown of the cannery for the season had begun at least twenty hours before. Swede removed only his shoes before he lay back on his bed and fell asleep.

Yet even in his sleep, he continued to run. Everything under his care needed to be considered. Had he really accounted for all of the cartons of tin cans filled with fish? Cans by the thousands. He raced among towers of boxes, checking destinations. And there to halt him was an officer in a green uniform—his chest high as bricks. He stared down. Demanded, *"Woher gehen Sie?"*

"Nowhere, sir!" Swede declared in Swedish and then added the same word in Norwegian, telling himself all the while that it would have been wiser to answer the officer in German, although he couldn't remember how. The officer seized his neck in a chokehold and propelled him toward an iron gateway. The grip held him entirely—helpless. His thoughts whirled: *Will they torture me with electricity, or fire, or something unknown and therefore worse?* Fire indeed glowed beyond the gateway. And screams came from the dark inside. Would he be able to keep the secret that this shipment of fish was not on the books? That it was to not be sent to Germany like the rest but smuggled across the border to the Norwegian fighters and never to be seen again? The officer's grip transferred to his shoulder, shaking him, a preliminary to the torture.

"Mr. Scorden! Sorry to wake you. Stuff here you forgot to sign."

Swede bolted upright. Had to shake himself to clear his head. He reached for the clipboard the man handed to him. "Ah. Yes. So." He scribbled his signature. "So. Yes. Good. Thank you."

Alone again, Swede tousled his hair askew then pushed it smooth once more. He decided not to try to sleep further. He tied up the laces on his shoes and walked deep in thought back from the cannery living quarters to the office. Rain spattered in his face. He welcomed it gladly.

Inside, Swede surveyed his Naknek office for the last time before closing. Furniture and flooring, now bare to the wood, looked already as bleak as the winter to come. Before he would enter the room again next spring to set it all back in order, cycles of ice would probably have lined the windows and frost would have glistened on the ridges of the desk. Rats would scamper here free from harm.

All creatures should be free from harm. He shrugged to dissipate the remaining cloud of his dream. Except fish, of course, killed mercifully for eating. Naturally . . .

Leave no loose papers—who knew what someone might find? A few irrelevant sheets of paper still lay in one of the drawers. He tore them up and stuffed the pieces into his briefcase. He'd drop them into one of the large, anonymous trash bins by the piers. He even removed the calendar from the wall—no use wasting its remaining pages when he now had an office at the cannery in Seattle.

Down the ramp by the main buildings, he joined the two trusted foremen who were to remain for the final closing of the processing and storage areas. Together they strode to inspect the deserted, echoing spaces where fish had been noisily collected and prepared just days before. All was clean, all scrubbed and disinfected—even down to the concrete flooring. Although, inevitably, there remained the faint odors of fish and machinery oils. Odors not that different from Father's fish plant so long ago in the old country. Before the German bastards took him.

"Yes. Good. Good. Okay," he declared, still trying to think past the dream. Nevertheless, he made it his business to stop once to point out a rust stain in the crevice of a heading machine and once for a fish scale stuck to the side of a flume—just to prove to the others that he was alert.

In a few days, a winter watchman would take over to guard against any pillaging at the hands of the villagers. The man had done the job for several seasons as a company employee. He'd fished once—had even prospected for gold, he'd said when he'd visited to arrange his quarters the week before. An unshaven, quiet fellow of the kind they called "old-timer," with tobacco-stained teeth. Who knew how he passed his nights? One rumor had it that a Native woman from the village moved in with him after everyone else had left. Well, why not? It might save the fellow from dreams, good or bad. Swede shrugged to himself. After tomorrow, the cannery wouldn't be his concern again until next April. Meanwhile, the company was sending him off to a different, most curious assignment. Just when he thought all had been settled, this new adventure came along.

Next afternoon, Swede flew from Naknek's airport at King Salmon to the island of Kodiak, where he'd never set foot before. The flight, which should have taken an hour, stretched into five—with hours of waiting time at the rudimentary airport because of bad weather. At last, with nothing to see along the way but gray clouds below, the plane reached Kodiak in heavy rain.

In the town of Kodiak, he'd need to learn the exact whereabouts of the trawling vessel *Deep Sea* and at what port he could meet it. His mission was not to spy, exactly. Rather to ascertain and report back to the company in Seattle. The vessel, owned and run by former cannery people, employed Scandinavians on deck, and this was the reason his own company's vice president for expansion had suggested they send him. Could the notoriously large king crabs—which until now most people had seen only in photos or as meat in tin cans with a Japanese label—become a viable American product?

All offices in Kodiak had closed for the day. After checking in at a hotel barely more elaborate than a cannery bunkhouse, Swede walked out into the rain. People brushed by him in slickers dripping water, joking and seemingly oblivious to the weather. Hardy people, even the women. The single main street had enough shops to raise it a notch above Naknek, but it had nowhere near the scope and variety as in Ketchikan. At least he found a restaurant that had tablecloths. With a flush of anticipation, he ordered the single crab dish on the menu. The crab, served as rounded chunks of meat—as if it had been sliced from a tube—, had a rich flavor that made the accompanying pink sauce unnecessary. *Yes*, he thought. This was crab that could be marketed.

Kodiak itself reminded him of a small Scandinavian town, with a layout facing the sea and its main waterway framed by hilly islands and a mountain. But there the similarity to the old country ended. Back home, even structures in the smallest communities had years and years of history. One dared not alter them without a lengthy period of consideration. Here the buildings were raw. Tear down one and another could take its place without concern. Yes, raw. Invigorating! Swede liked Kodiak at once.

Next morning he climbed the stairs in a weathered frame building to reach the office of the lawyer with whom he was to check in. The man waved him in past the secretary's desk, instead of leaving him to wait as Swede would have done. Held out a hand and shook Swede's warmly with, "Hi! Been expecting you. Grab a chair. Coffee?"

It appeared that the large vessel that had been outfitted to catch and process king crabs seldom docked in Kodiak, since it could refuel at small cannery towns closer to its fishing grounds. Its finished product could be stored and shipped from these places also.

"Weather's suddenly turned shitty otherwise you could charter a plane to Sand Point. These fronts can last a while." The lawyer continued

conversationally. "Tell you what. I know a skipper who's out here prospecting for these king crabs. Owes me a small favor. This guy's scratchy, but if
he'll take you, want to ride out with him a couple of days?"

So it was in America. Anyone could do anything. Swede nodded. "Good,
yes, thank you."

"Might be rough out there. What kind of sea legs you got?"

"Legs?"

"Small boat. Bad weather." To Swede, it made the proposition even
more interesting.

"I've endured bad weather, sir. No problem."

Soon after, dressed in newly purchased oilskins to guard against the rain
that continued to drive down, Swede climbed aboard the wooden fishing vessel
named *Kodiak Star*. Behind him, a familiar voice growled out, "What the fuck?"

There, staring him down, was the leathery, scowling face of Jones Henry.

Swede Scorden had, as management, not expected to work as a fisherman
again. Certainly in Sweden or Norway he'd never have done so as a fish plant
owner. Nor, he'd thought, in Alaska anymore, even though when visiting
Ballard relatives as a kid, he'd once crewed aboard their Puget Sound seiner.
And of course, after the war, he'd crewed for Cousin Nels out of Ketchikan.
But after all, Swede mused, it wasn't an unreal expectation. He had just
headed an entire operation in Bristol Bay with some hundred and forty
workers at his command and scores of fishing boats in his possession.

But here he stood idly aboard the small trawler while the three crewmen
worked hard. And one of them at that was the man Jones Henry, who just
days before in Bristol Bay had been dependent on conditions decided by
Swede Scorden himself.

By the second trawl-load the next morning, Swede was on deck assisting
where he could. In truth, the huge, trapped crabs they called kings were far
too interesting to only be watched from a hatchway. After all, they were why
he had come. He helped pull the net aboard. Then he assisted the others as
they lifted the crabs by their massive legs to store them in the hold. Sluggish
creatures, heavy. Soon he was handling lines, even jumping with the others

to orders barked from the rough skipper named Hoss. Shining with sweat
from the work, Swede was enjoying himself. This was America.

"So," growled Jones Henry as they rested behind the winch under shelter
from the rain. "Ever go back to Creek Street?"

"Jones, I am married!"

"So am I." Jones laughed in his way that seemed half sardonic. "To a fine
girl." He rummaged under his jacket, produced a single cigarette, and lit it
after striking a damp match several times. After taking a deep puff to get it
going, he offered it over to Swede. "Only one in my pocket. Here, share it."

Swede felt the generosity of the gesture, but: "Is this sanitary, Jones?"

"Suit yourself."

Swede quickly accepted the cigarette, drew on it until his mouth filled
uncomfortably with smoke, then passed it back.

"So. What's a cannery boss coming to Kodiak for? And out on a boat
like this? Them big crabs I'd guess. Or did they fire you?"

"Big crabs. Yes." Swede decided there was no secret to it, at least not
with one of his fisherman. "When the sky clears . . ." Now, as always when
he thought of it, Swede paused a moment to put his words together into
proper English syntax. ". . . I'm going to fly and visit a ship out west that's
famously catching and processing these crabs. I'm aboard here only because
the weather's too bad for flying."

"Wouldn't mind seeing that myself. If I didn't have to settle things here
and then get home." Jones took a drag of the cigarette. Drops of rain blowing in on an angle had put it out. He muttered without heat and tossed it
into the water.

"Hey out there," called Hoss from the cabin doorway. "Don't hurt to
rub a little soogie powder on the cabinets in here while we're dragging and
nothing to do on deck."

"Then do it your damn self!" snapped Jones and added in sudden humor,
"Marine."

"Might just do that," said Hoss in equal humor, and slid the hatch door
shut.

"Man needs setting straight every minute of the year," Jones muttered.
"Fact is, I'm tired of taking his shit now that I've seen the big crabs. Early
season yet, but I see the future. Skipper Hoss there says he's soon going to
put a smaller-mesh liner in his trawl, then go out to a bay here called Kaluda

or something. They say shrimp are packing in there like sawdust. Can't keep the man still. I understand that. Try everything. Out here's hopping with opportunity. But with the Chinook salmon starting to run back in Ketchikan, that's where I belong for rest of this season. Mebbe pat Adele on the head a little bit . . ." He considered, with elbows on his knees, looking out at waves turning dark in late afternoon light. "Still. Wouldn't mind seeing how they handle them big crabs when they keep coming. They say that Bering Sea's something to fish in, times."

The interval gave Swede time to consider. Why not? The chartered plane would be paid for. It would probably lay over at least to refuel before returning, time for Jones to have a look. Swede, having chartered the plane himself, could insist on further delay. And if anyone at the company objected, he'd insist that he'd brought this experienced fisherman along for his opinions. In Alaska the rules were flexible. And didn't he owe Jones Henry something for their friendship so long ago?

"Come see, Jones. As a guest of the company that pays for the plane. A quick look at this processor vessel before you return to Ketchikan."

Jones thought it over. "Paid for?" Swede nodded. "No strings attached?"

Swede enjoyed the fact that he understood this idiom. "No strings, as they say."

"Guess you are a big shot now. Well, I've come this far. Wouldn't hurt to see it all before committing out here."

At 140 feet in length, the ship named *Deep Sea* was a giant among the fishing boats a quarter of its size—at most. They were moored to the cannery pier by the remote village of Sand Point. The sea plane that had carried Swede and Jones floated in to an end of the same pier. The pilot, wearing hip boots, walked out on the plane's wing to toss his line to a worker. Within moments they stood at the gangway of the ship itself.

"Got your gear?" called a man from the deck above. "Come on. We've hung around for you an hour since refueling, but got to go. No profit tied up here."

"This man I've brought," called Swede. "He's only here to see what you look like. To take what you call a tour."

"He's welcome to look all he wants from down there. But we're leaving." Indeed, the ship's propeller now churned slowly in the water, and the Native man who had received the plane's line gripped the ship's hawser astern ready to cast it from a bollard.

"Jones!" said Swede. "I'm sorry. You can at least see how big the ship is before you return."

Jones barely considered. "Think they got berth for two aboard there?"

"Many days before they return somewhere for fuel, I think."

"I've come this far."

"Sir!" Swede called up. "We are not one but two coming aboard to travel with you."

"Yeah, yeah. Come."

They had barely ascended the gangway before crewmen pulled it up behind them. Within a half hour the Sand Point breakwater was a mere line on the horizon and the ship had begun to pitch through a heavy sea.

28

PIONEERS OF AMERICAN FISHING

The 140-foot vessel *Deep Sea* is part of Alaska's history. It caught and processed king crab from 1947 into the 1950s when the big crustaceans—destined to form the Bering Sea's most lucrative fishery in the following decades—were still an exotic product. Americans eventually would have discovered what a bonanza they had in these crabs, but *Deep Sea* pioneered the way.

Before World War II, the Japanese had harvested and canned king crab, mainly from the western Bering Sea, which their vessels dominated. Post-war, they joined the Russians fishing the crabs in the near-to-home Sea of Okhotsk to feed their hungry countrymen. In the United States, the incentive to harvest king crab came more from opportunity than out of a need for survival. Despite Americans' concerns during the immediate post-war years about the spread of Communism from the Soviet Union and about crippling domestic labor union strikes, this was a time when the people of the Alaskan and West Coast fisheries were riding high on optimism.

During the war, an innovative American cannery man named Lowell Wakefield had led government-sponsored exploratory fishing trials in

Alaskan waters to find new seafood sources. Thus, he saw what abundance the Bering Sea held. In 1946 he raised among investors—many of them back from wartime navy duty and primed for further adventure before settling down—an approximate $500,000 to build a ship that could both catch and process fish at sea in Alaskan weather of any severity.

Specs: The *Deep Sea*'s cost to build at the Birchfield Boiler shipyard in Tacoma, WA, came to $461,000 before equipment. Her length, as stated, was 140 feet, with a beam of nearly 27 feet. She weighed 550 tons and had a 420,000 pound freezer storage capacity. Her 10.3 foot draft deepened by some 2.2 feet when fully loaded. The engine was a GM two-cycle V-type diesel delivering 750 rpm and 1,200 horsepower. Cruising speed could reach over thirteen knots but averaged twelve knots, with a range of four thousand nautical miles before refueling. Belowdecks there were eleven staterooms to accommodate twenty-seven crew and four officers. The processing area included continuous production lines. Quick freezing equipment could take 1,200 pounds per hour in 15-pound blocks to a temperature of –25 degrees Fahrenheit.

Electronics on the bridge included the latest devices developed during wartime, such as radar, radio direction finders that could home in on buoys set earlier, and fathometers, while by 1950 loran (Long Range Navigation) was added after the Coast Guard had established reliable stations for this system in Alaska. A ship's intercom connected stations throughout the ship that could both receive and send.

By the summer of 1947 the ship had traveled from its Seattle shipyard to the Bering Sea, stopping in Ketchikan and Kodiak along the way to fuel and pick up final members of the crew. She carried a crew complement divided mostly between Alaskan Natives working in processing (Wakefield wanted this to be an Alaska venture wherever practical) and on deck, many of Scandinavian origin who had been signed on for their experience. At various times the investors themselves were also aboard. These were men still young and restless from wartime experience. They had shelled out their money partly for the adventure. Most were also well educated and had some means, recruited through contacts rather than through advertisements. When they weren't running things—sometimes the levels of shipboard authority became mixed and informal—they turned-to as crew. With twelve-hour shifts of cold and wet manual labor, and with the ship often rocked above deck by crashing waves, ice, and storms and below by brutally shifting platforms, the *Deep Sea* was a lively place to be for men who accepted hardship as part of the adventure.

The initial targets were sole, flounder, and other bottomfish. King crab was considered to be an ancillary catch. Then, *Deep Sea*'s drag net began to come up with as much big crab as bottomfish. The crabs had meat in them of a quality that would make them a luxury item in the United States. The trick was to preserve that meat in both attractive form and commercial quantity. This became the *Deep Sea*'s challenge.

Grabbing opportunity in hand, Wakefield and his associates experimented and developed an efficient way to flash-freeze the crab meat so that its taste and texture remained fresh. They led the way in proving that the huge king crabs of the North Pacific, previously harvested and canned only by Japanese and Soviet interests in the western Bering Sea, were a viable commercial product for the United States and its markets. In its first half-dozen years, the company Wakefield formed barely broke even—as is often the history of pioneering ventures. Eventually markets caught up with production and the venture prospered and was soon copied.

In time, Kodiak, as the location closest to the lower United States and abundant with king crab, became a boom town. It proclaimed itself, with reason, "The King Crab Capital of the World." But this mad success didn't happen until a few years after the still-early days in which Jones Henry, Swede Scorden, and Kiyoshi Tsurifune played their parts.

29

ABOARD THE VESSEL
DEEP SEA

Jones and Swede dropped their gear on deck and watched the shoreline recede. The man who had authorized their boarding had already left. Finally a passing man in coveralls said, "Get yourselves coffee, fellows. Galley's aft down that ladder. Watch the puke. Throw your bags to the bridge till we've squared away."

In the corridor below deck that led to the galley, they stepped around a brown swatch of vomit that gelled back and forth with the ship's roll, then made way for a man with mop and pail who muttered: "Shouldn't've let nobody ashore here, these dog-holes."

The messdeck was bright and clean. It had tables that sat a half-dozen each. Three men in rumpled dungarees slumped at one table with their heads in their arms. At other tables, sitting quietly apart from each other, were groups of Natives and a handful of whites.

Swede led the way to the coffee urn and filled himself a mug. He looked around at the men at ease and headed to the table where some Native workers sat. Behind him, Jones paused before following reluctantly.

"Good afternoon," said Swede. "Okay that we sit here?"

"Sure." One of the men nudged a chair out with his foot. Jones glanced at the table where the white men were resting, but he drew a place alongside Swede's.

"Long time at sea here, yes?" Swede ventured.

The man who had offered the chair chuckled. "Don't seem that long, till we come to land. Come to take fuel." His brown face was wide without being fat, his expression deliberate. He gestured over toward the three slumped men. "Then, booze. You see what happens. Guys there, they won't be no good for two days. Well. Then everybody's all right again. For another month. Till we come take fuel again at some other place that sells booze."

"Always like that," said Swede easily. "Everywhere." The others nodded agreement.

Another of the men volunteered, "Vladimir here, he's assistant village chief, sort of. Makes us stay away from booze when we come in some place for oil. Most of us. Makes sure we do right. Do our jobs so they keep hiring us. When there's a problem, it's Vladimir decides who's right, who's wrong."

"No fun," said another. "But we keep our money." The man named Vladimir shrugged, clearly pleased.

"Now and then," the first continued, "Maybe every three months, we stop at Akutan where most of us live. Then we sure have fun. Don't go back to work for a couple of days. Then everybody's okay."

"Yeah, yeah."

Swede laughed with them, then stretched, clearly relaxed. "On the processing lines, is it more fish or more crab that you work?"

"Crab, now. Since the boat's found the crab." Before they had finished their coffee, the men had described to Swede the steps they took to butcher the crab and to either extract the meat from its legs or to freeze and pack the legs with crab meat still inside.

Jones listened, amused in spite of himself. *Sharp fellow, that Swede.* By the time somebody came to say they'd better check up at the bridge and find where they should bunk, Swede had learned enough about processing the king crab to write his own book on the subject.

━★━

Swede, who had been expected—invited even—had a bunk with sheets waiting for him in one of the staterooms that slept officers and visiting shareholders. To make room for Jones they needed to clear cartons of soft drinks and engine oil from a top bunk in a cabin used for storage. Somebody found him a blanket.

For a while, Jones trailed behind Swede, conscious that he was no more than an unexpected annoyance forced on those who ran the ship. But his ambivalent position left him strangely at leisure. As a mere passenger assigned no real responsibility, he was free to wander where he pleased. In fact, everyone was so busy that no one challenged him.

The wheelhouse itself was so vast that they called it "the bridge." It resembled those on the navy troopships that had once taken him and fellow marines to islands for battle. He'd never been authorized to enter on those ships, but had occasionally snuck a look anyway. Here, he visited if he pleased. But he found this wheelhouse to be particularly alien territory. It was so far removed from that of his own boat, where the chow table practically bumped the steering wheel, that it appeared to be a whole other world. The electronic gadgets everywhere looked like a trade show display. He didn't even know what some of them were, or what the glowing green images on their screens meant. Fathometer, of course. And he knew of radar and radio direction finders from wartime, although he'd never needed them nor even been able to afford them on his troller. And what of this newfangled loran, with its need to adjust two wavy electronic lines called "slave" and "master," to get some kind of position?

No one seemed completely in charge. A calm, businesslike man named Bill Blackford was captain, but the man named Lowell sometimes examined charts and would issue commands. And two others would speak up as if they also had a say. Sometimes they argued among themselves. Most were guys about his own age—none over thirty-five. All of them full of energy. But they talked as if they'd been to college. It placed them apart, even though they were friendly enough whenever he ventured questions. All in all, he didn't feel at home on the bridge, even though its gadgets drew him in and Captain Blackford was nice enough to explain some of them when he asked.

The processing lines belowdecks were closer to his expertise, even though he'd never, of course, tied on an apron and fingered little pieces of fish and crab along some conveyor belt. Women's work. But here on the ship, men did it all. Most of them were the Indians called Aleuts, somebody told him, rather than the Tlingit Indians that had a village and totem poles on the outskirts of Ketchikan. He'd never looked at Natives hard enough to tell the difference. Some in Ketchikan had stumbled along the road around the harbor in a state of perpetual drunkenness. But others he encountered on the water were good fishermen, even though they kept their boats in poor shape—to judge how they were in constant need of paint. The Indians here were friendly enough, despite how they kept to themselves. With Swede having broken the ice, several nodded whenever he encountered them. They didn't mind working, he had to admit. Kept at it as long as crab parts bounced along their conveyor lines. Nothing like those drunk Indians who stumbled around the Ketchikan harbor.

The crab legs they handled were like the big ones he'd hustled live in Kodiak, waving sluggishly from their central body. The workers boiled the legs until the shells turned red, then packed them in trays that were sent down to a freezer. He soon grew bored of watching the process over and over. Why the hell had he stuck himself aboard this ship?

And then there was Swede—watching, taking notes, asking questions of the foreman. He even crawled below into the freezer spaces. He pulled out crab legs just boiled and packed, and long-frozen crab, to taste and compare the meat. Then he'd be on the bridge talking. Always busy. Next, down in the cabins with some of the fishermen who worked on deck, talking to them in Norwegian or Swedish with their arms in the air and big laughs at whatever they said to each other. So busy he barely had a word for Jones, even when they sat together for dinner just a few hours after leaving Sand Point.

By next morning the ship was pitching in open sea. And Jones, immune to seasickness aboard small fishing boats, felt the slow gyrations of the ship before he even rolled from his bunk. *This is bullshit*! he told himself. The door to the room flew open.

"You on this watch? Wake up call."

He'd been mistaken for a crewman, but what the hell. He responded without further thought, pulling on the boots and oilskins he'd carried aboard. Keeping balance along the pitching corridor, he avoided the smell of food coming from the galley and found his way to a hatch that opened onto deck. Waves outside rose high and black beyond deck lights that shone against a gray morning sky. A sea crashed against the starboard rail and bubbled into three men leaning over a net full of crabs. The men bent to the slap of water without losing their rhythm. Something metal clacked on the winch. Jones was glad enough for any noise, because in spite of himself he vomited. No one saw. He wiped his mouth quickly.

A strap on the trawl bag blew loose and skittered across deck. Jones walked out and grabbed it. He took it to the men at the net just as another wave cascaded over the rail and pushed him into one of them.

"Whoa there, who let you on deck?"

Jones stepped back, tensed to argue—even fight if necessary. Beneath the dripping watch cap and oilskin hood, the face frowning at him with half a grin was that of a man he'd last seen on the bridge discussing maneuvers with the captain. One of those who talked like he'd been to college.

"Ja, har har," bellowed another of the men. "Dot's de fellow come here with Svede. Come out here look us over, eh?"

At that, the three ignored Jones. They leaned in to pull crabs one by one from the heap dumped by the trawl bag and tossed them into a checkers hemmed by boards. Jones braced against another slap of water and kept his balance. He'd seen seas enough, but those beyond the rail swelled higher than most he'd ever witnessed. The wind blew foam off the waves and tore drops from the heavy mesh of the net on deck. Not so bad. For a marine who'd been through everything.

He didn't have gloves. But without further thought he joined the others. He'd pulled enough of the big crabs by now to know where to grip them free of the sluggish claws. The thick shells encasing their legs were cold and slippery. Solid critters. From deep below. But solid.

"Didn't see you at breakfast. You eaten?" called the college man over the wind.

"Just got up and came out."

"Well, glad to have you. Looks like you know what you're doing. Expect to stay? Long time before the next chow. Better go in and eat something."

"I'm okay. You just started?"

"Yeah, the watch is still fresh. Wait till the watch changes eleven-some hours from now. But I mean it. Fortify up if you plan to stick it out here. Or are you just sniffing the lilies?"

Jones snorted and glared at the others. Two bearded fellows, big and able-looking. He'd seen them joking with Swede in Norwegian. They watched dispassionately. Judging? "Expect me back here!"

On the messdeck, a man at the galley stove eyed him.

"Haven't seen you before. Breakfast or dinner?"

From a table that Jones hadn't noticed when he came in, Swede called him over. He was sitting with the Captain. Jones joined them, carrying a plateful of scrambled eggs and sausage.

"Got to get back on deck quick," he muttered. The food swam in grease. He mopped it up with bread, hoping it would stay down.

"So, Jones," said Swede. "Crabs here to fill a plate, eh? Got to create a market. Great future for such crabs!"

The captain looked Jones over. "If you're just pitching in for a bit that's fine. Swede tells me you know your way around a deck. But we lost a guy back in Sand Point who'd had enough, if you want to stay. Couple of our Native pickers too, they get restless and go. If you've joined the shift out there, I should sign you in. Not like the processing line where we pay 'em wages. Deck crew gets a share in the profits. But I warn you. Not much profit so far."

Jones considered as he ate. Ketchikan and Adele both crowded him. Even Bristol Bay, under his dad. And that driving asshole Hoss. Out here were big crabs, big waves, and open ocean as far as you could see. Gave him space to grab breath. Before settling back at home. "What the hell?" he answered. "Sign me on if it suits you.

Back on deck they'd found him gloves. The salt from the seawater the wind blew into his mouth helped the greasy breakfast stay down. Jones relished the salty taste in his mouth, the hard work for his hands. Nothing to think about or decide on. Guiding cable from the winch, they lowered the otter boards of the side trawl followed by the trawl net itself. Then, while the net dragged the bottom and caught the next haul, they gripped their catch crab by crab, snapped off the thick legs with clinging meat (a wrist-puller on the tendons that surely killed the critters), and with a shout tossed the legs down a chute to the processor guys. With the butchering over, they hosed each other of any crap and gurry not washed from their oilskins by the seas, then kicked the remaining mess over the side. By then it was time to bring aboard the next haul. Cold and numb after a while. And his wrists burned, when he had time to notice.

After it became clear that Jones knew his job, the college guy left. A while later Jones saw him looking down from the bridge. But at next chow time, he and two other of the college guys came on deck to relieve them long enough that they could eat and have a smoke. On the messdeck, Jones nodded to Swede, who sat again with the captain, but instead slumped beside the two Norwegians who now spoke in English to include him. No question that the plateful of hamburger, peas, and noodles stayed down. He plugged it with bread still hot from the oven, with some kind of orange bug juice drink, and finally with steaming apple pie. Soon, feeling much warmer, Jones was back dodging spray and hauling big crabs as a member of the deck crew. His wrists throbbed. But he felt good.

Temporary. Jones knew that well enough. His real world waited back in Ketchikan, or maybe over in Kodiak, with a boat he alone could handle and command, and ashore with Adele and whatever family they might be able to raise. Time spent aboard the crabber ship *Deep Sea* was only a breather from everything else. He rolled with it, or more truthfully, just let it roll over him. It suited him, the high waves under dark skies, seas frothing around his legs like hungry animals. For a while he was content being part of this new thing rather than separate and fighting against it all the time.

By the next day he was bunked in a proper cabin with others of the deck men, a signed-on member of the crew. They worked twelve-hour shifts. By each day's end he was tired enough to shovel in food and then sleep soundly. The others were all Scandinavian, and when Swede visited they talked in their lingo. At other times, like the shipmates they were, they spoke in English so as not to exclude him. They liked trying their English on him. Most expected America to be their home, although they lived in Ballard near Seattle where everybody still spoke like in the old country.

One, Thor, who had at first laughed at Jones on deck, had a wife and child in Ballard, and he declared himself frustrated that he wasn't getting enough money. Going to leave next time they went for fuel, unless the money improved, he declared. Others said they were there to be ready for the future when the big crabs started fetching high prices.

"They call it here 'ground floor,' Jones," Leif intoned. "Get in on the ground floor, ja? Get rich. Then invest. Buy houses, eh? That's what you should do."

When they inevitably quarreled on deck it was with shouts that had no heat or continuity, resolved often by wrestling or by lobbing crab shells at each other: buddy stuff. Jones had not felt so in tune since leaving the Marines.

He saw less and less of Swede, who stayed on the bridge most days but sometimes strapped on an apron and worked with the Natives on the processing line. It appeared that the ship's owners had learned to catch the king crabs that only the Japanese and Russians had thought to harvest in the Bering Sea before and had learned by trial and error how to freeze them without losing the crab's texture or flavor. They had not yet, though, figured how to market large crabs to Americans in the quantities they caught. Bills remained unpaid. The deck men on shares earned little for their hard work—a definite problem if they had obligations. And salaried Native workers on the processing lines grew homesick for villages where barter replaced much of what money could buy. But for the adventure—or more realistically, for profits not too far in the future—the ship might not have carried enough manpower to continue fishing.

On the water one day in early September, a cargo ship pulled alongside them to transship their frozen product to a land-based facility in Bellingham. By now Jones had found his sea legs. A pitching deck suited him. He leapt into the *Deep Sea*'s reefer hold and strapped up cartons for transfer. Then as the boom raised the load he rode back up standing atop them.

"That guy you brought with you sure is a pistol," he'd heard the captain say to Swede.

"Yes," Swede laughed. "Big gun all right!" From the bridge, Swede called, "Be careful there, Jones!"

Jones might have sneered if he'd been watching someone else ride the net, but the remark caught his pride. He glanced where the net was headed, to the cargo ship grinding against bumpers at their rail. A man over there was eating an orange. Jones gripped web and called to Lars at the boom controls, "Just lift me over with the stuff. Go inspect, mebbe."

"You vant to be bird, Jones? Ja, har har, okay, hang on."

On the brief trip between boats, the sea between them licked up spray that washed around his boots. Sea right there, waiting. Jones looked down and enjoyed the sight.

When, twenty minutes later, Jones returned in the limp, emptied cargo net, he braced one foot on a crate popping with oranges. He himself bit into an orange, skin and all as if it were an apple and casually spat out rind and seeds. Everybody watching from his own deck cheered. They had run out of all fresh food, let alone fruit, ten days before, and here this new man Jones had saved them.

"Those oranges are part of what we'd ordered," the captain said to Swede. "But if he wants to take the credit, fine."

"Ja, yes, good, let him," said Swede. "Jones doesn't much like to smile, and just look at him now."

"Glad to have a man like that on deck. Think he'll stay when you leave?"

"I don't know. I think that his wife wishes him home. My wife and his wife are friends, and this is what my wife says. Months ago, their baby died. Jones doesn't speak of it. But his wife . . . well . . ."

With all the activity, Jones barely gave a thought to Adele back at home. When he'd left for Bristol Bay the woman had said she might go south for a while to visit her parents in San Diego. He hoped so. Time she stopped crying at every little thing. Started dressing again in clothes that fit her, rather than that floppy housecoat that had begun even to stink. After the first weeks, when he'd held her and tried to give comfort, he'd sought his boat more and more. Dreaded going to the house and opening the door to that red swollen face. Lost the will to hold her for every little thing.

Little thing. The phrase started him on the baby, when he'd put it from his mind for days—weeks, even. Little bits of a kid, tiny pink toes one-two-three, toddling one stiff leg then the other. So proud to be on those little feet after a year of crawling. Happy enough to let out delighted squeals. Like a chirpy bird. Toddling across the room to his open urging arms, then her own warm, twiggy arms around his neck. So soft. Preferred him to anybody else—even Mommy. Wore that stiff little dress when she toddled to him, flower pattern smudged with baby food. A dress Adele had embroidered herself. The one they buried her in after the meningitis. Little dead bloodless face framed by light brown baby curls on that white silk. He'd bent to kiss Amy one last time, anticipating the sweet, light-soap smells and warm soft cheek when her arms had grabbed him. Instead, her skin was stiff and dry, cold as a fish. She had a hard, wrong odor something between vinegar and heavy perfume. He'd kissed the little cheek anyhow. Then held his blubbering until he'd found a tree outside to duck behind.

30

AKUTAN

OCTOBER 1951

Six weeks later, the *Deep Sea* had stopped once in Cold Bay for fuel. The crew had caught and packed king crab until the meaty legs waved in their minds, sleeping and waking. They had eaten crab legs so many times at mess that the sight of them in a steam tray elicited a delegation to the captain to give them good old hamburger. Movies played between shifts had been repeated so often that most everyone knew the lines by heart, and it was only the parts showing crashes or explosions that rated attention any more.

Jones had long ago settled into routine. A fist scuffle now and then broke the monotony. There was natural rivalry between the two deck shifts over both endurance of shitty weather and who caught the most crab. Removed from this, the Aleut crew who did the steaming and freezing were like people on a different ship a mile away. They sat apart at chow and at off-hours during movies and endless card games. Jones could tell only one of them from the rest—the lean-faced fellow named Vladimir—because sometimes at Swede's friendly call he'd join them for coffee.

Swede himself was hard to pin down. The man showed up everywhere—from the bridge, wearing a baseball cap, to the processing lines with a paper hat netted to contain his hair. Even a couple of times he'd come—in a wool cap—from the deck with one of the college types to help pick crabs from the net. One day, for once alone at coffee with Jones, Swede considered, then ventured: "Well, it's no secret. I've invested personal savings in this company. I am a shareholder in Deep Sea Trawlers Incorporated. These king crabs have a great future. Only three thousand shares available altogether, if you are interested. And we here, when we've paid our debts and finally made good the sales connections, we shall slowly become rich. This is the great American opportunity, Jones—right here in Alaska!"

"Any money of mine goes to a better boat. After I settle whether I move me and the ol' lady from Ketchikan to Kodiak. First find the money for that."

Swede considered some more. "I'm not rich, Jones. But I could perhaps lend you up to two thousand dollars. To buy a share in this company. In friendship. For your good future." He paused. "For not too long term, of course."

Jones flared automatically. "You think if I wanted, I'd need to borrow?" He curbed his resentment when Swede drew back startled. The man was a foreigner, however much he worked at being American. Didn't understand independence. Didn't understand that a man shouldn't go into debt—except maybe a man who'd served his country and could expect his government to lend money if he needed it for his business. "Well, thanks anyhow."

"Wise investment, Jones."

"You Norwegians ever think of anything but investment?" It suddenly seemed funny, probably because Swede never stopped being serious. "Like them squareheads I work with on deck. Good shipmates, I don't mean that. But, give us a couple minutes break between sets, there they are with paper and pencil—even if the paper's floppy wet from their pocket, talking how they should invest."

"Ja, yes! For the future!"

Jones began to feel restless. Missed his own boat. Missed Adele, although it was a relief to go to his bunk tired and not be awakened by the woman shaking with tears in her sleep. The truth was, he began to admit, the routine of catching and splitting the big crabs might be heady, but less so after a while if you weren't racking them one by one as personal money. Chow here was better than a can of cold beans, of course. Had lettuce and other

fresh stuff now and then when they offloaded to a Stateside ship or somebody came back from leave with a crate. But pay was only promised after
the crab got sold somewhere. Time to go home and face things. If he had to
move the old lady out of Ketchikan to stop her crying, they could come to
Kodiak and he could rig his boat to catch the big crabs direct. Certainly,
after crabbing with Hoss and now on the *Deep Sea*, he knew how to catch
them. Time to go.

Before he'd given up on her and followed his dad to Bristol Bay, he'd
told Adele: "Go back to work in that bank. Why'd you quit anyhow?"
Although he knew well enough it had been to prepare for the baby and
that he'd often declared there was no need for ever a wife of Jones Henry to
have a job when he'd made sure she had a house to take care of. This time
it was different. To keep her occupied. Then, when she reported that the
bank had hired another girl to take her place, he'd grumbled, "Well, go
join the other hens at the Elks and play cards or something. No call to
just sit here and wait for me to come in off the boat. All day. Every day."
Dumb of him.

"Hens?" she'd cried, and it started all over. "Oh you don't understand,"
and there she was crying again. "I do go out. I do, sometimes. But the girls
I knew at the bank are all married now, and they all have—. And what if
I wasn't here when my husband came home? With dinner waiting. Like a
good wife and . . . and mother?"

No answer for anything that set her off again. Sometimes after escaping,
he'd pass Creek Street and think how a few bucks got you a quick lay without having to coax a woman and listening to her talk about things like God's
punishment. She hadn't been like that before the baby. Or maybe he would
never have proposed. Even so, he'd missed her when he'd gone to Bristol Bay
and then to Kodiak and the *Deep Sea*. Missed the woman now.

By the time for the ship's next routine fueling stop, Jones had seen all
of other people's catches that he needed. Had slept alone all that made any
sense for a man with a wife.

"I, too, must go," announced Swede. He held two messages from the
radio room. "Company headquarters in Seattle wishes me to report. Then
quickly back home to Ketchikan." He hesitated, struggling with something
close to a grin. "Mary is pregnant. From a night before I left for Bristol Bay.
Not that . . ."

Jones saw Swede's discomfort. His own problem didn't mean that the world should stop. He slapped Swede's shoulder. "We're out of here. Both of us. Next fuel port. And . . . congratulations."

Jones joined Swede. They stood at the rail with Native men from the processing line who had no duties for mooring. Hours before, with the volcanic shoreline barely a ridge under low clouds, the processing room had been thoroughly scrubbed so that it smelled more of ammonia than crab. Now, still well before noon, they were close enough to shore to see that the Aleutian mountains swooped upward like waves. A shaft of sun broke through gray clouds. It glowed on a finger of snow that ridged the highest peak, traveled down past rock to slopes of bright green vegetation, and faded.

Akutan village lay in a strip below the mountains. Some of the Aleut workers might have murmured and pointed from the rail, but there wasn't much to see. High grass surrounded a spread of low-gabled buildings. A pole above one structure bore an American flag that flapped in the wind. There was a church, to judge by the cross atop its clapboard peak and the fenced crosses in the weeds around it. A few open boats bobbed along a pier of thick pilings. Not much else.

Men had started out to them in some of the boats. Vladimir, the spokesman, pointed. "That's my older brother there. Boat with red paint on the bow? He's chief. Coming out to get me. My wife and the other women probably inside cooking up a nice celebration." The ship tied at the pier of an abandoned whaling station across the lagoon from the village. Mooring lines had barely thumped down before men in some of the small boats had crossed to within shouting distance. They talked with the *Deep Sea* workers in a language Jones made no attempt to follow, since it wasn't English.

After calling back and forth to his brother, Vladimir declared, "Sure! That's what I figured since we've been gone from home here a while. Big party and dance tonight. Everybody's invited. The boats, they'll come back after they've taken us home who live here, to get everybody else for the party. Six o'clock, okay? Don't need to worry about dinner. Plenty of fish. And a pilot shot a moose over on the mainland and flew it in when he came, so plenty of meat."

"Local party?" Jones muttered to Swede standing beside him. "And since when did moose season open so early? Just fly me home."

But it turned out that no floatplane was scheduled to come or go that day, nor did any boat plan to make the trip across open sea to the larger island and airstrip at Dutch Harbor. A private single-passenger plane had dropped off some Japanese man earlier, someone in the village said by radio, but no one knew if it intended to return. Jones shrugged at the news, since nothing could be done about it, and Swede persuaded him to go ashore for the afternoon—something to do before the party that night. "For education," as Swede put it. "Every new place is an education."

"I already know all I need to about this place." Jones had retorted. But by two o'clock, with nothing else to do, Jones wore dungarees cleaned in the ship's washing machine and joined Swede and two of the Norwegian deck men waiting for the boat to shore. A ship's lifeboat had been lowered for the occasion, since most of the town's skiffs were smaller and slower, and it had already taken ashore one of the college types who knew the place from a previous visit. The sun had long ago disappeared. They made the crossing facing into a chilly wind that blew rain into their eyes. The upper mountains had turned as gray as the sky, although the green lower slopes closer to view showed misty dots of yellow and white wildflowers. By now, Jones had stopped fretting about Adele and what to do for her. They'd move to Kodiak. He'd catch king crabs. She'd settle in. He had even mellowed enough to shrug off the fact that Swede and the others began to joke in their own foreign lingo.

The village itself didn't look any more appealing up close than from a distance. For every one-story clapboard house painted white or yellow, another had boards weathered nearly to black. There appeared to be no formal yards, although washed clothes hung on lines in the back of some houses. Weeds and flowers sprouted together beside a couple of muddy roads. Large dogs, none hostile, roamed freely.

"Over here, guys!" called the college man named Tom who had come on the earlier boat. He stood at the back of a house larger than most. It had a store in front and a rear entrance sheltered from the rain. Jones had found the man friendly on the bridge—guy in his late thirties with black hair always combed it seemed. Gone to school with Wakefield or the captain, talked seriously about things like opportunity before it was too late, but seemed willing enough to have a laugh on deck whenever he pitched in.

"Don't worry, you're invited," Tom said. "But leave your shoes on the linoleum just inside." To Swede, Tom muttered, "I told you earlier about the man who lives here. Pretty well runs the village. Some of us always call here first, and he expects us. Scottish. Settled in years ago, married here, runs the main store, has kids all ages—so don't act surprised. Not the village chief, of course—he's Aleut. But the guy who pretty much calls the shots. It'll be his wife and a couple of daughters in the kitchen."

Inside, it was warmer by at least thirty degrees. Tom led the way through the kitchen, where a woman and two girls, all with Native features, stopped for a moment to acknowledge them, before beginning again to bustle. The counter spaces were crowded with opened cans and food in various stages of preparation, and gray sun streamed through the rain-spattered windows. Tom introduced the woman. She paused to wipe her hands on her apron, shake each of theirs, and declare, "You fellahs go right on into the living room and make yourselves comfortable."

The living room was as shuttered as the kitchen had been bright. It had a slight odor of kerosene, probably from a freestanding stove that radiated heat. Curtains, furniture, and rug all seemed to be of the same dark material. The girls from the kitchen followed, carrying folding chairs for the new guests. Sitting in the widest stuffed chair was the Scotsman himself. He rose easily although he was rather more fleshy than the others, shook hands with a firm grip as Tom introduced first Swede, the two Norwegians, then Jones, then settled back down, adjusting his sweater jacket. "Always welcome here, gentlemen. What's yer pleasure, tea or coffee?" When they all spoke for coffee, he nodded toward the girls, who had stayed a moment longer to watch.

"We were talking about king crab," Tom said. "Mr. McGregor remembers how, before the war, Japanese boats sometimes came all the way here to catch them. Of course they don't anymore. Oh. Sorry. Didn't introduce you over there." He gestured toward a man in the darkest corner of the room, who had risen. "I didn't catch your name, sir. From northern Japan, right?"

The man stepped forward with a tentative bow, hesitated, then extended his hand. "Kiyoshi Tsurifune, sir. It is . . . interesting pleasure that we meet again."

The two Norwegians shook the proffered hand. Swede observed politely, "Interesting to see you again so soon."

Jones remained with hands firmly at his sides. "You trailing us?"

The Japanese half-bowed. "Mr. Jones, uh, Mr. Henry. My happiness that we meet many times. Sir."

"Gotten to be more meetings than I can understand." Jones scowled. "What business have you got, all the way out here?"

"We wished in Bristol Bay to explore purchase market for salmon, sir. And now also I am sent to report on large crabs." Kiyoshi hesitated long enough to assemble the necessary words. "Sent to investigate . . . the sharing of great salmon and crab resource. Here in the great seas of America. Here where there is enough to feed everybody."

Jones snorted. "Yeah, that'll be the day." But as he looked around at all the foreigners in the room, he felt uneasy. What kind of war had he thought his country had won?

"Actually," said Tom, "from what I gather, Mister . . . uh . . . Surifurie here flew over this morning from Dutch Harbor because he heard our *Deep Sea* was coming in to fuel. Private plane'll come back to fetch him when he radios. Wants to look us over. Suits me. After we leave here, I'll take him back to the ship with me for a look-see." He glanced at Swede and Jones. "Wham-bam tour, nothing uh, proprietary. No harm in seeing what the Japanese market might want."

"Might want your balls and then some," muttered Jones.

"Sit, sit, everybody," said the Scotsman affably. "Make yourselves at home. You've met before, eh?" He called toward the kitchen. "Becky, lass, you hurry with the coffee now. And bring more tea for our Japanese friend." He swept out his hands. "Sit, sit. There're enough times around here when we've got to be standing."

"I see a few houses fresh painted," Tom remarked.

"Prosperity, sir. Thanks to the jobs some of our people have on your ship. Even the little church got painted. And some of the gold-colored stuff on the altar has been renewed inside, my wife tells me. Directed by Father Rostoff who goes from church to church down the island chain. Of course, I was raised Protestant and that's all Russian Orthodox, but no matter to me except people should be content and behave themselves, eh?"

"Part of *Deep Sea*'s charter, to hire locals." Tom glanced toward the window. "And a nice part of the world to be in, when the sun shines. Never seen such wildflowers."

"Well, sir, now's not a bad time around here, you understand. The days are still a wee bit long. Mosquitoes gone mostly. Snow not come yet."

Jones chose a chair as far from the Japanese as possible. Both men sat straight, even though the others settled in. Jones's narrow-eyed glance once caught the man regarding him likewise from across the room, before both looked away. *Dressed better than me*, he thought. *Maybe important. Face all blank like those people do, except for that shitty little smile that gives no idea what he's thinking. But he's up to something, just like in Naknek a month back. What kind of war . . . anyhow?*

The girl named Becky brought in a tray with coffee in cups that all matched except for one. Beside the cups was a can of PET Milk with a hole punched on either side of the top. Mr. McGregor leaned over to clear the table in front of him for the tray. He picked up a white inch-high figure and turned it in his hand. "Pretty little thing. From Mr. . . . our Japanese friend here." To the girl. "Take this, lass. Put it somewhere, eh?"

While he was speaking, a Native man entered and waited respectfully until the Scotsman was finished before asking about what he called "that ribbon stuff for tonight."

"Indeed, indeed." The Scotsman pulled a ring of keys from his side, detached one, and handed it over. "Storage locker in the loft. Bring the key back right away. Then decorate things right, my boy. I'll come by later to inspect."

"Yes, sir." The man left, slipping back into his boots at the kitchen door.

"And now, gentlemen. Can I help you with anything? After weeks of daily routine—months it seems—we have not only your ship here with some of our own people. From my radio, I learned that late today the Coast Guard ship *Sweetbrier* will dock over there beside you for water-whatever. We have a busy day, you see."

"Long as we're talking," ventured Jones. "I wouldn't mind to wet my whistle at a bar before this dance, if you can point me there."

"By 'tam," laughed one of the Norwegians. "Dis man's new here."

Even the Scotsman joined in a laugh as he declared, "New here indeed, I see! If yer bad injured, laddie, you'll come to me and I'll open my medicine chest a bit. But that's all, and I'm sorry for you then. Liquor with these people and they fall apart. So not a drop of it's the rule in my village here. Enforced by myself since I came. Since I saw what harm come of it. Even myself, and I sometimes miss it, I must admit. Better luck to ya over in

Dutch Harbor at that place they call 'Elbow Room.' Where otherwise good men go sloppin' in the streets picking fights, eh?"

There was a silence—what more could a hard-working man say after that? Tom ventured, "This is sure good coffee!"

"We save it for special occasions, sir. Like this day. Other days we drink tea." The Scotsman again settled comfortably against the crocheted doily covering the velveteen of his chair. "Now. You fellows all better have your dancin' shoes ready for tonight. You'll be needing 'em!"

From the Scotsman's house, Tom led them through the rain along a dirt road to the door of the village chief's house. Included in the group now was the Jap, who trailed far enough behind that Jones had no trouble keeping his distance. The chief's house was small, but fresh-painted. This time the man himself was waiting to receive them. He wore a checked shirt, newer-looking than the one he'd worn on the welcoming boat, and nodded to them with grave dignity. Also at the door was his younger brother Vladimir. Now, instead of the rubber apron and boots he wore when at work aboard the *Deep Sea*, he was dressed in a coat and tie, although he stood in socks, like his brother, and he had shaved. "You fellows come in, now. It's cold out there."

Only Jones needed a reminder to leave his brogans on the linoleum inside the door. Smells of fish blended with those of kerosene stoves. As at the Scotsman's house, but with less space, they were led through a kitchen where women bustled (but without introduction) and into a living room. Chairs had already been placed around. The chief motioned for them to sit. He himself settled into an armchair covered with blue cloth and adjusted a loose tasseled-edge of the cloth that that covered frayed stuffing. His brother Vladimir sat on a chair beside him. Behind them on the white-painted wall was mounted an icon of the Virgin alongside a framed certificate embossed with an American flag. A shelf underneath held a small vase, a china dog, and other knick-knacks. Unframed pictures on another wall depicted a thorn-crowned bleeding Christ and some family snapshots.

The Jap produced a small, wrapped box from his pocket and handed it to the chief with a slight bow. "For good friendship, sir."

Tom grinned at him. "Hey, how many of these you bring?"

"These only, sir. Netsuke they are called."

"Ahh." The chief examined the box, carefully removed the wrapping and folded it—for reusing, as Jones figured—then lifted open the top. "Ah!" He lifted out a tiny carved figure like the one given to the Scotsman, although the pose appeared to be different. He held it for his brother to see but did not hand it over.

Tom bent to look at it also. "Different little carving. Japanese shogun maybe. Looks like ivory. Even got an etched pattern on the guy's robes. Nice."

The chief spoke, and Vladimir translated, "My brother, he says thank you. He'll put it up on the shelf there with his other good stuff. But first he's going to keep it a while right beside him."

The chief called out something in Aleut. Immediately, a Native woman came in with a large tray that she set on a table. She wore a blue dress that looked new, printed with red and yellow flowers. He showed her the carved figure. She exclaimed, glanced at the Japanese, then left quickly. Two dishes on the tray contained chunks of fish with meat both reddish and gray. Some of the chunks had pieces of skin attached. The chief nodded to his guests and said something. "Eat. Please," translated Vladimir. "My brother says the salmon pieces with skin taste best. Of course, plenty more tonight."

Tom, who had apparently visited before, led the way once more by taking a piece in his fingers, popping it in his mouth, and declaring, "Tell the chief this is a good smoke batch, Vlad. Here, guys, dig in." He handed a plate to Swede, who followed suit in good humor, passed it on, and licked his fingers clean. At least these people know how to smoke a fish, Jones conceded after chewing a piece.

Vlad continued to translate. "My brother hopes you will enjoy the dance tonight. Everybody's fixing good stuff to eat." He grinned. "And some of us . . . well, we can make pretty good music. You'll see."

"Please expect us!" Swede declared. He glanced at Tom. "Maybe we should learn more about markets in Japan. Too bad Mr. Tsurifune will miss the party here tonight."

Tom shrugged. "If he wants to stay we'll put him up."

"Back at the ship we can radio your pilot not to come for you today," Swede said to the Japanese. "Go tomorrow instead."

The Japanese seemed pleased and excited, although he appeared to be trying to hide it. "This will be . . . very nice, sir!"

"Then what the heck," Tom declared and entered into the spirit of it. "Two ship's owners here, so I declare a majority. Maybe even serve you some of our crab and salmon. You might as well see we've got a good product." He stretched, and the notion seemed to grow on him. "Done. Stay the night. We have at least one bunk vacant that I know of. In the cabin where you sleep, Jones. And he's welcome to it, right, Jones?"

Jones tried not to show his anger and disgust since it was clear he had no say in the matter. Just get out of this Jap-loving place as soon as possible.

3 1

ALEUTIAN DANCE

A fter paying their visits to the two head men of Akutan Village, Kiyoshi Tsurifune accompanied the Americans by open boat back to the catching-processing vessel *Deep Sea*. What luck! When he'd engaged the little plane to fly him from Dutch Harbor to Akutan, it had been merely to familiarize himself with a Native village as part of his general reconnaissance. Dealing with their Natives might be a necessary component of doing business in this part of America. But now, by visiting their new processor ship, he could actually observe a new American seafood venture. Could report on how it competed with or might be of use to a Japanese enterprise.

Once aboard the vessel *Deep Sea,* the man Tom took him to a cabin and indicated a bunk. "You can sleep here tonight. I'll have them make it up with sheets. Get you a towel. Mr. Jones Henry here, he'll—. Hey Jones, where are you? Thought he was right with us. Well, anyhow, make yourself at home. I showed you the messdeck on the way down. Get coffee or tea any time there, okay? We'll all go back to that dance in two hours time, so rest up and get ready."

Left to himself, Kiyoshi exited the cabin in favor of exploring the ship. Before long he had found the processing compartment—now vacant. It smelled strongly of disinfectant. At the long preparation tables he counted out spaces for the number of workers who might line them. Looking around first to make sure he was alone, he pulled open the heavy, latched door of a freeze locker. He propped a box in the doorframe to make sure the locker wouldn't close on him and quickly pulled trays from a rack coated white with ice. His breath frosted. Big crab legs. And a red-fleshed fish that was surely salmon. Yes. Here indeed was product and opportunity.

"Lose something?" At the entrance to the locker door stood the man Jones Henry.

"Ah! Only . . . looking."

"So I can see."

Kiyoshi rapidly followed the man outside and closed the heavy locker door behind him. "Good product, sir," he ventured.

"Lose your way? I'll take you to the messdeck."

"So. Yes. Thank you."

A few hours later, Kiyoshi stood with Tom, Swede, and Jones Henry in the boat that took them from the processing vessel *Deep Sea* back across the lagoon to the village of Akutan. It was nearly dusk. Lights flickered in some of the houses ashore. Against the rain, they all wore borrowed oilskin coats that dripped water around their feet. Kiyoshi wore also the dark suit in which he had come from Dutch Harbor that morning, and the same shoes, although Swede had loaned him dry socks. Behind them at the old whaling station, the expected Coast Guard ship moved in to tie behind the *Deep Sea*. Its black hull, brown superstructure, and even its flags appeared dimly through the rain, but Kiyoshi could tell that this was a longer vessel than the processor that had taken him aboard for the night. Good fortune thus to experience both vessels and their crews in a single visit! Six years ago at war's end, American sailors had been kind and generous. Had given him denim pants—now patched beyond wear and folded in honorable retirement, never to be discarded. So, now, more American sailors. Would they still be kind to a foreigner?

Stay controlled. Despite the fact that he now represented a fishing company, he might see the men on this military ship in their uniforms and automatically bow to them as victors still. No longer should he be ashamed to be alive—a soldier defeated. The call for honorable suicide had long passed. He was alive. With a son. Yes, representing fishing vessels. Was treated with respect. His glance, as it often did, stole toward Jones Henry. He was of Kiyoshi's group, but yet stood apart from him. The American most important of all, to whom he owed his life. The man's jaw stayed rigid under a cap pulled down against the rain, his eyes cold whenever their gazes crossed. Perhaps the only American he feared. Unpaid obligation. However to repay it?

When the boat's engine stopped he could hear the chug of generators ashore. The tide was low. Kiyoshi followed Tom and Swede up the slippery ladder from boat to pier. Barely had he reached the uppermost planking when a large dog barked straight into his face. With a cry he scrambled back down the ladder and his legs tangled with the head of Jones Henry behind him.

"Watch yourself!" Jones cried.

Above them Tom laughed. "Come on up, he's not going to hurt you. Here boy, nice fellow. Look at that tail wagging." Trembling with shame and trepidation, Kiyoshi steeled himself to climb again and step onto the pier. If the others were so bold, better to have the terrible creature bite him than to show fear. To Jones Henry behind him he dipped his head—not bowed—in apology.

"Yeah, yeah," muttered Jones.

Two other dogs ran over, all of them barking. Large ugly black creatures! Kiyoshi pressed against his companions as much as he dared while they walked onward. But indeed the dogs did not bite. And, for what difference it made, their tails did wag. Tom strode ahead along a muddy road, past small, newly painted houses to a long low building lit brightly inside. As they approached, a nearby generator made an especially loud spitting noise and then stopped altogether. All the lights went out. A Native man came running from the door to examine it. "Guess we forgot to fill the tank again from the last party," he muttered. "We better go pump some more."

"Run then, lad," directed the Scotsman, who had appeared at the door. "Run! Run! The ladies inside are all bumping against each other in the dark." He saw the men from the boat. "Welcome. Welcome. Come in from the rain. I've exaggerated the dark inside, you see, to make him hurry or he might take all night, eh? Come. Welcome!"

Inside, with only a couple of windows to admit the fading daylight, it was indeed dim. As Kiyoshi's eyes adjusted he watched everywhere the shapes of people moving about. In another circumstance, perhaps only in a dream, they could have been spirits. Soon their features took form. Among those adjusting cloths and setting platters on long tables he recognized the women from the two kitchens he had entered. Busy at women's work. Some men shouted from ladders as they hung what appeared to be garland. Others opened folding chairs and lined them against the walls. A few men clustered on a small stage. Kiyoshi recognized the chief they had visited and his brother, the Native worker from the ship. From the sounds that followed, Kiyoshi guessed they were tuning musical instruments.

"Going to be a big night, eh?" declared the Scotsman. "Not only you fine fellows from the *Deep Sea*, but soon also the men from the Coast Guard cutter *Sweetbrier* just come in for fuel. After nothing but ourselves for weeks—nay since the last time *Deep Sea* tied here three months ago! And soon winter, and nothin' coming again till spring. So this is a night!" He wiped sweat from his face with a large cloth.

Kiyoshi stepped clear as a swath of glittering ornaments flopped to the floor. Tom picked it up and handed it back to one of the men on a ladder who had been trying to nail it to a beam.

"No, no. You fellows now, don't need to work. Hang your oilskins on that rack by the door. Then serve yourselves fruit punch over where the ladies are setting up. Find chairs and relax." The Scotsman turned politely to Kiyoshi. "Tea in a pitcher there, too, sir. My wife fixed it special, since that's what you people drink, eh?" He wiped his face again. "So! We'll have lights back on soon. And the music. And everything! Just be patient!"

Outside, the generator started to put-put. Lights flickered and died out again. Finally, the generator settled into a steady roar and lights suddenly glared in the hall. "Ah!" exclaimed several of the townspeople. Kiyoshi looked around. Indeed, there now glowed enough red and yellow from the paper garlands draped from the roof to resemble a temple at festival.

An hour or so later, amid the noise, Kiyoshi had found a chair near the doorway and settled in safely while people talked and moved around him. It was informative to watch. How at first the Americans stayed apart even from the Native men who served on the same ship, though both groups served themselves punch and food elbow-to-elbow at the table. How then the Native men up on stage began to play vigorous music on a violin and two accordions. How the Native women and girls from the village came, most of them shyly, to lead both sets of men to the dance floor. How then, gradually, the people intermixed. In Japan, if such an unlikely situation had ever presented itself, neither group would have combined with the other. Yet there would have been far more politeness between the two. Surely no laughs and loud calls back and forth.

He hardly dared admit how invigorating it would be to become part of such a thing. Certainly never admit it to the vessel owners back in Shiogama, or to his wife, or even to Father. None of them would understand. He himself barely understood. So just continue to smile, he told himself, while he watched two kinds of Americans deal with each other. Suddenly the door burst open. Snow blew in and with it, three sailors in uniform. They each carried a cardboard box.

"The Coast Guard has landed!" announced one of the men. Someone in the hall called out a welcome in good cheer. It was the friendly man named Tom. Another man from the *Deep Sea* vessel echoed.

"And what's that?" Tom continued. "Snow? In September?"

"Wet. Just all of a sudden. Won't last." The Scotsman hurried over and shook each of the Coast Guard sailors' hands. "Stuff for the party? On the radio they said you might bring something. Over here. Over here. The man said maybe ice cream, eh? And maybe hot dogs and lettuce that I said we've been out of since the last steamer?"

"Ice cream's already starting to melt, sir. We don't have dry ice, just regular ice."

One of the women opened a box and held up a chocolate-covered ice-cream bar. The music stopped. The stage and dance floor emptied as villagers crowded around. They tore off wrappers, some of which fell to the floor, and joked as they ate.

"Ah. And there you have a true party!" exclaimed the Scotsman as he pulled off an ice cream wrapper himself and bit into the dessert.

Others from the Coast Guard ship arrived, brushing wet snow from their coats. The sailors wore short black jackets and caps of either dark wool or of a rigid white fabric. They stayed together for a while, looking around as a group. Some of the girls came over, bashfully it seemed. Kiyoshi watched, apart as he knew himself to be, yet drawn to what was happening. Those sailors who paired to dance with the girls did not always return to their own group, which gradually scattered.

Then there were three officers, to judge from their longer overcoats and flattened hats rather than caps. They looked around, then headed toward Tom and the other, older Caucasian members of the *Deep Sea*, and soon were shaking hands. When the Scotsman joined them, they each shook his hand also. A few minutes later came two men in brown uniform rather than black. They entered no further than the doorway and stood against the wall near Kiyoshi. He turned only for a moment to watch them. One had eyebrows so thick and black that they looked like brush strokes, as on the makeup of a Kabuki actor. The man scowled, but his companion nodded to Kiyoshi, who kept his automatic smile but turned quickly away. He made himself concentrate on the center floor where some of the sailors had begun to dance. One of them hugged his girl close. Another pushed his partner an arm's length and then pulled her back while his own legs bent in time to the music. Her red dress had spare pieces of cloth on the shoulders that flared out when she twirled. In both instances the girls appeared, with their happy-seeming eyes, to be enjoying themselves. Were they not the girls working with their mother in Mr. McGregor's kitchen, those daughters who had brought out extra chairs? His own Miki back home in Japan, although forthright and lively in the privacy of their home, would surely never before their marriage have been so bold in public. Nor in front of strangers. And these men seemed so self-assured. They expected such behavior. Even if he wished to be American, he realized, there were barriers he could never expect to surmount. Nor ever wish to!

"If I wanted one, I'd take that blister in the red," said the Coast Guard man with black eyebrows who stood near him.

"You don't want to fool with these Native girls, Jimmy," the other replied.

"I said if I wanted one, cuz. That one looks less gook than the others. Didn't mean I was going to waste my cock in a hole like this. Where they might make you marry one if you knocked her up."

"You're always making jokes."

"I never joke about some things, Hancock. See you back at the ship."

"Come on, stick around."

"Need to do paint locker inventory. Or rope locker. Working buoys out there in shitty weather you never get the chance."

"That's work you tell your striker to do, man. What's eating you? Relax. This here's just a party with nice people. Other times there's plenty for the rest."

"Times ashore here in these islands, we ought to be out shooting birds or catching fish or whatever. Not dressed up and drinking lemonade. Not tit-wiggling with girls we can't shack up with."

"Just a nice little party, Jim. Look how they've gone to all this trouble decorating for us. How they're all dressed up for us."

"Yeah. In red."

Suddenly one of the Native women approached Kiyoshi and, without warning, took his hand. "You dance? You come on, now." Before he could reply she had pulled him to his feet and led him to the open floor. What followed was exhilarating, even though the most he could do was stumble in time to the music, trying to follow her feet in their bright green shoes. She never relinquished his hand. Fortunately, she never pulled him close to her as some of the others were doing. After a few minutes he was able to anticipate her steps better. By the time that the music stopped and she had led him back to his chair. He wanted to continue, and his smile was not plastered on to guard himself.

"Lookin' good there, buddy," laughed the American named Tom as they passed each other.

"Hai!" he panted. Tom's back was already turned when he remembered to say, "Yes. Yes!" instead.

He was relieved to see that the two sailors in brown had moved. They stood now by a table, loading food onto their plates. Seated again, Kiyoshi could hardly stay still. He glanced everywhere, enjoying all the sights. There were not only loops of sparkling paper draped from the boards of the ceiling, but strips of bright cloth fastened along the walls. Decorations even across the tops of the windows, where wind from outside made the material billow and ripple. His gaze traveled until it located Jones Henry. The man stood alone at another corner of the hall, staring straight at him. Kiyoshi nodded automatically. The stare continued with no acknowledgment. Kiyoshi looked away. So. Perhaps it was not so good that he would be sharing a cabin with this man.

32

FORBIDDEN HOOTCH

Look at him there, Jones Henry thought. The grin on his face could have been painted on an egg for all it told. That Jap smirk. As if everything he saw was as good as anything else. Treacherous. And the rest. Colored paper hanging like they were at some low-budget circus. Some of the ribbons had already flopped to the floor and been kicked around by the dancers until somebody ran out and grabbed it up. And that half-assed music from two accordions and a squeaking violin. At least a Victrola could have played records of real dancing music, like Glenn Miller or Tommy Dorsey. Not that he himself was any kind of fancy dancer, but just the same. Maybe if Adele was here hanging on his arm, and laughing for a change, it would be different. Be okay.

It was going to be a long night if the best thing they served at this so-called party was sugar water. Long past time to forget all this and go home to Ketchikan. Things to face there that wouldn't sort themselves out. The move to Kodiak would have to help. Best get back there and look for a place. A move he half wanted to make and half didn't, since it meant leaving the folks. Well, if it wasn't Kodiak where there was fishing for a man, she'd start talking California again, with her folks and a naval base and who knew what-all.

After the Coast Guard stormed through the door, things at the dance picked up a little. The wet snow they carried in on their shoulders seemed to signal a change of more than the weather. The older women setting out the table started giggling among themselves while the younger ones pulled at their dresses to smooth them straight. If only the Coasties had brought some booze along with their ice cream.

Most of the Coastie sailors were just kids, willing enough to dance if the girls approached them. Easy stuff he himself had long outgrown, back during the war when he'd first strutted in his uniform. The couple of officers homed straight toward the college types aboard the *Deep Sea* and soon were talking about things like . . . banks and opera, probably. Then there were the two chiefs he knew from Eva's on Creek Street all those years back. Guys who had inspected his bilge realistically and could tie a knot or two. His own kind, finally.

After a while, leaving time so as not to appear too eager, Jones strode over to one of the tables to pick up a piece of smoked salmon and then ambled to join them. He addressed the one named Hancock whom he remembered as friendly from Eva's. "Didn't know they let guys like you in here," he said.

"Seeing how they let you in," rumbled Hancock in good humor, "I guess they're already going to hell."

"Pretty far from Ketchikan for you Coasties."

"Shows how much you don't know." Hancock pulled a rumpled pack of Camels from his coat pocket and offered them around. Jones and the other chief each took one, then lit up on a single match that Hancock struck. "Coast Guard goes to Westward like this twice a year, one of our ships or another. Near six thousand miles round trip from Ketchikan for us. Do it in springtime after the ice, then early autumn before the shitty weather sets in. We load off supplies to all the light stations clear to Sarichef and Scotch Cap. Then out to other Coast Guard outfits like the loan station in Attu. Service harbor buoys and other aids clear up in the Bering to the Pribilofs. All that. Then do the same run again in early fall before shitty winter settles in. Navy and army might grease their guns in peacetime, but we go on doing real work."

"Yeah? Where's the Coast Guard station here in this dump?"

"Came to Akutan for water at that old whaling station. Could do it at the old naval base in Dutch Harbor next stop on the Chain, but the people here always make us welcome. Then there're the bars in Dutch. More problems with shore leave. What's your excuse to be here?"

Jones hesitated. Was there any secret to it? Finally: "Big crabs. Just curious."

The other chief looked him over coolly, pursing his black eyebrows practically into a straight line across his forehead. "Fishing, cuz? This far out?" He snorted. "Not enough that we pull your troubled asses from the water back in Southeast. Now you'll go sink boats all the way out here and expect us to save you."

At last, this was the kind of talk Jones felt at ease with. "Rather go down than trouble you," he said easily.

"Now, buddy." Ed Hancock turned to Jones. "Jimmy Amberman here likes to bitch. But you're in luck if he ever has to come save you. Providing you can stand his mouth."

Just then one of the Native men hurried over. "No smoking inside the center here. Didn't anybody tell you? Fire and all."

"Oh, sorry," said Hancock. "Should've remembered." Rather than stop smoking, the three went outside. Wet snow blew into their faces. The big flakes caught up a glow from the lights in a few of the houses. It softened the dark mountain sweep behind the village and blurred lights on the two ships across the water.

"Oh man," said Hancock, and he drew in on his cigarette. "Be glad to get back to civilization." He blew out a puff of smoke. "Watching this poontang I dassent touch makes me miss—never mind."

"Do it or don't do it, cuz," grumbled Jimmy Amberman. "Just stop bitching."

A head poked from around the building. "If you come out for a slug of this, don't think you'll get it at the doorway."

"That you, Kowalczyk?"

"Guy here just sold me some stuff. Says he makes it secret in his house. I wouldn't touch home-hootch if we was in Dutch where they got bars with the real stuff. But I'll say this shit has a kick."

At the suggestion, Jimmy came to life. "I hear church bells!" He laughed and tossed away his cigarette, heading for the corner.

"Won't hurt to see what he's got," Jones declared, and followed.

"Take it easy there," called Hancock. "This place is supposed to be booze-free."

"Then better come see for yourself, cuz." Hancock inhaled the last puff from his cigarette, then ground out the butt and trailed after them.

An hour or so later, the three—along with Kowalczyk, the quartermaster who had found the bootleg—leaned comfortably against the side of the building. They passed the bottle between them as they watched the snow slowly whiten a nearby pile of boards and, beside it, a wheelbarrow. The native who had sold it to them had slipped off to fetch another bottle—this one was already nearly empty. The wall they had chosen to lean on was opposite the musicians inside. Jones listened to the scrape of the fiddle and the accordions wailing. Calls and sometimes a laugh rose from the hum of voices and thump of feet. It all sounded better out here, he decided.

Amberman clung to the bottle longest when it was passed around. He handed it on without comment whenever one of the others muttered, "Quit hoggin' there, buddy" but held his hand ready to receive it back.

Suddenly Hancock turned to Jones with half-closed eyes that had lost their directness. "When they transferred me up here for a two-year tour, Ellie stayed down in Tillamook with her folks. Like I hadn't been away enough during the war. Maybe away too long. If we'd had kids . . . I figure they'll transfer me back after two years, then with my war record not mess with me no more until retirement. So we ought to keep the house there, I guess. But these long trips, even though I get a month home leave to Oregon afterward. I'm a man, you know. Need things a man needs."

"Should've stayed single then, cuz," growled Amberman. Through his growing buzz, Jones felt a sobering pang. Did he want to lose that girl back in Ketchikan? What was he doing so far from her? What kind of man was he to leave her for so long, just because he'd grown restless? What if she found somebody else back there? Somebody who treated her right.

Once started, Hancock didn't seem able to stop talking. He had by now decided that the Coast Guard's spring and autumn trips to Westward were at least sometimes interesting. "You want souvenirs? Some places where we kicked the Japs off, like Kiska and Attu, there's all kinds of crap they left before they committed harry-carry or whatever. And us—the USA! You ought to see the stuff we left behind when the war ended. Stuff just . . . left!

Not just ponchos and canteens and cots all in piles. Bulldozers, all yellow and rusting! There for the taking. Cheaper to leave stuff than to ship it back to the States, somebody at the base in Adak told me last year. So we just left it all out there to the rain and the wind."

"Don't mean they didn't collect up the guns and ammunition," muttered Jimmy. "Nothing left worth taking."

The initial burn of the homebrewed liquor down Jones's throat had lessened with each swig. His buzz was in full swing by now. "Canteen? Where'd you say? Wouldn't mind one of them things again. Always had my canteen back in the Marines. Wonder what happened to it?"

"Marine, eh?" Hancock turned enough to face him so that Jones could see in the dim light the heavy features glistening with snow melting down from his hair. "We took Marines in on landing barges. Near shit ourselves dodging Jap shore rockets to take Marines into—where? You name it. Iwo, Kwajalein, Okie. Then those guys waded in and took it. At least, if we wasn't hit we gunned back out of range until the next time."

Jones took a while to think it through. Jimmy and the quartermaster stood in black silhouette a few steps away, paying them no attention. "Well. You mebbe took me in to one of them beaches. Me and my buddies. If so, at least you didn't turn back. Till you got us as close in to shallow as you could." He took another swig from the bottle. It tasted less like rotten fruit than the swig before. "Them landing barges. Some dumped their soldiers short of the beach. Deep water where guys drowned. Packs were too damn heavy. Too chicken to take them all the way in. Guess you weren't."

"Not for lack of wanting to. No. Not for lack."

Jones stared up at the white-topped mountain that hemmed in the village. It seemed to expand and close in as he watched. Instinctively, he pressed back against the dancehall boards.

"Guts?" Hancock muttered softly. "Oh you guys had guts to jump off that barge and wade in."

Suddenly the vision opened fresh for Jones. "On the beach, some of my buddies," he blurted. "Guts all over the sand and rocks. Slipped in guts still warm, from my own bud—." The memory engulfed him. He began to sob in gulps beyond control. "Fuckin' Japs!"

Beside him, Hancock's voice turned husky. "Yeah. Yeah." When the Native brought them a second bottle, Hancock pulled the cork and handed it to Jones first. A windy gust blew the snow clear. A tarpaulin flew against the wheelbarrow, snagged, and remained flapping. The low peaked roofs of the village emerged like lines on a slate, and the sloping mountain behind seemed to retreat. In a moment the air turned colder.

"Weather's blowing worse," said Hancock. "We should get out of here, back to sea. Finish that Coast Guard's Westward run while we can. So it don't screw my Christmas leave back to Oregon."

After they had emptied the second bottle, they pulled themselves together enough to return straight-backed to the party. Laughing, Jones and Hancock steadied themselves with arms locked over each others' shoulders. Jimmy, who might have drunk the most, glowered and strode in, seemingly unaffected. Kowalczyk started with them, but vomited and instead wove off in another direction.

The stove heat and noise in the hall hit Jones hard as he entered. Hard even to breathe through the thick smell of kerosene and sweat. In the fudge of sounds, feet banged, a fiddle squeaked, people yelled. And all the colors waved. Silvery bands of tinsel blew in his face from the wind at the open door. He brushed them aside. But loops of red and green stuff from the bare boards of the ceiling swooped practically into his face. When he tried to wave them off they turned out to be far above his head.

People on the dance floor seemed to ripple as he watched. There lumbered two of the big Norwegian deckhands from the ship, clutching their partners and half stomping as if they wore heavy boots. And young Native guys, some from the *Deep Sea* processing lines, hopped with their girls past sailors in tight dress blues who danced smoothly with their own girls. They all blurred alike. Young and old. The chief. Even chuckling, fat old Native women who bounced and kicked their heels in time to the music as they held tight onto their men.

There was Swede standing in a corner with the captain and the owners of the *Deep Sea*. A Coast Guard officer was among them, and the Scotsman. All so like gentlemen. Holding cups of drink like at a tea party. Kissing each others' asses.

On the dance floor, one woman even clung tight to the Jap, pushing him step by step in time to the music while he smiled that Jap smile. What was Jones doing at this dance a thousand miles from his own woman? Should be home holding Adele. Have it again the way it was just a couple years ago, when she'd still leaned her head against his shoulder. Before the baby. He rubbed his head to clear it. Things weren't right.

Jimmy Amberman barely paused before he strode onto the dance floor. With barely a motion at all, he nudged the Native girl in red and took her from the *Deep Sea* Norwegian named Lars. Lars stood for a minute, scratching his head. Then he strode up, pulled Jimmy off by the shoulder, and resumed dancing with the girl. Seconds later, the two men had locked against each other, exchanging angry blows.

The music stopped. Jones and Hancock glanced at each other. They had both been weaving around the food table, filling their plates from bowls of potato salad, smoked fish, and hot dog pieces floating in stewed tomatoes.

"Party's over," Hancock announced. He laid down his plate and headed toward the dance floor.

"Over!" echoed Jones. He made it to the big Norwegian just as Swede and the Scotsman converged from another direction.

"Here now. None of that!" declared the Scotsman. But he didn't intervene. It wasn't easy to separate the two opponents. In the process, Jones ducked Jimmy's fist and it grazed his shoulder enough to hurt. The pain jump-started his anger enough that Swede had to pull him back against Lars the Norwegian. Lars mistook the action and thumped Jones hard before muttering "Oh ja, Jones. Fuck, sorry."

Separated at last, the two original combatants exchanged scowls. The girl for whom they'd fought slipped away as soon as Jimmy released his grip on her. The two watched her, then shrugged.

"Left hook not bad," Jimmy conceded.

Lars wiped his thick fingers across the blood on his chin, and with "Also you," he laughed his "har har."

"I smell alcohol," said the Scotsman. "You don't understand how dangerous it is here with Native people when you have liquor. Please, if you have a bottle of that stuff, remove it back to your ship. You don't understand the work I do here to make certain that—"

"Sorry. Sorry," murmured Swede. "We can't watch everywhere after so long at sea." He frowned at both Jones and Lars. "Kom," he said, taking Lars by the arm. And with a firm sweep of his head, he motioned Jones toward the door. When the big Norwegian seemed to resist, Jones took his other arm—clutched it rather—although he was careful to watch for a fist. But Lars had suddenly turned docile. The three lurched unsteadily toward the door. For a moment, it occurred to Jones that Swede gripped one of his own arms and Lars the other. That they were perhaps leading Jones himself away. In a blur Jones watched Hancock and Jimmy just ahead of them exiting through the door. The music had started up again. Others on the floor had resumed their dance.

Off to the side, the Jap stood watching.

"Well what are you grinnin' at," Jones growled in passing. Didn't the damn Japs ever leave off grinning? Poking their faces in the way? "Better not step on me in the middle of the night." He said it as almost a threat, but by the time Swede and Lars had dragged him through the doorway, Jones was too tired to care much. *Just sleep with one eye open.*

33

DECISION

Before Jones finally returned to Ketchikan, he shuttled from Anchorage back to Kodiak for a day. Saw again the big crabs. If he and Adele had to move, this was where they'd go, he decided. This was the place for a man to have his boat. And when scampering up the hill behind the harbor to view the lay of water, he saw a house with a FOR LEASE sign in front, he contacted the agent listed without a second thought. Hadn't Adele said herself they needed to leave Ketchikan?

Back in Ketchikan, there stood Adele on the tarmac. It was blowing a light southeaster with the typical rain. The flaps of her waterproof coat opened enough to show that she wore the bright green dress that he'd once said he admired. The minute she saw him descending from the plane she began to wave. For a moment, she seemed the eager girl of a half dozen years ago who had hugged his arm so tightly at that Fourth of July parade. He'd barely reached the ground before her arms were around his neck. Perfume smell. It almost embarrassed him, the way his erection popped up. Going to be again like the old days. Starting fresh.

Then she began to sob as she clutched him. He wrapped his arms around her slim shape and held her warm and quivering against him. Her fingers dug into his back. Let her hold, then. He'd escaped it too long. But he knew why he'd had to escape.

He readied to protect her. "Okay, honey," he said at last. "Good news. Couple of days ago I found us a house in Kodiak. Paid six months' rent, so we can pack and go. Any time."

Adele gasped audibly. "Why would we leave here?"

"Before I took off for Bristol Bay you said you were crazy to go." Jones reminded her gently.

"Did I? Did I?" She demanded. Seemed almost frantic. "What could I have been thinking! Leave little Amy's grave behind with strangers?"

"What about my dad and mom? They live here."

"My Amy was not their baby!" Adele snapped. "They've been sweet of course. I'm welcome to dinner any time I want. Even when your dad's away fishing. I mean, if Helen doesn't have some kind of meeting to go to. They're so busy. It's not like having my own parents nearby." She paused, chewing her lip. A stop in the barrage of chatter. "Yes, I want to move. They can transfer a little grave, can't they? But we need to go to California where my daddy's just retired. They'll have all the time in the world for us. And you're so smart. You could get a job anywhere. There's a whole machine factory or something right there. And you, a veteran, they'd probably make you a fore-man very soon."

Jones felt a wave of unease rising close to panic. His gaze swept beyond her shoulder, although he continued to hold her tight. Was she serious? Where the familiar wharf ended, familiar stores began. Joe Stanley, a fisher-man he knew from the boat *Lisa Jane* on the grounds, strode with an engine shaft over his shoulder. Grease smudged the oilskin jacket where the shaft rested, a cap pulled half over his eyes as when he fished, and he hadn't even bothered to change from hip boots. Didn't matter what anybody said. What would it be like someplace else? Leave here where he was known, for any other place?

Suddenly a pack of people moved down the street together like bees in a hive. People dressed for a party rather than work. One of the ships must have docked that shoveled in Seattle tourists for a few hours before moving on to Juneau and whatever. Their mass surrounded Joe, and when they had finally poured into a store selling souvenirs, he had pressed against a wall to avoid their onslaught. Even in Ketchikan, streets had crowds with no stake in the water.

"You'll like Kodiak, honey," he said firmly. "No damn tourist ships and geegaw stores. Place on the hill has a nice view, all the way past the islands to the open water. With a spy glass you'll be able to see me come in from fishing. Fish for crabs so big you'll think I—"

"And a place to bury little Amy?"

"Sure. Whatever you want."

And so it was settled. Jones and Adele Henry would move to Kodiak.

NOVEMBER, 1951

Amy's grave had been removed to the cemetery at Kodiak, not too far from the sea. Jones, in his cleanest clothes, and Adele, in that same green dress, stood at the foot of the little thing's headstone, sharing a moment of quiet in this out of the way spot. Too many memories to speak them all. Adele nestled her head against Jones's shoulder, like back in the old days before baby Amy had even been thought of. Jones held her while she sobbed, not so loudly now she used to, and when she asked to be left by herself, Jones took to wandering the rows of engraved stones and chipped wooden crosses. For a town so small as Kodiak, there were a surprising number of markers. Many of 'em fisherman that died in the frigid waters, Jones supposed. He wondered grimly how many bodies were actually buried with their names, and how many were left to float bloated, with eyes pecked by gulls, undiscovered at sea. Or worse, just a pile of guts and shrapnel lost in Jap-land. Like his own buddies. What were their names? Sokovich. Sugarmouth. His fists clenched. Jimmy Sleeves. Chuck. Callihan. All of 'em.

"Jones, dear?" Adele came up behind him. Grasped the arm he didn't realize till then was shaking. "Take me for a walk through town? Maybe it's time I get acquainted with it," she said and leaned her head against him a second time.

That night, they ate at the restaurant Jones had found with the tablecloths. As Jones had predicted, Adele ordered the Crab Louis. But to the waiter, she pronounced it with the hard "s." Jones corrected her. "That's 'Loo-ey,' honey. It's French."

"Loo-ey," she said, stretching the vowel. Clearly savoring the way the foreign sounds filled her mouth. "Louis."

"I hope you like the food as much as you like the name," Jones said, typically gruff, but with a shy laugh that made Adele smile. How long since he had seen that smile? Didn't just miss it while he was away first at Naknek and then Kodiak, but longer. More than a year and a half. Too long. Keep that girl smiling all through dessert, Jones decided—no matter how much it cost—and all along the walk back to their new home. Maybe even surprise her with something nice. Materials for new curtains, mebbe, like she'd been prattling on about the day before—if Kodiak had a store that sold stuff like that. Doubtful. Ah well, he'd make it up to her. For time lost while off with Dad, with Swede. He'd make her okay.

PART FOUR

34

DEPARTURE

SHIOGAMA, MAY 1952

Kiyoshi Tsurifune kissed his wife Miki in the Western fashion when he departed from their home with the last of his sea-going equipment. Later they might bow formally in parting, if she were to decide to change from Western dress to a traditional kimono when she would come with Kiyoshi's parents to see them off. The blending of their two ways, dictated by the occasion, had begun to be natural.

The fishing ship in the harbor floated with an air of readiness as people began to assemble below. He helped his father up the gangway. Father and son stood aboard, each with legs firmly apart, surveying the deck space around them.

The crewmen greeted them with respectful bows. For himself, Kiyoshi waved the bows aside and announced cheerfully, "No more of this. We're now fishermen together." Indeed, two of the men aboard had served under his command in the field of battle more than a half dozen years before. Happily, he now had the means and authority to employ both brave, reckless Satsumo and quiet, obedient Hito, both of whose fathers had fished for his own father before the war.

While Father had turned over all concern for ship repairs to Kiyoshi, he had kept for himself the selection of the crew. Every one of them was leaving a family on the quay, whether wife and children or aged parents. Father, in choosing from among more applicants than he could sign aboard, had considered both their youthful strength and their family obligations within the community. All had defended the homeland in some capacity. Father had not forgotten his own dead son Shoji, the heroic Kamikaze pilot, whose marker—lacking the comfort of ashes—he still visited regularly.

"Hah, see there," exclaimed Father. Some rust still flecked an underside of the trawl windlass.

"Ai! I'll tell the captain to see to it," declared Kiyoshi. It annoyed him that he hadn't noticed it himself. Through his own efforts, under the general approval of Father, new paint glowed on most of the superstructure, while belowdecks odors of rust and age had been dispelled and the crew cabins were made habitable. How could this small piece of rust have been overlooked?

Yet Kiyoshi could take stock without apology. Ever since his trips as envoy to America, the common people in town had treated him with deference. Even the vessel owners, his seniors, now fell silent when he cleared his throat to speak. All forgotten was any failure to die honorably in battle.

As for the nation itself, some in the big cities were still homeless, sleeping under bridges—as he could see from the train that took him to Tokyo for meetings. But in smaller towns, like his own, there had begun to be food enough at table, so that no one had to pretend to be full so others could be nourished. It was more than a year now since he'd commanded both Miki and his own mother to stop doing this and had with a laugh heaped their plates with more rice and fish than they could eat to make his point—even though to do so he had diminished his own portion.

On the pier, Miki stood with his mother, both holding the hands of his son. The son who carried the name of Kiyoshi's dead brother. Young Shoji, now nearly six years old, wore his school uniform. The boy had, perhaps, been allowed to leave classes for the occasion. He himself had been too busy with preparations to follow his child's schedule. Of most importance, the boy stood straight. Strong. Not fat of course. But sturdy.

Other families had also gathered. Fishermen from the vessel that was about to depart held their children and gazed at their wives in parting. It would perhaps be months before they would all see each other again, depending on the fortune of fish in the American waters that were soon to be opened to their nets.

One of the boys Shoji's own age was puny in comparison. His parents had not sacrificed enough during the hungriest years to nourish the growth of their precious young. His own Shoji stood in vigor like the American children he'd seen in Alaska only a few months ago. The cap on his head that was lettered ALASKA: THE LAST FRONTIER bought for him at the Anchorage airport, sat tilted loose on his head. Too big still, but he'd grow into it. The boy could even say "hello" and "thank you" in English, as coached by his father to the clucking delight of his mother and the admiration of his grandparents.

Kiyoshi held himself straight while permitting his gaze to travel over his vessel's machinery and superstructure. The winter months that had passed since his trip to the salmon and crab fields of Alaska had been eventful. A treaty signed by the governments of America and Japan had finally, officially, cancelled all documents of war between the two nations. He himself, as his town's envoy to the Americans in Tokyo, had helped gain consent for Japanese fishing vessels to enter the waters off Alaska. The waters of the Pacific Ocean off the far Aleutian Islands had been barred to Japan by war for more than a dozen years. Now, even waters enclosed within the Bering Sea and Bristol Bay, which Japanese vessels had never before entered in any number, would lie open to them. And he himself was to voyage across the Pacific Ocean, in a vessel bearing his family's proud name on the manifest, to participate in the opening.

Now that the years of struggle had reached a point of recovery, he could watch the progression of events with fresh perspective. America no longer knew whether to keep Japan dependent or to help Japan grow strong. Thanks were due to the new war that now engaged the Americans in Korea for it probably sped the process along. Fortunate also, perhaps—not certain yet—was the fall of China to the Communists three years earlier. No question now that America now needed its old enemy Japan to be strong, for America's old allies the Russians and Chinese had become feared threats. The dance that his own country played, like that of some maiden stuck between

Kabuki warlords, needed to be both bold and cautious, but in either case it no longer needed to be passive.

Russia indeed was evil. It had grabbed Japan's own Kuril Islands as war booty, after doing nothing itself to defeat Japan. General Douglas MacArthur, backed by the great American President Harry S. Truman had allowed this. Russia now harvested big crabs off the Kurils and begrudged Japanese re-entry into these waters of their own tradition. They continued to block Japanese interests as they had since the days of the shoguns.

Clearly America could not afford to keep Japan subservient and defeated. And thus to the advantage of the Tsurifune family, this great nation now needed Japan as its ally. But for that threat of China that America so feared, and for America's new war in Korea against a communist enemy supported by China, Japan's fortunes might not have turned so rapidly. Japan had begun to recover, even to prosper, and with it the fortunes of the Tsurifune family company that had seemed completely destroyed.

And now, beyond his dreams of only one or two years ago, a Tsurifune fishing vessel was on its way to be welcomed into American waters.

"He's arriving, Tsurifune-san and Kiyoshi-san," said the fishing master as he and the captain joined them. On the quay, the gathering crowd opened a path for a rickshaw that stopped at the gangway. Out of it climbed the priest from the ceremony two days before. With suitable gravity, the priest fitted a conical Shinto hat on top of his head, then straightened and rearranged the embroidered robe that had wrinkled around his open shirt. A man appropriately somber, as he had been two days previous. Leaning on his cane beside Kiyoshi, Father beside him grunted his approval.

On that afternoon two days before, at the side of the lifeboat that the crew was preparing to lower, Kiyoshi's father had touched his arm. "I'll stay here. It's now for you to assume full authority."

Kiyoshi now knew for certain that his time had come. Not only was he to be responsible for the physical welfare of Tsurifune vessels but also for their spiritual fortunes. For a moment he felt the panic of uncertainty. Then, in a voice of firm authority, he stated, "As you wish."

He stepped into the lifeboat along with his fishing master and captain. When he nodded, the coxswain half-bowed in return and pulled the cord to start the outboard engine. Soon they were traversing the harbor out to open water, then toward a low island rising far enough away that only the tops of trees spiked its silhouette.

In the harbor they passed smaller vessels that pursued a harvest far removed from the one he was chasing. Most were open wooden boats with only a single fisherman arranging the net or with a wife at work beside him, both with faces hidden under traditional conical hats. Neither party acknowledged the other.

A larger open boat carrying crew to the village set net slowed speed to give their own boat way, and Kiyoshi felt the eyes of the set net crew following them. All these were now older men, left behind from the days of starvation after the war when he himself had gone out to help pull a meager catch. Some he recognized with a nod. From the old-fashioned bows they returned, they acknowledged his change in status.

Younger men had now found other ways to live. The Tsurifune far-seas vessel had hired only the youngest of former crewmen for the voyage. So it was.

"We must face toward the future, Father," Kiyoshi had declared at the time, not without sadness for the decision.

"Yes. Yes." Father's acquiescence had been equally sad.

Their lifeboat passed the anchored fleet of steel high seas vessels like their own. These were still idle, but soon would become active again when America had opened its fishing waters fully. On one, where men were chipping rust, work stopped and faces followed their own boat's course. Kiyoshi knew what they were thinking. If his own vessel succeeded in the Alaska fishing grounds, their ships could follow.

When they entered a short patch of open water between the mainland and the island, waves lapped and the boat's bow sent up spray. The coxswain slowed the engine, although his passengers, scorning such mere spurts from a sea they would soon encounter in full force, had faced into the droplets of water without flinching. Pines on the island took individual shape as they neared. Before long, the boat was tied to a small pier. The party climbed up to the temple through a path overgrown by roots and heaped with brown needles.

The temple needed repair—that much was clear enough. There were not just the pine needles to be swept clear, but rotted posts needed replacing, and the carved entrance required fresh gilding. Even the wooden guarding statue of Ebisu the deity of fishermen—who held a fish in one hand—was weathered to the grain on top his head and was missing part of his chubby side. How long had it been since more than small coastal boats had needed a blessing? With overseas waters now opened again, it would become Kiyoshi's own responsibility as a town leader to see renovations were made. One more duty. Better indeed that he hadn't killed himself foolishly in the cause of a lost war.

Indeed the priest himself, although vigorous in body, appeared shabby and unprosperous. He scampered up the hill wearing torn pants, with sandals flopping, and quickly donned a patched robe embroidered in patterns of faded silk. Kiyoshi explained his mission while adding a few more yen to the donation than Father had instructed him to give. Inside the temple, they knelt at the altar, while the priest approached the shrine, the ship's omamori plank in his hand. *What is my job here?* Kiyoshi had wondered suddenly. *What had Father done?* Now, instead of only hearing about it, he was part of the ceremony itself.

It turned out that all he'd needed to do was to receive a freshly-blessed omamori and to bow with it before the altar when instructed. At length the priest declared, "It has been blessed so that your vessel will have safety and good catches. Place it securely in the vessel's shrine. I'll come there on the day of departure to ensure and complete the ceremony."

The priest ascended the gangway. After exchanging respectful bows, Tsurifune father and son led the priest to the wheelhouse. Kiyoshi opened the door of the shrine mounted on the bulkhead. Inside, newly purchased, were a miniature temple, a gilded bell, and filigreed lamps flanking a cup, along with a large bottle of sake and a leafing branch. The fishing master and captain had also followed to the wheelhouse. They crowded back against the box of new electronic equipment called "radar," careful not to jar it. The priest waved the branch over their heads, and they respectfully clapped hands to draw divine attention.

Kiyoshi followed his father's example. At first he participated with detachment while wondering what the Americans back in Alaska would say of such a ceremony. But suddenly he clapped with fervor—in case there were indeed gods paying attention. *Not all can be explained by Western logic*, he thought.

The ceremony ended. As Kiyoshi prepared to pay, Father stepped forward with his old authority. He gave generously, or so it appeared from the way the taciturn priest smiled before tucking the bills into a pocket beneath his robe.

"I'll stay," said the priest. "To bless the vessel as it leaves, then, if you wish."

"That is our wish," said Father. He spoke with his former upright power, as he had not spoken for years. Turning to Kiyoshi, he demanded sternly: "My son. Is your vessel ready for departure?"

Kiyoshi glanced at the captain and the fishing master for a hasty confirmation and then declared as if addressing a commander: "Tsurifune Vessel Number One, *the Shoji Maru*, is ready, Father. At your permission."

"Not my vessel today. But as I announce for all to hear: yours!" There was a murmur among those watching as Father bowed, not with a usual paternal nod, but low—as to a superior. "Go to restore the fortune of the family Tsurifune, that your own son may inherit, and his son after. I myself shall stand below with the women, and with the grandson you've given me to replace the heroically dead Shoji, your brother who has joined the spirits." Kiyoshi had no recourse but to bow equally low in acceptance.

Soon after, the vessel's hawsers were thrown from the bollards. Ashore, the watching families tossed streamers of colored paper to their men at the rail, while holding tight to the other end themselves. As the engines churned a wash from the propeller astern and the vessel moved slowly away, the streamers pulled taut. One by one, the loved ones ashore let go. Bands of yellow, green, and red paper flapped free and trailed in the widening stretch of water until the men at the rail slowly pulled them in.

Kiyoshi watched the figures of his family grow smaller. His fingers held especially to a white streamer that Miki had helped throw from the hand of their son.

35

FACTORY FLEET

The sea voyage to Alaskan waters took more than a week. En route, the waters of the wide Pacific Ocean seldom generated waves smaller than six feet high. Sometimes seas swelled above eye level—even from the upper deck of the wheelhouse. They rose higher yet during the few hours of a storm, when, in each wave cycle, the decks dipped from port to starboard and any unattached objects clattered loose, while the vessel's bow cut into roiling water that flew in spray against the wheelhouse windows.

"A calm passage. Every day of it," observed the captain, Shiju Tanaka. In days before the war he had seen this ocean through true storms, and he wanted his experience to be known. "It's nearly June by the calendar, Tsurifune-san," he declared, showing his teeth in an ingratiating smile. "Let me tell you of real January seas in waters like these."

"Ah? Perhaps you've forgotten," rejoined Kiyoshi, working to hide his annoyance. "You haven't been permitted to fish far-seas Pacific Ocean for— how long?" He stared through the wheelhouse window at a blackening sea that swelled past at a height high above his head and struggled to remain upright— as befitted a vessel owner. The vomiting had stopped three days ago, but as yet, food scarcely stayed quiet in his stomach. Had he fallen so out of rhythm with the sea? He who had endured a typhoon out of Okinawa only seven years ago?

Captain Tanaka, who had once served on one of his father's three fishing vessels, had subsequently risen to command of a small vessel in the Japanese Navy. His face was now lined from squinting at the sun, and his once-easy laugh had been replaced by that nervous grin that was perhaps appropriate for the gravity of his present position. After returning from the war, Tanaka had called on Father and declared himself able to be not only a captain, but better: a fishing master. Father had told him that such a promotion came only with proven judgment. In truth, two of Father's old fishing masters—men he knew could judge the whereabouts of a good catch—had also come to ask for employment long before any of his vessels were in condition again.

Indeed, Ebiro Takamori, the man whom Father had selected to be fishing master of this important first voyage, had proven himself many years ago to have been a good producer. Also, he bore a distinguished family name. Counted on the fact that he still possessed the ability to judge currents and sea beds for the presence of fish. The fortunes of the trip rested ultimately on his shoulders. He remained aloof while scanning the seas, studying old charts from years ago, and occasionally speaking on the radio to other fishing masters. His time to prove himself would come only when they reached the fishing grounds and he took command of the ship from the captain.

As for the fishermen themselves, they stayed belowdecks, biding their time until they could produce. They stood their watches, played card games, ate heartily—since all they wanted was provided them—and slept.

"Ha. There," said Fishing Master Takamori as he scanned with binoculars from the wheelhouse. "Coming from Kushiro up north, those vessels. We're not alone out here."

In the distance, two ships rode wave crests and disappeared into troughs. Kiyoshi knew that their trip through the ocean would be alongside others, but only seldom had they sighted any vessels making the voyage to Alaska. He knew that Takamori had spoken with at least four other ships via radio. Had the new fishing agency allowed by the governing Americans in Tokyo given too many owners permission to come, so that there wouldn't be enough fish to catch?

A voice spoke in English through the static on the ship's shortwave radio. "Japanese fishing boat *Shoji Maru*. Do you read me? Do you read me? Over."

Kiyoshi took the microphone. "Here. Yes. *Shoji Maru*. Hello." At least he could enjoy the fact that he alone of the men aboard the vessel spoke English. The others in the wheelhouse—fishing master, captain, and helmsman—all turned to watch him with respect. "Hello, hai, yes, yes?"

"Give us your ETA for rendezvous at north latitude . . . west longitude . . ." ETA? What did the speaker mean? But he understood the other words. He hurried to the chart that lay unfolded on a cramped table in the corner, studied the marks on it, and declared into the microphone: "Vessel *Shoji Maru*. Location, now. Latitude 46°-37' north. Longitude 35°-57' west. Okay?"

"Read you, *Shoji Maru*. Assume that's your present location. But I'm asking your ETA here. Estimated Time of Arrival. Over."

"Ah!" Now that he understood he could save face before the others. It was easy to answer since they had calculated their position that morning. "Arrival time. Shall arrive at rendezvous today number thirty of May month. May 30th. At afternoon time hour 1600." He enjoyed having mastered so many of their expressions and the look of respect it gained him from those watching. "Thus, arrival time vessel *Shoji Maru*, seven hours from this which is now present nine hours in the morning."

After a long pause: "*Shoji Maru*. The time you gave me, arrival time 1600, May 30th,—that's four o'clock in the afternoon—is nearly a whole day from now, not seven hours. Request that you re-calculate and clarify. Wait. Hold on."

When the radio activated again, it was a different voice, and this at last spoke Japanese. "*Shoji Maru*. Give me your position. Then give me your date and time." Kiyoshi complied. "*Shoji Maru*, I must inform you. You have given me Tokyo time and Tokyo day. We here, waiting to receive you, observe the time and date of our true location, in Alaska of United Sates. Your boat has crossed the International Date Line which divides one day from the next. Thus, you have entered back into the previous day and have lost a day of the calendar. Furthermore, you have in this process advanced five hours against the sun's passage around the Earth, making your day by the sun five hours earlier. Present local time here is 1400, 2:00 p.m., on May 29, not nine in the morning of May 30 as it is indeed now in Tokyo."

Kiyoshi glanced around at the others. Only the fishing master nodded with any comprehension, and even he was respectful. His own blunder in timing and position might not be held against him.

The radio voice continued, "If you wish to keep Tokyo time for yourselves, very well. But you must also at once prepare a clock for communication with Alaska where your vessel now speaks with officials here. For example, I'm now speaking from an office in Adak of the Aleutian Islands,

where I can look up to see a clock with the time that guides business here."
The voice in Japanese paused long enough that Kiyoshi thought he had
ended, but then spoke so quietly that hearing was difficult through the
static. "Listen. Not everyone in America is happy that we're finally allowed
to come here to fish their seas again. They don't understand that the seas are
for everyone, and thus that we are entitled to come take all we can from it.
A vessel of the United States Coast Guard is preparing to depart here and
meet your fishing fleet. Uh, to make you welcome."

"We come prepared to show all respect," said Kiyoshi as he glanced
toward the others and exchanged nods.

"If you'll take my advice, be discreet," continued the voice in Japanese.
"Follow their rules, especially at first. Americans don't realize the wealth
of their sea here. If they did, they might turn greedy and try to fish it all
themselves. If you and the others are discreet, you'll get rich from what's
here. So. Listen carefully to any rules they might want to give. And, hah! As
your first sensible step, set a clock to function in their time."

Several hours later the ship arrived at the gathering point where other
Japanese fishing vessels pitched and maneuvered. Beyond the enclave, open
sea stretched dark and empty in all directions. Truly this was water that
belonged to those who had the ability to fish it. By arrangement they lowered their smallboat to take Kiyoshi over to the mother-factory ship that had
been designated for official greetings. He dressed in a suit and tie that he had
brought for the occasion and completed the look with lowcut shoes.

"Put on rubber boots and a rubber coat for the trip over, Tsurifune-
san," Captain Tanaka suggested. "Otherwise you'll be dripping water."
Kiyoshi considered. Would these official Americans respect a man in common seaman's clothes?

"Coat, yes, since that can be removed. Boots, no."

In the smallboat, they had barely left the lee of their ship before the sea
gurgled over the rail and left water sloshing around Kiyoshi's feet. When
they reached the side of the host ship, Kiyoshi stood, gripped the rope ladder as it clattered toward him, and, with dignity, climbed to deck. Seawater
squished down from his sodden shoes. No matter. His shirt and tie were
only a little bit wet and would soon dry. The Americans would see him as
a vessel owner of authority.

Fortunate indeed that he had dressed for the occasion. Barely had he
reached the ship's rail when men with cameras began snapping his photograph.

—★—

36

CLASSIFIED SECRET

ADAK, MAY 1952

Swede Scorden straightened his tie, then tipped up a glass of beer and gazed out the window. Beyond low corrugated sheds and ships both military and cargo, there stretched the nothernmost edge of the North Pacific Ocean. Light from a gray sky played on the water's restless surface. Was this to become the seaway of his life—he who had once considered the Atlantic Ocean to be mankind's natural boundary? At mid day in the Adak officers' club, the tables were empty except for a group of women playing cards. On the evening of his arrival the day before, with John Stockhausen, manager of the company's new crab processing plant in Adak, a welcoming host, the place had been lively enough with filled tables and everywhere the white dress uniforms of the American Navy.

His present assignment was to observe and report, whatever his impatience. Events would occur in their proper time. Eventually he'd be home again. The Seattle company that had finally placed him second in command of its local cannery in Ketchikan, then in summers put him in full charge of their seasonal facility in Bristol Bay, now barely allowed him time to be home. Mary and the children might as well remain in Ballard, where they were visiting her sister, for all that their house in Ketchikan mattered while he pursued the fish business in remote corners of Alaska. Now when she returned, she and the kids would be speaking as much Norwegian as English from all the contact with their cousins down there. At a time when his own English, honed conscientiously, might now be taken for native-speaking American. He had even mastered profanity! Profanity only when appropriate, of course—only among fishermen and workers. He'd labored to become a leader. When he walked in town to the bank, dressed in suit and tie, people addressed him respectfully. All in English.

"Hi," said Stockhausen, and he pulled out a chair for Swede. When Stockhausen tossed his cap onto an adjacent chair, the man was revealed to be going gray, but he still retained the youthful American vigor that Swede so admired. "The club sandwich ain't bad, if you haven't already ordered."

"I had thought out here near the sea that people would gladly order fish."

"That's if you haven't been here long enough to get your fill of fried, creamed, baked, whatever with scales on it. But don't let me stop you."

A few moments later, a Lieutenant Matt Chivers joined them with a casual apology for being late. He, too, seemed driven by energy. "Can't stay long. You guys ordered?" To the waiter. "Halibut, fish, whatever's your special, but pronto."

Stockhausen introduced Chivers to Swede as one of the US Navy's finest young officers, whose present duties included communications with ships at sea. Chivers regarded Swede with only a casual interest. "Just looking around, eh? For some report back home? If you want to know, Stockhausen here's not doing a half-bad job. Joined Rotary—away and running you might say. Already on a committee with me there."

"I've come to observe the Japanese fishing ships, sir. When they assemble in water close by."

Chivers hesitated, then asked, "Where'd you hear that?"

"Come on, Matt," laughed Stockhausen. "The whole world knows."

The Lieutenant looked from one to the other and frowned. "Me, I don't know nothin'!"

"Nobody knows except everybody," continued Stockhausen. "Knows that some Japanese-American guy got flown in here yesterday to go greet the ships. And that some Coast Guard ship tied up down at the pier is set to take him out to go aboard and interpret. That one of the radio bands you think is closed to civilians has been buzzing in both English and Jap for two–three days now. That we're allowing the whole Jap fishing fleet back here."

"You sure didn't hear that from me, buddy."

"You deny it?"

"Shoot!" Lieutenant Chivers shook his head. "And they got me up at four this morning to decode a message from HQ in DC. Classified Secret. That's the official designation, last step below Top Secret. Took me over an hour, sliding strips in and out of the decoding board." He considered. "Things I couldn't tell you. But stuff that, maybe, you just told me. Washington lives in its own world back there. But you didn't hear that from me."

The waiter brought their drinks. John Stockhausen fingered his glass. "The thing is, Matt, we wonder if Swede here could go out on that ship that's supposed to meet the Japs. To observe whatever's out there. No use letting foreigners in if we can't do business with them. Swede here's doing American business. It's only patriotic to send him out."

"That ship, that I don't acknowledge exists, is Coast Guard, John. I'm navy here."

"Navy runs this base whoever comes. You're in the office that does all the communicating and arranging. I hear you've even got a Jap interpreter here talking to them on radio."

"Who said? That's classified."

"Adak Base might be run by the US Navy, but that don't stop navy gossip. See those women over there playing bridge? What do they have to do all day but jaw-jaw while their big men run the base? You think one of them wouldn't spot a Jap among all these white people? And start buggin' her husband when he comes home from a hard day's?"

"You think there's not a lieutenant commander over me, and then a captain, all answering to the navy brass in DC who suck up to, I guess, Congress and maybe the State Department?"

"And a Rotary election coming up for the new chair of the Steering Committee? Everybody knows anyhow, Matt!"

"Sorry, man. Washington, DC, comes first. Let the politicians talk when they're ready. Or play their game. I'm nearly halfway into twenty-year retirement, and I plan to get there with a clean ass."

Stockhausen considered, then shrugged. They ate in silence. The voices of the women at the nearby table continued in a lively murmur.

-★-

After the departure of Lieutenant Chivers, John Stockhausen exclaimed against keeping government secrets when everybody knew anyway. "First American boat that sees those Jap letters on a ship in our waters and calls a newspaper, the only people in the dark's going to be the bureaucrats. If Eisenhower gets chosen by the Republicans this summer, he gets my vote in November. This Democrat pussyfoot under Truman, or Adlai Stevenson or whoever else they decide to back, it's got to stop."

Swede had studiously read American newspapers, but still he was not certain. The bestial Germans who'd murdered his father were now being allowed to prosper again. China, the ally of America during the war, had turned Communist and become the enemy. Nothing bad was said any more by the American government about the Japanese, who'd started the terrible Pacific War. Japan had apparently become acceptable to do business with. Well, never in the Atlantic could he ever do friendly business with anyone speaking the detested German! But in the Pacific with Japanese? The war in Asia hadn't been his concern. If America now decided to make Japan strong, and he himself wished to be American, all he could do was participate and help his company get its share.

And so he shrugged and settled within himself to be patient when Stockhausen advised: "Stick around for a few days. The company's paying. Something might happen. You can at least watch my operation."

Swede wandered the compound of the Adak Naval Base. It was a dreary but clean place of long, low, prefabricated buildings. Why had he bothered to come all this way? They might have known when they sent him how secret the government was keeping this matter, and saved themselves the expense.

"I can't seem to shake you," growled a familiar voice. "Last year Bristol Bay, then Kodiak. Now here. You following me?"

It was his old friend, Jones Henry the fisherman. No mystery here. Jones wore one of his familiar frayed wool shirts and greased denims, with signature red-billed cap pulled low over his squinting eyes. His chin was blackened by a few days' stubble. A welcome sight in this enclave of clean military uniforms!

"On the contrary, sir," Swede joked heartily. "It is you who must stop following me!" He grasped Jones's hand, even though it was perhaps soiled from work. "I haven't seen you since you moved from Ketchikan last . . . November, was it? Moved to where? Here? How is your wife? And you?"

"Didn't move to this navy dump! Moved to Kodiak," Jones growled. Got a new boat. At least, one that's new-rigged. Out here now scouting for crab. Thing of the future."

"Good, good. And your wife?"

"Adele? The girl's okay now we've moved. Don't cry about things anymore." Jones took a moment to consider. "Already gotten mixed up in something to do with the town council. Keeps her busy and out of my hair. Livelier place than Ketchikan, that's for sure. Want to come see my boat?"

"Later perhaps. Later. I'm now trying to puzzle out a situation."

It turned out that Jones had come ashore to get fuel and water, as well as some odds and ends from the post exchange where, as an ex-Marine, he had permission to deal. Swede accompanied him. The PX, located in one of the longest buildings, turned out to be a veritable warehouse of goods more abundant than any Ketchikan establishment. As Jones observed: "Navy out here on this asshole island from nowhere's got to keep the wives happy."

"Now doggone. They must let anybody in here." It was the two Coast Guard chiefs whom Swede had met at the brothel in Ketchikan and then seen in the crowd at the village dance in Akutan. Vast Alaska was really so small! Now here they all were again in the remote Aleutian Islands.

Before the conversations had ended, they were all four seated at a club in another building—this one for non-commissioned officers—drinking beer and eating peanuts and pretzels. Swede had tried to hide his excitement, but now that they were settled in, he ventured: "You're aboard the Coast Guard vessel in the harbor, then? Why so far out from Ketchikan."

"Summer logistics," said Ed Hancock. "Some Coastie ship has to do it every year. Us this time. Got sidetracked for a little run out of here tomorrow. Then on to Attu."

Swede opted to speak boldly. "A run to meet with Japanese, yes?"

The two chiefs exchanged looks. "What did I tell you, cuz?" said Jimmy Amberman. "Word's all over the place about this Jap we're here to pick up. Wardroom steward told me he'd had to make up the extra bunk in the junior officer's stateroom, so you know he's not just crew. And they've even locked up our cameras so nobody gets a picture of whatever it is."

Swede leaned forward. "I wish to ride out with you tomorrow."

"Then quick enlist in the Coast Guard, cuz."

Chief Hancock shook his head. "I'd bring you aboard and show you the captain's door so you might persuade him, oblige you that. But from the way we're not being told anything I don't think he'll take you. Not often we see such hush-hush about whatever we're supposed to be doing."

Jones Henry turned to Swede with a mischievous grin. "You want a ride on my boat? We'll see what they're up to. Keep watch so we know when these boys go. I'll trail 'em. Follow on radar if they move off too fast. Only way we'll ever find out what's up, looks like." In answer, Swede slapped Jones on the shoulder.

Jimmy Amberman laughed. "Then I'll train something off the fantail for you, cuz. Nobody's yet locked up the bread crumbs on us."

37

No Secret at All

After Swede accepted his invitation at the NCO club, Jones had hurried to his boat to set things straight. Not that things weren't shipshape for a boat, but you never could tell with picky landlubbers. He fitted a clean cover on his own lower bunk mattress for Swede and he moved his own gear to the bunk above it. Best not to have feet clambering onto his face when the fellow gets seasick.

Then what to do about the crew? This consisted entirely of a kid named Lloyd whom Jones had taken on from the dock in Kodiak. "Putting you ashore overnight. This trip don't concern you," Jones said casually.

"You think I'm not up to anything out there, skipper?" Lloyd cocked an eyebrow, then flopped down on his bunk. "Thanks, but I think I'll just stay aboard."

Jones regarded the kid. Up from some stateside college for a summer's adventure, but not a bad worker, considering. Big attitude, certainly. Too big, Jones felt sometimes. Still, an extra pair of hands might come in handy. "Alright, fine. But you do as I say, no questions. And don't you be telling anyone where we're going or what you see. Not without my go-ahead first. Got it?"

The kid shrugged. *Take it or leave it, kid.* Jones thought, folding his arms over his broad chest—hoping he looked as no-nonsense as he felt.

"Yeah okay, skipper. I can keep my mouth shut." They shook on it.

"Just . . . take a nap or something," Jones said.

When Swede appeared, briskly ready, Jones was glad to see that he wore rough clothes instead of the usual suit and tie. Guy wasn't going to put on airs. Which was good since he wouldn't have gotten away with it.

Jones patted the lower bunk. "Make yourself at home."

Soon after, with Swede alongside, Jones watched the Coast Guard ship through binoculars. At length, he reported: "There go my two chiefs back aboard over the gangway. And an officer. With some fellow in civvies who looks . . . Damned if he ain't. That's a Jap! I knew they were up to some trick."

"Let me see," said Swede, and a moment later, "Yes, a Japanese civilian. And now there's a man on the pier throwing off their lines."

"Don't tell me they ain't pulling something!" Jones leapt the rail of his boat and started the engine. "We'll hang ready by the breakwater. No law says we can't trail 'em."

An hour later both vessels were in open water. Jones's boat came alive in that way he savored—pitching and rolling. He watched Swede, ready to enjoy how the man got sick. But Swede remained alongside him at the wheel, no problem.

The Coast Guard ship glided past them in the water, barely reacting to the waves. No question but that it would leave them behind. Yet Jones figured they'd remain as a clear radar blip for some fifteen miles, and by then, if they hadn't changed course they were probably pointed toward their destination.

Swede held tight to a rail for support, but he continued to talk as if they were steady on land. When a sudden cross-sea swept a loose shackle bumping across deck, he went out before Jones could stop him—braced with practiced sea legs—and retrieved the piece before it washed overboard. He returned inside, dripping wet. Plainly Swede had enjoyed himself.

Jones watched, chagrined to have left anything on his deck unsecured while grudgingly aware that maybe Swede was fit for sea after all. But nevertheless: "Mebbe should have let it go. Rough out there."

"A shackle costs at least three dollars, so you shouldn't lose it to the sea, eh?"

The further they drew from land, the higher the waves they encountered. Whenever the boat descended into a trough, they found themselves looking up at gray water. By now the Coast Guard ship was at least two miles ahead of them, with its black hull and brown superstructure dimming as it grew smaller.

"I can pursue if you want to rest," Swede offered. "This chase may last a long time, so we must stay alert."

"I'm all right. Mebbe you ought to lie down a while."

"During the war and the Resistance against the German butchers, I held wheels like this in bad weather. Worse weather. Escaping, sometimes. Spying sometimes. But often with life in danger. Maybe now I'm a company manager, but I haven't forgotten. This now's a pleasure, to chase without any consequence of death, but still with mystery. I don't wish to lie down."

Jones nodded. He liked this man, who only recently he'd begun to regard as something more than a mere company pisshead. "Well, I ain't sleeping either. But you take the wheel a while if you want. I'll make coffee—we might be here for a haul."

The chase, which began to appear to have no end, terminated abruptly in the sight of masts. The Coast Guard ship, which had disappeared from view for an hour except as a green dot on Jones's basic boat radar, could now be discerned near a vessel almost twice its length. Further out on the horizon bobbed the outlines of other ships.

The large vessel they gazed at lay huffing in the sea like a whale. Waves that pushed Jones's boat into constant motion, that rolled discernibly against the black Coast Guard hull, seemed barely to ripple against the high bow of this massive vessel. An outlet located barely halfway down its side poured a steady stream of wastewater from a height well above their own masthead.

"That vessel is well cared for," observed Swede. "It's new, or at least not very old. From the pictures my company sent me for identification purposes, this is a factory ship. A new idea on the ocean. Very interesting. Built to receive catches from smaller vessels and to process these catches at sea in the manner of a cannery on shore."

As they neared, Jones left the helm to Swede as he scanned the factory ship with binoculars. "What I see loud and clear is Jap letters on its side. Probably says something like 'Fuck you.'"

"More likely I think it's the name of the vessel as it's lettered above in English."

"Oh." Jones deflated. "You call that English?"

"Well, Jones. This is what I've come to see. To observe, eh? This, and those other vessels out there on the horizon. A fishing fleet, I suspect. More even than I had imagined. Good for American business if they catch and deliver to us. Bad if the fish are to reach shore only in Japan. I'm concerned that the US government is making this deal in secret because it's ashamed to admit to it."

Jones spat into the water. "If my boat had a torpedo, she'd get it. Sink you, like all you bastards sank us." He spat again, for want of anything else to do. "Sink every last one of you out there!"

"But we have no torpedo," Swede reminded Jones gently. "Do you mind if we go closer, Jones? If they allowed us aboard, would you go?"

"Sooner cut off my arm. And where would I put my own boat out here? But if they're dumb enough to say yes, and you're dumb enough to go, I'll wait for you. Don't hurt to see the enemy all the way I guess." He pointed his bow directly at the factory ship and revved his engine. "Let's ram the son of a bitch."

"Yes. Go. Pretend!"

In the water below the factory ship skipped a small open surfboat of the kind used by the Coast Guard. It was barely a sand flea in comparison. The two men in it wore dress blues beneath their lifejackets.

"Hey!" called Swede. "You're guarding against invasion I see. Or preparing to give a tow?"

The man who looked up was Chief Jimmy Amberman.

"Looks like we couldn't shake you," he exclaimed heartily.

Swede called over the sound of the waves, "Are you preparing to go aboard this ship?"

"Not me. Just waiting to take back our CO and Exec. They brought over this little Jap guy. Making a big deal of it, so they wanted to show some uniforms—even down here in the boat."

"An important official?"

"Fellow was too seasick to tell! Brought some bags with him, so I guess he's staying. But maybe that's a secret like everything else, so don't say I told you. Back on the ship they even opened our letters home before they mailed 'em off in Adak."

Swede gazed up at the ship's side. "I want to go aboard there. But I don't see a ladder."

"If they say yes, they'll lower a bucket for you like they did for our guys."

"Hey there," Swede called up. Two heads peered down from the rail. "Hi. Wish to come aboard." The two men above watched them in silence. At length one of them waved.

"Hell," said Chief Amberman. "You might be talking French for all they can figure."

Swede turned to Jones with a grin. "Please hold your ears, and forgive me that I've taken the trouble to learn a little Japanese." To the men above he shouted "Konichiwa!" and followed with other Japanese words accompanied by gestures.

The heads disappeared, and minutes later, a Jacob's ladder clattered down. "Guess you don't rate a bucket," Jimmy Amberman laughed.

Swede waited for Jones's boat to ride the crest of a wave, then jumped to the ladder's flopping rungs. He climbed quickly so as to be above the boat's rail on the next surge.

"Your boy knows how to do it," said Jimmy.

"At least that far," growled Jones. He watched as Swede, agile as a monkey, scampered up rung by rung. On the way up, his cap flew off and wind carried it into the ocean. At the top, hands waited to help him over the rail, but he swung himself over easily. The man would probably have made a good fisherman if he'd stuck to it, rather than going ashore.

Twenty minutes later, Swede's head of ruffled blond hair appeared at the rail. "Jones!" he called. "You're invited aboard also. Nice food here. They'll pass you a line so the boat can drift safely astern. If you wish."

"Jap line! Probably rotten and will break."

From the Coast Guard skiff, Jimmy Amberman called with gruff humor, "Go do it, cuz. See what all the secret's about for both of us. We'll mind your boat." Jones started to shake his head in an outraged negative, and then considered. Hadn't he come this far?

"Alright," he called. "I'll come up. But damned if I'm gonna leave my boat attached to some Jap rope and no one watching. Just wait a sec."

He dropped down into the cabin, where the kid Lloyd was snoring away again. Though he'd come a few times on deck and had exchanged some banter with Swede, for the most part he'd stayed below and out of the way. Not much for him to do anyway, Jones reasoned, before shaking him roughly awake.

"Need you on deck, kid," Jones said. "Be quick—need you to keep an eye on things."

Lloyd looked surprised, but swung himself out of the bunk directly. Something you learned to do quick out here, Jones mused.

"You going somewhere, skipper?"

"Not your concern."

On deck, Lloyd let out a low whistle. "That Japanese?" he asked.

"Mebbe. Just need you to keep your mouth shut and watch the boat don't drift away. In case the line breaks." The kid nodded and looked on while Jones climbed the Jacob's ladder, the rope joined boards clacking against the steel hull of the factory ship. At every third or fourth step, he paused to look down. Bad thing for a skipper to leave his boat in the hands of an unexperienced crewman, although it did ride easily on its line. What if the Japs cut it loose out of orneriness? Shouldn't've left it. Wouldn't have, probably, but for the Coast Guard skiff standing watch. And hell, ought to see for himself what the Japs were up to.

When his line of sight finally reached the level of the rail, there was Swede standing with some Japs. Jones shrugged off an offer of assistance, but he hadn't even swung a leg over to deck when cameras started clicking. He scowled automatically. "What's this?"

"Don't worry," joked Swede. "Photographs are for newspapers back in Tokyo, not here."

"Well I guess their cameras're going to break if they take much more of me." Jones kept the scowl. It wouldn't do to be shown here enjoying himself, wherever the pictures went.

He had barely put both feet on deck when another Jap came forward and grasped his hand to shake it. "This is Captain Mitsuboshi," Swede continued. "He's come to greet you personally and welcome you aboard. Then he must return to his duties."

Jones took the hand. It had little grip. "Yeah, well, okay. Hello, captain."

Swede explained that someone was about to give them a tour of the ship, after which the captain hoped that they would be his guests for refreshments. Jones began to ask why they were being treated like VIPs and what did Swede tell them in their lingo, exactly, when Swede shot him a warning glance. When the captain had gone a few steps forward, Swede lowered his voice.

"Just act like you belong here, yes? They think we are part of the American delegation. Don't give them a reason to be suspicious of you."

"Us, you mean."

"Ja, Jones, us."

Jones had ridden crowded troopships, so the size of this ship was nothing new. But the rest was out of some fantasy book. Little Japs scampered everywhere. Many wore the squashed caps he remembered from their prisoners on Okinawa, and some even wore parts of uniforms. On deck, men in black rubber suits hosed sections of a cargo net. Inside, down some steps and through corridors that Jones noted were fresh painted, a bunch of them sat at long tables on a messdeck, clacking chopsticks over bowls of food. Down further metal stairs, from doors surrounded outside by sandals and boots, others looked up with their blank Jap expressions from tiered bunks in crowded staterooms: hard to count how many with all the clothes and towels draped everywhere. Down further, entire lower decks were taken up by machinery and shining metal troughs. With a final flourish, their guide announced: "Very good capacity!" and threw open the doors of a freeze locker, empty but for swirling ice clouds. The space was bigger than that of Jones's entire boat. "Soon filling with product!" announced the guide proudly.

"Ja," muttered Swede. "Yes. Many men. And they are prepared for fish." Their guide seemed to understand. He nodded with one of those people's typical blank smiles.

"Hai! Full equipment. Very modern. Ready for product from gillnet vessels!"

"You will look happy, please," said a man they had not noticed, followed by a camera flash.

Jones kept the scowl that had settled on his face. "That guy been trailing us?" he muttered.

"No," replied Swede. "I think he was waiting here for us. But they're taking pictures everywhere."

"Yes, now again," said the photographer. "You will look happy, please." Jones glared in the direction of the camera.

Their guide conducted them back to the main deck and across into another housing that extended up to the windows of the bridge. "For officers," he explained. "And for officials."

Again, the corridors smelled of fresh paint. They were led to a room with a few tables covered with clean blue cloths. At one side, under portholes, was a longer, covered table holding tureens and an open platter of food.

Seated at one table were two Coast Guard officers, the Japanese captain, and other Japanese. The captain rose and beckoned them over. At once, Swede assumed a more formal bearing. He nodded to the two Coast Guard officers and shook hands saying, something in Japanese as he was introduced to the others.

Jones remained standing. He felt out of place. Wasn't one of those Japs the fellow who had gotten in his way a couple of times in Bristol Bay the summer before and then at that village dance, now with hair slicked and wearing a tie?

"And here," said Swede smoothly, "Please meet my friend Mr. Jones Henry, a famous fishing captain."

"Ah!" exclaimed one of the Japanese and extended his hand eagerly. "A great pleasure, Mr. Jones. You will have fishing information for us." He introduced himself as the representative of a large company in his nation.

The Jap Jones probably knew eyed him directly, gave a little bow, and said in a respectful voice, "Again pleasure that we meet, sir."

"Yup. You get around."

"I represent the fishing enterprises of Tsurifune and others in my town. As also in Bristol Bay and in Akutan village. I hope that you have had good fishing."

"Can't complain."

Two other Japanese came in, carrying cameras. Under the polite direction of the ship's captain, the Americans were placed among the Japanese officials for a group photo. Then the captain declared: "Friendship!" and went to each American and shook hands while the cameras clicked.

Jones hesitated when the captain reached him. At last he accepted the man's limp handshake for the photo but didn't relax his scowl. *Let 'em figure that one out back in Tokyo.*

Another Japanese joined them. "Pardon me," he said in clear English. "A bit seasick for a while, I'm afraid. John Kobayashi, American research scientist in the US state of Washington." It was the passenger from ashore who had come aboard with the Coast Guard officers. The man continued, speaking to the others in Japanese that at times seemed a bit halting.

Captain Mitsuboshi clapped his hands, and soon a bowl of steaming noodles in broth had been placed in front of each man. Jones, offered his choice of utensils by the steward serving them, waved aside the chopsticks and took a spoon and fork. He picked through the noodles and sorted out the slippery black objects that might have been mushrooms but just as probably some kind of beetle or even chopped rat. Swede, using chopsticks, ate the black things without hesitation. So did the others. Not his business what others put in their mouths.

The Jap he knew named Surifooly or something began to speak politely to the American Coast Guard. After a few sentences, the Japanese-American

John Kobayashi held up his hand and explained: "Now that I'm here to interpret, this representative of the fishing vessels wishes to tell you the following.
I'll try to give it exactly. But I must explain that I'm an American citizen and
don't often speak Japanese anymore." He spoke in Japanese to the man, who
replied confidently, and then with "Okay, I'm getting it right. I think" translated sentence by sentence.

"Mr. Tsurifune says: 'It's very good that America has finally decided to
share its sea wealth because oceans belong to anyone in the world uh . . .
efficient enough to catch fish in them.'" Jones watched the Surifooly Jap grow
confident as he spoke. Despite his fancy clothes, the man wore no shoes, only
socks, but he stood straight and looked directly at the Americans as if he were
addressing equals.

"Might ask him how many fishing boats have now come here from
Japan," said the younger of the Coast Guard officers. "It's our job to monitor
you." The gold stripe and a half on his sleeve showed that his rank was lieutenant junior grade. Jones regarded him with the detachment of an enlisted
man. Junior officer who needed to watch his ass. And the captain of the
Coast Guard ship, with two full stripes, was only a full lieutenant. If they
were climbing a career ladder in the shadow of a military base as large as
Adak they still had a long way to go without screwing up.

The Japanese began to talk again, and again after a few sentences,
Kobayashi held up his hand. "Okay, I'll translate further. I'm afraid he didn't
answer your question directly, even though I asked it twice. But he says:
'Don't worry. The wealth of the sea is bottomless. We'll place our nets effi-
ciently in the agreed areas so that we'll miss nothing for our efforts. You will
be able to observe how we keep order in the fishery. And in a few weeks, new
fish will have come to take the place of those we have caught.'"

"Yeah, I'll bet," said Jones. "Ask for the number again. I'd like to know
how many of their boats have just come over here and might be bumping
against mine."

"Sir," said the Coast Guard captain. "Whatever the number, it's classified. I'm not sure what your status is to ask."

"Except that it's my water, not theirs."

"International waters, sir."

"I don't need to look very far north from here to see Alaskan mountains."

"But the United States can claim control of only three miles from shore
at low tide, just as with any other nation."

Jones snorted. "Then we'd better shag ass to change that."

"I've read that some in Congress want something like a twelve-mile jurisdiction," said the Coast Guard executive officer. "Not that any law's been passed."

"Don't wish that, Mr. Sawyer," the Coast Guard captain replied. "We've got enough on our hands to patrol and enforce in the three miles that are allowed."

The Jap spokesman started speaking again. John Kobayashi bent to listen closely, then said "Goes like this. 'America has no use for the great sea resource off Alaska. I've seen no facility here to catch it in the quantities the sea produces. Millions of food creatures here have lived and died without benefit to anyone. Therefore it makes good sense to allow others in the world in need of food to harvest here whatever we can. Don't worry. We will proudly set you an example of efficiency that you may wish to follow. With the sea's infinite resources, on continental shelves such as America has in abundance, there's enough to share for all the world.'"

The Coast Guard captain nodded. "Well. Our people aren't taking it all, that's obvious."

"Excuse me, captain," said his exec, who was younger and more intense. "Nothing's infinite. With too many ships fishing out here—"

"I think our people in DC know what they're doing better than we do, Mr. Sawyer."

John Kobayashi tilted his head toward the Americans and suddenly his manner changed. "Slick case he makes. Take it or leave it, gentlemen. I'm only translating."

The Japanese captain signaled to a steward. The meal aboard the factory ship continued with fried squid, then tough beefsteak, which the Japanese cut into with gusto.

"This is special meat for guests," John Kobayashi translated for the captain. "On most days, everyone on the ship will eat what they catch from the sea." He grinned, and his official veneer changed altogether. "Personally I'd take the salmon if this is the best they can do on meat. I could get it better at any corner grocery in the States."

"Remember, we're guests here," said the Coast Guard captain mildly.

The exec studied Kobayashi. "You seem more American than Japanese, despite your face."

"American citizen, but interned with my parents when the war started because of my face. Finally served in the United States Army, although my parents remained interned. At home in Seattle we did speak Japanese, but not with these northern accents. It's a struggle to understand everything they say."

"Kind of divided, aren't you? Must be pretty rough."

"Finding my way through it. I'm an American citizen, although some in my country America still treat me as the enemy."

"Yeah. Well," said the Coast Guard captain. "We've got another problem." He turned to Jones. "You the boat that trailed us here?"

"Might say that."

"Like to ask what your purpose is?"

"Interest in what's happening. My being American."

"I've got to inform you that you're observing a mission that our government has classified 'Secret'. A matter of national security, you might say."

"I don't see no guns."

The Coast Guard exec leaned forward. "We have the authority to impound you and your boat for a while."

Swede turned to him, shocked. "This would be terrible. I'm the one who brought Jones here with his boat. Are you going to arrest me also? Here in America?"

"National security, sir."

The Coast Guard captain turned to his junior. "I think if we got their word they wouldn't radio anything about this, Steve . . ."

The man paused. "Your call, Captain. But in light of the classification level DC's given this mission, I suggest it's our duty to report it before this man's boat is released from our control. Right now he can't go too far without refueling with us back at the base."

The exchange had probably not been understood by any of the Japanese, although possibly they noticed the tension. Little more was said by anyone.

38

INUNDATION

Japanese fishing ships did indeed return to the grounds off Alaska where they had fished unchallenged in the 1920s and early 1930s. The Truman Administration opened the way cautiously in mid-1952. He did it for pragmatic reasons that were justifiable given the post-war climate in China and Korea, but he did so in secret. National presidential elections were just a few months away. (Nevertheless, Republican Dwight Eisenhower won over Truman's Democrat successor Adlai Stevenson in the November election.)

Priorities in Asia had shifted since the Allied defeat of Japan in mid-1945. China went Communist in 1949, and Communist North Korea invaded South Korea in 1950. Suddenly it had become the United States's best interest to have a strong, economically stable Japan instead of one still vulnerable and recovering from chaos. Yet anti-Japanese sentiment remained understandably strong among American veterans who had fought the Japanese just a half dozen years before.

At the time (at least for those not in the marine biology business), the great seafood resources off both the Pacific and the Atlantic coasts of North America appeared endlessly sustainable. Teeming on these vast continental shelves was natural protein for the taking. Indeed, there was more than American or Canadian fishermen had ever been able to harvest. In retrospect, this was because up until that time, the waters had been fished solely by boats with only limited technology. It did not take into account any catching done by factory fleets, which used huge nets guided by such electronic wonders developed during World War II as radar, loran, depth sounders, and electronic trackers. Nor did they account for the development of power machinery to haul in bigger nets made of stronger materials than ever before.

The first fishing nation allowed in post-war Alaskan waters was Japan. The Soviet Union followed on all North American Pacific coasts. Then came Taiwan and South Korea. In the Atlantic, the Soviets and West Germans were the first to seize the opportunity. They were soon followed by Spain, East Germany, and Poland, along with a host of others.

The author was a junior officer aboard the Coast Guard ship that formally welcomed the Japanese back into the waters off Alaska on 1 June 1952. I stood on my ship's boat deck, ensuring against photographs from any cameras on board. Only our two most senior officers went by smallboat to make the greeting. They escorted a Japanese-American marine biologist, whom we had picked up at the naval base in Adak, and delivered him as envoy to the waiting fleet. As communications officer, I had decoded several messages from Washington, DC Headquarters concerning this event. Labeled "Secret" (second in classification only to Top Secret) the messages contained the details of our rendezvous with the Japanese. Weeks later, our ship returned to home port in Ketchikan to find casual news coverage of the event that had been handed to us as a heavy military secret.

Whoever the traitor was who broke the story to the American public, it hadn't been one of us. We were too militarily indoctrinated to risk our necks leaking a story. However, the news provoked no particular outrage throughout the nation. Alaska was still remote for most Americans—a territory still years from achieving statehood, while Americans were more preoccupied by the spread of Communism than the state of its abundant seafood shelves.

Japan may have been humbled by losing its war, but this had not impaired the ability of its fishermen—goaded perhaps by hardships back home—to take full advantage of an opportunity. The Japanese fishing fleet that we had secretly welcomed back into Alaskan waters turned out to be anything but modest. It consisted of three mother-factory ships, each with its own fleet of catcher boats. The largest ship of these (of which I have the most specific information) was supplied by some thirty catchers, each with a crew of about twenty who fished their nets around the clock. More than half a century after the event, I established contact with the Japanese-American whom our Coast Guard ship had escorted from Adak to the Japanese fleet. At the time of our 1952 encounter, he was a young man (as I was) just beginning a career that had not yet been fully defined. Since then, Dr. Francis M. Fukuhara has become a distinguished marine scientist with a veritable library of publications to his credit.

Recently, Frank Fukuhara graciously consulted his old notes and furnished me with firsthand recollections. They indicate an extent of preparation and organization beyond the average American's ken at the time. Perhaps even beyond the ken of the officials in Washington who were keeping the event quiet.

According to Fukuhara, writing of only the mothership complex he had experienced among the three that had come over, each of the 3 catcher boats would set about 5.5 miles of drift net per set, but many would actually set as much as 10 miles of gear every night. If each of the vessels set 5.5 miles of net, the entire 30-boat fleet would have almost 165 miles of net in the water each night. And this was only one of three mothership complexes!

The mothership complex was perfectly organized, with nothing seat-of-the-pants about it. According to Fukuhara, it consisted of two main groups: one that fished and one that processed the caught fish. The leader of the fishing group had a team to establish fishing strategies by analyzing fishing, weather, and oceanographic data. The fleet's fishing vessels were then deployed in strategic patterns. A fleet manager oversaw both fishing and processing. Proper communication was vital to coordinate the deployment and logistics of the fishing boats, and it was necessary to maintain contact with company headquarters in Tokyo. The fleet carried such supercargo as a licensed physician and several Taiyo Fishing Company officials. On another front, vegetables and other food items were regularly brought by refrigerated supply ships. These ships were designed to bring supplies to the fleet and afterward to transport the finished fish products back to Japan.

This was in 1952. Japan might have needed permission to return to the waters off Alaska, but the United States and Canada protected only the waters within three miles of shore for their own fishermen. The foreign fleets had harnessed technologies developed during World War II to make their catches efficient. It seemed that the only backward fishermen were those from the host waters of North America, who went to sea in boats still as modest as those of their fathers. In many cases, the foreign fleets simply overran domestic nets and bullied smaller domestic boats aside. It could be watched from the shores of Alaska and New England.

By 1975, according to US Department of Commerce figures, there were 3,477 foreign fishing vessels working off Alaska, over two thirds of them Japanese. Also 475 off California, plus 382 off Oregon and Washington. Off the Atlantic coast were 2,339 foreign vessels, over half of them Soviet. And our 1952 welcome to ships from the hungry but strategic Japan started it all.

Only with the 1976 passing of The Magnuson Act, which took charge of US waters within two hundred miles of shore, was the foreign presence controlled. Canada had taken similar action a year previous.

By then, American and Canadian fishing ships were beginning to be able to handle their own country's sea bounty. They did so, often with continued overfishing. Even now, more than a third of a century after The Magnuson Act, much of the sea bounty off North America still remains depleted.

All of this is another story. But it started with the need to use one of Earth's natural resources to feed hungry people.

39

ADAK RAIN

Jones Henry returned his boat to Adak harbor to deposit Swede Scorden and to refuel his boat. By now, the sight of the volcanic mountains that seemed to rise from the sea had become routine, as had the green-swept hills in places where land had eroded beneath the cones. This wild country suited him.

At the fuel dock, before he could lift a hose, a navy boatswain and several seamen converged, all wearing sidearms. The boatswain declared, "Sorry, sir. Orders are to impound you for a couple of days. But I'm directed to see that you get a room and a meal ticket for the time you'll be here."

"What the fuck?" Jones raged. "I'm a goddamned American citizen."

"Yes, sir. I've got to come aboard and direct you where to tie up. And then to see you're taken care of."

"I'm sorry to have pulled you into this," muttered Swede. He was visibly upset. "I'll go at once and speak to the commanding officer here. Any loss to you, Jones, I'll pay from my own pocket if my company doesn't."

They even pulled the spark plugs from his engine and put a padlock on his cabin door. Jones Henry would have been more outraged if they hadn't treated him as well as they did. As it was, he'd barely been taken to a plainly furnished room in one of the enlisted men's buildings when a young ensign entered, apologized for the mistake, and led him to another building. Furnished quarters with a bed and private bathroom. Swede stood in the doorway of the adjacent room. "We're VIP guests, Jones. Not mere fishermen. I called strongly upon the commander of the Base, showing my credentials. Accommodations together. All paid. So. Let's enjoy the sights of Adak for a while. I see from a menu that they're serving famous king crab in the officers' dining room tonight. Okay?"

Jones shrugged. The sea had been rough, and a hot bath wouldn't be so bad. A full meal waiting afterward. But then he remembered: "My crewman's still in the enlisted men's quarters. Make sure he gets good treatment, okay? Name's Lloyd."

The young officer nodded. "I'll take care of it, sir."

"Okay then." Jones stretched, suddenly in a good humor. They couldn't keep the Japs out there a secret forever. And right now, the exactness of a military base appealed to him: everything in order. Besides, Jones was no longer a sergeant and didn't have to salute every kid officer. "They'd better have a lot of that crab. I'm hungry."

At dinner that night, Jones trailed Swede, who had joined some officers he had met previously. After fancy drinks with olives, he barely glanced at the menu before saying to the waiter: "Just bring me some of each way you fix that king crab."

"Soup first? Salad, sir?"

"Crab only. Since I catch it I'm going to see all the ways it gets fixed."

One of the officers laughed. "Give our guest what he wants."

While the others ate broth and greens, Jones was served lumps of crab with celery and mayonnaise, followed by cold crab legs smothered in a thick rosy sauce. Then, while the others were given sides of vegetables, he was served long, spiny crableg shells from which he extracted tubes of white meat to swirl through melted butter. Halfway through, the richness of it began to bother him but, having committed, he continued eating.

"Maybe they can fix you king crab ice cream for dessert, sir?" the officer commented, amused at Jones's tenacity.

"Not bad, this crab. But heavy, ain't it?" Jones admitted finally.

Hours later, the rich crab remained in his stomach like a lump. Certainly don't puke it up. Although that would have been a relief. When Jones finally fell asleep, he dreamed of Jap soldiers stomping over his body while he lay in an endless field of mud. Jerking awake, he rose and paced the room, hoping the dream would dissipate. A window looked out over low roofs to the sea. In the blowing rain, no lights shone out on the water except for a couple of buoys bobbing up beyond the breakwater. Wherever the Jap fishing fleet had gathered, it lay beyond the horizon. Damn Japs. And his stomach still growled.

By 4:00 a.m. the rain had stopped and the easterly sky had brightened, although a set of hills blocked the glow where the sun might be rising. He needed to move, not sleep. He dressed. Craving sweets now, Jones ate part of a candy bar he'd bought at the PX, stuffed two others in his pockets, and headed out for a stretch. Between buildings the streets were deserted, although streetlights still glowed in the early dawn and reflected in puddles. After a while, he found his way to the pier where they had impounded his boat. There she bobbed, almost breathing as the water surged around her. The padlock on the cabin door held firm when he tugged it.

Fucking Japs. To cause a man's boat to be tied up by the very Americans he'd fought them for! If Jones had been the kind to write letters, there'd be one to his Senator. Maybe he'd write anyhow. Adele would approve of that. The girl enjoyed getting herself mixed up in things.

Nothing to do but wander the base if he didn't want to go back to a stuffy room. The whole place had a spooky air in the early half light. Back in harbor the Coast Guard ship had a pale shine on its rain-slicked superstructure. Buildings were featureless blocks of gray. The green hills beyond had scattered quonset huts that took shape and melted away through patches of mist. The only thing steady and solid was the beacon from an airstrip laid out on flats beyond the structures.

His walk from the docks had soon encompassed the rest of the base. At land's edge, he faced a muddy road that led up into the hills. High, sharp-edged grasses bushed out along its track. White and yellow wildflowers popped through their fronds. It was dense and wet enough to discourage a free romp beyond what had been cleared. The road twisted with backtracks to conform with the hill. At length it degenerated into paths. He stood still, with clear views looking both up and down. Way below, the base's long, boxlike buildings sprawled like fish spines. Close by stood a gutted foundation with blackened posts, twisted metal, and a solid staircase leading up the side of a hill to nowhere. What remained must have underpinned a large structure. Beyond this ranged a cluster of quonset huts, most of whose long metal roofs had caved in.

Only one hut remained in good repair. Its long arched metal roof caught gray light in the parts that had avoided rusting. The weathered wooden door was padlocked. A sign stated: PROPERTY OF LT. CMDRS ASHCROFT AND WARREN. The wind blew a light rain in his face. Jones ignored it, as he wandered further upward toward other huts along a path that cut through the brush. The long roof of the first had collapsed and its wooden base was rotted, but others of them seemed to be in stages of repair and also bore padlocked doors with signs of possession.

Outside the fallen beams of a larger building, heaps of things lay rising from the weeds. Jones caught his breath. Ponchos, speckled in camouflage designs, were layered into a mound. Close by rose separate piles of canteens with their covers peeling off and a helter-skelter stack of folded canvas cots. Government issue that he'd known well, back on the islands fighting the Japs. Stuff still intact and usable. But when he kicked absently at the cots, one of the wooden crosslegs snapped like butter and poked a hole into the rotting canvas. *Usable like hell*! He picked out a canteen, slid off the wet remains of its cover, and ran his fingers along the smooth aluminum. Just like the one that had carried his last lifeline of water, while he ducked in and out of foxholes and traps. He took it for a souvenir.

Half hidden by the grass and wildflowers that had begun to entwine around them lay heaps of dark green cans. Combat K-rations! Dog food, Jones remembered, gobbled cold in fear. *Never again*! He heard himself yell and felt his foot kick into the middle of the pile. Only when the cans scattered did he pull himself together.

Had the men here even needed to fight? Had their daily lives gripped the line, or had they passed the days fighting off boredom while they cleaned their rifles on the ready? He'd sweated both. No more, except in restless dreams. Hard to believe.

It began to rain in earnest. Jones pulled a poncho free and slipped it on. Wet and clammy, but it still shed the water that suddenly poured in sheets and blew into his face. The poncho had odors. Old earth, old grease, mold, indefinable decay. Here he stood, shivering in the Adak rain, yet sweating from memories of the jungle and glancing for snipers. Nothing here to be afraid of, he told himself. Yet he still felt a tight grip on his stomach.

The war. Fucking war. Men he'd shared it with in blood and jokes. In piss-fear! Their faces came back as he muttered their names. Part of what he'd never wanted to think of again, and now he stood alone and missed them. Guys he'd never see again. Missed them. The rain slashed across his face. At least he couldn't feel how his eyes watered.

"Hey, buddy. Come on in out of that shit." A man was at the door of a nearby quonset hut in fairly good repair. His civvies resembled the canvas clothes that Jones would have worn when hunting.

Jones pulled himself together. "Don't mind if I do." He walked a straight line through high wet weeds, scorning a roundabout path, and at the man's invitation ducked through the doorway.

Warmth! An orange wood fire flickered in the opening of a potbellied stove. Rain drummed on the curved metal roof above them. Everything inside was ordered, organized, in stark contrast to the chaos of the tumbled huts outside. Along one side, cots were made up with sheets and blankets. Two other men sat at a table. A kerosene lamp shed light on their faces as they affably gestured him welcome.

"Join us, man. Having our wake-up slug for breakfast," said the man who had called to him. "We're just headed for our first eagle bust of the day. Take it neat or with water? Don't worry. It's Old Grand-Dad, straight from the PX—not somebody's bathtub."

Jones barely considered. "Neat suits me fine." He slipped out of the dripping poncho, glanced around to see coats bunched by the doorway, and tossed it with them.

"I'm Jack Stevens. Over there's Bert Gillis and Tom Wells."

"Jones Henry." He shook their hands.

"New here on base, Jones? On our way up here yesterday I saw you being checked into VIP quarters."

"Fishing boat. Out from Kodiak."

"Hey! A civilian! Come in, come in, man. Tell us what you're fishing!"

It turned out they were all junior navy officers, restless with their desk assignments, unhappy at being stuck on Adak, but not so bored as their wives. They had commandeered the quonset hut and fixed it up themselves as a hunting lodge.

"Eagles! You know?" Jack Stevens said lightly. "Keep 'em away from the dump. Same for those scavenging ravens. Anything that moves, actually. I brought down one eagle just before dark last night. Down somewhere. Never found him. Didn't look too hard. What's a big dead bird when you've already got two of 'em stuffed and your wife complaining that they take up too much room?" He handed Jones a drink and raised his own. "Routine rainy morning in crummy Adak! Chug, man!"

The man named Bert, whose stomach bulged slightly through his checked shirt, topped off Jones's glass when he set it down half-drained. "Never let your glass be empty up here with us, man. Fuckin' bugs might crawl in the glass and take over if you don't keep chuggin'." The others joined his laugh. The drink went readily to Jones's head. He leaned back in the chair they had offered, raised his hand as if in agreement while he warmed himself, and through a growing buzz, watched them without needing much to talk.

"Ass-end of the world up here," Bert continued. "Of the globe. Of the fuckin' universe! When we could be in Japan living high, or at least off in Korea getting real career points. So you do what you can."

"We come up here more to get away than anything else," explained the man named Tom in an easy voice. He had a carefully trimmed mustache that he kept tweaking with his fingers. "Get away from the movies every night—ever had to sit through the same Bob Hope thing three times before they shipped up a fresh batch of films! Work out at the gym every day, but how many times can you run the same treadmill? Friday–Saturday dances at the club, wives bitching, kids yowling. Anybody who went to war was lucky. They got adventure. Promotion! Out here we just have to mark time, you know? Stay ready. Kiss each others' asses. Watch the rain blow."

Officers. Young assholes. Without a clue. The man named Jack took over. "Now say, what kind of fishing you do? Tuna, marlin, anything big? Hey! How about taking us with you? Give us some action." He lowered his voice. "You have anything to do with those Jap boats out there? I guess it's against the law to shoot Japs anymore. But no harm to sight in a few."

"Shut it, man," said Tom. "Those Japs are a secret."

Bert yawned. "Secret the whole base knows. Secret we keep right here in Adak, end of the universe. Mum's the word, eh, Jones?"

Jones shook himself alert. So this is what the war he'd fought had come to. It took all his energy to bang down the glass and rise to his feet.

"Hey, old-timer. Need to take a piss? Just do it outside the doorway—don't need to get wet. If you need to shit, there's a little outhouse we dug fresh, just up the hill. Shake in some lime from that bag by the hole when you're through."

Jones didn't bother to speak. He walked out the doorway into the rain, then uphill through undergrowth that tangled in his feet.

"Buddy!" called Jack. "Outhouse is the other way. And you forgot your poncho."

Whatever. Jones continued to climb. Water streamed down his face and sogged in his shoes. He paused, panting, only when he stood high enough to see the hut roofs below. The one that he'd just left puffed smoke. At the doorway, Jack called, "Hey Jones. You don't need to go that far to take a piss, man! You'd think that ol' boy had a bear on his tail!"

The long buildings of the base further down misted gray. The sea beyond undulated dim rows of waves. He pressed on until his feet had stopped pulling at vines and only moss covered the rocky ground. With nothing to break its drive, a gust stronger than the steady blow tattooed rain in horizontal streaks. The force made him sway before he leaned into it. For a moment, the sky cleared enough to show a peak whitened by snow, then closed again. Top of the world. World gone spook.

At least with the wind, he couldn't hear any more if they were still calling him back. Men in authority that were really nothing but kids dreaming of war. Boozing, bitching, shooting creatures just to ease the boredom—when they hadn't a clue what they'd been spared!

Dripping wet suited him. He felt bent to the raw weather like the weeds and brush. With sudden energy he planted his feet apart, spread his arms, and shouted "Fuck!" to the wind. "Fuck! Fuck! Fuck!" until he needed to cough. All the buddies he'd held dead, while their blood burned his hands! They'd left him alone to booze with kids who wanted war because they didn't know what it was. Left him alone and alive on a mountain of tumbled quonset huts. "You hear me, guys? I'm alive and you're dead. I can't help it. That's just how it turned out! Callihan! Jimmy! Chuck! Sokovich . . . Sugarmouth! You guys hear? You died, and I'm alive with kids bitching 'cause they don't have a war! Ahh!"

There was silence except for rain pelting against metal and a distant foghorn far below.

"Sir. You are sick? You must come in from the storm."

There stood a figure at the entrance to the nearest collapsed quonset hut. Jones squinted to clear his vision through the rain. "Who the hell is that?"

"Sir. You come in from the rain."

Jones took a step closer. A Jap. Maybe an ambush, and his hands were empty. He glanced around. Not even a branch to grab.

"Sir! I am friend." A face he knew.

"What're you doing up here? Saw you back on that ship—where you belong."

"Arm broken, sir." The Jap held up the cast. "From a sudden fall when not looking. The Coast Guard vessel returned with me for a doctor at the hospital. Now I must wait for return to my fishing vessel."

"I can't shake you, can I?"

"Shelter in here from wind and rain. You come, please." Sure it wasn't an ambush? Even with that arm in a cast, it could be a trick. Jones felt his mind clearing, although the whiskey still made objects swim. But nothing he couldn't handle.

"Well. For a minute." His legs led him to the entrance. A half-rotted door hung by a single hinge. He tensed while he peered inside, checking all around. No question, drink or no, he could handle more than one Jap if it came to an ambush. Never trust them. But even in the dim light he saw the long interior was empty except for scattered junk. No hot stove like in the other hut. Halfway along, the curved roof had fallen in. Rainwater sluiced from it to splash on the blackened canvas of a half-opened cot. Weeds poked through a hole in the floor where the water continued down. Jones entered. Musty chill inside. But at least the wind was blocked.

"You wish to sit, sir? Please." The ridge of a chair pushed against his leg.

"None of your tricks! I'm standing." It flashed in his mind. Here was a place where American soldiers, maybe even Marines, had waited to fight Japs. Waited ready for Japs. And now a Jap stood safe where those men might have died. "Who said you could be up here?"

"Climb up, from the hospital. No boat back for me for two more days. Doctor tells me walk where you wish. This after I hear him say to a nurse how things are so different now than back during war. That he had hands not for helping stupid Japanese that fall down. Thus, yesterday, dinner forgotten. Up the hill." He stopped, eyeing Jones. Seemed to consider, then changed direction, speaking softly, "War long ago, sir. But in this place I feel still the spirits from war. From terrible long ago. I wandered up whole side of hill—have passed all huts and felt the many spirits here in this place. Sometimes I wish to go down. But then also, I feel spirits. Thus, I do not wish to leave."

"Been up here all night? Before dinner? No coat. Ain't you cold?"

"Cold, hai. Not important. Many times cold in wartime. Did you come to search for me, sir?"

Jones looked at him, wide-eyed. "Why the hell would I do that? Fuck no. What's your game?" Jones regarded him with something of his old suspicion, but spoke less gruffly than he might have done. "You keep showing up. On that Jap ship a couple of days ago. In Akutan, in Bristol Bay almost a year ago, sucking up to Swede at the cannery. And before that. Mebbe even in Japan."

"Hai?" The man watched him squarely, not with that sneaky turn of the eyes.

"You people all look alike. You know?"

"You people also, sir."

Neither man looked away. Outside a wild bird cried. A gust of wind blew rain through the doorway and rattled a loose piece of metal dangling from the caved-in roof.

Jones felt hungry. He pulled a candy bar from his pocket and peeled down the wrapping. Started to take a bite, considered, then snapped the bar squarely in the middle. "Here. Your half. Breakfast." The Jap put out his hand, then hesitated. "Take it. Take it!" Jones snapped.

"I do not have in return."

"Ain't a gift. Just a piece of candy!" Jones took his own half and shoved the rest into the man's hand. "Eat it or throw it away. All the same to me." He studied the face that was watching him. The man broke off a piece of the candy bar and put it in his mouth.

"Thank you. The flavor is . . . delicious." He finished it ravenously.

"Just a chocolate bar. Mebbe not all your faces are the same. Just the way memory plays." Jones bit into his half of the chocolate. Chewed for a few moments in silence before saying, "You coming over here now—think you'll grab all our fish?"

"Only to share, sir."

Jones took a minute to consider. Swallowed the last bite of the candy. "Share, bullshit," he growled. Then announced, "I'll be there watching. You might be catching all the fish for now, but I'm in Kodiak and I'll be watching. Just you wait, I'll be coming to get 'em back. Here. You look hungry." Jones rummaged in a pocket and pulled out his last candy bar. "Peanuts. You people eat nuts? Look, you chew 'em first. Take it." He waited until the man's hand closed around the candy Jones proffered. "Least you didn't just come up here to shoot down eagles, appears. Not bitching about how you spent the war." Jones looked up angrily, glared at the rotting door they had trudged in through. Behind him, the crinkling of the wrapper as the Jap opened the candy sounded like the crackle of radio static over the storm. Jones felt his shoulders sag, his frantic energy ebbing away.

"Spirits, huh?" he asked. "Like buddies dead and who won't leave your mind?" The Jap—Tsurifune, his name was?—he nodded. "Mebbe we're together on that one."

Jones watched as this man named Tsurifune looked up at the caved-in ceiling. Closed his eyes and seemed to be listening. Jones listened too, to the rain dropping heavily on the corrugated sheeting, to the wind whispering past with those voices he'd tried to forget. Maybe the Jap was right. Maybe there were spirits wandering this place.

"That one at least," Jones muttered. "At least we're together on that one."